OCEANSIDE PUBLIC L
330 N. COAST HIGHWA
OCEANSIDE, CA 9205⁴

D0407298

OCEANSIDE PUBLIC LIBRARY
3 1232 00752 4996

THE PRIEST OF BLOOD

THE VAMPYRICON

THE PRIEST
OF BLOOD

DOUGLAS CLEGG

ACE BOOKS, NEW YORK

OCEANSIDE PUBLIC LIBRARY
330 N. COAST HIGHWAY
OCEANSIDE, CA 92054

THE BERKLEY PUBLISHING GROUP
Published by the Penguin Group
Penguin Group (USA) Inc.
375 Hudson Street, New York, New York 10014, USA
Penguin Group (Canada), 90 Eglinton Avenue East, Suite 700, Toronto, Ontario M4P
2Y3, Canada (a division of Pearson Penguin Canada Inc.)
Penguin Books Ltd., 80 Strand, London WC2R 0RL, England
Penguin Group Ireland, 25 St. Stephen's Green, Dublin 2, Ireland (a division of
Penguin Books Ltd.)
Penguin Group (Australia), 250 Camberwell Road, Camberwell, Victoria 3124, Australia
(a division of Pearson Australia Group Pty. Ltd.)
Penguin Books India Pvt. Ltd., 11 Community Centre, Panchsheel Park, New
Delhi—110 017, India
Penguin Group (NZ), Cnr. Airborne and Rosedale Roads, Albany, Auckland 1310,
New Zealand (a division of Pearson New Zealand Ltd.)
Penguin Books (South Africa) (Pty.) Ltd., 24 Sturdee Avenue, Rosebank, Johannesburg
2196, South Africa

Penguin Books Ltd., Registered Offices: 80 Strand, London WC2R 0RL, England

This is an original publication of The Berkley Publishing Group.

This is a work of fiction. Names, characters, places, and incidents either are the
product of the author's imagination or are used fictitiously, and any resemblance to
actual persons, living or dead, business establishments, events, or locales is entirely
coincidental. The publisher does not have any control over and does not assume any
responsibility for author or third-party websites or their content.

Copyright © 2005 by Douglas Clegg.
Text design by Kristin del Rosario.

All rights reserved.
No part of this book may be reproduced, scanned, or distributed in any printed or
electronic form without permission. Please do not participate in or encourage piracy of
copyrighted materials in violation of the author's rights.
Purchase only authorized editions.
ACE is an imprint of The Berkley Publishing Group.
ACE and the "A" design are trademarks belonging to Penguin Group (USA) Inc.

First edition: October 2005

Library of Congress Cataloging-in-Publication Data

Clegg, Douglas, 1958–
     The priest of blood / Douglas Clegg.— 1st ed.
        p. cm.
     ISBN 0-441-01327-9
     1. Soldiers—Fiction.   2. Crusades—Fiction.   3. Vampires—Fiction.   I. Title.

   PS3553.L3918P75 2005
   813'.54—dc22

                                                                    2005047183

PRINTED IN THE UNITED STATES OF AMERICA

10   9   8   7   6   5   4   3

FEB 1 5 2006

For Sharon Gamboa

With thanks to Raul Silva; my agent, Simon Lipskar; my editor, Ginjer Buchanan; and to Susan Allison, Leslie Gelbman, Andrew LeCount, M. J. Rose, Matt Schwartz, Mick and Anne Schwartz, A. J. Clegg, Tracy Farrell, and especially to Jeremy, Jacqui, Caravaggio, and Vivy Caniglia.

The Invocation

◆

Sing to me, Falconer, of what was and what shall be. Blow the victory ram's horn and recall the destiny to which you were so cruelly taken.

How you came to us in the night of your soul's despair, on the rocky ledges and fallen citadels of the Eastern kingdoms. Roar the story of the warrior-youth from the West, who came to plunder the treasures of Antioch and Kur-Nu and was himself plundered . . .

Here is the story that has been kept secret for more than eight hundred years, suppressed by the Keepers of the Veil, hunted by the humans who came after the Falconer, and buried by those he most trusted.

The shroud of history is upon humankind and those born of the Serpent as well, and all has been lost from the past, but you will invoke it now that it might live—

Speak the prophecies of Medhya, and of the secret wars that would not have begun without the appearance of the Maz-Sherah—

And remember the tale of the Priest of Blood, who brought you to this desolate and wretched and noble state . . .

BOOK ONE

MORTALITY

I
THE FOREST

◆ CHAPTER 1 ◆

The Words of the Blood

◆ 1 ◆

MORTAL life is an echo of footsteps heard in the halls of the dead. Despite the adventures glimpsed at Death's Threshold, we turn toward life, as if that echo were all.

Within life, the blood is sustenance, the flesh is our cloak, but it is the breath that is the life—of eternity—itself.

◆ 2 ◆

LONG before my birth, and well before my initiation into the mysteries of vampyrism, there were prophecies written in blood on a parchment made of human skin. These were rolled, as a scroll might be, bound in goatskin, placed in an urn, then sealed.

Servants of the fallen ones buried the urn beneath the earth to protect its secrets. The servants were slaughtered, with the last taking his own life, so that no one might ever know of the prophecies and the power they possessed.

The Earth itself wished to learn of the urn's secrets, and so after many years, the Earth crushed the urn. Dirt and crawling insects spilled across the words of blood.

From this earth, grain grew, and whispered the words to the air.

One who harvested the grain heard the words as wind swept the grasses. This man came to know the power within the words of the Blood, and became a great priest of his tribe, and when he passed to the Threshold that exists between life and death, he returned to life and raised up a kingdom of his own. He had many daughters in his former life, and they grew in power themselves, stolen from him and from the shades that gathered to those who held the power of one called Medhya, who had made the prophecies with her own blood, and the parchments were her own flesh.

She had been a great queen of a distant country that the ancients called Myrryd, which now lies somewhat in northern Africa and in the sea, for it is one of the Fallen kingdoms of the world.

Medhya had power and wisdom in her youth. It was said that the Serpent, which was sacred to her land, told her the secrets of the Earth and of immortality, stolen from the lands beyond the Veil. With this illicit knowledge, she brought about prosperity and heaped all manner of blessings on her people. Three distinct priesthoods grew about her as her kingdom grew to encompass many kingdoms—the Myrrydanai, the Kamr, and the Nahhashim, to gather worshippers to her throne.

But she grew corrupt with her immortality and became a tyrant to her followers. When foreign invaders finally destroyed the thousand years of Myrryd, her priests discovered the source of her immortality and stole it for themselves.

They took her flesh from her, to wear as a cloak, and her blood to drink, leaving only her shadow, which was dark as midnight.

The ones called the Nahhashim preserved her words in her blood, on her sun-dried skin, as her shadow lingered with them, whispering prophecies that maddened them and brought them death when her whispering was done. A tree grew among their graves, and from it a flower with juice that was poison. From the tree, a staff was cut, and the priests called the Kamr, who likewise drank of Medhya's blood, took the seed of the flower, and the priests called Myrrydanai tasted of her flesh.

But the prophecies were unknown to them, and the shadow of Medhya was upon them, both a curse and a powerful force.

The first prophecy told of the days to come when the blood would sing within the cupbearer, and all who had drunk of the cup would know her secrets.

The second prophecy spoke of a great bird that would come to devour the snake and so become a dragon and raise up the Fallen Ones of Medhya.

And the third prophecy of that terrible and powerful immortal was that the bloodline of Medhya would drink the blood of the dead and dying until All became the One, and the One, All.

There was one more prophecy, but the one who heard the words on the tips of windblown grain did not reveal it. All that anyone would know of it was that it spoke of a great war that would be like no other, between those of the blood, and those of the flesh, and it would return Medhya to her place of power.

There are those who say Medhya walked the Earth for many thousand years more, calling for her flesh, weeping for her lost blood and for the children of her children, cursing those who stole the source of her power, searching for a doorway from the world of shadow into the world of flesh. She is nothing but shadow by day, and by night, she is the whispering darkness itself.

Against her will, but from those who stole her blood and her secrets, the race of vampyres was born, from the Curse of Medhya and her Sacred Kiss, which drinks, resurrects the flesh, and passes the soul from mouth to mouth.

She seeks those who stole her secrets.

She hunts the night to bring Hell to her children.

She is the mother of the tribe of vampyres, and the one who wishes to bleed them for eternity.

These prophecies and this legend were unknown to me until after my nineteenth year, when a vampyre named Pythia took me.

• 3 •

WHEN she murdered me, her sharp canine teeth savaged my throat. I can still remember the pain: it was the pain of birth. I saw a vision of shadows in darkness, as of men of some authority gathered around, shadow against shadow. I felt my blood rise up to the bite, as if meeting Pythia's lips and tongue. The smell of her—at that instant—was the musky perfume of the grave itself. Her beauty changed from the maiden to that of the corpse, the drying leather of skin pulled taut against her skull. I saw her as she was. I saw her for her flesh and not for her spirit. Her eyes opened, milky white and diseased. Her jaw, wolflike, as she tore into me. Her weight, heavy on my chest. I froze, paralyzed, unable to fight, then the awful sucking sounds as she drank me.

I remember the beat of my pulse, as if it were a heavy, slow knocking at a wooden door nearby.

I saw her true beauty, as the life poured from my veins into her mouth. Her eyes, like burning sapphires. Her hair, thick, dark as night, flowing from her alabaster face, then the flush of pink in her cheeks as my blood nourished her.

She became my mother, and my lover, and my savior, and my murderer, and my demon.

It was not intense pleasure I felt then, in the Sacred Kiss that burned on my lips. The pleasure came after, when I experienced my first resurrection. The pleasure of opening myself up to the night, to creation itself, to the flesh in full.

The pleasure arises when the body comes fully alive again.

When the thirst for blood begins.

The curse of the thirst is not the thirst itself, but of the memories it stirs. Each drop of blood brings forth, once more, the memory of my mortal life.

Red is for remembrance.

• 4 •

THERE is another world, and until I tasted of it, it remained legend.

I am vampyre, but have not always been. Once, like you, I was someone's child, and the world seemed an eternal spring to me.

There is a history you do not know, nor have you seen, except those who have torn the Veil, which is the juice of a rare flower, known to the ancients by other names. The world you believe existed in my mortal lifetime is a forgery, committed by the monasteries whose monks wrote much, and lied more, and by great men who proclaimed their great deeds in order to store up their treasures and create dynasties. But like a blanket of mist on marshlands, the past has been hidden to remove the power of those who were not men. And even the past is its own fog, for beyond it lies the Otherworld itself, the Veil's secret world that exists with the one of mortals, and yet we do not see it. You cannot conquer a world if your chronicles tell of your failures and defeats and of the blood on your own hand. You can only conquer when those who come after see you as the holy victor, as the anointed of God, a victim of devilish evil, of plagues, and of monstrous invaders. But the truth resides with me, and others like me.

And so, I will tell you what happened in those dark times.

I write this from my tomb, in the present century, having lived (in the way that I live, which is not living but not dead) for these hundreds of years. I have lost some of my provincial touch, the air of the peasant boy from what is now called Brittany, the uncouth youth who spoke in crude, barely decipherable phrases, the child of a mud-and-thatch hut that I once thought of as a cottage, as home, without education, without a hope in Hell, as it were. Should I lapse from the tale, or forget a detail of history, you will forgive such ignorance, for too many years have passed from my birth to this date, and I remember it as if through my current sensibility.

I picked up my language from the past hundred years or so. I did not learn the art of writing my name until I was nearly three hundred years old. My education—at the great universities of mankind and among ancient profane documents hidden in caves from the eyes of man—did not begin until the last days of the nineteenth century. Laggard schoolboy that I am, it was not until the twentieth century that I comprehended the vastness of this world, of its literature, of the inventions of man, and the passing and rebirth of the Gods in this, the Forest of those who hunt in the dark.

My understanding, also, is of this new age. The past is a territory of mirrors and tricks of light. Should I fail in my depiction of the battles in the Holy Land or the chateaux of my home country, then so be it. It has been too many years, and memory piles upon memory. And yet, of the truth of it, I remember all. And the smells, the tastes, the touches of those whose lives were intertwined with mine. I write of the history of the soul. There are history books you may consult, although most of them lie, but if you wish to know the date of battles, or the banner flown by a knight, or the ins and outs of the strategies that toppled the Holy Land, then untoppled it later, I suggest you find a history of my first century of life. There are maps. There are treasures locked up in museums. There are tombs. There are the accounts of the kings and dukes of the world, as they affected the politics and legends of their eras. Some of the history is true, some of it false, and most of it, hidden.

There were greater wars than human wars, greater races than the mortal, and greater histories than those of the kings of men.

So, I will write as well as I can of all that I remember, beginning with the road that led me to the Priest of Blood.

Blood is my sustenance, and my glory, but I am not its Priest. I am but a servant of the Veil and its creation, once a man who was then re-born of the Great Serpent in his nineteenth year.

Since you asked, I will tell of such things as my immortal life has experienced. I will show you the great Temple of Lemesharra and of the Netherworld called Alkemara, and the towering citadels of the Veil itself and yes, its murky inhabitants, as well as the abominations known to many as the Myrrydanai, those plague-bearers born from the corrupt wombs of the Chymers. I will tell you of flights across the seas of the Earth, and of the rocks that speak, and the blood that sings, and of the eternal newborn who sleeps within the sacred waters and whose dreams kill all who approach it. Furthermore, I will tell of that which I have seen through a Second Sight, of others who played their parts in the tale of my existence, of paths I have not taken, and those that have led me to the darkness and the truth. I will show you the secret of the life of the Blood itself, and of Pythia, and of her jealousy. And above all this, I will tell you the history of the Fallen Ones of Medhya, and of the tribe that was once vulture and jackal, which became falcon and wolf and dragon.

I will tell because I know.

• CHAPTER 2 •

Born in Ember Days

◆ 1 ◆

I WAS born from blood, and to blood I return.

We are all, who are flesh and blood, born from a violence of that same flesh and blood. Just as the cat screams as the barbs of the brutal phallus of its impassioned lover tear its innards in order to bring new kits into this nest of life, so my mother was torn by men that I might be born. Her inner body went to war with her desire. I learned later that she tried to rid herself of me, using potions and flowers known only to the Wise Women of the forest, fragrant but deadly white petals stewed in water poisoned with insect's venom. Tried to use instruments of the midwives to draw me from her innards and crush my skull, as she had done with my less fortunate siblings, buried, it was said, at the edge of the barley fields of my home country, where the sedge grew wild.

But I resisted within her and grew to term.

◆ 2 ◆

AS such, many hundreds of years ago, I came into being in a spot on Earth that has captured my imagination and heart as no other ever could. It was a place you would not recognize, though histories have been written about my first century, of its wars and kings and territorial disputes. I arrived in a land of the Bretons—which is known now as Brittany. My ancestors were varied, for, being of a lowly family, born of a bastard line, I was a mix of Gaul and Celt and Briton and Frank on my mother's side. My father, my natural father, was, by legend, a Saxon merchant. Only the very wealthy could say for certain who their parentage included, and even that was suspect. Because of my ancestry, I was considered racially mixed, as were many of the peasant families in my world.

If England was not fighting for control of Brittany, France was, and if neither, there was some foreign invader at the shores, notably the Norsemen. By the time I was born, Armorica, Brittania, Bretagne, my Brittany, had become a wasteland in parts, overforested in others, abandoned by many in the Church, or by the great chieftains. We lived at the edge of the Great Forest, and heard many tongues spoken at the crossroads of town and wood. The French language had begun to take over the Breton tongue, and families such as mine had lost everything over the past few generations. We were the vanquished of a vanquished land. An abbey had been built perhaps two hundred years before my birth, then a village grew around it, and somewhere in its history, my mother's family had fallen from some height and taken up residence squarely in the mud.

There was not yet the sense of a great Mother Church, but instead, we had Christendom, and in her skirt hems the Old Ways still continued, and orders of nuns and monks who would later be called Heretics, who believed in a Christian God that was not quite the one believed in today. It was an embattled territory, but my memory of it coincides less with history than with the world of a little boy. Despite our Breton blood upon the land that would one day be France, we still had ways of our tribes and clans, and were closer in tongue to our kinsmen in Wales and Cornwall than to those who lived far to the east, in Paris. Thus, my name had a decidedly English cast, as did most of my siblings' names. Aleric. I had no sense of national identity, nor of the invasions that must have been constant.

My world was the only world that existed, and it was not full of the high history of books, but of the lowly and simple and humble and mean. It was a daylight world with a beautiful sun, its jewels strewn upon the slanted, thatched roof, the sod and mud and sheep manure between my tiny toes even as I dropped from between my mother's thick legs, out of that darkness, into a cradle that was no better than her womb.

(Do not think ill of me for insulting my mother in this way, for you may guess that I might have had reason to feel this.)

Thus, I was born in the ember days, a new year, after the solstice, into the frozen world of life. They say that my mother was in the village, a half day's foot travel from our home at the edge of the Great Forest. Heavy with child, she had taken rest by the village well, along its smooth gray stone edge. When the hour of my birth had come 'round at last, the frost of the day drove her to a stable. Like Our Blessed Lady, as she has been called, the Maria, Mary, Notre Dame, mother squatted among goats and sheep and asses and perhaps even a sunk-backed horse and no doubt several spotted dogs, and out I came, into the encircling snake of life, into the hoop of time. My mother grew sick in that place. I have no doubt she thought, for a moment, that she might kill me and bury me in the dung, to hide her shame and her sin. No barleyfield for me, my early grave was meant to be the home of flies and vermin.

But something stayed her hand, whether the law or her own conscience, I can't be certain. Perhaps it was Fate herself who kept my mother from braining me against the wall. I can even hope that she felt the maternal warmth of a cow for its calf and she let me suck at her teat. Perhaps she held me close and wept over me with love and a sense of her unfortunate life. Perhaps a midwife had been there, too, helping to snip the cord and give me first milk from a more generous breast. Perhaps my mother had, for a few moments of her life, kissed my cheek and whispered a lullaby.

Perhaps the Great Mater was there with her, Matter, Mother, Mutter, the Earth that cradled me, in some invisible way, guiding her hand as She had guided so many hands before.

A kind merchant put Madonna and squalling brat into the flat of his wagon and drove her back over snowcapped slopes to the one-room home that I would come to think of as little better than the stable in which I'd been born.

My name was at first Alaricald, and then changed to Aleric, and my full name Aleric Atheffelde, which is not the patronym it may seem, nor was it pronounced as written. In fact, neither my siblings nor mother had a name passed down, either from mothers or fathers. It is easy to forget the pains of bastardy, and the lengths to which good folk kept away from it, and kept all bastards from any number of endeavors, including attaining a name of any distinction. Atheffelde simply meant "At the field," and that is, in fact, where we lived, although more appropriately "In-the-Marsh," "Felding," or "Attheforet," as some families had it, or even my stepfather's name, which was Simon Overthewater, for his work in the sea.

You will detect the Saxon influence in our names—for while we were Breton by culture, we were the mutts of that world, between Saxon and Breton and Norseman and Gaul, as well as other influences. Years later, when the French language took us completely, those called Atheffelde would become Delafeld, as well as other variations. We were not fixed in our names except as they were recorded at the church. Some of my siblings had other names, depending on the mood of the priest and the neighbors and my mother. The village folk often had names passed down from antiquity or from work, but such as my family was, we simply were of the land itself. In homes such as mine, the children might go on to change their names as they discovered life. Whenever one from our region ventured to other countries, we were generally called as if by one family name, LeBret, The Breton. Thus, my name, too, would one day change based on my talents and travels, but as a baby, I had no such influence.

My mother told me, when I was older, that she nearly went to Heaven the night after my birth, and that my stepfather, a brute whom I was lucky enough rarely to lay eyes on after the age of four, called me a whelp bastard and thrashed my mother for bringing another mouth to feed into his home. I might hate him for this, but I barely knew him—he was often off to sea or to the rocky coast to gather shellfish and the ocean's harvest for months at a time, returning with very little in his pocket but a dried fish or two. My mother, I soon discovered, was often abed with the local men of the village, lifting her heavy brown skirts, drawing back her scanty and torn underthings, whenever she chanced to wear them, giving to get something in return.

As a result of her wantonness, my brothers and sisters and I barely resembled each other except, perhaps, in our lack of fat on our bodies and in the generally sleepless look in our eyes. Even the twins might've been sired by separate whorehounds. As a child, I hated her unholy, if brief, alliances, and it was only when I spied her in the chapel of Our Lady, her dimpled sun-browned thighs wrapped around our local prelate, a look of absolute sacred radiance on his face, a reddish glow to his tonsure, that I realized that we all must do what needs to get done in order to put bread in our mouths. If the fish and mollusks were not a-plenty, we would go without, but not so long as our mother prayed on her back and brought home bread and sweets and mutton. Everyone who is mortal must work at some trade, and my mother's was more arduous than most, but possibly pleasurable, if damnable.

Certainly, the local monks did not think it a damning offense.

That week, we got a finer share of the Poor's distribution, a charity taken in by the Brethren of the monastery for the families in need.

My brother, Aofreyd, who I called Frey, would place bets with me about where we would find our mother a-lying on a summer afternoon. She was, nine times out of ten, pressed into some haystack with a local farm boy half her age. Those nights, we often drank fine milk and had fresh eggs. When the plague came through each year, bringing with it terrible nights of praying and endless Masses that lasted past midnight, and my father stayed away for the season, at sea, my mother often brought her men home, believing that we were too ignorant to understand why the planks in the cupboard creaked. At night, Frey and I would lie together on our mat, listening for the sound, and giggle together at how the men always seemed like dogs, growling, barking, whimpering, and how what they did sounded as if it could not be pleasurable at all, but was, indeed, what the cats in heat must feel when Old Tom mounts them.

Once, when Frey threw this in her face, furious that he had to defend her at Market from being called the Whore of Babylon by the local boys his own age, she gave him a whipping and told both of us that she worked for God, and those men were Saints come down to Earth to bring a message from Heaven.

At the time—I was seven, perhaps—I believed her. Frey did not. My brother spat at her in the face and told her that she was the kind of woman who should be dragged through the streets and beaten on a gibbet until every bone in her body was like honey in a goatskin. He pointed to little Franseza, with her tangled black hair and the raised bumps on her face. "She is dying in front of you, and you lie with strange men. Look at Aler"—as he called me—"he is bones and hair and not much else. You let those men use you as a sewer for their cods, then you bring another bastard into the world and watch as they suffer." I knew this was bad talk at the time, although I didn't understand it.

My mother took a hot pan from the fire, full of oil, and threw it at him. It hit Frey on the left-hand side of his face. I screamed as if I had been hit. But Frey made no sound. He put his hand to his forehead. He kept his eyes on her.

That was the night she locked him in the root cellar, and I lay atop the locked wooden platform and whispered to him that it would be all right, that he would be out in the morning. We touched fingers to each other that night through a crack in the wood. Frey told me that he would never forget my loyalty and our kindred (even if we shared the same mother, but perhaps not the same father), nor would he remain at home another day. "She is not a bad woman," he said of our mother. "But I cannot live here."

"I hate her," I said. "Sometimes."

"It's better to pity her. She has some cause for her anger in life." Then, he told me a story about our mother, and my grandfather, and how our family had become outcasts of the village. It made little sense to me, for I was too young to understand how prejudice might arise even among neighbors. "I need to leave," he said. "She is angry because she knows I must go."

"She's mad," I said.

"She has her reasons." His words made me curious about our mother. When I asked him more about her, he told me to keep quiet. "She is as she is. I am as I am."

Frey was twelve years of age when he left home for good. At dawn's first light, he dug his way out of the cellar trap, taking with him some roots and apples, wrapped up in his ragged shirt. The left side of his face was scarred and full of raised bubbles of skin where the oil had struck him. He kissed me on the forehead and swore that should we ever meet again, in this life or the next, that he would greet me as brother and friend and allow no one to harm me.

I thought that I would never see him again. We all knew that if any of us left, abandoned our home, Death would surely follow. Frey knew this. We had heard of what happened to boys who ventured into the world without any means. I said many prayers for my brother the morning I watched him running along the path at the edge of the Forest.

It was the saddest day of my young life, and though you may judge my mortal days as misspent and full of vain pursuits, you must always remember that, for a child, the world is meant to be wondrous. When it is not, it becomes the realm of shadows and of nightmare. In the mud of that world, I did not know one day to the next if I would eat, or if I might die, or if one of my sisters might fall dead.

It was quite natural for a boy such as myself to dream of great things, to believe in the lies told me by other dreamers, and to want more than simply the filth and disease of the hovel called home—I wished for Heaven in that lifetime, a sweet place where dreams and hopes were fulfilled.

The Forest was my place of dreams, and the birds, my messengers to Heaven.

◆ 3 ◆

I must tell you of the Forest, a place of dreams and wishes in my young mortal life—as well as nightmares. They said that in the center of the Great Forest there was a tree older than all the others. It was called the Oak of the Priests, or the Devil's Tree, depending on whether a peasant or a monk mentioned it. It was said to be the Father of all trees, and its roots went down into the Earth and from them grew all the trees of the world. This was just one of the legends of the wood, and I grew up with the magick of these stories.

Although it went by ancient names as well as Christian names and names of conquerors and chieftains, those of us who lived beside the Forest knew it as the Great Forest. It was a fortress unto itself, and was bordered for us with marshy land on all but one edge of it, that could mainly be crossed easily in the summer or during particularly icy winters.

To the west were the great caves in which the group of Sisters, Brides of Christ, had built into the rock their quarters and chapel, at a grotto. They were known as the Magdalens, nuns who shunned material life and, more importantly, sunlight itself, as part of the world of matter that corrupted the spirit. In those days, Christendom encompassed a variety of what were later called heresies, and a century later, the Magdalens of the Languedoc were hunted down and slaughtered in their chapels, but during my young life, they were simply part of Christendom's variety.

These good women lived mainly on the food brought them by pilgrims, for the grotto and its springs were said to restore the sinful to a state of innocence by virtue of Mary Magdalen's blood, which had, by legend, been spilled to create the spring. They had a relic of the Magdalen, supposedly a bit of her heart, dried and kept in a wooden box at the foot of the statue of the only female Apostle. The Magdalens, although friendly with the local abbey and its abbé, kept their distance from all, for they were meant for a solitary life of contemplation and prayer, as well as bestowing a blessing upon the rock ledge within which they dwelled. But the good Sisters were the farthest point in our land that I then knew of, and the Forest and its marshes were of much more interest to me than a nunnery and pilgrims.

In the spring and fall, one had to find entry points through narrow, muddy paths. The marsh and bog led to streams into the woods, and an area we later came to know as "The Devil's Teeth," which was a series of large stones standing upended in a circle—as tall as many men—that were said to have been there since the beginning of time. It was a mysterious and wonderful place, although the priests and monks often warned us to never go into the Forest except from necessity, for the Devil lurked everywhere among its branches and roots.

Our storytellers spun many tales around firesides of the ancient heroes and damsels who had met their fates within it, of the creatures and monsters that had once walked among its great trees, and the nymphs and faerie queens that had lived along its bogs and among the caves. There was a legend of a sacred poisonous tree—its fruit would kill whoever tasted of it, save for those purest in spirit. I heard a story once of a man who went foraging for his family and drew a root out from the earth, and the root was shaped as a man, and screamed so loud when the good man pulled it that he went deaf from the sound.

At the center of the wood (as all legends went) an ancient ruin of a castle rose up from fern and thicket, home to a Celtic queen, who once ruled all the forests of the world. An old Roman wall, half-torn, half-lost, ran among the overgrowth. There were legendary fountains, and lost treasures buried centuries before; other great tales of magick and history mingled in its green darkness. Although the Duke claimed the woods, and, of course, the Baron, partially, in the name of the Duke, there was not a family I knew of that did not occasionally risk the punishment for poaching in order to feed themselves. And although there was a great cry from the abbots and priests and nuns, there were still known those who practiced fortune-telling and healing within the Great Forest.

When my mother had taken sick, I often accompanied her with my grandfather, on a journey into the woods, where my grandfather knew how to call the crones of the wood. They would come with a poultice or a tea for my mother to drink to help with her fever. When I cut my foot on the edge of an adz, which was a kind of ax that we used then for woodcutting, my grandfather carried me deep into the Great Forest to the crone who I knew as Mere Morwenna.

Although she was not my mother, we called her as such, and she gave me something that tasted like licorice and mint, then had me eat a disgusting chunk of rye bread covered with a gray-green mold. The candy-flavored treat helped me swallow the pieces of bread, and within two days, the infection and its accompanying fever had vanished. Like all the Wise Women, she wore a thin veil that seemed to me to be made of spiderweb, for once, when I touched it, it seemed sticky to my hand.

We of the fields knew them as the Forest Women or the Wise, but they called themselves the Women of the Veil, and so, they wore this to cover their faces from the nose to the chin. Mere Morwenna had a young child whose entire body was veiled, for it was said that too much light would kill it. It was little more than a baby when I was a boy. My mother told me that it had a great deformity of some sort and that Mere Morwenna had to bathe it hourly in a bog at the center of the Forest, a bog in which grew berries that cured the ill or poisoned the healthy, and which was only known to the Wise Women. "Her baby needs these hourly baptisms to cure it, or else it will surely die," my mother said. "She is a very good woman, despite what villagers say."

Once, out of curiosity, I drew back the veil slightly and looked at the baby's face. It had a level of ugliness I'd never before seen, although its eyes were like pools of clear blue water. I heard the word, "changeling," now and then, and that the child was not truly Mere Morwenna's but had been discovered tucked into the opening of an oak that had been split by lightning. The Forest women's stories were all like this—there was nothing of the ordinary about their world, and I loved every visit to them.

We knew then that sorcery and witchcraft were outlawed, but those who lived outside the castle, out in the mud, did not turn against the Wise Women of the Great Forest. Brittany was not so rigid in its thoughts, nor were its people far removed from the Celtic ways of old. While the world of Christendom was our life, and the Christian gospel our salvation, although none could read it save the monks, the fever to destroy that Old Religion had not yet arisen in as violent a way as it would, soon enough.

Mere Morwenna was our midwife, and with her assistant sisters, Brewalen and Gwenvred, would come to a home when the cries of labor had become too great. They were of value to us country folk, and they did not curse the priest or the Holy Mother when they were spoken to about matters of the spirit. Mere Morwenna had a hand that felt like fire when it was cold, and her eyes were small black rocks at the center of a wrinkled but kind face. Her hair was white from age, and when I was very young, she'd rock me on her lap after my mother had fallen asleep with my new little brother or sister. She told me of my birth, and how she had not been there to deliver me, but that once I was brought to her in the Forest that she foretold great things for me. What were these great things? I asked her often enough.

"A prophecy told to the one who must fulfill it is a destiny interrupted," she said more than once.

"But you must tell me," I insisted.

She took my hand then, when I had thrown a fit over not knowing of my destiny. She kissed the center of my palm and peered over the whorls of my fingers and the lightly creased pathways between fingers and down to the heel of the palm. "All I can see that can be told is this: from the smallest, greatness may come."

"Will I be great? One day?"

"Perhaps," she said, peering into my eyes. "We live in a world where those who seem weak are the strongest. And those who seem strong are without true power. Someday, when you seem to have great power, you must remember this, for it is at your greatest moment of strength that you will also be at your weakest."

I laughed at her, for I was too young to understand this, and she laughed, too, and went back to cradling her little veiled baby in her arms.

Mere Morwenna told me more tales of the Forest, of an ancient well and a great, fearsome beast with wings that had been trapped by some hero of old; of a fountain that was hidden from all men, but from which waters flowed that could heal the sick and make those who drank of it either die a sudden painful death or remain eternally young; there were streams within the Forest that went underground, into the caverns beneath it, and ancient drawings adorned the rock walls in those dark, dank places, telling of other worlds that had yet to be remembered; the trees themselves were thousands of years old, far older than mankind, planted by the giants that once walked the Earth, the same giants who brought the giant stones that existed along the plain at the center of the Forest. She also told me of the Faerie Queen whose castle still stood by the golden lake at the center of the Forest, although I had never ventured far enough to see it. I could well imagine a lake of gold, and she told me that if the wrong person put his boat upon the lake, it became a lake of fire. "Seven princesses sleep in the castle, waiting for seven youths to come and break the spell," she would tell me and my brothers and sisters as she tended my mother's birthing fever. "Each night, the princesses turn into ravens and fly up from the Forest, out to find the brave youths who will risk the lake to rescue them."

She told us on one occasion a tale of the True Bride, which made sense to me even while I did not entirely understand it.

"So the maiden went to live in the great castle, and married in the church the handsome prince. When the moon waxed, she would return to garden in the moonlight. She would stand beneath the pear tree and call to the golden bird. Soon enough, the bird would fly down from the sky, carrying in its beak her silver wedding dress. And she would wear this at night, for those who came to her knew that she was the True Bride. But when the prince's father, the King, returned to his home after many years at war, he did not like his son's choice of wife. So, he had brigands tie her and put her in a great cauldron. This, he sealed, and bade them throw it into the deepest pit they could find. Then, he went to his son, the prince, and told him that his wife had been unfaithful. He brought another maiden to him, this one rich, and lazy, and spiteful. She would glance at a person and judge him without thinking twice. When the prince, after many years of waiting for his Bride to return, finally agreed to marry her, she became more demanding of him, and of the entire kingdom. But we should not hate her. She was from another land, and she missed her people. Still, she caused much heartache and only some good. Her jealousy enflamed, she would have her husband declare war on his neighbors. She punished the strong and just, and rewarded the weak and vain.

"One night, the prince, now King, went to his garden, so beloved by his first bride. He remembered how she had called the bird, and he did the same, for he missed his true love. When the bird came, down from the silver moonlight, it brought with it the silver dress in its beak, as well as a diadem of gold. The bird told the King of what his father had done, how his first wife had begged for her life, and, feeling pity, the brigands released her but swore that she would die if she ever left the Great Forest. The King was inconsolable, but the bird told him that he must have faith. 'Keep the gown and the diadem, for she will return when her strength is in her. Remain with your new wife, but when the time is right, you will see your True Bride again. She will come from the Great Forest, so you must protect it and its creatures. And when she comes, bring out the silver gown and the diadem, and embrace her and celebrate the True Bride when you see her.'

"And so, one day, when the King was very old, and his second wife had died of a fit of anger and bitterness, he stood in the field and saw the True Bride step out of the woods, naked and beautiful. On her forehead, a crescent moon. On her arms and fingers, the secret gems of the Earth. She was as young as she had been when he had last seen her, and although he barely recognized her because of the years that had passed for him, and his memory had waned like the moon, still he welcomed her with warmth and love. He gave her the silver gown and diadem, and she clothed herself in these. She had no anger for his father, who had betrayed her, nor for him for taking a second bride. Together, they returned to the castle, for the time had come for the True Bride to take her place with the King of men."

None of us understood this strange tale, but Mere Morwenna looked at each of us, deeply, to see if we had pictured it in our heads. Had we? Yes. "Good," she said. "The Forest stories need to live. For just like that King, you each will need to recognize the True Bride when she returns to the world of men. She is hidden now, but she will return, and you need to have her clothes and crown at hand."

I was too ignorant of my own homeland to know that the True Bride she spoke of was the worship of the goddess of Nature herself, gone into hiding in the Great Forest when the new god had invaded and sought to destroy her.

The Great Forest's trees were ancient oak, but even between these were a jungle of other trees and plants such that it seemed always green, even in the depth of winter. If I chanced upon a salamander along one of its streams, as a child, I imagined it as a faerie cursed by a sorceress; and a hedgehog might be a princeling who had not been pure enough to cross the lake of gold or fire. It was a place of imagination, wonder, and danger, and the source that sustained us through hardship.

Once, when my older sister and I went hunting for berries in the wood (knowing that we risked punishment of the most extreme kind if caught by any authority), we came across what looked to me like part of a ruined castle. It was covered with vines, its stones interlaced with fern that grew from it at strange angles, and I entered through its little doorway. Although a mess of mud and brambles met me within, I saw the roof of it—a dome-shaped place, with faint paintings upon it of naked women who danced among strange beasts with heads like eagles, hindquarters like lions, and the wings of dragons. My older sister Annik told me that we should leave this place, for it was an ancient one, of the Old Ways, of the ways of the Devil.

• 4 •

BEASTS were my childhood companions, outside of my grandfather.

My first loves were the dogs, great wolfhound mutts that were the extra coverings on winter nights between and among my brothers and me. My second love were the birds of the air. My grandfather often led me to the edge of the Forest to teach me birdcalls, and the names of each winged creature, how to find a falcon in its nest, how to raise it from the egg and teach it to hunt for you; how to train a raven to speak several words, although I never completely mastered this. My grandfather kept doves, both for food and for companionship, and I remember him best, standing on a rock at the edge of a long meadow, the white wings of his birds flapping along his arms and above his head as if they might take him to Heaven.

Of all the children, I was the only one who took to birds.

There were six of us, plus two girls who were babies by the time I left my family.

You must know of the place birds had in our lives then, for they were as important as our eyes in many ways. Goshawks and falcons were hard to come by, and hard to train, and knights throughout Christendom demanded falconers to travel with hunting parties. It was said that the Duke of Brittany had a hundred falcons for his hunt; our local Baron had few. But none of this mattered to me as a boy, for I took to birds, and soon enough learned how to capture a newly hatched falcon from the nest without its mother tearing at me with her piercing talons and beak. My grandfather taught me much of this. He had learned the lore of the birds and of falconry in distant lands during wartime. I suppose that, as a boy, I aspired to greatness, beyond my natural station in life, because of my interest in falconry, for poor boys were poor hunters, and the great birds of prey were meant for nobility.

I had my eye on the Baron's household from an early age—I wanted the horizon beyond the mud that was to be my inheritance. What blood I had within me was the blood of a scrappy, dirty, undisciplined, and selfish boy, an inheritance from a long line of the scrappy, dirty, undisciplined, and selfish. But I wanted more than the dirt and the marsh and the woods. I wanted all the world could offer, for I saw it daily in the great castle upon the hillside. I wanted to know the inside of that place. I wanted to watch the nobility of the world, the knights and ladies, the great halls and the kitchens full of meat and bread.

My grandfather fueled these fantasies of mine to some extent. He was a tall, spindly man, unusual for a Breton, with hair white as the marsh and a nose that hooked like a falcon's beak. His eyes were warm and bright as a hearthfire, and my earliest memories of him were of his shadow, which sat beside me as I slept among my brothers. As I grew a bit, I sought him out to hear his tales of the past and of the days when the Great Forest covered the entire world—when birds spoke, when trees held treasures, and when the moon itself was a stag that crossed the night stars. Some of the elders of my childhood visited him for wisdom, for he was eldest among them and knew both the lore of the wood and field and that of the castle.

He often told me stories when I lay down to sleep at night, on straw that crawled with lice in winter, with my younger brothers close by me, nestled in each other's arms like cherubim.

"Once, many years ago, we owned land, to the south, down at the great mountains," my grandfather told us. "We are descendants of a most royal family, lost to misfortune, having crossed the sea to come to this rocky land. A woman, heavy with child, whose man had died in another land, brought up the grandfather of my grandfather's grandfather, and kept secret the lineage. But we were once, our folk, greater than even the Duke. Greater, I tell you, than the kings of men. And we may be great again. You, you Aleric, you boy of birds and hounds, may one day rule this land. You have a talent for what nobility craves, and even when you hunt down a rabbit or rat, I see the mix of your ancestral blood in you. Royal blood runs like gold beneath your skin." He might grasp my small arm and hold it up to candlelight. "Do you see the blue there? Beneath your skin? That is the blue of nobility. We are meant for this. You are destined for great things, grandson."

"I can be king?"

"King, or prince," he said. "You have the bloodline in you. Do you not talk to birds? And understand their language?"

I laughed when he said this, for I did know the language of birds, although it was not magickal in any sense. My grandfather took me out in the spring to take eggs from the nests, and to keep them beneath the pit of my arm, using a sling, to warm the eggs. When they hatched, days later, we would feed them with a worm, cut, and impaled upon a slender hard grass, thrust into the baby birds' throats. My grandfather taught me in this way to train birds of all kinds, and they would follow us as we went about our day—whether geese or dove, raven or falcon. These last were forbidden to us to raise, by order of the Baron, for he and his huntsman were to own all falcons and goshawks. Because my grandfather gave well-trained falcons to the Baron's household, he was never prevented from capturing and raising the birds himself.

"In my grandfather's day, all was different," he told me, while we taught a young falcon maneuvers of the hunt with me crouching low to imitate a rabbit (and sometimes being cut by a young bird's too-sharp talons!) "Folk came to him for the secrets of the earth and sky. You have his face, you know. You do. You have the pale skin and the rosy glow and the smile of him. He could read the leaves, which foretold the end of the Forest's strength. He knew, by the flight of sparrows, where the storm might begin in the sky, and how soon it might arrive for us. He was a remarkable man."

"And my father?" I asked.

His eyes grew shadowed. "The fisherman?"

"My real father," I said. "The one who has gone away forever."

"A scholar," my grandfather told me. "From distant lands, and to them, he returned." The cloud had not left his face, and when I tried to speak more of my birth father, he would return the subject to his grandfather, or to my mother as a girl when she "looked like the spring itself, bedecked with garlands of wildflowers, and riding a wild horse along the marsh as if she were a Briary Maiden. And me, her father, proud of her, happy that she had so much life in her. Ah." Sunlight seemed to shine across his face as he spoke. "You must never grow unkind to your mother," he warned, shaking a finger at me, his eyes squinting as if searching my face for any sign of disagreement. "She has suffered much, and has done much, despite what it may seem. She saved my life once and paid a terrible price for it."

But I wanted to talk of more exciting things. How I wish I could go back and beg him to tell me more of my mother's past, of the young woman I never knew who might have paid such a price that it had changed her forever, from a beautiful maiden on a horse to a wanton among the fields with children all around and begging for bread daily.

I grabbed him around the collar and told him he was the most wonderful grandfather in the world. He, in turn, embraced me, holding me so close that I could feel his tears on my neck. "We are born to this world to find our destiny, my dear boy. You are of the bloodline of the Great Forest, and of those who knew of its gifts before even the Romans came to this land. No matter what misery the world offers

you, do not let go of that love you have now. Do not let go of all
that you were born to do. All is good and bad. There is no one or the
other. You must look at the bad and see the good in it. And when you
see the good, do not forget that it contains the bad, as well. Do you
understand?"

I murmured that I did, though I did not then have the experience
to comprehend what he told me.

"All that is good, has bad in it. And if you forget this, you will feel
betrayed when you should merely have understood the nature of the
world."

I drew back from him, smiling.

I recall how much my love for him shone above all other loves.
Every crag of that face, every white hair on his head, the way a knot at
his throat bobbed up and down when he spoke. I could live in the mud
and the cold, put up with my mother's darkness, which erupted now
and then, so long as I could be with this old man whose wisdom and
warmth raised me up and held me aloft, above all that threatened to
drag me under.

"You were once a king," I said.

"Not a king," he corrected. "Not in the way you think of kings. I
served a greater being than any king could offer. As did my father, and
my grandfather. What we once did . . ." He leaned forward and kissed
me on the forehead. "Once upon a time, in the long ago. That world is
gone. The wind has taken it to sea." A jewel of a tear arose at the edge
of his eye. "Gone. But you, you are from a great bloodline. Magnificent. That you must never forget. We are children of this Forest. We
planted these trees, and our souls remain here."

It was a fabulous history of our clan, and no one believed it, but he
clung to it, and I dreamed from it. He spun it like a spider's web for
me. I suppose that's where I got my hunger for better things, for a
finer life. Why the stink of the pigsty and the smell of the rotting fruit
in the orchard vexed me. The disgusting gust of befouled odor that accompanied the fisherman's trade when my stepfather returned from
his distant journeys. After months of being away, he would arrive with

the chilly rains, his eyes as round and empty as a halibut's, his mustache like a carp's, the malodorous stench of gutted fish on his rough hands. That life had never held any allure for me.

But I knew of that other world, and it might have been out of reach, but early in life, I determined that I would grasp it. While my grandfather lived, I held the dream of happiness. I overlooked my mother's ways. I sometimes saw her as a faerie princess who bestowed wishes upon wild men.

I spent so much time with my grandfather that I soon forgot all other duties. We would train the birds. Teach the ravens to speak. Gather up the eggs in spring and keep them warm in various ways so that the hatchlings would follow us. He sold them to the Baron and to the abbey in exchange for food. The geese of the abbey honked their greeting whenever my grandfather and I came onto the grounds with new hatchlings.

When I imagine the boy that I was, I remember the smell of mud, the grass-stained tunic, the scalp that itched, and yet none of these troubled me. For my grandfather and his birds lifted me to the heavens. I flew with them above all my troubles.

We walked along the path at the edge of the marsh, me running ahead in the exuberance of childhood, while he hobbled along, leaning into a long branch of a tree he'd carved to help him walk. He led me to a great oak that was dead and yet stood thick and tall near a gushing, clear stream. A falcon I had trained the previous winter perched on my shoulder, digging into the leather pad wound there just for protection.

Grandfather had wanted to show me something, and had promised all winter to take me to a particular spot in the Forest "where the treasure grows."

At the tree, he stood upon his toes and pulled away the roots of some thick vines. He lifted me up so that I could see what he had found.

"Put your hand inside it," he told me.

In front of my face, a knot in the oak.

I reached in, my hand nearly too large to make it through the small hole. I felt around, and there was a smooth stone. I drew it out.

I opened my hand to look at it as he lowered me to the ground. I noticed then that he was out of breath, and began to worry that I had tired him.

The stone was a deep blue, but pale and broken at its center, and amber seemed to blossom within it.

Taking deep breaths, my grandfather said, "I told you once of your bloodline. This is a sign of it."

"You must not speak," I said. "You are tired. We can rest. I can bring water."

"No," he said. "Just sit beside me."

He patted the fern-covered ground to his left, and I plopped down, eager to hear a new tale. He cradled me with his arm. He took the stone from me.

"It is worth little now," he said. "But it once was a sign of our family. Before the invaders, our blood ran in the veins of these woods. My grandfather's grandfather's grandfather planted this tree. In those days, there was no abbey. No church. We are now the vanquished. But you must never forget who we were, for it is in your blood to be more than what this world has forced upon you. And what your true father has done."

"My father?" I asked, but when his breathing became labored again, I begged him to rest a bit before speaking.

But he would not. "My birds are the last of my own childhood. They will fly away. But you will remember this day, won't you, Aleric? You will remember me?"

"Always," I said, and I took his hand in mine and leaned over to kiss it. "But you won't ever leave." How young I was to say such things! How ignorant of the pulse of life itself! For, surely, the old man was past the years of hope for life and had managed to survive merely from luck and his love for his family. I could not know then of the disease that had begun to ravage him a few years earlier. That his breathing and his complaints of soreness of old wounds had all been part of the beginning of his demise.

"All who breathe upon this earth," he said, "must depart the flesh. This does not mean that we are not here. The soul flies, and nothing should stop it from spreading its wings, just like a dove. Its journey is known to it alone, not to the one who possesses the dove. Here"—he brought my hand over his heart—"feel the way it pounds, lightly, feebly? Like a drummer marching into the distance?" Then, he brought my hand to my own heart. "Yours is strong and just beginning its journey. But one day it, too, will slow. It is a gift to die, Aleric. You must always remember that. We return to the arms of this." He glanced up at the ceiling of leaves, the deep emerald of the forest. "And the soul flies like a bird to a new nest."

I resisted the sorrow his words brought to me. I pressed my face to his heart, trying to hear it. But it was faint. He stroked the top of my head. "Your falcon has flown," he whispered. "He will be free in the Forest now, for he seeks a mate. He is the age of mating and of the hunt. You will be of that age soon. It is an important time. You will forget the Forest. You will even forget the birds. But you must fight the world, Aleric. It is important to remember. This stone, from the tree. It is of little value in the world. But it is an ancient stone of our people. It was once possessed only by great men and women. We were once of a line of the priests of the Forest. No one speaks of our kind anymore. Many were hunted. Many killed. Many left to become priests in the church of the new god. You are of a priestly caste, my boy. Your talent for the birds shows me that you are closest to the forest ways. You have been taught the woods are full of devils. But you know they are not." As he spoke, his strength seemed to return. I felt the beating of his heart increase, and was glad of it for all the talk of the past and of death and of stones and priests made me think he had but moments left. "I want you to remember this. Your father was a man I despised. Yet he had greatness in him. He was not of our kind, nor of any country I know. He chose your mother because he understood that she was the daughter of the Forest, though she lived in the mud and gave herself too freely to men. He changed her forever. You must forgive her all, for he had power and terror in his gaze. And yet, for all that, he had goodness, as well. That goodness is within you."

"Who was he? Where may I find him?"

"He will find you," my grandfather said. Then, when he had re-gained some of his strength, he lifted me up to put the stone into the oak's knot. Yet, I did not do as he wished. I was afraid that I might never find the tree or the stone again. I slipped it into the leather pouch about my shoulders and did not tell my grandfather I had taken it. The badness of this act did not haunt me until the next morning, when my mother cried out that her father stood too still in the field.

<h2 style="text-align:center">• 5 •</h2>

B Y the time my older sister and I had run out to him, he had already fallen.

"Grandfather!" I shouted, feeling for his heartbeat, while my sister cried out for others to come. I wept over his body, not wanting to be-lieve he had died, not wanting to look at his lifeless face again. I wrapped my arms around his neck, tears flowing too easily.

I heard the birdsong at that moment—just a lark in the field.

As I let go of him, I saw a flock of wild birds flying out from the Forest, across the marshes. Although it may be a trick of memory, I was sure I heard the geese in their chattering sound as if they were praying; and the two ravens he kept circled the sky above us. These did not leave the heavens until my mother had removed his body.

The birds had known. My grandfather had breathed his last, and the birds had taken his soul with them as he had taken them up in his hands at their hatching.

The soul flies, and nothing should stop it from spreading its wings, he had said.

After his death, I grew ill, and feverish. I kept the stone a secret, and rubbed it with my fingers in the night as if wishing for my grand-father to return.

One dawn, I awoke feeling better, but in my soul, anger had grown. I began to see things darkly, I began to view the world as a de-vourer of all that was good. I no longer could find forgiveness for my mother, nor did I find comfort in my siblings. I felt as if all love were lost when that old man dropped in the field, and only my love for the birds remained.

I wanted nothing more than to leave that home and get far away. It became like a thirst that could not be slaked, or a hunger with no fullness after a feast. I could not escape the feeling that I had to get away, the way my older brother Frey had done.

By midsummer's eve, I found a way to leave and still remain close enough to my family to help them when I could.

· CHAPTER 3 ·

The Huntsman

WHEN the Baron's men went looking for a new boy to serve the hunt and train the falcons and goshawks, I begged my mother to take me to the midsummer's fair. It was a league or so up the road, where peddlers sold wares and music played and the huntsmen of the Baron tested the skills of local boys of talent. After the fuss I made over going, my mother relented and took me.

I stood in line behind many other boys, most of whom were of better lives than I had known, but I had prayed to Our Lady and had left a birch twig at the edge of the marsh with a wish to the Forest crones themselves. I had rubbed the blue stone from the oak tree and walked backward at the crossroads in the marshes, which was considered good luck. I had cleaned myself well before the trip, and stood tall and proud as the other boys my age did.

When it came my turn, a broadax of a man with a booming voice and brusque manner checked my teeth and the way my legs moved, in case there was disfigurement, and then my scalp for lice. He commented greatly on my fair hair and red face to his compatriots.

"The Baron likes boys who are rough-and-tumble," he said. "You seem soft. You have hair like a girl's, full of bird's nests, and you smell like a barnacle."

With this comment just out from his lips, I kicked him hard in the shins.

He looked at me, eyes wide with shock, and the next thing I knew, his hand came down for my face. I flew through the air in the next moment, backward onto the grass.

Then, he began to laugh, and gave me a hand up again. "You're a tough little mudlark," he said.

So, this huntsman liked me, and enjoyed my scrappy demeanor. He had me demonstrate my use of the bow and quiver. He asked me how I was at running with the dogs. I told him that I often slept with dogs, and felt they were my cousins. He laughed at this, but I could tell he meant to dismiss me. "And what of your mother? Would she not miss you?"

"I am not a girl who would stay by dung-fire tending the rat-stew," I said, boldly. "I intend to be the greatest of hunters one day. And my mother is a whore." I said this last part without any sense of judgment, for I was used to thinking of her this way. When I said this, the men around us roared with laughter, some of them clapping their hands and a few asking after my mother and whether or not her hair was like mine.

"The Baron would not want the son of a whore in his Forest," said one of the men, who looked like a great bear. He laughed loudly, as if it were the finest joke he'd ever told.

"My father is a great fisherman," I said, allowing the lie to slip off my tongue far too easily. "He has a fleet in the sea, right now, and dives for pearls in the southern sea in the winter. He has made a necklace for the Queen. He finds rare jewels in an ancient city, beneath the waves, and brings them up for the Seven Princesses of Spain."

I can, even hundreds of years later, recall the burning of shame on my cheek that day, as I spun a tale that I hoped would save my reputation as a wellborn boy. I heard myself, as if from a distance, recite the very lies of noble birth and ancestry that my grandfather had taught me, as well as his stories of the Lost City beneath the sea. Even as I said it, I could see it in their faces: not just bemusement or even annoyance at my boasting falsehoods.

They had lost interest.

I had to somehow get the attention of the huntsman again. He seemed kinder than the rest, although his face had something of the aspect of an ogre, and his nose, a serrated blade. But his eyes had a keenness to them as I spoke. I had not just yet lost his attentions. I understood in that moment why my mother, with no means at all, might do anything to entice men to give her what she needed to feed herself and her children.

I needed him to want me working for the Baron. It was my only escape from the life I hated as a child.

I took a deep breath. I prayed to the Lord for guidance. Then, to the Devil for a magick trick.

"If you give me one night in the Forest, I will bring the Baron the most magnificent hunting bird he will ever find." I am certain that I didn't use words quite so well placed at eleven. But I said something as formally and awkwardly as I could to put my point across.

"What kind of bird?" he asked.

The lie came easy, and I convinced myself even as I spoke. "The most magnificent bird, a gryphon, with talons as big as goat's horns, with a wingspan as wide as the castle walls," I said, quite seriously, and nearly believing every word.

His men laughed, but the huntsman nodded. "A wager from the mudlark." He winked and patted my hair, calling me "Yellow bird," and told me that if I could bring him back the finest hunting bird in Christendom, this gryphon of monstrous glory, the following day, I would be the bird-boy in the Baron's hunting party.

"But," he said, "if you do not, if you have lied to me about this business, I shall cut out your tongue. Do you see this?" He drew a small, curved blade from his belt. He held it in front of my eyes until I saw the sunlight glinting from its edge. "I have cut off a man's hands with this blade. I have cut a baby from its mother's belly with it. I have even gutted a stag with it and held its beating heart in my hand. Open your mouth, boy. Open it."

I did as I was told, but had never in my life felt quite so terrified.

He reached forward, and grasped the back of my neck with his left hand. With his right, he brought the blade to the edge of my lips. "Your father is a great fisherman, who dives for pearls in the Southern Sea, say you. Do you know how he takes his blade and cracks the oyster shell and digs in to the squirming meat of it? How he presses the sharp edge at the back of the thick slimy creature, and saws, to and fro, slowly, carefully, to dislodge it from its home?" As he said these words he made slight motions with the knife, its curved end inside my open mouth, not touching anything, but nearly. And then I felt the razor cut of its edge—slight, but painful.

I tasted blood. Metallic as the knife.

Then, he tucked the blade back into his belt and let go of my neck. "Shut your mouth, mudlark. Look at me."

I gazed first at his boot, then at his middle, and, finally, up at his face again. His eyes were pinched and small and like shiny stones.

"Tell me again about this gryphon, for I have heard of these creatures, although I have never seen them. I would like to have one in the Baron's menagerie, both as a hunting bird and pet."

I then had no reason to doubt that this was a sincere interest on his part. The legends of gryphons were everywhere in those days. I knew of one, although I had never seen it. I had been warned away from an ancient sacred well that was far off the path in the Great Forest, entangled with vines and encrusted with the roots of trees to the point that the well—which some called St. Vivienne's Fountain—was barely visible for the green growth around it. My mother, when she heard me mention it, forbade me to speak of it. She told me that it was of another race of people. That it was of an old time, before even the churches had been built, and that it was no Saint that had been martyred there. But she would not tell me the rest. But Mere Morwenna had told me about it, when she found me in the woods at the old ruins, training my birds.

"There is a great bird at the well's bottom," she had said. "As large as a dragon. It has claws that will rip a man to pieces, and a wingspan that can take over the night sky. A thousand years ago, it fell and broke its wings, and so it lies at the bottom of the well." She showed me the well, and told me that the pagan Romans had martyred St. Vivienne there as well. Her story had a profound effect on me, and when I asked my grandfather about it, he told me that if it had such a wingspan and such powerful claws and was an immortal bird, that it must be a gryphon, for that was the only beast with such qualities.

So, with the huntsman and his party surrounding me, I began to sputter on about gryphons and great beasts that had remained unseen by men, but we of the country knew them, of wolves the size of dragons, and dragons the size of mountains, and the poisons of the witches that grew in the shadows of the great oaks. I felt as if I were drowning as I spoke, as if my tongue would soon unfurl and grab his blade from beneath his belt and cut itself off rather than listen to the wild stories I let loose.

The huntsman drew his hand back and slapped me across the face as hard as he could. Knocked me down. In the dirt, I looked up at him, coughing. He bent over, grabbing me as if I were an ash sack, lifting me up from beneath my armpits, and hefting me above his head, all the while keeping watch on my eyes as if to catch the imp of perversity scuttering about inside my soul.

"When you lie," he whispered, "the angels weep. The Devil himself has not lied so much as you have in these precious minutes. Will you tell the truth, Bird Boy? Will you?" As he spoke, he shook and rattled me in the air, and I was fairly certain he would toss me into the crowd before too long.

I felt it was in my best interest to change course.

"I will tell the truth, sir," I said, solemnly. As I spoke, the fair around us disappeared to me, the men beside him vanished, and I felt as if there were just the huntsman and I in all the world. "I am a poor boy, and I have not a trade. Nor is my father a good fisherman, nor does he hunt pearls. My sister took sick and died last winter, and my little brother went soon after. My mother is a wanton, and sleeps with even the clergy for scraps of mutton and pork, but I do not blame her, for she has many mouths to feed. I have but one small talent. And that is for falcons and doves, sir. The birds of the air. I speak to them, in my own way, and they understand me. And they hunt with me."

"So please God if you lie now, I will do more than cut out your tongue," he said.

"I do speak to the birds."

"They listen to you?"

I nodded. "The rock and mourning doves. The falcons, too. I trained a raven to speak by splitting its tongue, and I once raised a hawk to bring fish from the river." This was all true, and had been taught me by my grandfather when I was barely able to speak. The only lie within it was that the birds usually escaped to the Forest once they were of an age, although I could call them to me through whistles and caws now and then.

"Tell me, what did your raven say with his language?"

"He repeated the 'Ave Maria,'" I said, which was true, and made the huntsman laugh like a crash of thunder. "Not every word of it," I said. "Just the first part. His Latin is not as good as our priest's. He flew beside old women as they knelt to pray at Mass, and it was the only thing he would learn. The farmers nearby think he is the spirit of a damned soul, for he now haunts the old burial grounds, repeating the words again and again."

When he had stopped laughing he lowered me to the ground and scruffed my hair with his rough fingers.

"I would love to meet this praying bird," he said. "You hunt in the Forest?"

◆ 2 ◆

IT was against the law to enter the Baron's Forest, despite the fact that I—and all in my family—had been doing so since my memory had begun. A family of bastards might all be slaughtered by a servant of the Baron or the Duke if caught with a boar's head in the home. Poachers, if discovered, were hanged or drowned, depending on the availability of a gibbet or a pond and a sack. Now and then, a poacher was allowed to live as an example to others, and I'd seen one once, his hands cut off at the wrist, his nose also cut off. There was a man named Yannick, who wandered door to door, begging for morsels, because he'd stolen a rabbit from the Great Forest. His hands had been chopped off, as well as the toes on his feet, and his left ear. I did not want any such fate to befall me or my family. One did not break the law lightly. So, I lied a bit.

"No, sir. I hunt in the fields by the cottage. I hunt rat and rabbit and other small creatures of the marsh and field that are not owned by the King or Baron."

"You speak well for a meadowlark."

"My grandfather taught me to speak well."

"Your grandfather is alive?"

"No, sir."

"What was his name?"

When I mentioned my grandfather's name, the huntsman nodded. "Tell me, how did the old man die?"

I told him of the day in the field, and of the ravens and doves, as well as the flocks of birds that seemed to be everywhere at his death, though I, perhaps, exaggerated the tale as it went.

"Did your grandfather mention his time in the Wars?"

I shook my head.

"I knew him," the huntsman said. He half smiled. "Ronan was a fine soldier of his day." Then, his mood darkened. "And your mother is his daughter?"

Again, I nodded.

"Armaela." When he said her name, it sent a slight chill through me. I had never heard a man say her name without trying to bed her. "I knew her, many years ago," he said. "You must not speak ill of her. Your family truly was once a great one. Perhaps you have greatness in you, though your kind has fallen from favor in these present times. Let this be an understanding between us, boy, should you think ill of any for whom life's fortunes have turned. Misfortune is the world. Those who are kings today may be knaves by sunrise tomorrow. Those who are peasants without means may become princes of the world. Only you and I know this to be true, for I have seen it come to pass, and remembered, while others forget and believe that we are each born to our station and remain there until death. Remember this moment in future years. Remember when a man plucked you from the mud and brought you into a better life."

He glanced over at his compatriots, and roared for them to go off and drink or wench or devour roasts, but that he was going to go with me to the Forest to see how well I called the birds. He told me to call him by his name, not the haughty French name of his father, but by his Breton name, which was a fairly common one of the time: Kenan. His father had been from the south, by way of France, and his mother had lived her whole life in the castle, and died there while he was still a boy, sent off to fight Norsemen along the coast. When he had returned to his home, it had changed, and he no longer hungered for war and adventure. Although he seemed old to me then, Kenan could not have been more than his late twenties. Yet, he had a kind of halo of age around him, as if life had been too hard on him.

I took him down a well-worn path. Once we had gone into the murky part of the woods, where the bramble grew thick and high, I tied his horse to one of the old oaks. When he'd dismounted, I took him by the hand and led him in among the giant ferns and the roots rising up like low cottages among the part of the Forest. Running within the overgrowth, the remnants of an old Roman wall. My grandfather had told me that many years before, when his great-great-great-great-great-grandfather had lived, this had been a military outpost when the Romans fought the true people of the land. I showed him the stones that were the markers of the dead.

"Is this where your birds speak?"

I nodded, and cupped my hands to my mouth and let out a whistle and a call that I had learned from too young an age even to know where I'd learned it. Within seconds, a giant raven swooped down from the dark green canopy above us and came to rest on one of the ancient stones.

I held my arm out, and chirruped for the bird, and it flew to my shoulder. It was always a jolt when it grasped me, and I had to steady myself, for the bird had grown large over the past year. I pursed my lips, and my wild pet cocked its head to one side, then another, and leaned over and pressed its beak to my lips.

"Sing to me," I commanded.

And then the raven began reciting the "Ave Maria," but in the poor accent and mispronounced words as I might do it myself.

Kenan roared with laughter, which scared my dark friend away. The bird flew up again, and although I whistled for it, it had become skittish around this stranger.

I looked up at him.

"And what of the gryphon?" he asked.

"I have never seen it," I told him. "But I know where there is an ancient well, and at the bottom of the well, a gryphon lies, immortal, but broken-winged."

"And who told you this?"

"A crone," I said. "Her name is Mere Morwenna. Although she raises a young child, she is ancient. She is bent and hobbled, a friend of my mother's, and has some pox across her face so she lives deep in the woods so that she might not spread her plague. Her child is hideously deformed. Yet she has wisdom, my mother says."

"She has a plague but has lived long?"

I nodded. "I have never seen her face, for she hides it with a veil. But once, she came to our home to offer the leaves and bark of the birch tree to help my mother bear the birth of my little sister. She told me then of the creature in the well. She has told me never to visit the well, but I have gone once or twice and heard the gryphon crying out, at midday. It is the saddest sound." This last part was something of a lie, for though I had been near the spot, I had never actually heard anything from within the well itself. Still, the lie added a nice glow to his face, and a bit of a light grew in his eyes.

"And if you were to capture this beast, how would you do that?"

"I would first ask for a large fisherman's net. Then, a rope. I would tie one end of the rope to a hook lodged at the top of the well. Then I would climb down the well, with the net. When I reached the bottom, I would cover the gryphon with the net and have someone—perhaps you, sir, draw me back up."

"That wouldn't work," Kenan said, a grin on his face. "The gryphon would be too heavy for you to bring up. And it might fight you. And it might hurt you. Kill you."

"Might," I said. "At midday the gryphon is weak. It has not eaten for many years, perhaps centuries. It has no fight left in it. And I, sir, am very strong."

"You must show me this well one day, mudlark," my huntsman said. He put his hand on my shoulder. "You may have been born under a lucky star. I believe you may have work with the hunt." He told me that if I proved able with falcons, I might end up a huntsman just as he had become one from being a boy who worked with the horses once. He mentioned a brief memory of knowing my grandfather, yet Kenan would not tell me much of what he knew of him.

That night, I drew out the blue stone that my grandfather had shown me at the oak tree, which I had stolen to keep near me at all times. I rubbed it for luck, and for hope, that I might prove myself in my work and help my brothers and sisters in some way. I kissed the stone, remembering my grandfather's face, feeling a twinge of guilt that I had not returned the gem to its rightful place, yet comforted that I drew the memory of the old man into it and held it there.

• 3 •

FROM that day forward, I went to live within the Baron's household. Although I knew my huntsman to be named Kenan Sensterre, I was instructed to call him "sir," or even, "Master," for the sake of the castle.

Now the castle was not the enormous fortress of history, but a fairly simple structure of wood and earth, grand in its own way, yet fairly primitive in others. Very little of it was made of stone, except the chapel and beneath it, the kitchen, and beneath that, underground, a dungeon of sorts to hold prisoners. The structure was pentagonal in its interior, but from the outside, palisades seemed curved in a circle. It was built upon a low, smooth hillside overlooking the Forest and marshlands, close enough to the abbey and the village if there ever was an attack (for truthfully, the abbey was a better fortress if trouble neared). The village beyond it was protected by the Duke, then the great King, whose name was never spoken to me but was simply known as the father of our universe, next to God.

The Baron was simply called "my lord," if any were to see him, but in the first weeks of my employment, I rarely spoke a word to the great man. The Baron himself was perhaps the richest man within one hundred hectares of land, which today I suppose would be a thousand acres or so. Treveur de Whithors had been the name he'd been known by as a knight in one of the Crusades, and he had returned from years of battle to his storehouse of land and coin, married quickly, and had three sons. All had gone to war but the youngest, who was still a baby, and remained with nurses and maids, and was treated like a pampered pet. He also had three daughters who, as they grew, were capable of running the castle by themselves. His wife took sick after her last child had been born, and this lingering ailment brought a kind of unspoken grief to the household that shadowed its halls and etched lines in its quarters.

I felt the brunt of the Baron's anger at times, as passed to me by other servants; I also felt his generosity during the Christmas feasts. I felt as if I were a princeling, even so. I slept in a room with the other boys who worked under the Baron's household, and at Holy Days and in seasons of plenty, I was able to take bread and fowl to my mother and little brothers and sisters. The work took me from dawn until midnight some days, and it was thankfully constant, so that I always had a roof over my head and food in my belly. I raised doves, swans, and falcons from the egg, and trained them for the needs of the castle. My name "Aleric" was soon lost, and I became first Mudlark, then Bird Boy, and finally, Falconer before my first working year had ended.

The other boys were often envious of the attention that my master gave me, and one in particular named Corentin Falmouth, who some in the castle took to calling Foul-Mouth, seemed to enjoy tormenting me in the few hours of sleep I had.

Corentin first came up to me when I had laid claim to the straw mat in the corner not far from the fire, and told me that a boy had burned from lying too close to the hearth. "You should sleep in the back, with me," he said, pointing to a pile of bedding in a dark corner. "I can be your protector."

I soon learned that he believed protection meant keeping me from being beaten—by him.

Like me, he was a boy from the country, and reminded me somewhat of my older brother Frey, and what I imagined he might look like then. Handsome, and not particularly charming, Corentin at first seemed as if he would be my guide and confidant. There was something of the familiar to him, and to his manner of speech—he was a youth who had come from the marshes and woods, as had I. We spoke some of the Old Tongue, as well as the New. He had been educated a bit, as far as working boys could be, when he went to work with the Brothers, cleaning their quarters and learning bites from their lessons.

He told me that the Brethren had taught him much about the world and its workings, and how a boy might rise in station further than he could imagine if only he would put himself under the care of the correct guide. He placed his hand on my shoulder and whispered to me that I should not be afraid so long as he was nearby and would be my guide. At first, I thought this delightful and part of the goodness that life had to offer me. I soon learned that he exacted tribute from those of us he considered his vassals, and that he was nothing like my brother Frey at all, nor much like any who might be called country people. He was not particularly adept at companionship. He would crawl onto the straw-stuffed bed, and tell me of the tortures that the Baron put to boys who lied or disobeyed.

Corentin was older—perhaps sixteen—and he was the unofficial leader of some of the other ruffians with whom I shared quarters. Most of them had not come from families as poor as mine, but they bemoaned their lives as if they had been dealt the worst fate that had ever been conjured. Most were the second and third sons of noble blood, with no estates, no legacy, and many of them were destined for the monastery in a few years if they were lucky. Corentin himself claimed to have no living family, and perhaps I could feel for him in his lonely misery, but he insisted on tormenting me.

"Your mother is a whore. She is known throughout the village, and the priest takes pity on her when he allows her to Mass. I heard from a courier that she slept with his horse for a tankard of ale."

The most frightening thing about his voice and his words were that I had thought of my mother in the same way. And yet, it incensed me to hear this from him. My heart grew dark with hatred of him. I had to resist wrestling him to the ground, although I didn't resist nine times out of ten, and we'd roll around on the floor of our chamber hitting and biting and tearing at each other. Corentin, the stronger, the larger, the older, had the better of me. I often ended up bruised and battered at dawn, but still arose to get out to my birds and my work.

I was determined not to allow anyone to stop me from proving myself and moving forward in life, though Corentin did his best to tell me that Mud-hens (for that was his own nickname for me) never rose higher than I had, and that when I reached sixteen, I would be sent back to the filth from which I had been born. "Or else you will be sliced from nave to chops," he said, making a motion with his hand from his sack to his chin. "And your head will be stuck on a pike."

This last part terrified me, for I had seen the heads of criminals on pikes during certain months when treason had been discovered.

I had gone to the executions of the depraved and the indigent and those who had cursed the Church or those who had committed adultery. I had seen three children—two brothers and their younger sister—all hanged at the gibbet just outside the Baron's castle, none of them more than six years old, for stealing food from a family of good lineage. Mud-hens, indeed, could be hanged, or their heads severed from their bodies and thrust onto pikes for all to see the faces of those who had broken the law.

Corentin's words gave me nightmares when I had thoughts against those surrounding me. I had to keep my humours balanced and my emotions buried, or else I might, one day, wind up spinning slowly on a rope or sliced with a hand ax for having sinned in some great or small way. Although I had seen Death before with my family, it was among the boys of the hunt and the stables that I saw it pass by, and often. A chill would come, and suddenly three of my cohorts would catch fevers in the night, and no amount of fire in the hearth or soup in their bellies drove Death away.

I began to see Death as a great King, perhaps the greatest Fallen King of the Earth, for Death ruled all, was feared by all, and yet, had no worshippers in any chapel. Death was the unacknowledged visitor in every household. Corentin reminded me of how Death could arrive, and I hated him for it but could not get far away from his words. I was the most humble and most impotent of the boys in the Baron's household. If Corentin, who outranked me in position as well as age, had decided that I had committed a terrible crime, he could let it be known to the Baron, and I might be dead before the next morning. While I didn't live in fear of this, I knew that the possibility for deviltry existed with Corentin, and his word would be taken over mine.

Thus it was that when Corentin one night came to my bed and pressed himself into me, turning me onto my stomach, holding my arms such that I had no movement in them, that I cried out into the straw and not for others for help. A boy who was thus used would certainly be thrown out of his occupation, and perhaps worse would befall him. He might even be found as guilty as the perpetrator of the deed itself. King Death might visit him next, for whether the sodomer or sodomee, the crime reflected both as evildoers. There were no innocent parties. Sodomy was considered the Devil's worst offense, and although I would later find out of its acceptance among certain warriors, in that world I occupied at twelve, to be named a catamite was to be as good as burned alive. Although I tried to fight him, he overpowered me and had his way. It was not a sexual impulse on his part; even then I was aware of this. He was pissing on me, the way a dog might piss on something to mark its territory. To keep the pissed-upon from rising up. To somehow damage me. His laughter afterward told me that. He was interested only in destroying me. In pushing me aside. In ensuring that a Mud-hen would not rise above his lowly station, and that if one would rise, it would be Corentin Falmouth himself, whose father was the third son of a Breton family that had risen in their fortunes since God had decreed it many centuries before, then fallen all too swiftly—or so he claimed.

I bore the shame for weeks on end, and slept little but kept watch for my nemesis. But it was the last he ever came near me or spoke to me for a long while. I began to hope that he might be afraid of me. That something in his vile act upon my body had terrified him. I can only guess that he felt he had done his work on me.

But he had not.

And no matter what ill he wished me, I prospered despite his taking of the last remnant of my childhood from me, which was not my innocence but my love for all mankind. I would weep for the child I was, but I truly had fury in my heart, as well as innocence. My grandfather had warned me to take the good with the bad, and never to forget that all within life had both. I, too, had both good and bad. But Corentin seemed completely evil to me, and I saw no good in him.

Truly, I wanted to kill him and keep him from hurting others as he had hurt me. I wanted to cut out his tongue so that he could not say the words of loathing of my mother, though there were times when I felt them in my heart, as well. He was like a shadow that I could not rid myself of—for when I thought of evil, when I held the idea in those years of all that was terrible about the world, Corentin's face came into view, whether in my mind or before me in one of the chambers.

And yet, I dare admit to myself that even then, part of Corentin was too much like me, as if he were me, a few years ahead, having taken a slight turn in the path of life from where I would stand one day. Had I been sharper, perhaps I would have seen in his demeanor a caution to me, a mirror of what I might become: a predator in the world, and more than that, a predator who made all around him into prey.

From that moment, I went to the boys and the esquires who worked with the knights, and watched as they lifted their swords. I intended to learn to fight like a man, and, if necessary, kill a man well in order to protect myself from any who wished to harm me.

I would kill Corentin if given the opportunity.

I would risk the gallows to stop him from ever harming me, or anyone I knew, again.

⋆ 4 ⋆

A ND yet there were sunny days as well as the murky ones.

The huntsman, my master, Kenan Sensterre, had a masculine grace about him, and despite his boisterous appearance and occasional moodiness, he and I grew close as I ran alongside his horse, twin falcons on my leather-strapped arms. He taught me much about the bow, and about hefting the sword in such a way as to increase the strength of the shoulders and arms. He took me to the machine that the knights used to train, and we spent an idle hour simply running at each other so that he could show me proper technique. Our hunts together seemed unforgettable to me—he had the prowess of an archer in top form, while I knew the paths through the Forest where the wild boars rooted. We hunted boar and rabbit and stag, and I showed him many byways and paths across the treacherous marshes that were rarely crossed by any but poachers. He asked me if I had ever seen those sacred nymphs of the Old Way known as the Briary Maids. I laughed when he said this, for I knew them as imaginary tales told to the young.

"They are girls of the wood who seduce and destroy youths," I said. "By calling them to the edge of cliffs and down into deep bogs covered with briars." I told him that they couldn't possibly exist because if they did, many more young men would go a-missing. But there was, of course, truth to the legend, for whenever a young man was found, by himself, drowned, or having thrown himself from a rock ledge to his death, it was said he was called by the Maids of the Briar, rather than that he had killed himself. The Briary legend was at least as old as the Forest itself, and sometimes I wondered if Mere Morwenna and her hags were not, in fact, of the Briary themselves. In the village and the Baron's household, Morwenna was often called Morwenna Bramblebog for just this reason. For it was thought she was no longer a woman at all, but a damned spirit that roamed the woods and marshes, calling out to those who were weak in faith to come join her and her sisters in their deviltry among the oaks and birches.

You may wonder how the Old Ways and the New could live side by side, yet if you look around the world, even in the most intolerant land, there is some tolerance, particularly when those being tolerated have no land and no coin to steal. Charges of witchcraft were rare in those days, and when they were brought, underlying the charge was theft, or a poisoning, or adultery, where bewitchment may have been the action of the accused; but it was not the crime that committed the woman to death. But things were beginning to change, and as the abbey and its monks grew richer, and the Baron sold more of his knights off to the Crusades for a mercenary's share, I began to notice that the whisper of sorcery and witchcraft was growing stronger among those in Christendom, as if an enemy were growing in the ranks.

Kenan told me about his fears of the witches in the Forest, and how even hunting the stag, he had once seen something that utterly terrified him and made him rush to the church for a blessing and a Mass from our Pater. "We chased the stag for three days, deeper and deeper into the woods. This was so many years ago, before you were even born, and I was still a boy, training with my own master. We did not understand how one stag could have the energy to keep running, without stopping for eat or drink. Exhausted, I ran with my master into a clearing, and there we saw our stag—which was snow-white and with a great crown of antlers that were of so many twists and turns that it seemed impossible. And there, the beast went into a bog that was as black as night.

"My master and I cut through the brambles, and waded into the bog. I had a spear, and he had his bow, but when I entered that water, I felt as if I might burn—it was so hot that bubbles came up from beneath its surface. Still, my master entered the water, though I stayed near the muddy land. I called to him to leave the stag to its fate, for the beast waited at the center of that terrible bog, as if watching the both of us, taunting us to follow it in. Then, my master took one step farther as he aimed his arrow for the stag's neck, and in that one step, his fate was sealed. He slipped, and went beneath the surface of the water.

The stag went to the other side of the bog, slipping back into the woods. And I waded into the bog, calling to my master, wondering where he had gone. Finally, he came up, and he nearly thrashed me, thinking I was some demon.

"He told me that when he went beneath the water, he saw such things as he thought never to have dreamed. He saw a war on Earth of demons and sorcery, and a woman whose cloak was the night as she swept down upon the world of men and made them tremble. He forbade me to tell this to anyone, then we returned to the hunting party to tell them that the stag had gone too deep into the Forest to be tracked.

"The worst of it was, I, too, had seen something in that water. I never even told my master. Before the stag departed the bog, it spoke in some language I could not understand, but I knew it was a corruption of the Old Tongue. It spoke to me, directly, although I could not understand it, still, I knew its message: we must never come to this place again, and were I to do so, I would die. I remember how unnatural that beast was, Falconer, with its white coat and its antlers that seemed like brambles themselves. The priest told me that the demons of old lurk where the Church has not yet consecrated. The deep of the woods is a deadly place, and the servants of Satan are everywhere there, waiting."

Despite the chill I felt at his story, I admit that it intrigued me, for I was not afraid of bogs or stags, and I wished to have great adventures. Perhaps my head had swelled in the years I had eaten the Baron's food, but my childhood in the mud-and-straw hut seemed another life, a dream I, a huntsman's apprentice, the Falconer, had once had— a nightmare, perhaps. I had even, in my mind, created a family from the Baron's house, with Kenan Sensterre as my father, and my mother as the rarely seen matron of the castle, the Baroness.

In many ways, my master seemed to be the kind of father that children only dream about, although he did not suffer idleness or stupidity or falsehood without drawing a whip out and tying one of the working boys to the post. I had even suffered under this punishment, but it was meted out with such efficiency that I could not take offense, for I often stole an apple from the kitchen wench, or fell asleep at the edge of the pond when I should have been herding the swans to the butcher's block. I took kindly to my benefactor. As I grew older, I showed him the secrets of teaching certain birds—mainly blackbirds— to speak. He told me that in his travels, he had seen birds with long tails singing songs in pitch, and promised that if he ever traveled to the southern mountains again, he would capture one and bring it back to me. Later, he decided that he couldn't encourage this, because of the fears of sorcery that abounded, since many believed that talking birds were the Devil's emissaries.

I revealed the secret of my trainings of the falcons and where possible, even the swans: being there the moment they emerged from the broken shell in their nest. "You must be the first they see," I told him. "Even the falcon's mother cannot be the nestling's first sight. You must be the one. Your face. Your voice. Your eyes. Then, the bird will follow your every move and will not leave your side. It is impossible to train them well if they already have flown from the nest."

Then, one day he asked me again about the gryphon. "You told me more than a year ago of a legendary beast at the bottom of a well," he said. "I have since heard of this well, although my kinsmen do not know of its location. Tell me, Falconer, were you telling me the truth about this?"

I nodded. "As far as I understand what is true, sir."

"Then, take me there," my master said. "I must capture that creature."

• CHAPTER 4 •

The Gryphon

• 1 •

IT was a day of fog and omens of foreboding. The sun emerged only in a round aurora, the outline of pale disk against the tattered white sky. We watched as an owl flew out from the gassy marshes, like a ghost in the misty air, although neither of us spoke a word about it. A family of beggars met our horse on the road, and this, too, was a sign of ill tidings for beggars were considered blights and presagers of turns of luck. We passed by them, and I glanced back at the man, hobbled by nature, in a cart pushed by his too-weary wife and their three young children. I thought of my own family, and how close we were to being such as they.

The enshrouding mist grew thicker as we passed along the swamp. My master now and then said a word to me about the silkiness of the water and how it seemed deep for that time of year. I glanced down from the horse, and thought I saw faces in the cloudy water alongside the raised paths. We rode into the arms of the Great Forest together, me in front, leaning back against his body. I shouted directions as we came to the verdant path that twisted and turned and looped between trees and over hillocks. The mist lessened the deeper we went. His horse bounded over rotting logs and continued to gallop along what had once been a road but now was covered with fern until the Forest grew too thick around us. Then, we dismounted, and he led the horse a ways before tying her up just before the last thin line of grassy, rocky path that ended completely along a gully.

"This wood is dangerous," he said. "The wolves are hungry this year. You have ventured this far before?"

I nodded, pointing off through a bramble thicket. "Through there," I said. "They call it the Forest Door."

"Who are 'they'?"

"Folk," I said, for lack of a better word.

"Ah, commoners." He grinned. "They're not afraid of these woods?"

"At times afraid," I said. "At times, not."

"There are folk who live here," Kenan said. "They are full of old deviltry from the days before Christian charity. They cling to sorcery." His voice took on a distinct tone, as if he were afraid to speak like this surrounded by the trees. "My father told me once of these folk."

"I have seen them," I said. "But they are not devils. They live more humbly than even my brothers and sisters. And yet they are richer than kings in some ways."

"If they live in this Forest, they are trespassers and poachers," he said, sternly, but again, I detected a quiver of fear in his voice.

I jumped over a mossy stone and stepped into the emerald darkness as trees began to block the sun above us. I cut my arms and face a bit on the brambles. Kenan drew his knife and slashed at the branches, which were full of a purple berry that I'd been told all my life never to taste. Then, past this sentry of Nature, we both saw the ancient stone wall. It had more gaps in its masonry than when I'd been younger, and the overgrowth of vine and fern had all but devoured it.

"It is not too much farther," I told him, and ran to the wall and scrambled over the top of it. On the other side of the stones, I glanced around the thickset trees, and located the mound that I believed to be the well. When Kenan and I stepped up to it, he said, "This is a Devil's Fountain."

I laughed, and he reached out with his hand and slapped me so hard I fell to the ground. Rubbing my cheek, I looked up at him.

"This is the well I have heard of," he said. "It was sealed so long ago that I thought it was simply a legend. And you say there's a gryphon at the bottom of it?"

I nodded, rising, not sure whether or not I should near him again. "I heard it once. It wailed, but was weak."

He leaned over the mound and began tearing the vines from its top, using his knife to cut away at the roots from nearby trees. "Get over here!" he shouted. "Boy, get over here!"

I did as I was told, and went to help him clean off the well. If there had once been a seal to this well to block its opening, it was long gone. Instead, we both looked down into its darkness. A stench unlike any I'd before experienced wafted up from that pit.

He whispered, as if afraid of being overheard. "Are you certain there's a gryphon?"

I nodded and whispered to him, "With a huge wingspan." Then, to prove something to him, I leaned over the edge of the well and shouted, "Gryphon!"

My voice echoed back up to me, then faded.

I watched the round darkness and thought that if I could not prove my gryphon to my benefactor, he would likely tip my legs up and throw me down the well as punishment for a lie.

But as we both listened, a sound came back up from the depths of the well.

It was a faint "oooo," then a screech that truly might've been the rasp of a great bird.

◆ 2 ◆

KENAN organized a party to go out into the Forest the next day, with me, the captain of the hunt, running on foot beside them. Rather than merely cut the brambles of the Forest Door, they brought torches at midday and burned most of it, managing to contain the fire so as not to overtake the Forest itself. What had been the Forest Door was now a desolate, blackened floor that still smoked with ash as I walked through it.

I had begun to think that I had done wrong by leading the huntsman there. I saw in his gang of hunters an odd bloodthirst. They shot arrows at rabbits and other small animals they encountered, leaving the dying creatures where they lay—it was a pleasure kill, which I never understood, given the hunger and want of my own upbringing. Then, when they reached the ancient wall, rather than simply leap over it, they wished to ride on through. So, with several of these fellows, I had to help pull down stones from the wall, which was heavy work, and which exhausted my body and spirit. But still, we pressed on, and came to the well.

Kenan was the first down from his steed, then came a young man just married named Reinald, who had come from the southern countries to claim his dowry and take up a station with the Baron. He dragged down the net he'd brought, and a trident made of iron that was used to bait lions, he'd told us. "This will subdue any creature," he said, his voice a muted growl.

I admit that I got into this sport, and became excited as all the men gathered around and tied a rope about my waist and shoulders, with another between my legs with a small plank as a seat of sorts. The gleam in the huntsman's eye told me that there would be a rich reward for capturing a beast that few had ever seen. He passed me a torch and warned me about burning myself. I was to descend to the base of the well and see in what condition the gryphon remained, then they'd toss the net down. I was to secure it around the gryphon, then take one of the ropes at my waist and attach it to the noose at the edge of the net.

"Use your fire if you need a weapon," Reinald said.

Only then did I become a little frightened of what I faced; but I saw the crew with their courage and bravado, and felt that this would be the crowning moment of my life if I carried it out.

Down, down, down they lowered me. The light from my torch brightened the dark descent. I saw scratches and strange symbols scrawled into the damp, mossy stones. The smoke from my torch made me cough, and now and then I had to grip it tight for fear that I'd drop it below. They lowered me slowly, but it seemed like hours before I reached the bottom of the well. It was muddy, with perhaps less than an inch of water. I glanced up to the entry of the well, and it seemed like a pale coin above me.

What I first saw as I brushed the torch about was that the well was wide at its base, like a large round room.

I saw the creature off to one edge of it. The beast lay, curled, forming a circle, with wings that encompassed its form.

I glanced up to the huntsmen above me, but was afraid to shout to them for fear of stirring the gryphon. I waved my torch as if it were a flag. As I did this, the torch's fire diminished. Perhaps it was the damp air that took away the fire, but before I could do much more than stare at the creature, my torch had nearly turned to a soft ember.

Then, I heard a *whoosh* above me, and the distant shouts of the hunting party. I looked up, and saw a twisted ball fall from above. It was the net. I moved to one of the cavernous recesses of the well, and the ball of netting dropped, unraveling slightly to the wet ground. I quickly ran to get it, and began to unfurl it so that I could somehow get it around the creature. I touched something sharp and hard with my foot, and using the last bit of torchlight, looked down. Were they bones? Had other creatures been trapped in this well, along with the gryphon?

Then, fearing that I had awoken it, for I was sure I heard a slight rattling noise, I glanced back through the shadows to the beast. Was it sleeping? Had it died? I didn't know. I could not be sure, although I heard no breath from it. My torch diminished to little more than a spark, giving off a feeble candlelight so that I barely could see my hand in front of my face. I walked slowly to the creature, but in the growing dark, it seemed simply to be dead, and the stench I had smelled was a sulfurous odor off its slick wings.

I took nearly an hour getting the net around it, greatly relieved that it hadn't stirred. Even dead, this gryphon would be a prize. Just as I got the net sealed at its noose, my torch went out completely.

I did my best with the ropes, tying them to the noose, attaching it to the rope from which I'd been lowered.

Once I felt it was set, I gave a high-pitched whistle. As I did so, I thought I saw movement within the net.

The men above began hauling the rope up, and it went fast because the gryphon was not as heavy as it had looked.

Soon after, the rope dropped, and in the dark, I felt for it. I knotted my seat and strap into it, and was lifted up again.

When I reached the lip of the well at the top, I saw that all but the two men who had drawn me up were gathered around the beast in the net.

My master's face was ashen. He drew his sword, holding it aloft.

Other men cut away at the net.

The wings were not as I had expected. I'd been told that gryphons had wings with gold feathers like a hawk, but with a great shine to them. But these wings were like a dragon's, and seemed like an eel's skin pulled over arched bone. The wings were ragged also, but if, as legend had it, this beast had been in the well for as long as any of the crones' memories, it no doubt had torn itself on rocks and the stone wall of the well trying to get out.

The huntsman said, "It is the Devil himself."

I looked at him, shocked, and the others. This could not be the Devil. It could not be. The man named Reinald, using his sword, drew back one of the wings.

Beneath the enormous wings, a man's body. It was shriveled and dried, like a corpse, and naked. He had barely an ounce of fat to him, and seemed a bag of bones. But when the wings had been drawn apart, his eyes began to open and his lips, ragged and parched, parted slightly. His eyes were pale white, and I saw for a moment his teeth, which were like a wolf's.

Swiftly, Reinald took his sword and raised it up over the creature's throat, bringing it down, then sawing to separate the head from the body. Then, he plunged the sword into the breast of the creature, twisting it as if searching for its heart. He drew his sword out, and it did not drip with blood at all, which seemed more than miraculous to me. It was a chilling sight to witness, and I daresay that all of us had that feeling of ice in our veins at that moment.

Then, Reinald tossed his sword to the ground as if it were cursed.

He looked first at the huntsman, then to me, pointing at my face, "You have brought us to the Devil's Jackal, boy. This is damnation."

I stood there, shaking, confused, until the huntsman came to me, and said, "I have heard of these creatures, Falconer. I have heard of them, but did not believe they existed. The wars brought this one here, I'm sure, from the East along with other pestilence. It is a demon that brings plague with it."

"I thought it was a gryphon. I did. I thought it was," I said, feeling as if I had committed the worst crime.

"We must burn it," Reinald announced, and went to get one of the torches from his companions. "Then, we must scatter its ashes so that they might not ever find their way back from Hell."

He set the torch on the body, jabbing it into the chest. The oily skin of the creature quickly caught fire, and the fire spread out to the wings.

We all gathered around the burning demon, the stench a mix of sulfur and venison, and, on our knees began reciting the Nostre Pater.

• 3 •

THAT evening, we camped briefly, for the men had lost their courage upon the sight of the winged demon. It was a terrible omen for them all. Though I had not known what lay at the bottom of the well, I could tell by their glances that I was held responsible for bringing them to this unholy spot, to this demon place.

When I went to grab a bit of bread from one of the men, for I had grown hungry during the day, Kenan hefted me up by the collar and dragged me back from them, among the trees near the well. "Do not speak to anyone of this," he said, after dropping me to the ground. I felt as if I had done something wrong and looked up at him as he returned to the well. He stood there, glaring at me. "Do you know what you've done?" he asked.

I had no voice in me to respond.

"You've cursed us," he said. "You brought the Devil into our camp. Those men, my men, they believe the plague is coming. Do you understand?"

"I . . . I didn't mean to," I said, weakly. "I thought it was a . . ."

"I should have known," he said, closing his eyes, and beating his fist against his breast. "I should have known. When your mother . . ."

Opening his eyes, he seemed to have calmed slightly. He whispered something, and gestured for me to draw close to him. As I approached, he swiftly picked me up and swung around, holding me over the well. I became frightened, nearly out of my wits, sure that he would drop me to my death in that awful place.

"You do not know why you are with me. You do not know what your mother has done in her past. But had I known you would bring us to find a demon, I would have left you in the mud, no matter how well you speak to birds, boy." His harsh words beat against me, and I fought back tears. I did not understand this sudden change of heart. I did not understand what curse this winged demon brought with it.

Finally, he set me back on the ground, and spoke softly. "I have seen demons before," he said. "They bring ill winds upon those who witness them. I know it is not your fault. But it may be in your blood to know where they live. To bring them into the light of day."

He spoke more, about the Devil, about what he regretted without mentioning these regrets by name. I felt as if I watched a man I had admired and respected grow mad, mumbling words about the past, about his youth, and the wars he had seen when he had been but little older than I.

Finally, wearily, he began walking back to his huntsmen. As he passed me, he gave me a cold glance and said, "Corentin was right about you. From the start."

The words chill me now as they did then. My worst enemy had

begun to destroy me in small ways, and my greatest protector had begun to turn against me.

• 4 •

THE story of the demon spread like fire across the village and abbey. Fears of plague arose, then died down again, as no one seemed to be getting sick, and though a woman died from drowning in the marsh, and at first this was seen as the Devil's work, such rumors were whispered rather than shouted. The priest and the Brethren blessed the land and the abbey and the village and the Baron's household, and soon all returned to normal for us.

Except for me. At the time, I could not know what mechanism had turned my master against me, other than Corentin himself. Days went by when Kenan did not speak to me, nights passed when I could not sleep, rubbing my grandfather's blue stone, praying that my master would have a change of heart.

One cold morning, my mother arrived at the courtyard, riding in the back of a wagon with other beggars. When I found her, I went to get bread and what scraps of meat I could find, for she had nothing to feed my younger brothers and sisters. But when I returned to her, Kenan Sensterre was there, waiting for me. He came up to me, slapping the food from my hands and pushing me to the cold ground. "She is a bad woman," he said. "Do not feed her. Do not clothe her."

I gathered up some of the bread, hiding it under my cloak. "Why have you changed, master? What have I done? What has my mother done?"

Without answering, he left me there, and I took what I could to my mother, who shivered at the gates.

"He cannot forgive," she said.

"What have I done to him? And why should he hurt you?"

I remember her face so clearly: it was filthy, but shone with an inner light. Her hair, though matted, seemed to catch the sun's glow, and her small hands held mine briefly before taking the bread from me. She had the heat of fire, even in her cold hands. "He has helped us. Even though he is angry now. He has blessed us. Do not forget that, ever."

She leaned into me to kiss me on the cheek, but I drew away. I felt confused and unhappy, and unsure of anything I had believed. "You must accept life," she told me. "The way it is."

"Grandfather once told me we were from a noble line," I said.

"He was a liar," she said, and what light I had seen in her eyes grew dark as she turned to go. Her feet were wrapped in bandages, and her cloak was torn and ragged.

"I will come one night with shoes, and clothing," I told her.

She glanced back, briefly. "Do not risk your life here for my sake. I wanted this for you. You must forget you ever knew the field and its misery."

I blurted, without meaning to, "You must stay away from Mere Morwenna. And the Forest women. There have been demons. It is a dangerous time."

She smiled, as if about to laugh at me, but then thought better of it. "The demons of the world wear men's faces."

As she stepped beyond the gateway, a sharp call from my master brought me back to my duties.

• 5 •

CORENTIN taunted me one night by the fire. "They say that common folk worship the Horned One. They say that those pagan demons are still in the Forest, and all of them need to be burned. I bet you are from a family of witches," he said. "They think you want to bring the plague into the castle. Some believe that your family is unsanctified."

"I was baptized just as you," I spat back at him.

"They say the Devil looks like an angel when he wants," he said. "I would not be surprised if the Devil has been baptized in order to fool village folk."

I went to the village priest and asked for forgiveness of my sins, though I was not certain that I had many. He took my confession, although my penance was minor, and asked me why I was so vexed. I told him of the demon in the well, and how my master had changed toward me, and my mother's words, and he began to read from the Bible in Latin, none of which I understood, but it sounded holy and magical and I felt Mary, the Queen of Heaven, with me. The priest assured me that he would light a candle for my soul.

Kenan Sensterre remained distant from me in a way that he hadn't been, and I never again felt his touch on my shoulder, nor a kind word from him in the hunt. I wasn't sure then what great sin I had committed, but these were fearful, ignorant times.

There were times when I saw Corentin walking with my master, and I felt rage and shame that my greatest enemy should take the hand of him who had once been my only friend. I wondered what Corentin had told him, what nastiness that enemy of mine had perpetrated. In those days, when I was still young, I did not understand what my grandfather had told me about the good and the bad, and so it confused me further to think bad of Kenan when he had been so good to me, once.

Corentin had grown handsome and thick of arm and leg in a way that ladies remarked upon. It was as if the sun lit his hair during the daylight hours, and in the night, his face shone bright in the torchlight. I could see that he was being favored, not just by Kenan, but also by many others.

One who favored him greatly was the Baron's youngest daughter.

◆ 6 ◆

H ER name was unknown to me when I first caught a glimpse of her against a bloodred sunset. The sky blackened from smoke from fires at some distance from the castle, beyond the haystacks, for it was a frosty autumn day, and the bonfires had been lit before a celebration. She passed by on horseback, riding as I'd never seen a woman ride, leaping over bundles of hay, and between the stacks, then up along the rim of the hill. Were it not for her garment, I would have thought her one of the gypsies who yearly came through with their carnivals and dancing, or even one of the Forest women.

She had no attendant with her, no handmaiden, which was unusual and perhaps even dangerous, for young women of breeding were never seen without protectors around them of some kind. Her fine dress, crimson and white, was in tatters along its hem, her feet were bare and dirty. She clung to her horse as if it were a lover. I heard her laughing gaily as she rounded a curve of the road and brought her horse to jump over the low walls surrounding the sheep meadow. Although she wore the clothes of a woman born to wealth, and pearls and rubies beringed her throat and arms, her hair had torn free of its restrictive braids and flowed as if from an angel in flight. She took the horse across the barren hillside, admonishing it to go faster and faster.

I could not help but smile as I watched her. What was she celebrating? What happy circumstance had come to pass?

I had been closing the swans up in a pen for the evening when I saw the blur of motion as she rode—for at first I couldn't see even her lovely fiery red hair but that it seemed like a trail of fire in the last of the sun. I cannot say that there is love at first sight, but I can say with certainty that there is something in the human soul that recognizes the kinship to another soul, even at a distance. This, I felt for her, though I knew little of her, nor was she my equal. Perhaps it was her beauty, which was unfettered and striking.

She was my better in nearly every way, and I had no hope for her. A girl of her station and beauty would have been contracted to wed for many years—perhaps as early as birth, depending on how the Baron conducted his estate. She had a spirit that none of her sisters possessed, for I had seen them, two others, tall and dour-looking like Roman Fates, ready to spin, measure, and cut their own destinies.

But she was like a faerie princess, escaped from some goblin's lair.

Alienora de Whithors was her name, and I whispered it in my prayers at night once I'd heard it. It seemed exotic and spun of gold, that name, the evocation of an angel when I dared to say it aloud. She was not much older than I, and she sometimes laughed when she saw me herding the swans as she passed across the courtyard on her way to her own chores (for yes, even noblewomen had work to accomplish, for few were idle in those days, for idleness was believed to be, by some, the source of plague.) To say that I found her enchanting would be an understatement. I had felt an intense, cruel heat when I chanced to see her. She destroyed me with a pleasant glance, and honored me when she ignored my attentions as she rode her pony along the fields or when she sat with her sisters at the windows overlooking the courtyard.

My master forbade me to speak with her, when he saw me glance her way. "She is betrothed to a nobleman older than even the Baron. A man of wealth and power from the north. Know your place, Falconer, and you shall be content with the serving wenches, who are comely and handsome."

But one sight of Alienora could turn my thoughts to Heaven, and to Hell, at the same time.

My predicament became worse when I saw her speaking with Corentin, for I saw in him his plan, which was to gain her affection and improve his status in the Baron's household. He had used the monks to learn the rudiments of reading and writing to further his ambitions, and now he would use a pale young girl to continue on this journey to the stars. I felt as if I could read his blasted heart, and as much as I despised him, I could not help but recognize my own ambitions in his. He and I had been born out of fortune, and we lived in a world where fortune either smiled or scowled. There was not much to be done about it, unless one were clever. Corentin Falmouth was clever, and although I knew his heart to be that of an eel, I felt a pang of jealousy that he might win the young maiden's favor before me. Although he would have no hope of marrying her, I hated to think that he might entertain a thought of seducing her at all. He would ruin her, if she allowed him even to steal a kiss. He would take her maidenhead and her purity and dash them to the ground.

This was a genuine fear of mine, for it was not uncommon for noble ladies to take lovers from among the household as it suited them, in secret. Only those of us who worked in the halls and fields would be the wiser, for those of noble breeding never seemed to be aware of these couplings. They lived as if what they did among the servants had no effect on their piety or chastity, and they did not see us as entirely elevated beyond the state of animals, to some great extent.

I saw Alienora de Whithors as more pure than any other young lady of the household, even her pious sisters, and did not want to believe that Corentin Falmouth would try and bed her. I felt ashamed that I had even had those thoughts. Her skin was pure milk, and her lips, like bloodstains on a swan's wing. Her hair that red, like fire, like the sunset itself, reminding me of her mother, who was from Viking blood. Once, I saw Alienora walking with her youngest brother, holding his hand, and as she walked by, I smelled what could only be hyacinth and spice and citrus, and it made me nearly swoon as if I were some weakling. I looked at the back of her neck, as the ringlets of hair fell over that alabaster skin, that place that I longed to draw aside and press my lips, just once, just one kiss there. One kiss was all I would press upon her, then, perhaps, I could sleep. Then, perhaps, I could forget her, if I had but one such chaste kiss.

⋅ 7 ⋅

I saw the Baron, often, from afar, on the hunt, where I followed the men on horseback and helped flush game from the thickets, with long sticks and shouting, and called to my falcons to aid in getting the smaller creatures for the Baron's table. When wolves had attacked the Baron's deer, I helped carry the torches for my huntsman and his men, as we flushed out the creatures and sent them racing from the Baron's Deer Park at the edge of the Forest.

Eventually, having shown my bravery among the wolves more than once, the Baron had my master bring me to his table and sit with him as he ate from his trencher. He was a twisted man, with one arm bent always, it was said from many battles to have been broken and thus mended in that position. His nose, also, moved to the left when he laughed or when he snarled, and he had only one eye. The other was milky yellow, as if diseased, although he kept the lids so closed that it was hard to catch a glimpse of it. Yet, despite this, his wealth and goodwill gave a handsome, amiable cast to his features, and I was not even a little afraid of him.

"You are famous for your bird knowledge," he said after a bit. He leaned closer to me. "I desire for my dear wife, the Baroness, a little bird that will sing for her when she is sad in the winter. Might you find one for me?"

"That is easy enough," I said. "For the lark has a sweet song, and

I have raised many." It was true—many ladies of breeding enjoyed having a caged bird to bring them music during the harsh winter months, and I had captured many songbirds from the field.

"I have heard that you can teach a bird to pray," he said.

"It is not so much in the teaching," said I, "but in the bird's talent to mimic. The birds suited for this are the raven and the daw. I do not know of any other that will speak."

"She has been ill a long time," he said, a shadow crossing his face. It was a secret grief of his, and although it was known within the household, none of us spoke of the Baroness's illness lest we bring her and us bad luck. "I want to lift her spirits. Might you not train a daw to speak soft words to her that she might laugh? I would love to hear her laugh again, or even smile."

I worked industriously, setting traps in the marsh, until finally I captured a young blackbird that had only just left the nest. I had learned in my years that my grandfather had been mistaken about the splitting of the tongue—it was not necessary, even for the raven. I learned instead that the bird must trust the teacher, then words had to be repeated again and again. I spent two months with the little dark bird, feeding it from my own lips, and the only words I could think to say were, "I love you, dear lady, with all my heart," and although it resisted its lessons, finally, in the days when I had begun to give up hope that this little bird would learn, it began to repeat the words back to me, with a croaked version of my own voice: "Dear lady."

I built a tall, wide cage for the bird, which I named Luner, a name that always made me laugh when I heard it. Then, I presented it to my master, who took it to the Baron and his wife. I lay awake at night imagining her in her room, covered with a winter fur, by the fire, feeding bread to her pet, Luner, as the bird said, with my voice, "Dear lady."

One afternoon, a servant came to me, commanding me to go visit the Baroness in her chambers. When I arrived, in awe of the enormous hearth opposite the large, wide bed, covered with the furs of every animal imaginable, the beautiful Alienora stood there at her mother's bedside, beckoning me with her hand. Her eyes shone with tears that she held within, and when I reached her, she grasped my hands in hers. I felt warmth and fear in her touch.

I gasped as I saw her mother, who lay shrunken against the bed-clothes as if she were slowly vanishing. She seemed much older than a woman who was mother to children no older than nineteen should be, but she wore a slight smile on her face. Sitting in its cage, next to her, Luner, the bird I had trained.

The Baroness crooked a finger toward me, and I leaned down to hear her. She whispered, "Thank you for bringing me this sunlight, into a room so dark."

I felt better than I had in a long time as I stood there, listening to the bird speak, and seeing the wan smile upon the old lady's face. Alienora looked at me as if I had just given the most wonderful gift she had ever received. A single tear, what must have been a diamond of grief and joy mingled together, rolled down her cheek. I stood there by the bedside into the night, speaking with the Baroness about the Great Forest, and of the birds and the marshes.

◆ 8 ◆

By the time I reached the age of seventeen, in the estimation of many I had risen too high. A mudlark was not meant to be a falcon. The others grew jealous of this peasant boy who had come to wear finer things, who trained the falcons most beloved by the Baron, who had even trained a falcon that was sent as a gift for a foreign prince, and was now called Falconer. I had lost much of my childhood as I consciously tried to become what I felt was a better person. Although I still sent food to my mother and her children, I did not spend time in the field seeking them out. I had grown cold and a little empty, and my hatred of Corentin ruled my heart at times more than my burning but unrequited love for Alienora.

I could feel the jealousy of some of the others my age, when I was called to care for the Baroness's bird, or when, on the hunt, I rode on a horse beside the lead huntsman, two falcons on my arms at the ready. Kenan Sensterre had remained aloof from me during those years, but none could deny my abilities on horseback and with the falcons, and so he remained a distant but approving presence in the hunt.

In those years, superstitions about country people were on the rise, and as the village grew, a wall of stone was built between it and the field, further separating families like the one I'd come from, and those who were of a better class, despite the general poverty of the area.

I do not like what I remember of myself then: I had turned to stone in order to gain favors, to build what career a youth might in that cutthroat terrain where one might be executed for a stolen loaf of bread. I had once been a boy full of love and life, the boy who loved his storytelling grandfather, who spoke to birds and loved them and the Forest as well. I had become a product of the household, of walls, of chambers. I had grown dishonest in the way that those do who follow rules too closely—I was ready to blame others for minor sins, quick to bend before a better in order to rise up beyond my station. I worried at times that my soul had begun to erode as I sought to escape my origins. I had begun to forget that I had ever come from the woods and the marshes at all. I cannot judge that youth too harshly, for he lived in a world of rats and lice disguised as noblemen and ladies, of servants who would slice him open if it meant a crust of bed and a mat near the fire. The boy named Aleric—the one I had been and the one I had become as I approached manhood—had lost the Forest and its verdant life for the gray and the brown, the dead wood of the castle, the place of infestation.

And yet, I saw it as beautiful and wonderful then, for I had a nearly full belly at times, and the company of those who had fine garments and spoke a language that had been unheard in the outer world.

It was only when I met a boy two years younger than I was, named Ewen Glyndon, that I remembered what I'd come from. Like me, he was of the field, but he had become a shepherd to the household, as a debt from his father who owed much to the Baron. He was handsome and strong, but seemed in desperate need of protection. A night came when I saw Corentin begin to treat him as he had once treated me years before, and Ewen had no defense in him.

I crossed Corentin then and there, and whispered in his ear,

"Should you hurt that youth, I will find you one night, in your sleep, and tear you open with my bare hands. And when they execute me for your murder, I will be happy that I watched your face as pain poured from you."

It was enough, that threat, for Ewen to remain free of Corentin's darkness. After that, Corentin did not bother Ewen, and the young man followed me whenever he could as if he owed me his life, though I reassured him that he owed me nothing. But from this, we became fast friends, and when I opened my heart to him about my secret longing for Alienora, he grinned broadly, slapping my shoulder, and whispered, "She does not deserve one so fine as you."

• 9 •

SINCE the incident of the speaking bird, Alienora had stopped me in my duties now and then to ask a question about birds, or about fish, or about the Great Forest, or about why the marshes stank during the spring. I detected that, beneath the question, she offered a spark of interest in me.

Still, she kept some distance, and I did not approach her to speak but merely waited for her to come to me. She had become as pious as her older sisters, each of whom had married but whose husbands were off in wars. Rarely seen without her Bible, Alienora read it aloud in Latin in the morning, in the courtyard, with her older sisters. We began to talk of her faith and her blessed purity, those of us who saw and admired her. I suspect that seeing her transformation from beauty to saintliness changed even Corentin, who watched her nearly as close as did I. I learned from Corentin himself that her piety stemmed from the death of the man to whom she'd been betrothed. He had died in the north, on his way to meet his future bride for the first time. Alienora was to have married him in her fourteenth year, but this had been delayed because of wars and troubles beyond our little country. Now, at eighteen years of age, Alienora had decided to go to the convent to live. Soon enough, she would have to bid farewell to the castle forever, in exchange for the nunnery that existed to the west of the Great Forest, its chapels and rooms carved into the belly of the Earth itself by an anchoress who had seen a vision of the Holy Mother in the rock.

It seemed a tragedy to me that such an angel should lock herself away. I wanted to be near her, constantly, when I wasn't working. I began to go more frequently to the chapel to stand in the doorway and watch her pray beneath the altar and statue to Mary as well as of Saint Blaise. Alienora's purity had seduced me, finally. God's Heaven showed through her face, and in her eyes, I saw the light of eternity.

I had no lust. I had no desire.

I simply did not want ever to live in a world where I could not watch Alienora pray or recite Latin or stand at the parapet, watching the horizon, as if waiting to see God Himself in the setting sun.

By my eighteenth year, I would take unholy advantage of that fair maiden, I would face a terrible truth, and the worst that might happen to any I loved would come to pass. That one year would set the course of my life and start me along the path that led to my soul's damnation.

But the most terrible moment of my mortal youth happened early in my seventeenth year, when an official of the village had my mother arrested on charges of sorcery and consorting with the Devil.

◆ CHAPTER 5 ◆

The Accused

◆ 1 ◆

THE village had grown by leaps and bounds in the years since I had first burrowed beneath the Baron's largesse. Shambles of houses topped the earthen-and-wood palisades of its gate. Beyond it, and yet somehow surrounding it, the abbey itself loomed like a very different castle. It was full of monks and the priests and who tended to the sick and the poor as well as the rich and mighty. The road broadened within a few years, and we had pilgrims from foreign climes, and even the Bishop from Toulouse came once to bless the Barony of Whithors, as we were now called.

The stories of war were always on the tongue, for battles to the north and south and east and west raged, yet our Forest home was untouched by much of this in those days. Knights rode out, or rested in the Great Hall of the Baron, and young men like me went to be the foot soldiers of the Heroes, as we called the men of wealth who went to fight the Saxons or Norsemen or Spanish or those of the Southern Heresy. But I was not called to fight, for my value with the hunt was great. Although I had learned a bit of swordsmanship, poor boys such as I would not wield a sword but a spear or a bow. I had no real skill for warfare, and my only weapons of excellence were the sling and the dagger.

On my trips outside the Baron's household, to take grains to my mother, or what were then called mint-sweets to my little brothers and sisters, most of whom I barely knew, I began to notice how merchants from Normandy and the south had come and brought to us the promise of foreign goods. My mother's home, however, was the same as it had always been—an earth hut, with thatch for roof and only a little wood to create structure to it. When I entered it, I saw a dark, smelly rathole, and felt that if I could, I'd try and bring my remaining siblings into the service of the Baron. It made me happy to think I might do so, and I made plans for ways of shepherding them into work in the castle or grounds. The older children from my family had all left, and either had begun their own families nearby, farming as tenants and subsisting on a small portion of what they were able to produce from such efforts, or, like my brother Frey, they had just disappeared into the night, no doubt to seek their fortunes in war. My mother had a total of eleven children, and I barely saw a reflection of her face or mine in any of them.

My stepfather stopped returning from his trips to the sea, and my mother had become exactly what I was afraid she would. She slept with too many men, and her payment for these beddings had gone from food to drink. She was often sick, and I could look in her eyes and see that she was not a woman who would live much longer. She told me that she often went to Mere Morwenna for cures, for she had bouts of fever and a foot that would swell up often after she'd been bitten by a venomous spider. I am ashamed to say that I felt no real love for her but an obligation and a duty to console her when I could. I spoke to the local abbot and priest about possibly allowing my mother into that order of nuns that lives to the west, in caverns, anchoresses. There, she might find peace and the arms of the Lord before her death. But these men of the Church were not sympathetic and believed my mother's soul had already been lost in the battle of righteousness. I saw men in the Church who had taken their liberties with my mother, and yet they still retained their piety, while she had been cast from God's saving grace.

I had told my mother that she should not see the Forest women so much, that the world had changed since her girlhood, when the midwives and the herbal teachers were part of the village. I could tell that the tide was changing as I saw the priest speak out against the Devil in the midst of what he called the "ungodly wood," and although there were not yet accusations, I had heard of men and women of the country claiming that witchcraft had begun to curse the crops, and that the Devil had killed a child sleeping in its cradle.

When news reached me that one of the Forest crones had been arrested on the charge of fortune-telling, I was not at all surprised. Relief passed through me when I learned that it was not Mere Morwenna, but some hag whom I did not know. But I was startled at the way the abbot dealt with this old woman, for she was bound and thrown in the marshes. Being an old woman, she died there, for it was winter, and they had not clothed her.

But when my mother was accused, and arrested, it was a shock to my system so deeply felt that I flew into a rage when I first heard.

♦ 2 ♦

"HOW do you know this is true?" I asked my companion, Ewen.

"Corentin told me," he said. "He was at the abbey, bringing with him the pups from the Baron's litter as gifts for the monks. Your mother is held there, against her will."

"They will release her," I said.

"They say she murdered a child," Ewen added, and he said it with such compassion that I nearly wept. "I am sorry to be the messenger of this news, Falconer. I could not keep it from you, for you have been my friend since I arrived here. But if I had known it would make you suffer like this, I would have held my tongue."

"No, thank you, my friend, my only true friend," I said, and embraced him in goodwill. "You are right to tell me that I might go change the course of this terrible mistake."

I went first to seek out Corentin. He seemed to be at the center of any base untruth, of any evildoing, and I had become the protector of the other boys against his wickedness. He by then was held in too-high esteem, both by my master, and by the Baron himself. I would not be-lieve a word he said, but I needed to face him and discover exactly what he knew before taking this up with my master.

I found him in the stables, not working as he should have been, but atop some hapless milkmaid. I drew him up by his elbow and pushed him against the wooden slats. "What do you know about this vile gossip?"

He seemed a little frightened, then began laughing. The girl ran off, out into the yard. He said, "What in the Devil?" Then, he boomed, "How dare you, Mud-hen, come in and demand of me." He had a blade sheathed in a short scabbard that had been a gift from some lady. He drew it out and held it in the air between us. "Do not come near me, or I shall ruin that pretty face."

"My mother has been accused of witchcraft," I said. "What do you know of this?" I used language then that I'd held inside myself. Curses and oaths that I had not yet uttered in life. They flew from my mouth like locusts in the air.

"I am sorry, Mud-hen," Corentin said, but there was no sorrow in his voice. "I am sorry. This fate should not befall even you. Your mother and a midwife of the Forest have been taken into the abbey. They are accused of sorcery and murder."

"Did you cause this to happen?" I asked.

His eyes widened. He slashed his dagger in the air before me, so close that I could smell its metal and the filth of his hand, yet it never touched my skin. "Go to your mother, Mud-hen. Do not waste your time with foolish chatter. If she is a servant of the Devil, they will find it out soon enough. If she is innocent and Godly, that, too, will reveal itself."

He held the dagger up in front of my face until I turned and left the stable.

◆ 3 ◆

I could not simply rush to the abbey to see my mother. I had to wait until work was done. I went to the small chapel in the household to seek solace and find an answer through prayer. The chapel was dark, but flickering with candles.

Alienora knelt near the front of the chapel, deep in prayer. When she saw me light a candle and place it at the Virgin's feet, she came up to me and put her hand on my shoulder.

"I feel the Holy Mother's presence here," she said, softly. "What troubles you, Falconer?"

When I looked into her eyes, I felt the maternal warmth of her being. Her face was like an arc of light in my dark world.

I told her of my troubles, and she took my chin in her soft, warm hand. "Have faith. If your mother is as you say, then she will be found innocent in the Lord's eyes. Our priest and abbé know what is of Heaven and what of Hell."

"You do not understand," I whispered. "And I dare not tell you more."

"Please," she said. "Please tell me."

"If I tell you, will you promise not to be angry with me for this? For the telling?"

She nodded. "On the Blessed Mother's womb," she said. Then, she went and kissed the statue of the Virgin, first at the feet, then at her womb, as was then the custom of maidens who sought the Virgin's protection.

She brought me to kneel on the hard stone floor and clasp hands together in prayer. "Tell me," she said. "Tell me what strikes fear in your heart."

"You have lived in comfort," I said. "You have, since childhood, known no want. You have known no care. When you are sick, you are healed. When you are sad, you are made gay. When you desire meat, it is cooked for you. Drink, it is there. You adorn yourself with jewels and fur, at which price someone must go hungry, but you have not met whoever hunts the bear or barters for the gemstones or captures the wild boar and slaughters and dresses it for the feast. I am one of those who pay that price. I have known a different life.

"When I was a child, there were days of hunger. Long nights of fever, while I watched a sister die slowly, and without any help, except from the Forest crones. Here, in your home, it is warm in the wintertime. Where I lived, we simply froze. We slept with dogs and each other for warmth, upon straw thrown on the frozen ground. My mother is old before her time. My life, to her, seems like the life of a prince, and yet I sleep in a place that even your hounds would not venture.

"If you were accused of this crime of sorcery, your father would pay tribute to the abbey, and you would soon be released. But my mother does not have a father to protect her. She does not have powerful friends. She has no influence in the village, and she has been kept from Mass on too many occasions. I dread saying this at the foot of the Virgin Herself. But she is a whore, and has many children to still care for. She is not someone who, like you, would have others to speak for her or to pay the jailer's bribe. I am afraid that she will die."

Alienora leaned forward and kissed me gently on the cheek, right where a tear had fallen. Her lips must have tasted that tear, for when she drew back from me, her lips shone with it, and her cheeks were flushed with red where they had been snow-white a moment before. "Your love for your mother is strong," she said. "I will help you. I will help her."

She reached up to her neck and drew a pendant from over her head. She asked me to open my hands, cupped. I did so, and she placed the pendant in them. "This was brought to me by the man I was to wed. He died in the Holy Crusades, but this was a gift he had sent to me before his death. They call it an encolpion."

I looked at the image on the medallion. It was the face of the Virgin Mary, Mother of God. Above her, to her right, a small white dove. It had a Byzantine cast to it, and gold filaments within the metal. On the other side, was a picture of Our Lord, surrounded by gold, holding the Bible in his left hand, his right hand raised up. There were strange figures written below this, and Alienora told me that it was a prayer for safety and glory.

"You must wear this for me," she said. "Wear it and Our Lady will speak to her son for you and for your mother, as she watches out for all mothers and their children."

I put the pendant around my neck, slipping it beneath the cloth, and felt Alienora's warmth in its metal as it struck my chest. "Alienora," I said, then faltered, remembering my station in life. "My lady."

"I must go," she said. "I will aid you in this. Your mother needs you more than I at this moment. But take one thing with you tonight that will be not for you, but for the one who brought you into this world." Then, she leaned forward and bestowed the slightest of kisses on my forehead.

❖ 4 ❖

ALIENORA first went to her sisters, all of them pious maidens, and when she had rallied their support, they went to their sickly mother. Then, to their father and begged that he might show his mercy to help the Falconer's mother in this time of terrible trial. Generously, the Baron consulted with my master, Kenan Sensterre, with whom I had chilly relations at best, and the huntsman came to me within the hour and told me, gruffly, "You have worked your own kind of sorcery on the Baron, Falconer. I am to give you a horse, and a bag of coins. You are to ride to the abbey this evening, and speak with the abbé himself."

My heart gladdened at this, and I felt hope rise up in my soul. But as I rose to take the small cloth sack of coins, I saw an undisguised disdain in my master's face. "Sir, if I have offended you in any way, I ask your forgiveness," I said. "You have been good to me all my life, and if I have repaid you with sorrow, I would like to know of it and atone for this sin against you."

His eyes grew cold and distant. He whispered something that sounded like an oath. Then, he said, loudly, so that I would not mistake his words, "Honest Corentin has told me of your kind of mischief. I had known your mother in my youth, and I had assumed that she was a victim of the world. But you, the spawn of her womb, are the worst sort of man. And your grandfather had been a great man. How your name has fallen in the world and in my estimation. If the Baron had not commanded me to give you these coins, I would have thrashed you and thrown you out of the castle.

"You return any favor I have offered you with lies and with trouble.

And now, your mother has murdered a baby as it was born, and you expect to save her using the Baron's good faith and the piety of his daughters. Do not ask for forgiveness where you shall get none. I have only the memory of a young woman named Armaela, your mother, as a girl who was full of love and innocence once, to stay my hand from throwing you into the marshes. Pitiably, she has returned to the perversions and deviltry of her bloodline. Your grandfather may have been godly in his old age, but your kind always comes through."

• 5 •

I rode out of the castle with confusion and pain in my mind. What had Corentin told him to make Kenan believe that he was Honest Corentin and I was worse than a thief?

But even these questions had to wait, as I rode down the hillside, toward the abbey. I felt bolstered by the faith of Alienora, and of her gift, the encolpion pendant that swung against my skin, beneath my shirt. The coins from the Baron would no doubt buy my mother's safety, if this were at all possible. And Alienora's words about Our Lady watching over my mother in her innocence of this horrible charge, these thoughts also gave me comfort.

I arrived at the abbey at nightfall, and asked immediately to see the abbot. "I am sent not merely as a dutiful son," I told the brother who came to me at the gate, "but as a servant of His Lordship, as well as of Our Lady of Sorrows."

The monk, who was young and seemed frightened by my approach and demeanor, scurried off to find the abbot. Soon enough, I was ushered into the abbot's quarters, and sat with him at table. He offered me wine and game bird as we spoke, but I could not touch any of his food, for thoughts of my mother and her pain swelled within me.

He told me of the charges. They had come from an official in the village, who had come to the abbot because of a curious story he'd heard from one of the prominent if humble families within the abbey's protective reach. It seems that a woman named Katarin Luhan, a good woman of virtue, had been giving birth when she erroneously called out for her sister to go find a midwife. Had she called for one of the

Sisters, the Brides of Christ, perhaps none of this would have come to pass. Katarin experienced great pains, but could not deliver her child. An old woman of unknown origin who claimed to be Brewalen du Tertre had come soon after, along with my mother. They had spent many hours trying to help Katarin deliver her child, but realized that either the child would die, or the mother must. Katarin's sister heard clearly words said between the two women that the mother must live and the child must be sacrificed. Other words were also spoken, in the ancient tongue, and her sister believed they invoked demons, for the baby itself, born dead, had another child attached to its scalp.

Thus, Katarin and her sister brought the charge in the village, and the two women were brought to the abbey to be examined and determined if a trial was necessary.

As he spoke, I felt my heart pound with fear. A fever was beginning to sweep the country—a new plague had been reported to the east—and when these plagues and miasmas came through, the Devil was often to blame, and the women of what I have come to think of as the Old Religion were considered to be the emissaries of Satan on earth, though I knew them not as such.

I must add that I did then believe in a Devil, but my belief must not have been strong, and this news of my mother now had me doubting anything I had ever believed about Hell and its minions. I knew the Forest women as good folk, knowledgeable of herbal lore, difficult only in that they did not mix with the village or town, and no one could ever remember them in the abbey or at church or chapel.

I gave the abbé the bag of coins, and he took them with some delight. "Of course," he said, while counting them, "if your mother is a friend of the Baron's, then we must be very careful with this case. Our Lady will show her as innocent, I have no doubt about that."

I asked if I might see her. First, he asked if would be willing to disrobe so that he might make sure I took no weapon or poison to her. I balked at this, but quickly enough decided that this was a small price to pay for seeing her. I had no masculine modesty as some young men seemed to exhibit, and was perfectly content pulling off my breeches and boots and tunic and standing before him naked, except for the pendant my lady had given me. He asked me what it was. I drew it from my neck, and showed it. He came over to me, far too near, and took it from my hand. He turned it back and forth between his fingers. "This is the Eastern Heresy," he said.

"It was a gift from her betrothed, now in Heaven," I told him. "Although it may be from Constantinople, surely you can see that it is Our Lord and Our Lady."

"Yes," he said, and the "s" of his "yes" drew out too long. "I must keep this while you visit her. It is a precaution. It will be returned after."

He then reached over and touched the edge of my scalp. "You are unusual," he said. "A fair youth when most of your brethren are dark."

I nodded and said, all too proudly, "My father was from another land, I am told."

"A Norseman?"

"I have heard he was Saxon," I said, "though even that may not be true."

His fingers lingered too long in my hair. "Turn around," he said. I did as I was bidden to do.

He had a peculiar gleam in his eye when I looked at him again. I went to dress. He watched me the whole time. It made me feel dirty and lower than my station, which was low enough as it was. I did not like putting myself on display for this man, nor did I enjoy his fish-eye stare.

Then, he rang a bell for a servant, who came and escorted me to quarters beneath the abbey, where my mother and her friend were imprisoned.

To call them "quarters" was too kind, for it was little more than a tunnel into the earth. Without windows, and with very little light, my mother and Brewalen might have been buried alive down there.

I was able to bring them out into a room above, to talk. I felt my heart gladden when I saw my mother's face, for she seemed to have hope and some sense of purpose, the like of which I'd never seen before in her. She held my face in her hands and told me not to be afraid for them. "The Lord will help us," she said. "I am certain."

Brewalen was less faithful. She began to talk of Katarin and the baby with another body attached, and how in the old days, this would not have been considered amiss.

"You killed the child, then," I asked, surprised by her manner.

She nodded, her pockmarked face filled with hate. "As would any of these Brides of Christ. She was to die if that baby were to live. And that baby would die before it reached its first morning of life, after the mother died. We had to. I used an herb called by some the Beautiful Lady, and I put it in my mortar and crushed it with the juice of the mandrake root. This is not sorcery, Aleric, this is simply healing."

"It is not healing to kill an unbaptized newborn," I said.

She gave me a look of scorn. "You are too much like the Baron himself. I knew you as a little boy. I saw in you a terrible future. I saw on your forehead a mark, and it meant something too awful to contemplate then. But now I see it more clearly. It is the mark of the betrayer, Aleric. You may yet wash it clean off." Then she put both hands on me, as if seizing me to throw me. This was somewhat laughable, as she was a thin, frail hag, but I felt strength in her hands as she grasped me.

"Even the anchoresses, when in the birthing room, will smother a newborn child if it has deformity. They will not baptize the child, so Katarin's child would also have not been anointed with your Church's sanctity. It was a terrible choice to make. But there was no choice. If I had to do it again, knowing what that woman and her sister did, the charges they brought, I would have let her die and saved the child though that child would be dead before sundown. But had I done so, and brought that child to the baptismal font, our priest would have dashed its brains against the stones beneath his feet. And now, I am afraid, I will be murdered simply because I did what was necessary to protect a life."

Her eloquence was startling in its simplicity. Her anger had not made her thoughts ragged. She let go of me, then went to my mother and put her arms around her. "Do not weep, Armaela, my sister, do not shed one tear for these people who do this to you."

"I have come to save my mother," I told Brewalen. "Perhaps I can save you, as well."

Brewalen smiled then, and nodded to me as if she acknowledged that I had some small spirit. Then, she said, "It is already written that I should die, Aleric. My body has dark humours within it now, and I awake with blood and sleep at night with pains. I am not afraid for my own life, for I know that my spirit will return to the Forest, and I will awake a moment after the death of this body. But for your mother, who has children, whose body is not ready to die, she needs your protection. Do what you must."

Then she retreated to her prison, and I was left alone with my mother.

"Your brothers and sisters need you," she said. "Please help them. I don't know what they will do. I don't know how they will eat . . ."

"I will make sure they have what they need," I said. "And you, as well."

"Son," she said, her voice a bare whisper, "there is so much I want you to know. So many things I have hidden from you. I did so to protect you, as the life I have led has not been one of purity or sanctity. But everything I have done, it was so that my children might live a better life than I have. And I am proud that you are here now, favored of His Lordship, with skill and talent."

I felt a chill as she spoke. It had not simply been skill with birds, or any natural ability of mine, that had secured my fortune of working for the Baron. She herself had done something to help ensure my placement. I tried not to remember the men whom she had bedded, thinking that she had even done that to help her children. Had she slept with Kenan more than once, simply to ensure that her children would find work and food? I recalled the phrase my grandfather had once used, "a terrible price," that she had paid when a maiden. What had it been? I longed to ask her, but knew this was not the time for it.

She held my face in her hands as if I were still her little boy. "You must not be near me when I die. You must keep your distance, for you may lose your position if you show me affection. You are the child of an accused witch. You do not need to lose all you have for my sake."

"I do not care about position," I said, willing my own tears to remain within my eyes. "I do not care about them. I am not one of them. No matter how much I want to be. We are different. Grandfather said we were of a bloodline of priests of the Forest."

"If you speak of that," she said, her voice dropping to a whisper, "they will, one day, burn you as well. Forget the past. Forget our home. You have younger brothers and sisters to feed. Although Annik and Margret will take them in, and others will help, they will need their older brother's favor in the castle to survive."

"I will do all I can," I said, and no longer held back my tears.

She began weeping, as well, and covered her face with her hands. Then, her tears dry, she took my hands in hers. "They will burn me. Or drown me. Or they will keep me in that burial chamber beneath this floor until I die of plague. I am not afraid of death for myself. I only wish that I might take care of my children who still need a mother. I have been changing how I've lived. The crones of the Forest have been teaching me the skill of midwifery and of healing plants. I am an outcast of the world, but not of the Forest. If I die . . ."

I shushed her, and promised her that I would find a way to gain her release, and God willing, Brewalen's as well.

"No," she gasped. "Please, Aleric, do nothing for me. You cannot risk this. I did not do all I did so that my sons would return to the dirt."

"I will do what I must," I said.

Then, I kissed her and bade her pray so that God's light might shine upon her and bring a spirit of grace to her and her companion.

I left the Abbey that night feeling heartened, even victorious. With the Baron and his beautiful, pious daughter requesting my mother's freedom from the abbé, surely by sunrise, she would be released.

◆ 6 ◆

I rode home across marshes and along fens, and kept to the path by the light of the moon. But as I crossed a narrow way, at a crossroads between the road that led beyond our homeland and the one that led to the castle, I saw a strange figure with a small bundle in its hand. I tell you, I felt it was a phantom of some kind, for its cloak was long and hung in front of its face like a mask. Beside it, another cloaked creature that was only a few feet tall.

My first reaction was to ride by fast, for crossroads were terrible places, where the unbaptized were often buried and where oaths to the Devil were made. But as I rode near, I heard a woman's voice call out my name.

I brought my horse to a slow trot and turned about. The moonlight struck the face of the figure. It was not a stranger at all, but Mere Morwenna herself. Beside her, that misshapen changeling stepchild, now perhaps ten years old, clinging to her like it was a monkey. I dismounted, and the crone shambled over to me. The child, veiled from head to foot, clutched at Mere Morwenna's skirts as if afraid that I might bite it.

"Your mother," Mere Morwenna said. She reached to embrace me, and I fell into her fragile arms as if she truly were my blood kin. "I am sorry."

"I've just been to see her," I said. "And Brewalen. While they are in good spirits now, the charges against them are serious."

"Yes," Mere Morwenna said. "My child saw this." She glanced down at the veiled creature. Her child pressed closer into her cloak and skirt as if trying to disappear there. "She has the Sight. She told Brewalen of the trouble that might come."

I looked from the veiled child to the crone. "Why, then, did Brewalen take my mother to midwife the newborn?"

Mere Morwenna said nothing. She drew back from me and took my hand in hers as she had many times when I had been a little boy. She turned my hand over so that my palm caught the moonlight. With her index finger, she followed the curves of slight lines on my hand and pressed an area between my thumb and fingers that causes me slight discomfort. "There is much that can be seen of the future. But it is like these crossroads. We know the destination of each, but to get here, there are a hundred choices that must be made first. You are still the boy of birds. I see a crossroads ahead where you will rise up like a dragon. Or you may not, Aleric. You may instead marry the girl you love and live far away from here. But wait, I see in your future something entirely different—you will die at the hand of a beautiful woman. You will have a child. A boy. No, a girl. Your child shall die. No, your child of some future year lives."

She looked up at me from behind her veil. Her small eyes seemed shadowed and bright all at once. The wrinkles of her forehead and around her eyes seemed deep, drawn creases. "Do you understand?"

I nodded.

"The Sight offers the crossroads, and the destination, but does not always follow the journey we expect."

"Is there nothing that can be done?" I asked.

The veiled child stepped out from Mere Morwenna's moon-shadow, and said, in a voice that was older than her years and yet still of a young child's timbre, "You stole a relic from a great oak. You brought up the winged demon and had it slaughtered. Your destiny is dark, Falconer, and your journey will be on a thorny path. I see a hundred fires along these marshes. I hear the screams of women and men. I smell the burning flesh and smell the wood of ancient oaks as they blacken. And from your loins comes the fire."

I shivered as I heard her words. I wished my mother had never grown close to these Forest witches and their Old Ways. I could not get back on my horse fast enough. I did not want to think what deviltry they were up to in the marshes, where the roads met. I snapped, "What is your name, little accursed one?"

"She is called Calyx," Mere Morwenna said. "For she was born from her mother's side, with a caul covering her body, and within its bloom, a child who brought with her the wisdom of another world."

"Is this why she is a misshapen thing?" I said, feeling bile and bitterness in my throat. "Who is her mother?"

"Her mother is dead," Mere Morwenna said. "She gave her life that this child might live. She is born from the Veil itself and brought into this world as a cupbearer for the goddess."

"She is no changeling," I said. "She is deformed. Children are often killed at birth, so your friend Brewalen tells me, when they have these deformities."

"I may be deformed on the outside," the cloaked girl said, "others hold their misshapings within. Some are like castles—beautiful and fair at a distance, but within the walls themselves, there is pestilence and poison that has not yet been torn at by the ramrod. Do you trust the outer beauty or the inner? Do you look for that which will corrupt with time, which hides darkness, or what is timeless?"

"You disgust me," I said, and glared at Mere Morwenna, also. "You and your kind are truly witches and lovers of the Devil. How else would my mother be accused of such a crime if she had not fallen in with your lot? How many other peasant women go to your herbs and healings and come away with the mark of the Devil upon them?"

The rage that filled me, the wanting to blame them for my mother's imprisonment, grew from an enormous fire within me that I needed to expel in order to breathe the night air without feeling the smothering burden of helplessness. I felt as I hadn't in years—on the verge of tears, yet I would not let them fall from my eyes. "Had she kept to her life, though it were the life of the lowest whore in Christendom, she would not await a terrible judgment, both here and in the world to come."

Mere Morwenna drew back from me as if she had encountered a viper.

The veiled one called Calyx stepped forward, pointing her finger nearly up to my face. "You have seen a demon yourself, once. You have seen what you are meant to know."

Mere Morwenna reached out, clutching the girl, drawing her back to the folds of her cloak.

"If you are a witch, then work spells to release my mother from prison. Bid the Devil free her!" I shouted as I returned to my mount.

"Give your mother peace," Morwenna said before I rode off.

When I returned to the castle, Alienora stood along its slender parapet, as if she'd been there all night, keeping watch. Her beauty against the torchlight inspired me with affection and took away much of my anger. She was purity. She was love.

In her form, I saw all that could be made right of this world. I left behind that Forest world of witches and devils, and hoped that the purest light of love could overcome the darkness.

◆ 7 ◆

I first sought out Corentin, and found him drinking before the hearth in the Great Hall, surrounded by hounds. I leapt upon him, nearly pressing his face into the fire. His eyes glowed with the flames, and I saw fear in his soul.

"What have you done?" I asked. "Why have you turned my master against me? Of what crime am I accused by you?"

"The crimes of sodomy, and blasphemy, and thievery," he said, and then began laughing. "And should you kill me now, all would know of it. Kill me here, by the fire, with drink in my hands, so that it might be known that you are vermin. That you are the monster that I have said you are. That you are the murderer, like your mother. It is in your blood, Mud-hen. That is what I have said of you. But do not be so angry with me, fair one, for although I said the words, it is your master who believed them because he knows your true parentage. He knows from what sin you are born. He knows the stain that is upon your brow that causes you to be a twisted soul."

◆ 8 ◆

I risked my life, but I ran through the castle, up and down corridors until I came to my master's chamber. I awoke him, in his bed. He lay there with a woman whose nakedness made her lighten the darkness. Kenan drew a robe around his shoulders, pushing me into the corridor, then shutting the door behind him.

"I have heard the lies from Corentin himself. I have heard what poison he has planted in your brain. Hear me out, sir. Hear from me what I have suffered at Corentin's hands. Do not speak, and when you do, you may cut off my hands if you wish. But only after I have spoken my part."

Kenan, fury in his face, grunted an acknowledgment to me.

"I came here, sir, an innocent. You remember me then. You brought me to this place. I thought it to be a world that would be better than my own home. I thought that the marsh and the mud were left behind when I entered this castle. But instead, I found soon enough that mud not scraped off at the threshold could be brought within even the better households of the land. For within a fortnight of living here, Corentin came to me and forced himself upon my flesh. You may remember me then. I was puny and slight. I had not had the food that Corentin, older and stronger, had been fed since his birth. Neither did I have strength then. Who do you think could have been the victim? The puny pale filthy boy from the marsh, or the strong boy who took what he wanted and did as he wished? I risk my own death and my own reputation by telling you this. I swore that I would never tell a soul for fear of the shame such a revelation would rain down upon me.

"And thievery? Have I stolen anything? Has gold gone missing? Or silver? Has a horse vanished from the stable? A swan from the pen? Have even the roasters been taken by any other than the fox? If something was stolen, I would look first to Corentin himself, for he has proved himself a knave to me many times over. And blasphemy? How does that stand against me? I am at Mass each Sabbath. I am in chapel for morning prayers when not called away on the hunt." Then, I stopped. Looked at him. I could see that his mind was trying to grasp all of this at such a late hour.

Then, he said, "You have had a long night. Go to bed, boy. There are other concerns in the world than yours at the moment."

"You must tell me, sir," I said. "You must. Where have I fallen in your eyes? How could one man's words to you, lies about me, change your good opinion of that boy who you knew? Corentin told me it was because you knew who my father was. I demand that you tell me."

"You demand? You *demand?*" he said, and came at me with both fists. His hand grasped my collar, lifting me against the wall, and he hit me hard in the jaw. I struggled, but he was strong and fierce, and I felt myself fall to the ground. He kicked at my ribs once.

He stood over me.

I lay there, clutching my side.

"You are the bastard of an evil man I once knew well. A man who delighted in perversions and worshipped the Devil himself. A man who took the woman I loved from me. From *me*. From my arms. And he destroyed her. And from their union, you came. I thought I could love you as I once loved your mother. As I once saw her, so beautiful and young and happy and innocent. I thought by saving you from that misery, I would make amends for what I left her to in years past. But then, you had to destroy my own son. My own *child*. With your father's sins and deviltry. And now you lie to me. Like a serpent in the field, if I had a sword right now, I would cut you down and not think the worst of it."

"Sir?" I pled, weakly. "How? How? I do not know your son."

"I have many bastards. But only one that I have brought up and given help. He is your brother whom I took from his mother's arm as a baby to save him from that accursed rat's nest. And he is my son. His name," my master said, "is Corentin."

Then he turned and went back into his chamber.

• CHAPTER 6 •

The Blasphemy

THE night's events troubled me such that I found no peace in sleep, nor could I return to my quarters, where I would surely find Corentin if he were not abed with a serving girl. I felt battered and worn, and I did not know where to turn for solace. I went to the chapel and prayed before the Virgin for guidance in that dark time. I lit candles and went to sit at the foot of the statue. I placed one small candle in the palm of Our Lady's hand, and it extinguished too soon. I lit it again, and put it in her stone hand, and again, its small flame went out. I began to wonder if I might be cursed, or losing the battle for my soul within me. In those days, the priests told us that both angels and devils vied for our immortal souls. We could not control such battles, nor determine the outcome. We were at the hands of the invisible agents of the Divine and the Damned, and I felt that night that my soul had been fated to Hell.

Sometime in the night, perhaps just before dawn, the only angel I had ever met came to the chapel. Alienora. She, too, had been unable to sleep.

"I saw the light here and thought our guard might be praying," she said. "What vexes you that you cannot sleep?"

"I would ask the same of you, my lady."

"I have been troubled by dreams," she said as she knelt beside me. "Dreams of which I dare not speak."

Boldly, I put my hand against her cheek. I felt a feverish heat in her, which shocked me to my core. I had imagined her a chaste and pure angel, but this fire on her face was of the animal. My hand warmed against it, and the warmth spread up my arm to my shoulder, then throat, and my entire body went from a frozen winterland to burning.

I looked into her eyes and saw there a desire I had not expected from one so pious. Her lips seemed parched. She whispered something to me then, and I did not understand it. I watched her lips as she spoke. I listened again as she said, "I dreamed of you."

I leaned over, pressing my lips against hers. My lips moistened hers, and I felt a gentle softening of her mouth, as it opened against my rough pressing. Like a rose blossoming, her lips parted. My hands went to her face, holding her in that kiss like I held a wineskin to my lips, unable to stop drinking from it. I felt wetness from her tongue as mine played against hers. As her lips parted farther, a bit of ash from my internal fire leapt into her mouth. Her arms went about my neck, and my hands roamed from her face to her beautiful hair, and I drew back and caught my breath as I looked at her. She gave me that look of the animal in mating season. Her eyes were blurred and clear at the same time. She looked both at me and through me. She seemed to have donned a mask, and a sly smile on her face showed fear and yet daring. Was she as chaste as she seemed? How could I know? Would I be murdered for the liberties I took with her now?

I caressed her throat, kissing to her shoulder, then pressed my lips to the nape of her neck. She smelled of lemon and herb and evergreen. She took my hand and brought it to her throat, and then to her breasts. I began undressing her, my mind no longer my own, my body no longer a servant of my soul but of that animal instinct that raises up and lays low all people in the spark of youth. Her breasts were small and perfect, flickering with shadows from the candlelight, and I took each nipple in my mouth; hearing her gasp slightly, I glanced up at her face, which now seemed to burn with lust as I had never before seen in a woman, virgin or whore. She grappled with my outer garments, tearing at them when they would not come off. Soon enough, we'd created a pile of clothes and she had begun licking my chest, pressing her face into the center of it as if she could find my heart to kiss it as well. My manhood grew enormous to me, and I felt powerful as she whispered her love for me in my ear, licking around the whorls of that part of my flesh that was so sensitive to a woman's touch.

I pressed my hand against her flat belly, then wandered to that thatch of hair that crude men call names of affection but which I thought of as the source of power over men. My hand felt moistened as it found her center, and I heard the gentle purring sound in her throat and the tender gasps and moans as her hips pressed up against my fingers. We kissed long then, and I held her and roamed her body with my hands, and she brought her hands down to my maleness, caressing it, feeling its length, bringing out its own moisture into her fingers as she played with it and became familiar with the slight sway of its movements.

I had no doubt now that she was not the virgin she had seemed and that she had been taken by at least one other in the household, whether it was someone unknown to me, or perhaps even the loathed one, Corentin, who had stolen my own childhood from me and been revealed to be my mother's child from before my birth. But these thoughts troubled me not, for her heat and her handling my erect phallus had taken my soul into darkness while my flesh sought its own natural home.

I was the one to moan and gasp when she took me fully in her mouth, kneeling before me as if I were a Saint, but her worship was of lust and pleasure. I found, with my left hand, her backside as she thus brought herself to my need, and with my right, played with her beautiful red hair. Then, I was the one to bring her legs to my face and I kissed and worshipped there as no man had before, wanting to meet her fire with my own, wanting to incite her pleasure to the brink of wild, unimaginable lust, to unleash something within us both through my mouth and her opening.

Then, we kissed, tasting of each other, a communion of passion, and her legs wrapped around my hips, and I plunged into her with the abandon of one who understands a woman's readiness, the moment at which the vessel is at its brink of fullness, and as I did so, I felt the barrier within her. Before I could even realize what I'd done, I felt my phallus push through it, opening her, and I heard her cry out. I covered her mouth to silence her, and knew that she had, indeed, been a virgin before I had entered that sacred space.

Rather than wince in pain or beg me to stop, as some maidens had done in my youth, I felt her hips rock against me, and she whispered for me to continue, to increase my fury inside her. I had never experienced this with a lass, and it incited my body to heights I had not known before. I felt myself lengthen within her, although this was impossible, I felt my member grow fat in that small secret space that is so protected by maidens. She brought her hands to my buttocks and held them against her body as if to draw all of me into her.

And then I felt the supreme moment. Before the waves of pleasure. Before that final exultant second of loss.

We held time hostage in that moment. We were still. Inside her, I was still. She, too, was still.

Our vision locked in a dream together.

Frozen.

Held.

Silence.

And then, release came, and I began kissing her face as I withdrew myself, and felt that awful breaking of the thread, of the stream, between us, that moment when the cat turns and spits at its mate, and the rabbit fights with its beloved.

So, she looked at me with a kind of horror, then up to Our Lady's face.

She drew back from me, weeping.

I could not console her. I, too, felt that animal coldness that all mating brought when it ended. It was a recognition of death, I think, of the fact that we were indeed animals, and the illusions of the world of men were nothing in the face of the moment after the fornication had ceased. We, in our world, believed we had been created in the image of God and that we were above the animal kingdom. But that damned moment after the breaking of the thread between the two bodies brought the understanding that we were as doomed as the sheep in the meadow, as the stag in the forest when the horn of the hunter blows and the dogs begin to howl.

♦ 2 ♦

WE parted at dawn, weary from our efforts, drained of life it seemed, and although I told her of my love for her, she did not return the words. But when night came again, she found me at the last of my labors and asked that we might talk of our affection. Although she did the speaking, what I heard from her was both encouraging and dreadful. She loved me, she told me, with all her heart.

"But I am the Baron's daughter," she said. "You work in the field and in the hunt. Although my betrothal to a man I never met ended in his death, I did not then feel cursed. I do now, for I believe we violated that most Sacred Lady's sanctuary. We forgot ourselves, and our bodies befouled that place. I have prayed to her who has never understood the sin of lust and asked her forgiveness. She answered my prayers with the atonement I should make, and I shall do as she has guided me."

My heart pounded in my breast, and I wanted to embrace her to me and beg her not to speak of atonement and sin when my love for her, and my desperation for her arms and the longing for that scent of evergreen and lemon in her hair, had become overwhelming.

"I am going to take the vows," she said. "The Sisters who live in the caverns in Laseur will welcome me, and I shall bring my dowry to Our Lady herself. This is the only atonement and expiation for the sin I committed. I must become a Bride of Our Lord, and in doing so, I shall also pray to the Virgin for your sake and for your mother's, as well."

I stood there, stunned, unmoving, and could say nothing to dissuade her. It was believed that the only way to restore virginity to a maiden was to take vows with the Church and to serve Our Lady as a nun. The Sisters in the caverns lived an ascetic life, with few comforts, and some, anchoresses, had not seen the light of day in many years. There were rumors of leprosy that had been cured by what were called the Virgins of the Rock, and that Our Lady had herself been seen many years before, in the sky over the entrance to the caverns of Laseur.

Her flesh and her purity would torment me for days and nights after this.

♦ 3 ♦

EWEN went with me to take food to my little brothers and sisters, whom I had never come to know. A neighbor, who had lost a child from fever, took in the youngest baby and nursed her. I arranged to send eggs and some grain to this kind woman, and she told me that she would care for the baby until such a time as my mother would be free to return home. I felt heartened by the hope she offered.

I slept in the stables rather than my quarters with the others of the field, so as to avoid Corentin. I spoke nothing to my master and spoke little to others during those days of shadows. I could not visit my mother in her cell, nor could I speak again to the abbé and priest while my mother and her companion underwent the inspections and interrogations by a man sent from Toulouse who had experience with what was called the Great Heresy, the Old Religion that had not died completely in the Great Forest.

♦ 4 ♦

WE were a poor country backwater, and it surprised many that a scholar-monk had come all the way out to deal with this question of witchcraft and murder. I had heard stories of what happened to those who were thus accused, and I worried myself into a strange ailment with all that had happened.

Within a few weeks, I was taken to bed and fed only clear broth. A serving wench acted as my nurse as a fever took me, and I wondered if somehow I had received the plague from Our Lady for my sin of taking the virgin and righteous maidenhead from Alienora one terrible and wonderful night at the chapel dedicated to the most sacred of virgins.

And then, soon enough, my mother's fate was determined. I awoke from my fever, having lost weight, weakened, and it was Alienora herself, who had not yet gone off to the Sisters, who was the messenger of it.

"She is to be burned in the marshes, along with Brewalen of the Forest, for the crimes of murder and sorcery," she said, as she wiped a warm, wet cloth against my forehead.

"I must go to her," I said. "I must stop this. She is not a witch."

Alienora folded her hands as if in prayer. "You love your mother greatly, and for this, the angels weep, Falconer. I love you now with a charity I had never before known. I wish for you only the light of Our Lady to guide your steps. But your mother has confessed. She has described her meetings with the Devil, and with his emissaries. I do not know beyond that."

"But will she be burned for this confession?" I knew well enough that if a witch confessed, she might be pardoned, although imprisoned for the crime. While in prison, a confessed witch might still be tortured and die within a dank miserable cell. But alive, she might have hope, and I might be able to rescue her from that awful fate.

I felt a surge of strength in my bones. Soon, I rose and went to the Baron himself, pushing my way past his guards, who raised their swords against me. I did not care if I were cut down. I needed the Baron's protection and authority if I were to help my mother.

While the Baron listened with compassion to my entreaties, and held his tongue until I had finished, he showed me with his words that he had washed his hands of this as surely Rome had washed its hands of Christ's crucifixion.

"It is the murder that is the charge that commends your mother's body to the flames and her soul to God's judgment," he said. "The sorcery charge is a lesser one, and her confession would have rescued her from the fire, truly. But a child has been murdered in this instance. And two women, midwives no less, drowned the child in the same barrel of water in which it was meant to be first washed. Pray for your mother's soul, boy. That is all that can be done."

"If I have to, I will go to the King himself," I said.

"You will waste the last hours of your mother's life riding on horseback to his court, then," the Baron said. "For she has been sentenced, and she will burn this night."

• 5 •

I N those days, witch-burnings were not as common as they would be years later. Although ecclesiastical law was such that a woman or man could be executed for what was often called Devil worship, it was rarely enforced, and had not yet become the firestorm that took over all of Western Europe soon enough. In fact, if my remembrances are not too clouded with later centuries, few believed that witchcraft was a threat to any. Yet, there were those among the villages and abbeys accused of a crime, with worship of the Devil and the sorcery attached to it, who would be burned for their own redemption, sometimes by a mob if famine or plague had swept through. I had never seen it before, but I had heard of distant, ignorant villages and towns where this might occur.

I didn't think it would happen in my own home. The heresies of country people had not yet been seen as a threat within Christendom, although the winds would change within a hundred years, then, later, the burning times for the witches would begin. But my mother's case was one of the many isolated ones, where locals and others felt that sorcery and murder had occurred, and any form of execution other than public burning would not cleanse the community of such deviltry.

My mother and her friend would be set ablaze with a large crowd watching, for it would be considered sinful not to attend such an event. The murder itself had grown in rumor from the death of a child with two bodies, to the Devil and his infernal angels gathered around, conjured from the blood of the infant as the sorceresses drank from its throat the last of its life. Katarin, the mother of the dead child, went from being an ordinary woman of some means to being sacred to the Virgin Mother in her aspect of Our Lady of Sorrows, who cried nightly for children who had been sent to either Limbo or Hell itself. But none of these wild rumors mattered to me.

I saw my mother when they drew her along, tied to the back of a horse. She had to run in the mud, and she went too slowly. I could clearly see the marks upon her of the interrogator, the scars from her tortures, though I did not dwell on this much, for my goal was to pray to the Almighty to intercede on her behalf. When she finally slipped to the ground, it was my own angel, Alienora, who went to her with a cloth and a cup of water, lifting her up and whispering some prayer to her. My mother clung to her briefly, until a soldier drew her away again. Where was her companion, Brewalen? I wondered. Where was she who was elderly and frail? I did not know, nor did I ask anyone in that crowd of villagers who stood near a hastily constructed pavilion, lit by a hundred torches.

Within the pavilion grounds itself, before what would be my mother's funeral pyre, the Baron and his household stood, as well as my friends, the few I had, including Ewen. I went to be with him, and he told me, "The other one, that they call Brewalen, died at the abbot's hand. Folk say she cursed him as well as the priest and all of the village. Maryn told me that the old crone said that from the abbey itself and its corrupt minions would come the only Devil known to mankind. Do not think me an enemy for bringing you this message, Falconer. I do it only so that you will know from a friend."

"We are still friends," I said, embracing him, thanking Our Lady for one good friend among the crowd.

"I do not know how you bear this, my friend," he said. "I do not believe she is a witch. And yet the child is dead, and the blood is on her hands."

When I heard his words, something in me awoke. My health had not quite recovered, but I knew I must do something to stop this night's horrible event. I looked through the crowd, hoping to find a sympathetic face. Even for Alienora, there with her sisters, at their father and mother's side. There were others to think of besides myself, there were children that my mother had given up as orphans, now without a parent to protect and care for them. Soon, they would work as virtual slaves to such as the folk in the village, or would be sent into ovens to clean and into rabbit holes in search of food for their cruel masters and mistresses. And that was only if they were fortunate.

The other way they might go would be to the Great Forest itself, for it was commonly believed then that Our Lady watched over innocent children, and so common folk did not often take them in. Innocence could overcome evil, as that belief went, and children who had been orphaned might be blessed with the Savior's patronage. It was all absurd, and no one truly believed it. But of that time, it was accepted as a way to avoid taking in those who had no father or mother. I resolved to gather these children up, my half brothers and half sisters, and do what I could for them, but even my time at the castle was nearly up, though I did not then know it.

I fought back tears as I stood among my neighbors, watching as my mother was bound to the stake.

And then, I could take no more. I ran through the crowd, fighting against the guards. Their hands grasped at me, and I felt the slam of some cudgel against my shoulder. Yet, I felt a strength that had never before existed within me, and pressed through them, to the stake itself.

A roar of surprise went up, but I had deafened myself to these enemies of my mother's. I reached the kindling that had not yet been set ablaze. The abbé held back the soldier who held the torch that would begin this execution. I wrapped my arms about my mother as she wept against my shoulder, and I begged her to help me loosen her bindings so that we might somehow fight our way through this terrible gathering.

She whispered to me, as close as she could press her mouth to my ear, "Get away from me. You must. Do not show them you care for me. I am a whore and a witch, Aleric. Let me be, do not put yourself into the path of this fire. I would not risk your life or the life of any of my children, Aleric, my love, my son. I have grown sick in that prison. I have learned from Brewalen of another world. Before she died, she offered me dried and twisted root, which is now beneath my tongue. She told me that if I press it between my teeth at the moment before death, its juice, which is powerful, will overtake my senses. I will be transported to a certain place, though it is not the Heaven of which we have learned from the priests."

I kissed her cheek, and wept upon her, "Please tell me what can be done. I don't want you to die."

"A secret has been kept from you," she whispered. "A secret of your father and who he is. He . . ." I felt an iron grip on my hand. I turned, and saw the same monk who had me disrobe before him. He drew me away, and I struggled against him. Two guards rushed up to us, each taking my arms and lifting me while I fought to return to my mother's side, shouting for justice and for innocence. It took four men to subdue me, and still I fought them, regardless of what might happen to me as a result. I lashed out at them, and kicked, and pulled, tugging my arms free, but still other men grabbed me and drew me back into the sea of faces that watched my mother.

My mother cried out to me to have a care for my brothers and sisters.

A soldier lit the kindling that surrounded her, a crown of thorns at her feet.

Her lips moved, and I knew she had bitten down on that root of which she spoke. Her eyes went up into her head, with only the whites showing. Smoke came up, from the kindling, and it drew up around her body. The rags in which they'd allowed her to be burned caught fire fast, and though I could not watch, I heard screams from the crowd. I opened my eyes to see her belly rip open from the fire, and her entrails pour out.

And yet, upon her face, a smile or grimace, and her eyes looked toward Heaven. I can only believe—and hope—that the root's juice had sent her on her journey to eternity without the pain that was her body's fate.

For my part, my eyes were dry of tears. The spectacle of the column of smoke and fire lit the night, and I watched as others, people I had worked among, those I had called friend and enemy alike, seemed to become entranced with the white and black ashes as they rose up into the sky, a human bonfire, reminding me of the tales of the ancient burnings of sacrifices to the Pagan Gods of Old.

This night of burning terror changed me forever. What love I felt for the world went with the black smoke of my mother's flesh and bones, up into the heavens, blown by a bitter wind.

It burned away anything good within me, though I fought to cling to my sense of love and curse my foolishness at spending my childhood and youth pretending to be of the castle when I was of the Forest itself.

I had betrayed my mother by not moving heaven and earth to free her, even if it meant murdering the monks who held her, taking a hostage of the Baron himself.

I saw myself then as a monster, bad as those who had accused my mother. Armaela, the witch. And her son, the Devil himself.

I thought of my grandfather's words, about the good and the bad in all things, all people.

But as I stood there, a young man, I knew only the bad. I saw only the bad among those folk as they watched the spectacle of my mother's burning.

❖ 6 ❖

THAT same night, the Baroness grew more sick, and also died, although it was not discovered until dawn, for the Baron's family had not returned to their quarters until the sun's light had risen. Although I did not see this, the story swept through the Baron's household that she held in her hands the cage to the little bird named Luner. It was open, and she had, before she died, let the bird go. Her servant told others that the bird flew up first into the rafters, then, finally out the window, into the purple light of morning just as the Baroness breathed her last words, which were, "I am free."

❖ 7 ❖

OTHER particulars I would later learn had some effect on me, soon after my mother burned in front of the Baron, his household, and the village and the Sisters of the Magdalen caverns, and the abbey and its monks.

It would seem that a conspiracy was afoot regarding my own being, although at that moment I would not know whose hand made the first gesture toward my demise. Certainly my outburst at my mother's execution played a role, for I was seen as untrustworthy and possibly in league with her, though there were those who were touched by my devotion to her in her last moments. I heard whispers of words about my grandfather, too. He had been a great soldier in some long-ago war, but had also been of the Forest folk and not of the Church. Still, other forces were at work. Corentin was involved, as was my master, his father, my mother's early lover, Kenan, and perhaps even the Baron himself. For that small pendant that Alienora had passed to me, which had been owned by her betrothed, had been reported stolen within the household.

I knew Alienora herself would not have done this, but I suspected that she had confessed her love for me to the local priest. Despite the sanctity of the confessional, when word got out that a nobleman's daughter might have been taken beneath the consecrated image of Our Lady the Virgin Mother, in full view of the Saints and perhaps the Savior himself, it would probably get back to the Baron and his wife, or at the very least someone in the household who might have a particular friendship with the priest or one of the Brethren at the abbey. The ridiculousness of it all seems laughable now, but in that day, it was a matter of the utmost gravity.

Additionally, having nearly flung myself upon my mother before her death, I was no doubt viewed as a suspicious and derelict personage to know, for little understanding existed of how a pious son would love a mother who consorted with demons, unless he, himself, might be among the throng at the Witches' Sabbat on a Lammas Eve.

All I know is that my dear beloved, who had given her body to me and her soul to the Almighty, came to me one dawn with the news that I must leave the castle with as much haste as possible. Although I begged her to go with me, she told me that the Almighty planned her life. She would enter the convent and take Holy Orders before Christmas with the Magdalens.

"My love for you is strong," she said. "I will seek your safety in my prayers. They say if two hearts who have bound as one drink of the water of the Fountain of St. Gwynned, then they will never truly be parted."

We went together, under cover of darkness. She had bribed her servants and guards, and as I had seen her on that first night, she climbed astride a stallion as if she had been doing so since a child. It was hard for me to believe that this young woman would ever remain a Sister of the cloth, for she seemed wild and gay as she rode her horse across the marshy land, following the road until we reached St. Gwynned's Grotto and its Font.

We approached the entrance to the carved and settled cavern where the anchoresses dwelled, living in an ascetic darkness within a cave that had been carved into a series of quarters and chapels for worship, lit occasionally by the sun and moon when the rock ceiling opened up. St. Gwynned's Grotto was covered in a fine mist that caught the full moonlight that had emerged from behind clouds. It was like a metallic blue light, and it made the mouth of the Magdalen's cavern—which looked less like a cave than a rock chapel—glow with a midnight rainbow of purple and white. The grasses had grown tall around the Font, and we spread ourselves out like children on a picnic there, at the edge of the water. I leaned to kiss her cheek, but she drew away from my love.

She would not let me touch her, nor would she allow me to speak of plans or of ways of stealing her from her family. She simply cupped her hands in the water and sipped of it. Then I leaned over her cupped hands and drank the rest of the frigid water before it dribbled out from between her fingers.

"If we did not live in this world," I said, "I would take you for my bride. We would ride out to the sea and travel to other Breton lands, and live freely. We would raise children, and I would build an earthen house and keep the fire burning so you would never know want or lack of desire."

"If we did not live in this world," said she, "I would go with you, taking jewels from my mother's furs to pay our way on a boat to those lands of which you speak. And there, like the lovers of legend, we would spend our lives in bringing to each other happiness and freedom from the sorrow that is our mortal life. May it be so in the life hereafter, when our eyes shall be opened on the Day of Judgment." I had already lost her, I knew. Lost her to a suitor I could not fight, could not even challenge. I had lost her to God. At least, that was my feeling then. I still retained hope that I might draw her back from a decision to leave the world for the confinement of this rocky nunnery. But I had to let her go for the time being, I knew.

We rode back to the castle, and my heart was heavy. I had sent Ewen Glyndon to my mother's house, and with him, the charity passed to my brothers and sisters from the Baron's wife. He returned and told me that many of my siblings were gone. Still, the neighbor had taken two of the youngest and had promised to raise them as her own.

I had no family, and soon, I would have no love.

Nor was hope rising within my heart, and my mother's death weighed heavily on me.

I had just passed my eighteenth birthday, and I felt as if life held nothing but misery. I could not see beyond my present pain, despite my having drunk of the sacred water with its legend of lovers bound forever.

✦ 8 ✦

AT the castle, we were surprised by guards, who took me prisoner and swept Alienora away, off her horse even as she struggled. She cried out for me, and I for her, but it was too late for us. I knew they would not hurt her, but simply return her to her father's care though I worried for her reputation and safety, even so.

I was taken to a room I had never before seen. It was beneath the ground and smelled strongly of dung and blood. In it, were implements of torture and restraint. The dungeon. Three guards fastened shackles made of iron to my wrists, and more to my ankles. I was bound in such a way that I had to sit uncomfortably on the dirt floor, with knees bent, head and shoulders forward, almost to my knees. After I was secured thusly, a guard took a strip of cloth and thrust it into my mouth to keep me silent.

Into the room came Corentin himself. He wore a soldier's garb, and I knew immediately that he had managed to raise himself in the Baron's estimation and might now be a guard or even sent off to fight in the Duke's army. It was an honor for him, although it often meant death to the men who were thus passed from the Baron out to the foreign wars.

"I have brought you here, dear Mud-hen, because your time on this Earth will be short. You are accused of a crime," he said, although he did not inform me what that crime might be. Neither could I ask. "And you have been poisoning a young maiden's mind with obscenity and blasphemy. Because of your mother's crime, the Baron and the magistrates have some care for your being, despite the fact that your life is worth nothing. However, when I told them of how you had taught a bird to blaspheme the Holy Virgin by repeating the 'Ave Maria'—surely this was of the Devil himself—they felt that you should be dispatched before another night goes by. You made things worse for yourself with kidnapping his daughter and stealing a horse, but your master has spoken out on your behalf. He has, for reasons unknown to me, taken up your cause, though I do not know why."

As he spoke a small ray of hope lit up the dark of my mind. Kenan, my huntsman, had spoken for my goodness. He had, perhaps, saved my life. Yet, at that moment, I did not care for life at all. What had life to offer me? I was truly a Mud-hen, I had no family, I had no hope for the love of my heart, and this despicable Corentin, who had done everything within his power to ruin my life and destroy any chance of happiness or decency I might have, ruled the last of my existence.

He taunted me with his tales of Alienora and how he intended to take her for himself now that my flesh had damaged her. He tormented me with stories of our mother's wantonness, and then struck me several times as I crouched there, unable to fight back. He lay on the dirt before me, and wore a grin of idle wickedness as he said, "Your life is truly in my hands, little brother. I knew of our relation when you came here, and I could not stand to see our mother in your face. I still cannot stand her, though she is nothing but ashes in a field. But I see her in your face, and I see your father as well."

At this, I started, and tried to spit out the gag in my mouth. He saw this action and reached over, pushing the cold palm of his hand against my lips to keep them closed. "Your father was an infidel who had gained favor with the Duke many years ago. He had his own kind of witchcraft. Few knew him, but all took pity on our mother, for he had raped her, and you were born from that heinous act." He smiled, nearly pleasantly. "Didn't you want to know? Your father was a monster. He abandoned your mother as soon as he had his way, and I've been told that it was then that she lost her mind with grief. Then that she began to spread her legs for food. She was not like that before. He changed her, and disappeared before you were born. Everyone knows, but few would tell you of him. My father tried to kill him, but could not. My father led a party to hunt him down, but he used his sorcery to elude them. All took pity of our mother, until her own witchcraft came out."

I glared at him, wanting to shout that he was a monster, for she was his mother, as well.

As if reading my thoughts, he said, "I did not care for her. She was a bitch, giving birth to litters of children. I was merely in one of those litters."

He spat more poison at me, speaking of the tragedies I had heaped upon him, upon the Baron, and upon Alienora. "If you are found here in the morning, you will be arrested on charges of theft and of sorcery. I requested this night with you so that I could tell you how, after you're gone—gone from this country—I will know carnal pleasures with Alienora. I will think of you, as I enter her. I will imagine how your lips took each nipple, and I will bite them as I do so. I will force myself upon her, and she will acquiesce, because I will tell her that your life hangs in the balance, and should she not pleasure me in every way I can devise, then I shall see to it that you are murdered instantly. And she will not even know that I don't have that power, nor would I ever hurt you, little brother. I will let others butcher or enslave you. I imagine you in some prison in Byzantium, living on rats, raped nightly by a filthy Turk. Or deep in the land of the Rus, a savage winter taking you in its frozen embrace. And all the while, think of the roaring fire in the hearth, and how I shall bend Alienora to my will because of the purity of her love for you. How I will enter her, thinking of your suffering."

I wanted to pull free from my shackles and cut his throat as he lay there before me, spinning out his hellish heart.

"You and I are children of the same womb," he said. "You see me as everything you are not, but I see how alike we are. Do you cringe at my ambition here, in the castle? It is the same as yours. Do you fear how I will take your beloved and make her suffer? It is the same suffering that you brought her. You are not as good as you believe. And I am no worse than you, my brother. We share the same sin."

When he was done with his poisonous words, he called the guard back and a cloth sack was placed over my head.

I felt blows to my back and arms as men with cudgels pounded at me. Then, a blow to my head, and another.

I was thrown into darkness in my mind and thought as I went that I must be dying.

II

THE WORLD OF MEN

CHAPTER 7

Abducted

· 1 ·

FATE had not yet taken my life, though even I assumed she would at any moment. How little I understood of life and death in that mortal realm, for I wept in darkness for my mother. I prayed to see her face again. To see my sisters and brothers, and to feel the arms of my grandfather about me, with the wings of doves fluttering like those of angels. I wept at my memory of Alienora, and the fate I had brought upon her. I began to understand how I had brought about the destruction of others around me, how Corentin's words had at least half of the truth to them. How, just by not having a care for my mother, I had allowed her death. And Alienora—if I had truly loved her, would I have so let my animal urges run free in the chapel of Our Lady? Would I risk her reputation? If I had truly loved her, not just wanted the Baron's daughter, but genuinely loved her soul, could I not have held back from the temptation to have her? All my pain had come, I felt then, from my not knowing my place in life. I had believed, as my grandfather had taught me, that I was meant for greater things than the mud. I believed that I was as worthy of the Baron's daughter as a prince might be. I believed that my mother was lower than a dog at times. I had been blind to her goodness until it was too late. I had only seen what was bad in her, and I felt the burden of loss and of my own vanity. Was there nothing of Heaven within me?

I would die like a dog as I had lived. I would suffer for these many sins, for the foolishness of my childhood dreams, for the way I had not cared enough for my family, not honored my mother in any way until it was far too late to matter. I remembered my grandfather's kindness, then how I had stolen the small stone from the oak tree, thinking that it would somehow bring me fortune, when it was meant to remain within the tree, a memory of past generations of our bloodline. I could not blame everything of my life upon Corentin, who had begun to seem like a foul shadow of my own being. He was more than half brother; he was half soul in some unspeakable way. I loathed him the way I loathed part of myself, and wished I could take a dagger and slice myself away from this shadow.

I lay in a smelly, dark, small prison, and remained battered and barely conscious, wishing for death, wishing for vengeance, wishing to be clean of the sins of my past. Although I was later told that I regained consciousness soon enough, my memories of that time blur. I remember being in a small, dark, enclosed space, still shackled, dryness about my lips. I remember light, but briefly, and water. I remember that my bodily functions proceeded, whether or not I could stand and find a place to relieve myself of them.

I did not wonder if this were Heaven or Hell, but knew that it was the beginning of my voyage from home, away from that terrible hearth near where I slept, away from my beloved. I felt as if I had been packed in ice, not merely from the dank atmosphere in which I found myself, but also from the winter in my heart. Mere Morwenna had told me as a boy that the only hell that existed was separation from the one most loved, and she had been proved right by me: I thought of nothing but Alienora, the Lady de Whithors, the maiden who might at that moment be suffering for the sin I had thrust upon her in my lust for her body.

I tried to conjure her face, thinking of that sacred water we shared on our last night before the sorrow of parting forever, hoping to see her in my mind's eye, but instead, I conjured darkness. Another face came to me: my mother in her last moments. My sweet mother, who had been trampled by the world, and had to suffer the fate of the ignoble and the damned before the entire community that I had once thought of as home and hearth.

The memory of my mother's burning body at the stake still left its yellow-and-red echoes within my soul, and I doubt I could ever wash that in the river of forgetfulness. Her eyes, so full of Our Lady's own grief, as we kissed briefly, before I was torn from her. Before the executioner's torch came to the brambles around her feet. There was no justice in the world. There was no honor. Perhaps for the Baron and his family, perhaps even for treacherous snakes like Corentin Falmouth there might be victory and conquest; but justice was something sold to the poor, which, like the mud and thatch of a roof, had no value and might melt during even a mild storm. These images and thoughts plagued me from my cramped barrel, and I wondered at what cruel fate awaited me once I was set free from it, or if I would lie there until dead.

I arose from a deep but troubled sleep to see what at first I thought was torchlight but soon discovered was the light of a fresh, fair morning.

The lid of my prison removed, someone yanked me into a fresh sea air. The thick arms of a man of swarthy complexion, and long, ragged beard. His dark beard was braided as the looters from the north often did, and he had a bushy brow and a scowl upon him that made me think of a badger. Let me now think of him as the Emperor, for that is the nearest I could come to pronouncing his name, a foreign one. He unlocked my shackles and threw me into an ice-cold sea, at the edge of the land.

What land was this? It must surely be my country, only the water was clearer than the Atlantic, and the rocks along the shore towered above me. My arms had been set too long in my dark prison, such that

I could not swim, and felt myself drown. The Emperor splashed into the water after me, a burly bear of a man, dragging me to shore. I lay back and looked up at the sun. It seemed brighter than it should have been. The Emperor laughed at my pains, and spoke to me as if I understood him. Then, he brought water and a bit of rabbit, which he roasted over a fire while I longed to grab it off the spit and gobble it down, my hunger being so intense.

I could not estimate the days I had been in my dark prison, but it seemed an eternity. I can also guess that I had been somewhat cared for, even in the barrel, for I no longer wore my breeches and tunic, but was dressed as if for a pauper's grave in a cloth that barely covered my loins. Clothes were brought—these were not as fine as the ones I'd had, but once I washed up more, another servant threw a proper tunic and shoes to me.

The Emperor didn't treat his servants badly, nor did he dress me as someone who would go to work for him. Instead, he pointed to a great ship in the harbor. I gathered from his motions and a word here or there that I would be taking a long voyage.

When I had regained some strength, he secured the shackles at my ankles; all the while I was too weak to struggle against this. I accepted my fate. I would never see Alienora again. I would never see the Baron's castle upon the hillside. Or the marshes that guarded my beloved Forest. Nor would I be able to help my younger brothers or sisters. All was lost.

My mother's ashes floated above me as gray clouds moving eastward.

I looked to the ship, which was being loaded with cargo and on which I saw others like me, hapless youths being sent off to some unknown fate.

On shipboard, with the Emperor working beneath the commanding officer, I was soon in yet another darkness—the hold of the ship, crowded by more youths and men, many of whom spoke my language. I learned of tales of sorrows of the younger boys, sent or kidnapped as was I or enlisted if they sought fortune in the wide world. We were headed toward Byzantium, or the Holy Land, or faraway end-of-the-Earth countries with names that could not be uttered in our own languages. We would fight for the Pope and for the King and for the glory of Sir Ranulf, a rich knight who desired to fulfill a Crusade to stamp out a heresy in a southern city that was not yet occupied. We were not to be Crusaders, or gain wealth ourselves, although this was the mythology that many of my companions had on that long and arduous journey east. The Emperor had been, I learned, a pirate of sorts, but had discovered the Savior on an island in Greece and had determined to serve him in this way: by enslaving and kidnapping and bringing into the Lord's Service those youths who would bring him the most coin.

♦ 2 ♦

W HILE I had many adventures aboard that ship, and I saw a boy of fourteen cut the throat of a man of twenty, most of the journey was tedious and without horizon. We ate hard, salty bread, and drank what tasted like bilgewater. I grew sick some days from the sea's motion, as did many of my companions. One man threw himself from the ship, taking his shackled companion with him, willing to drown rather than continue the journey. But I remained hopeful—not of the foreign land upon which I would set foot, but that my love for Alienora, and her love for me, would sustain the both of us through any trial that we would encounter, separately or together.

When we finally came into port, and our shackles were taken off, I had already accepted this new fate and this new world. I had begun believing that I was a servant of the Holy Cross, and that I must gain my fortune, however meager, from this endless war with the East in order to prove myself worthy of one so far above me as Alienora. I was not to be a mercenary soldier of the lowest caste, but one of the infantry, which was called a Badge of Honor by those above us in rank who took treasure and honor at will; but to us, being the infantry meant we were the unpaid slaves of a Holy War.

We would have no weapons but those we took on the battlefield from the dead infidel, and we would only find food and water after the knights and soldiers had their fills. Men talked incessantly of remission of sins and of the death of honor as a pilgrim-warrior, and there were monks who were handsome and bright who told those of us—some as young as eleven or twelve, in truth—that we were doing this for the honor of Jerusalem, which was the center of all Christendom, which the heathens of Satan had defiled and blasphemed for too long.

There were so-called papers of transmission and manumission from the Baron, as well as a passage of armor. That was not to say I would be well armed, but the papers would be sent on to the Knights Hospitaller, to whom my Baron sent me. I would never hope to be part of that Holy Brotherhood of Knights, but no doubt, I would be doing some fighting on their behalf as a servant-soldier. As a bastard, my life would be fodder for the Glory of the Most High. My lot in life had been thrown in with other serf and peasant youth—our lives were part payment to some King from the Baron. Other boys and youths like me had been sent off, as well, and I was overjoyed to see my companion Ewen Glyndon, the shepherd boy, among those in our group.

His face was dark with grime, and his hair a tangle of bird nest, but I recognized him through his eyes, which had not dimmed in their warmth. I could not believe that we might've been on the same long voyage and had been within arm's reach of each other the whole time without recognizing each other at once. I embraced him as if he were a younger brother. I held him, wishing not to have to lose even the smell of him for a moment to this strange land and these strange people around us.

He laughed, and told me that he had been sent along on my passage by his own request. "Kenan Sensterre wished me gone, and I begged the Baron's daughter for help in this plight. She thought you had been murdered, but when she learned that you were to be sent to the Holy Land, she bade me kiss your cheek so that you would feel her love. I am here as her message to you. She will never forget you, Falconer. She will always seek your salvation and safe return." Then, Ewen pressed his lips near my ear, by a wisp of hair that hung down from my scalp.

"Do not fear for her. She is safe," he whispered. "She told me to let you know that there is a token of love she holds for you so that she might always remember you."

I thought of Alienora, and felt gladdened by all of this. I felt as if the Fates watched over me, and over my beloved, and Ewen was a messenger from them to let me know that the love between Alienora and me could not be ended by war or exile.

I did not appreciate, at the time, the great sacrifice Ewen had made for me, nor did I understand the full extent of his friendship; but if you have ever been sent to a foreign land, to face certain death if not hardship, and you had seen a familiar face, you, too, would keep that person at your side at every moment.

As I looked at other youths, similarly sent to soldiers, I realized that all of us who were from among the poor and subservient had the look of the vanquished upon us, no matter the land of our origin. We were payment for the debts of war. I have since learned that much of mankind's security and comfort is built from such payments, and the wealth of many human nations has been built on the backs of such as I, sent off to fight without weapon in hand, for the glory of others. I counted myself, and Ewen, as lucky for having survived the trip with only a sense of the heaviness of the burden of life and the charge put to us to help with the bringing of the land of the Cross back under the holiness of Christendom.

I did not lose heart. Alienora's face remained within my mind, and I felt as if I could speak to her in my dreams, and she would hear me.

Nor did I lose hope when we docked and went overland some hundreds of miles or more, many of my fellow soldiers dying along a sunburned roadside, keeling over from fever or thirst or hunger. There was little in the way of supplies until we reached an encampment of Holy Knights at the outskirts of a stone castle called Kur-Nu. Many in my company were calling it the City of the Miracle, for it held, according to legend, the cloth that had wiped the Lord's face when he went to his crucifixion. If you had told me that we were far away from Jerusalem, the center to our world then, I would not have known. Our commanders had told us that we were about the work of the Lord and

of the Pope and of the kings of Christendom. We traveled to the
south and east. On some days, over a mountain pass, I could see the
blue of the distant sea.

I was young, still, and I believed more in goodness than I did in
evil, despite what had happened with my mother, despite Corentin
and his dark heart, and despite the betrayals I felt from my master, Kenan. I had lost a sense of justice, but I still believed that benevolence
could come from the darkest shadow. After a skirmish along a trade
road, in which we took camels and supplies from the infidel, and during which our commanders slaughtered every living enemy, I found
myself with a weapon. I took up the sword offered to me—a double-
edged broadsword that had belonged to one of the recently killed infidels we fought.

Ewen and I quickly learned how to wield it, as well as the mace,
which was a weapon of the Saracens, though the knights would not
then touch it, nor would the sergeant-brethren. Most of us in the infantry had daggers, another instrument of battle that the superior
knights sneered at. Knights had the great swords, with legendary
names, blessed by saints and the Pope in Rome, passed down from
King to knight with magical Christian properties. Those of us who
would fight on foot simply had ordinary weapons, and I was honored
to be given the broadsword, despite the fact that it was no use in spear-
ing. Still, I learned to wield it, to cut and hack at the enemy, and my
muscles built fast as if they'd been waiting for years to grow from my
scrawny shoulders.

My waist narrowed even as my chest expanded, and the running
and marching that we had to do during the campaigns and sieges built
up my endurance. When the days were on fire, I ate little and fasted and
prayed on the marches through the desert; but when we took an enemy
encampment or came to a castle that already held Hospitallers, I ate better than I ever had. The Hospitallers, our patrons, knights and soldier-
monks who were our masters in every way, promised that among us,
even a serf could rise to become a sergeant-brethren if we proved ourselves in battle, and that to die while on this holy pilgrimage would

mean immediate remission of sins and entrance into Heaven. Ewen and I both determined that we should use this Holiest of Crusades to make our fortune and take our place in the world.

I had, at last, become a man, and felt the blood of life within me as I never had before. The love of my brethren—the infantry as well as our decorated commanders, the Brethren and the Knights Hospitallers, and the banner of my own Duke of Brittany, who had offered his services to the crown of France and to Rome for this Crusade against the unholy of Byzantium and of the Holy Land, all brought my love of mankind back to me. We were one—a fighting force, and we lived and died together. I buried myself in our brief victories, finding the wenches of the foreign hordes to be as soft and delicate as the Breton women of home, although none made me forget my beloved, my sacred pain of love for Alienora de Whithors.

Ewen was not as good at battle as was I, so I always made sure to stand before him, and when we marched, I kept him to my side and a little back, so that if a blow were struck from nowhere, if the whistle of the arrows flew toward us, I might protect him. I was quick with the shield I had acquired, and even faster when it came to striking and turning and watching him even while I fought. Many of the youths were so young that they should not have been fighting, but the world was the way it was, and I watched many of our own die in Christian honor alongside the infidels that we slaughtered. Do not ask me too much of our military campaigns, for I was low in rank and took orders without understanding their nature. One of the monk-knights told us of our Christian Love, and how, in killing the enemy, we were bringing the love of our Savior to their souls, for in killing for the Holy, we brought the infidel into God's embrace.

We heard from the brethren and knights of the Hospital that we must keep to the fires at night if we were at camp, for the tales of demons were rampant. They came in the dark and ran like wolves, grabbing the dying up in their jaws, taking them from where they lay before any could rescue them. We were told to stay near the banners and the great crosses that the monks kept, as well as with our fellow soldiers when the sun set. "These demons are sent by the infidel," a monk warned a group of us, "and we must take in the sick and bury the dead well before nightfall."

"Do they only take the dying?" I asked.

He looked at me with interest, as if he had not expected a question from anyone. "A strong youth could cut one down. They avoid the quick. I have been told that fire and the ax subdue them. I watched one burn."

His mention of burning made me ache for a reason of which I was not certain.

"I saw a demon once," I told him. "In my home. I was a boy, and with several huntsmen, we drew it from a deep well. It had wings like a dragon."

The monk smiled. "That I have never seen. These are weak demons, and the locals call them Ghul. Our prisoners fear the thought of them coming in the night. Devils are everywhere in this land, I'm afraid. We are bringing the light of God with us to chase them into the shadows forever."

• 3 •

WITHIN a few weeks, I had already seen battles and bloodshed. The Hospitallers had a reputation for caring for the sick, and so, after a battle, one of my many tasks was to find our men who had survived but were heavily wounded and carry them to the tents that were set up for the purposes of care. I often sat by with a rag to wipe at the blood from a countryman's breast that had been savagely cut open, or to hold the oil lamp so that one of the brethren-at-arms might see better as he stanched the flow of vital fluids from a soldier. Despite my weariness and exhaustion, I felt an excitement about life I had never before known. I was lean and muscular, and nearly nineteen years on earth. I had begun to prove that I was worthy of a higher station, and I had managed to rescue Ewen from close scrapes with death at the hands of the ungodly. When one particular battle was over, after a full day and night of attack against a walled city, during which the Knights Hospitallers and the Teutonic Knights brought their infantries together against an infidel stronghold, I looked through the terrible yellow-brown dust smoke, smoke from a fire we'd set to burn infidels in their place of worship.

There, I saw a face that looked nearly like my own. I became certain what I saw was not a man, but a ghost.

· CHAPTER 8 ·

The Ghost

◆ 1 ◆

WHY a ghost? I have not yet mentioned the thousand tales of legendary terror in this land of dust and sun. It was our Holy Land, but also the place of the Devil, who lurked in the abandoned citadels of legend, like the famous leprous city of Hedammu, called also the Devil's Horns, which overlooked the southern sea. Other foot soldiers who knew of it called it the Mouth of Hell, for there were tales of demons and treasure there. Our commanders talked of sending an expedition to it simply to see if it lived up to its reputation as a place of hidden treasure. It had been held once by Knights of the Temple, and by the Teutonic Knights, but now had been abandoned as an unclean city. It was said that our enemies had powers to summon spirits from the battle, and I was as susceptible to this superstition as any of my companions. The stories of the creatures called Ghul had passed among us, for some claimed to see them feeding on the dead or sick just before dawn.

So, when I saw what I was sure was a ghost, it made my heart beat fast and with great fear. We were at the rim of Heaven or Hell in this land, and at any moment, demons might appear to take our souls.

This strange visage terrified me at first, for I thought it might be a sign of my own madness or of some infidel demon trick. We had been warned of the godless sorcery of the enemy, and of their crimes against Nature and Heaven. I had heard of strange burial mounds where creatures called Ifrit and Ghuls and Djinn, the demons of this world, supposedly attacked wayward travelers. We were truly frightened of such things, although our monks—many of whom took up the sword as well—told us that the Savior and Our Lady would protect us and send us to Heaven to keep us from these demons.

So, when I saw this face, I first thought that I was seeing a ghost, then a Ghul, some trickery of the enemy. And yet the man I saw could not stop watching me, either. Soon, as the smoke continued to cloud the air, I moved through it, toward him, stepping over bodies and those who had fallen but not yet died. I had no fear, yet my heart raced. A great smile lit up his face, and in an instant, each of us recognized the other.

He gave out a shout, "Bird Boy!"

And I laughed and ran to him, recognizing him mostly in his voice and then knowing the face and the man immediately. It was my brother, Frey. In the years since I had last seen him, he had grown tall and stout, but his eyes and his smile were the same as that little scrawny boy I remembered on his last night in our home before he left for the great wide world. He wore a kerchief of sorts just to the left of his face, wrapped around his head—covering the scars where our mother had burned him in anger with oil. We embraced long, and I felt tears in my eyes, for here was more than my lost brother. Here was a sign from God Himself that good could come from bad, that happiness could exist in the darkness of life. I was surrounded by friends and brothers and comrades-in-arms. This was truly the place where I most belonged.

My brother Frey smelled of onions and dust, but it was the most fragrant perfume I could imagine. There is something about your kinsmen that is indelibly pressed into you, into your blood, into your memory, and the smell and feel of them is like no other. It was like coming home, to feel his arms about me, and when we let go of each other to laugh and talk, I felt as if life had blessed me with this fate rather than cursed me, for where my brother was, there was my fortune.

After we'd put up our weapons and gear, I brought Ewen into our circle, and we sat and talked of our adventures. I told him, sorrowfully, of our mother's fate. Ewen added that she had met her death well, and that she had not dishonored our family despite the charges brought against her.

Frey kept a hard eye upon me, and when I was done with the injustice of the abbey and village, he told me, "Our mother had her faults. She drove me from the house, yet I was ready to go. If she had not, I would not have become a man, for I traveled much. A monk took me in. He taught me of the past and of all that has been lost in the world. I have loved many women and have two bastards in the Languedoc, and now am a warrior where I once was a country fool. I have this in remembrance of our dear mother." He reached up and drew off the kerchief that hid the left side of his forehead and cheek and ear. In the fire's light, I saw the scarring that had occurred from the boiling liquid my mother had thrown at him in a rage.

"At first, I felt she had cursed me with this as I began my journey into life. But soon enough, this was my protection from men who wished to kill me, for on the road, I was viewed as one watched over by Our Lady. Strangers who felt it was their Christian duty gave me bread and wine. As I said, I lived with monks for a time, and then among vagabonds. Then, in a great city, I learned of knights who sought soldiers for battles. I became apprenticed and learned how to wield a sword and an ax and to run for days with messages. I lied about my heritage, and my family, so that my mean origins might not be discovered and held against me. I have seen countries that you might only imagine, and have been with beautiful women on islands only spoken of in dream. And I learned of my talent for war, and thus, I became prized as a soldier, and now carry the banner for Sir

Ranulf le Bret. But all these years, brother, I have felt empty, no matter what wine I drank, no matter what bread and meat I devoured. And it was for home. And now, you, my home, are here. Let us praise our dead mother, and our many fathers, and hope that in the hereafter she has found her peace."

We raised our wineskins and drank heartily to this. As if this question were always on my mind, I asked him, "What of my father? Did you know him?"

Frey did not look at me when he answered. "I remember a man who was bad to our mother."

"Corentin said he took her with force."

He looked at me carefully before answering. "You believe him? He could not remember your father. That scoundrel was little more than a baby when he was taken from our mother."

"Tell me about my father."

"I barely remember any of the fathers," he said. Then, his face brightening, he added, "But you, my little one, and our sisters, I remember well. How are they? I remember a baby we called the Marsh-child."

I could not speak of the fate of our brothers and sisters, and thinking of it vexed my soul, but there was nothing that I could then do for them. I told him of my life since his departure, and of my love for Alienora, daughter of the Baron.

He nodded, laughing at me as I spoke of this lady. "You must somehow break your thought from hers," he said. "For you are young and will bed many women, but the likes of us shall never wed a lady, a daughter of a nobleman."

"She will wed no one but Christ," I said.

Remembering the curious sect of nuns of the caves, he said, "Is she a Magdalen?"

I nodded. "That is what I've been told."

"They are a most fanatical order, with peculiar conduct," he said. "Our mother took me to them, once, to beg for bread from the pilgrims' offerings. I saw their lair. They live like anchoresses in the dark and rarely come out into the daylight except to meet with pilgrims who come to drink from the springs. They have a statue of Holy Mary Magdalen the Sinner, which is carved from the blackest stone and covered with garlands of dried wildflowers. It scared me more to see them as a boy than to see Mere Morwenna and her hags. There are those I have met since who believe this sect of Magdalens is not of the True Church. I worry for her, being among them."

"We drank together of the grotto's waters so that we might always be together," I said, boldly romantic in a place—a foreign land full of dust and blood and the cries of the wounded—that was about anything but the love between man and woman.

Again, he laughed. "You must put the past aside, Aler, in order to enjoy the pleasures of what is left you. The past is death itself. God and the Devil, and the angels and demons that fight for your soul determine the future. The present is the only life."

But I brought up another ghost from the past. Our half brother, Corentin, whom I had never known. Frey had known him, and remembered him well. "He was the worst of our lot even as a squalling brat in rags," Frey said, a tinge of bitterness to his voice as he stared into the embers. "Our mother loved him dearly. His father visited often when I was but three and six months, for I remember Kenan Sensterre well. He was kind to our mother, and to all of us children. But once he took the baby, I did not see him again."

"I hate the man," I said. "It is he who saw me thrown out of the castle. It is he who believed Corentin Falmouth and not my word."

"Falmouth? That is what he calls himself?" Frey began laughing. He had become such a large, overly muscled young man that his laugh was like the bellow of a bull. "That is such a fine name for such a dirt sack. Quintin Atthefeld has become Corentin Falmouth. Soon enough, we will discover that he has been knighted for his bravery. By God's wounds, his father has protected that bastard much."

"May all bastards such as us find protection," I said, laughing along with my brother.

Ewen, sitting beside me, laughed also, then began weeping, for our talk had made him miss home. Even the most courageous soldier might weep if for home and hearth, and we said a prayer to Our Lady to guide the hands of our knights and our brethren in Holy War, that we might one day return to the land of our fathers.

◆ 2 ◆

A ND now, I must tell you of another met during this campaign. He was a lad named Thibaud Dustifot. Although barely eleven years old, he was an ancient soul, and brought skins of water for us on the road or at camp. He didn't know his real name, but we called him Dustifot for the dirt on his oft-bare feet. He was terrified of battle, and begged me to watch over him. "I-I will bring you water and share any bread I gather," he said, a slight tremor in his voice. As I got to know him, and saw how he helped others on the battlefield, I grew to understand his fear of those older than he was—for many of the soldiers treated him like a dog despite the many kindnesses the boy provided. I could not resist his smile or his promise of help, and was reminded of children I had known as a boy.

The Hospitallers considered the boys who served in the ranks as Holy Innocents who brought good fortune to battle, and yet the children in the camp were routinely beaten over theft of a bit of bread or dried meat. Thibaud was also of the Old Ones of my native land, more pure in his blood than I, and like the Old Ones, of smaller stature and swarthy of complexion. He had the full Celtic blood in him, and although he called himself a Breton, from our homeland, he had come from a family in Cornwall. I mention him now, because, like my friend Ewen, I became protective of this little boy with the enormous heart and spirit.

He spoke to me in the Old Tongue, some of which I understood. My people revered his kind, for he was the link to our ancient world, when Bretons flourished, before even the Romans. Although he was Christian, he knew of the Forest women and of the legends of the Briary Maidens. He even knew of the sacred stag of Cernunnos, the white deer that lured hunters into the Old Ways, and of something that was rarely spoken of, the ancient bog surrounded by thorns. It was the legendary swamp where all that was evil festered, and to gaze into it was to lose your very soul. How entertained Thibaud kept us, with his knowledge of tales. Had he remained home, he no doubt would have become a village storyteller, earning his keep by the variety of stories he remembered from an older storyteller.

In battle in a foreign country, the best he had was us, for the knights and commanders had no interest in Breton boys who spoke too freely.

I had to rescue him from being severely beaten by his master, who fancied himself a knight but was, in fact, not much better than any of the rest of us. I saw this man beating with his fists upon the little boy's back and scalp, while Thibaud crouched down as much as he could to ward off the blows. I lifted the man from his violent attack, and threw him to the earth. I drew my sword, but needn't have. Men who attack the less able seem to be more terrified than any others, and so, Thibaud's former master ran like the dog he was, off to his drunken compatriots and the few brother-soldiers who would protect him.

"You must have angered him greatly to deserve such a beating," I said as I took him to the washerwomen who would tend his wounds better than would the Hospitaller monks themselves.

"I stole from him," Thibaud said. I demanded he show me his goods, and the boy drew out the tiniest scrap of meat, of a pitiful size that would not slake the hunger of a newborn.

"You do not need to steal anymore," I told him, and brought him under my protection. "You may eat from my trencher, and drink from my cup." Although his master came back for him, each time I saw the man, I raised my weapon to greet him so that he would know that to get the boy back in his service, he would have to fight me first. He never accepted the challenge.

On long marches, Thibaud Dustifot regaled Frey and Ewen and me with tales of ancient heroes, of Arthur, and Lancelot, and of the Faerie Queen who had built a castle from the dreams of the dying upon a lake of mirrors within the heart of our Great Forest. For a child, he had an enormous ability to spin stories of straw into fine gold. I hesitated telling my own stories of the Forest, but knew that I would one day sit with him and tell him the tales even he had never known.

◆ 3 ◆

BUT I paint too kind a picture of my travels with the soldiers.

The battles happened often, and a day was a fine one when I saw fewer than ten of my brethren-at-arms slaughtered.

The smell of blood of that time is one I shall never forget. It was not an intoxication, but was a stink of rot and sourness, and had a milky consistency, mixed with dirt. To see a battlefield of rock and dust, laid out as if in a carpet to God of my compatriots and fellow Hospitallers, their arms sliced off, heads separate from bodies, the little boys slaughtered on pikes and spears, as well as the bodies of the enemy infidel similarly displayed—it did not make me wish for yet another battle in a day's time.

The days of siege were long and terrible. The blood ran to our ankles in the worst of a day that seemed to never end. I remember there was a man of twenty-five or so who clung to my leg, even after his torso had been sliced down the middle. And yet, that was simply a moment within the blackened smoke of war, for I tugged myself free and continued to wield ax and short sword as I took down those who came at me to bring me to the grave.

◆ 4 ◆

IT was a world of blood, and what was not blood, was the coal black smoke of the charnel house. The ash of human death seemed to hold the gates of the city closed as much as it did the horde. The mournful sound of the horns sounding along the battlements—and the strange chants and songs, so foreign and godless to the soldiers below whose commanders had plotted out the day and night and the day next, and planned the deaths of many, and the victory of few.

From one of the great cliffs by the sea, a bird swooped down, spreading its dark wings over the field of soldiers lined in a near amphitheater of war—below the bird, a buzzard, the only victor of the coming battle.

I glanced up to the dark morning sky, seeing the majestic creature of ill omen, remembering my falcons and doves, and thought not of my own death, but of those I would slaughter that day in the name of righteousness. I felt afire with the potency of a war-lust that I had learned from my brother. My love for my mates and for my country and for the maiden who waited for me in a distant land, all conspired against my own natural fear of what was to come. Yes, I thought of Alienora, my sweet, who had lain with me in the chapel and had drunk sacred waters of bonding so that our souls should always be as one, even though the world kept us apart. I saw her face when things got too terrible for me to bear. I saw her face and felt the warmth of her hand on my cheek when death got close enough to singe me with its icy breath.

I breathed in the fear of others beside me. I glanced at Ewen, and felt the need to make sure that he survived another day of war. Thibaud, too, although he was often at the camp during the worst of the battles, for his talent was for healing and not slaughter. It brought me strength. It made me feel as if I were no ordinary nineteen-year-old foot soldier. My hands were large, used to the heft of the blade. I had sprouted—as if they were wings—strong, broad shoulders—and was a head or more taller than the others beside me.

I tasted fear, coppery on my tongue, hoping it would bring me more power that day.

The smell in the air was of dust and sweat and a distant and unfamiliar perfume, as well as the stench of the unburied dead. The battlefield stretched out across an endless wasteland of rocks and towers and the savage and alien world of the infidel at the great towering fortress of Kur-Nu. But Kur-Nu would fall—we and others like us had been laying siege to it for years, with the precision of a Roman phalanx. We were a small piece of the larger puzzle of the fight for this castle of legendary treasure. Walls had tumbled, the rubble spread like frozen lava along the valley between the jagged and imperious cliffs. Carcasses of horses and men lay in a heap near the ash pits of destruction; still, the smell of some aromatic flower wafted on the viperous air, taunting me as I awaited the first signal of battle. The men around me, some barely men, others too old to be in battle, were covered in the yellow dust from the windstorm that had passed the previous night, unable to clean it from our bodies, tunics, armor. It was as if the earth had begun taking us down into her womb, into the dust that we would soon become.

It was a game of men and Death, and only Death won in this game. But I would not die, I knew.

To Frey, more skilled at battle and more bloodied by it, it was all a joke. He had been at this war long, and had grown into a husky, powerful man with it. He knew the use of five different blades, and had, by his own account, lopped the heads of the best of the enemy. Had he not been of lowly birth, he no doubt would have been a great knight and commander. He had told me just the evening before that what he loved most about warfare was the feeling of invincibility that arose within him, the knowledge that should he die, his reward in Heaven awaited, and there would be no death for him until he had reclaimed the Holy Lands.

I was less skilled, and less confident. This was no game, no match. This was a chaos of cries and torments, and a vision of any hell that might exist.

I tensed, waiting for the cry in the field. My muscles ached, but I held my breath in a prayer.

With the first battle cry, I shouted to my brother for victory, and he back to me. This stirred our blood, and even Ewen joined in the great war whoop that went up from the infantry as the battle began.

Raising his ax, my brother ran ahead on foot as the first arrows flew over our heads, and over the hordes of descending infidels. Frey turned about like a windmill, swinging out at the enemy, taking one, then two, then three down. His laughter seemed that of a madman; I caught sight of him when I could. He brought down several more men, like a lion taking down a herd, their spears and swords falling as he slit their throats or hacked arms free of shoulders.

The arrows of the archers struck the great gate ahead of us. The sergeant-brothers and the siege machine, which we had come to call the Bad Neighbor, had moved into position, and the first great stone was flung against the enemy line along the battlements. We would come to know these gates as the Gates of Hell, for it was the most powerful enemy who held within them the torture chambers of others from the Holy Crusade; the stories of how the men would be roasted on spits or tied together with ropes and then starved to death until it was rumored that one man would begin to devour the other while still alive . . . the horrors were ungodly in that terrible place, even if our own men had done that or worse with the enemy. But we were all; they were nothing. This is the way of war. This castle and city needed to burn and be destroyed beneath the feet of the Holy Crusade.

The heat grew intense as flames danced across the enshrouded sky.

I felt enormous power as I swung my sword against the enemy. There was the brutality of violent death all around, but I felt above it, or so inspired within it, seeing the absurdity of all human pain and suffering, feeling like I was playing the game of the gods. Twice, I hacked at an infidel who nearly took down Ewen. I grabbed the youth by his waist and flung him forward so as to keep him from harm's way. Ewen returned the favor threefold, scoring men with death as he went, hacking, hitting, stabbing, grabbing up a mace from a fallen enemy and using it to bring down a great bull of a man.

Too many men fell around us. Too many boys died at my feet. Death traveled, touching the shoulders and necks of soldiers, and I nearly felt it myself. My mission here was to kill or be killed, to move forward by my commanders' signals, so that by the end of the battle, my companions and I would still breathe and taste of the delight of life itself.

The human storm raged, roiling winds of man against man, cross against crescent, sword and spear and ax and arrow swirling in the acrid smoke of the burning fortress gate. The land had been cut with the rubble of other battles, and we added a new wound to it. The armies of the Cross were going to be victorious, I could feel it. I could feel the great swell of the ranks as we pushed toward the goal. I felt that we would take this castle, then have peace. I truly believed it.

I could not even see the fire at the gate, for the bodies of both living and dead and the dust they stirred blocked all sight beyond a few yards. I lost sight of everything but the infidels who crossed my path, and of Ewen, who had managed to fight well and take few injuries.

My brother rode out on horseback—a fallen knight or commander's horse had loosed itself, and he had grabbed it before it could gallop off or be killed. Frey, astride, jabbed and speared at the horde that circled around him.

An infidel leapt up onto the horse itself, a curved blade aimed to slice my brother's throat.

When I remember it, it is as a moment frozen. A mere mote of time, where all else faded into sulfurous yellow around the outline of my brother and the jackal that had held his life in the shiny crescent of metal.

"No!" I shouted, as I cut the infidel before me down. I swung my sword in a neat arc through the oncoming flesh. Its double edge, like canine incisors, met flesh as if it were a reed slicing through water. "Frey!"

Frey turned at the shout. I was certain that he raised his hand to me, in need of aid, for his own sword had fallen. Frey reached at his side for his ax or a dagger.

I could not have seen his eyes, but I feel, in memory, that I did. I remember his gaze, as if he were not a man at all, but a stag in the woods, taken by a hunter.

I leapt over the dead, but felt as if I were moving against a strong current.

Frey's eyes widened, his mouth opening in a battle cry. The enemy warrior sliced his throat, and in the next instant, threw his body from the horse.

"Demon infidel!" I cried out, my tears mixing with sweat as I turned on the enemy.

I brought the sword down across the man's shoulders, cutting in deep. With all my strength, I drew it out again. My muscles twisted as I turned the blade. And brought it down again. I sawed my weapon in and out of the enemy, then brought it out again, with blood spraying from the wounds.

The man who had murdered my brother fell to the earth. The

horse my brother had been riding took off into the billowing smoke. I took my hand ax and began chopping at the dead man until he was no longer in the form of a man at all, my anger unquenched even as I obliterated the body of the murderer.

I searched among the dead and dying, in the blood-caked rocky ground.

Frey lay in the dirt. I got down on my knees beside him, clasping his hands. "Don't die, brother," I wept, unaware of the battle raging around him. I pressed my face to my brother's hands as I held them together. "You shall not die, brother. By the power of God and of all the gods."

But the wound was deep at his throat, and blood had burst from him like a long red cloak.

"Aleric!" Ewen called out. He ran toward me, pulling me away from my brother's body. "He's gone."

Tasting gall in my throat, and fury in my blood, I rose up. I pushed Ewen away from me, and began to strike blow after blow to the oncoming enemy. I felt power in my arms, and a strength in my chest that beat against my cage of bones as if it were a bird of prey within me seeking release.

Something sparked like a flint against stone within my soul. With wide strokes I slashed across the oncoming infidels, and only an instinct for life kept me from falling into despair.

My sword sang in the air that day.

It cut through flesh after flesh, and my face and body were spattered with blood as if I'd been baptized in a sea of red.

I leaned to the left, plunging the bloodied sword into the next man's side. I had only a vague awareness of those around me—Ewen and the other soldiers fighting with daggers and great batons clubbing at the enemy; the knights on horseback, swinging mace and sword and lance and poleax; the archers to the rear shouting each to each as another shower of bolts from their bows found release.

From behind, I felt a knife dig into me, just beneath my shoulder blade. I spun about, ignoring the pain, and hacked my sword into the shoulder of yet another of the faceless infidel.

✦ CHAPTER 9 ✦

The Horns

✦ 1 ✦

THEN, it was over. For a full hour or more at the end of such a day of attack, there was a terrible silence on the field, and the billows of smoke blinded us to any sight of conquest or victory. The only sound might be the whistling of wind, but on that day, the air stilled, and only yellow-and-black smoke rose as if carrying souls to Heaven.

"Aleric! Falconer!" It was Ewen's voice, breaking through the last of the silence. I glanced up, and Ewen raised his ax high with victory. His face streamed with the blood of the enemy; his scalp was dark and wet as well. His left shoulder had been cut, and he limped, but he had a look of elation. He had become a man in war, and I could see upon him the mark of death as surely as if the Angel of Darkness stood behind him. His happiness at the end of a terrible day's fighting should have gladdened my heart, but it did nothing for me.

We would all die there.

All of us would be dust and smoke, soon enough.

Like my brother.

The world took from man. Took, and took again, and the only way to live happily was to pray for Heaven and give up on this world.

But for me, there were no prayers, and no Heaven.

◆ 2 ◆

I turned away from him, dropping my sword in the dirt. I stood, brushing dirt from my tunic, from my knees, feeling the itch of lice, which was common enough among us. The blood on my skin and clothes had caked with mud and sweat, and flies had begun hovering over the battlefield and around my form. Above, the vultures circled the blackened air. All of life was parasitic. All fed upon all. I glanced through the throng of men, then, up to the sky as if it contained answers.

The heat of the sun beat down upon me. We had fought for hours, but it was not yet nightfall.

One of our commanders rode among the crowd of victors, sword raised high. His horse's flankard was bloody with the life of fallen infidels. His cuirass, dented where the spears and sword thrusts of the enemy had failed. With helmet still upon his head, this great knight held both hands aloft.

In one, his sword.

In the other, the fresh-cut head of our enemy's chieftain.

Tossing the head onto a pile of corpses, he roared so that all might hear and speak of it. "Christendom has conquered the Legions of Hell!"

I felt a stab beneath my heart—it was not from an enemy, but from within. I fell to my knees from weakness. Dirt in my fingers felt like the blanket of my own grave. The memory of my brother's face faded from me as if it were as insubstantial as smoke. My mother's face, too, seemed a fiery yellow memory and did not possess any feminine feature that I could recall. The faces of my enemies were more powerful in my thoughts: from Corentin to the Baron to Kenan Sensterre, to the infidels. Even our commanders seemed to be enemies to me, for they brought us here.

Only one memory of hope within me, but it was nearly dead:

Alienora's sweet, pure face, as I had last seen it when I had kissed her lips. Yet, she would never see me again. Those who held power and sway over others—and God and the gods—had commanded that whatever love I kept in my heart for her would wither and die as my love for all mankind must.

The sounds of the earth died for a moment.

I hated all mankind. I hated its works. I hated that I had been born in a time and place, cursed from birth onward, which sent me and my brother and my friend to this hell for the benefit of the knights. For those like the Baron, who would watch my mother burn but would train a dove for his sick wife, who would keep Alienora from me. I burned with anger over this world—the world that God had ordained and all must accept. I hated that I could expect no more from life, nor would life offer more, that even in the life to come, the kings and dukes and barons and knights would remain powerful, while such as myself would be a servant even unto the end of days.

I felt a fever overtake me in this anger. A ringing in my ears began, blocking out all other sounds. The world seemed to grow into a whiteness, as of snow. I smelled a burning of oak, as if I were in the Great Forest, around a campfire. Was I going blind? Deaf? Why could I hear only a distant ringing as of one bell tolling in a long, drawn-out tone? Why the light that ripped at my vision of the world? Then, I heard a strange voice, almost as if it were within me, whispering. Then, it grew louder. It was a woman, not Alienora, but some stranger. *Come home,* she said, and I tried to remember where I had heard this voice before, but I could not. It was of the Old Tongue, but I could not recall it. This phantom inside me said two words, again, and again, *Come home.*

The moment was broken. The smell of bloodied dead, of sweat, of human pain, all around again. The dust still rising, obliterating the gates of the great city before our throng, a city of purported riches. The men around me, cheering their heroes, raising the whoop and cry of the battle well won.

The boy, Thibaud, found me by the torn banner that our men had raised among our dead. Piles of bodies lay there, as if for a feast of some terrible demon from Hell. The boy searched among the dying, and after a time, trotted over to me, raising a skin filled with water. "Are you wounded?"

"In my shoulder," I said.

Thibaud ran about and touched both my arms and shoulder. He tore at my coverings and tunic until I lay there, bare-chested. "There is no cut here. You have but an old scar."

What infidel magic is this? I thought. For I was certain I had a wound from the day's fighting. I could not remember an old scar at all, but then, when he touched the edge of it, I remembered my beating at the hands of Corentin before my journey to this desert hell had begun.

The old wound of that beating had been opened again, and if I lived longer, would rip apart each year of my life.

• 3 •

LATER, when I had some strength, I reached out to Thibaud Dustifot for support as I stood. "Frey is dead, boy." I had no tears left, and no feeling in my body or soul.

"No," he said, and began weeping in a way that I had forgotten there could be tears at all. He wept with the innocence of his age and his heart, and in his eyes I saw all that I had lost on my journey through the world.

I could not comfort him, for I had begun to travel in my soul to a place of ice and fire that was beyond any human feeling.

• 4 •

WHEN the camp had been set, for we had not yet opened the great gate of the Kur-Nu, but simply damaged the outer walls of its fortress, I sat with Ewen and Thibaud and whispered to them of what I meant to do. I tell you now that all I wanted was to be dead. I had no love for life, and had even begun to resist the idea of one more day of battle. Yes, I would desert my countrymen and the Hospitallers, and I knew the consequence of this act. I did not care. I had watched the world take my family from me, and my only love, and I had no faith left.

"Before dawn," I told them. "I will go. I am unclean from this battle."

"If our unholy enemy has cut down your brother, would it not be better for you to avenge his death?" Ewen asked. "At least for the sake of your country?"

"I have no country," I said.

"What of Our Lord?" Thibaud asked.

"You remember the Old Ways," I said, noticing the glimmer in his eye. "What of those gods and goddesses? I have no faith. I am lost."

"You have the stubborn streak of your blood," Ewen said, wise beyond his years. "As well as its doom. You must not let humours destroy you. You must not, Aleric. I beg of you." His face had taken on a reddish hue as he spoke, and his words were more impassioned than I'd heard from him previously. Yet, he meant nothing to me, nor did his words have an effect on me.

I grinned, more grimace than smile. "I will never see my homeland again, I will never see my beloved. I am a man who will bring to doom those who carry me in their hearts. It would be best if you abandoned me to this, both of you, friends."

The boy shook his head. "I am your servant. I go where you go."

"As do I," said Ewen.

"Where I go—" I covered my face with my hands. "Where I go, friends, is to the end of my days. When the feast begins tonight, and the boasting and calling, I will be gone."

"But the Ghul," Thibaud said, a shadow crossing his young face. "They are out there, master. I have seen them once."

"Have you?" I said. "Perhaps I shall meet one of these Ghul, and he shall make quick work of me."

◆ 5 ◆

To desert the Hospitallers was to court death in many ways. First, deserters would be executed on sight, if found, as they would in any military order. Additionally, because I was part of a payment from the Baron to the Hospitallers themselves, I might even be given a torturous execution to further discourage other servant-warriors from imitating my flight. Although I had never seen it, we had all heard the tales of those deserters and traitors who were roasted on spits while they begged for mercy. I did not intend to find out if those stories were true. Additionally, the enemy might take me at any moment on my journey from the Hospitaller encampment, and the foe would be happy to find a soldier wandering unguarded so as to slit his throat or perhaps take him back to their city for a slower death.

But worse than all this, was the land itself. It was a land of hills and crags and desert and boulder and the intense heat of a sun that seemed to rise from Hell each day and carry with it brimstone and fire. I had nearly starved to death along our march, and the sunlight could parch even the most well drunk soul. I knew I was going to certain death, and I embraced that. If I had had an ounce of genuine bravery, I would have cut my own throat to end things there, but I felt as if I needed to find a place to die. To be away from all mankind. To find a hiding place among the endless caves and rocks of the wasteland beyond the citadels.

I could not discourage my friends from coming with me. Though I didn't feel that Thibaud should risk his young life at my expense, he felt as if he owed me his allegiance. Ewen had become as much like a brother to me as had anyone, and as they both slipped away from camp with me, under cover of the dark, I felt as if I had burdened them with my grief and hatred and oncoming death. Hours into our journey along the vast emptiness, I turned to them, drawing my sword.

"You must return to camp," I said. "I will kill both of you here to save you the hardships of the days to come. You are not part of my hatred. You must live and return home to those you love so that you may not fall in with the wolves of darkness, as have I." I truly saw my world as one of wolves, not men. I meant to be done with it, and I cursed God for the life given to me.

Ewen shot me a sharp glance. "You are more than brother to me, Falconer. You have saved me more than once in the past. I cannot abandon you to this darkness you hold."

"You must," I said. "If you love me. If you care for my soul, you will allow me to make this journey alone."

"I pray that you will find peace, and return," Ewen said. He approached me, and we embraced. I felt the wetness of his tears upon my neck. Though he had just reached manhood, he was still only a boy in his heart, a boy from the fields of our homeland. I could nearly smell the sweetness of spring grass in him, and as heavy as was my heart, and though rocks seemed to weigh my soul down into dark water, I could not help but hope that he would find a better world than the one I had seen. I ached for home, for love, for happiness, for some peace. But my brother, dead, my mother, burned alive, there was nothing but ashes and smoke in my world.

Ewen whispered in my ear as he held me, "Losing you, my friend, I feel as heartsick as you must have felt when your brother fell. Do not do this to me, or to the boy. I beg you."

When he withdrew, he turned his back on me and began walking back to camp. We said nothing more.

The boy stood, watching me, as if trying to understand my resolve. Finally, he said, "With you, the wind," which was an old saying of the Bretons on voyages outland. "And the birds, to find your way home."

"And with you, the earth," I gave the response. "And the forest."

The parting of friends tore at me, but I could not then recognize the love and affection of any. I was set on my course, and had perhaps only been interrupted by the voyage to the battles. I would never see Alienora again. I carried guilt for my mother's death, and for my brother's as well. I did not then understand the powerlessness of mortal life against the greater forces in the world. I blamed myself for much, and saw no good in mankind nor in myself. I pitied all, and spurned what little remained in my heart of kindness and love and hope.

I felt I had already died before I had even met Death.

◆ 6 ◆

I had heard of a place, and hoped it was not simply a falsehood, a mirage created by soldiers who dreamed of darkness and cautionary tales in this foreign land.

It would take me nine days to find the place where I would die. It was a place I had only heard of in legend from other soldiers who had been in these wars for a decade or more. They told of a Plague City—a city of the Devil Himself—called by some, the Devil's Horns.

◆ 7 ◆

HERE is the legend of this place of the Devil, the great many-towered city that was also called Hedammu. It had been a great stronghold of the infidel, then had been taken by an order called the Knights of the Sword. They had begun as an order of warrior-monks, very much like the Hospitallers and the Templars.

But the Devil's Horns had changed them. Enchantment and bewitchment were said to be afoot within its walls. Within it, it was said, was a great relic that contained healing and prophetic powers, and which had seemed to be of holiness, but had been revealed to be the head of Baphomet, the reviled and sinful.

The enemy had returned to poison its wells, and had sent in harlots full of disease, whose lips and breasts had been painted with an elixir that smelled of almond and cinnamon, but which brought a slow, burning death to the soldiers who tasted of these women. Soon, all had died within the towers, and the citadel remained uninhabitable. The infidel had razed the land with salt and spices that were poisonous in nature. It was said to be cursed and the mouth of Hell itself, thus the nickname of the Devil's Horns. In the many years of this war against the unfaithful, more than one great city had met this fate. They became known as the Unclean Places, for disease and pestilence were their only legacy.

They became places where we, the soldiers of the Cross, were forbidden on threat of eternal damnation.

But what light of faith had I left? All my belief in eternity had diminished. All of love had been stolen from me. All of hope. I had been reminded of my lowly station, of my bastardy, of the shame of my mother's life and execution, of the deceit and betrayal by my master Sensterre and his son, my half brother, Corentin. And just as I thought this foreign land of war and holiness had returned my sense of justice and mercy, I had watched while my beloved brother was cut down, and I had truly grown sick of all the machinations of mankind. I was not for this world, so I needed to enter the next.

And I would do so at the mouth of Hell itself.

I knew the place on sight, for its towers seemed pristine in the last light of day, and its battlements perfect yet in places crumbling. It had remained untouched by all, and was known as a symbol of the wrath of God upon all who had taken to vice and debauchery.

It would be my final home: I wanted nothing more than to drink of its poisons and taste of its damnation.

◆ 8 ◆

THE first dawn, as I wandered just over the rise from the main road, so as not to be spied by either enemy or friend, I had the feeling that someone followed me. I began imagining it was an enemy, then I half hoped that Ewen dogged my steps so that I might not feel this terrible loneliness—the solitary end of my days approaching, torturing me with thoughts of the past and fear of the world to come.

All that day, I stopped, ran up to whatever rise or rock was within easy distance, and glanced back along the road, but I could not see anyone within the shadowy overhangs of rock along the ridge of the hills. As the first night approached, I became more certain that I had a tracker, and wondered who would be following me so far, for surely I had traveled too many leagues to make it worth tracking me and bringing me back in shackles to the camp.

I squatted among a clutch of rocks and waited for the spy who followed, and when I saw a movement, I drew my short sword and leapt down to attack my pursuer.

The one who followed me emerged into the moonlight, and I nearly fell backward rather than cut him down. It was Thibaud, my little friend, a child of the war itself. "You?" I shouted, perhaps too harshly.

He sprang forward, drawing his dagger. He had a fury in his face, the like of which I had never seen except in battle.

"Did you follow me to kill me?" I asked, laughing.

"I mean to serve you," he said, sheathing his dagger.

"Why do you follow me?" I scowled at him.

"Is there not treasure where you go?" he asked, a gleam to his eye.

"Why, you greedy little thief," I said. "The only treasure ahead of me is death."

"Is it made of gold?" he asked.

"Yes," I laughed. "Golden death." I raised my sword again to try and scare him into returning whence he had come.

In the moonlight, this scrawny scrap of a boy seemed even more wan and hungry—and I was taken aback by the sorrow in his eyes. What had this world done to one so young? What world was this? He said nothing, but brought out a bit of dried meat and offered water from the skin that was slung over his narrow shoulders.

Once we had made camp for the night, we sat before the fire, and I told him he must return the next morning.

"No," he said. He and I stared at each other a bit, I trying to understand what had driven him to desert, and he, no doubt, becoming more resolved to accompany me to my death.

"What of you?" I asked. "You cannot give up on your life so young. I will not allow it. You have a master among the knights."

"A terrible man," he said, then looked deeply into the fire. "Kill me if you must. But I will not return."

"You must," I insisted. "You have more life ahead of you."

"You are my only master," he said. "You saved me." He spoke no more that night. We slept, he covered by my cloak, while I sat up, on watch, truly unable to do more than drift off a bit just before dawn arrived.

Well before the sun rose, we continued on toward the cliffs overlooking the sea. As the afternoon wore on, and a terrible thirst overcame us both—though I allowed him a ration of water and felt best doing without—he stopped in his tracks and turned back, as if listening. "I am afraid others follow us."

"If they do, we will cut them down," I said. "And roast them for our dinner."

He laughed at this, and ran ahead of me along the narrow rocky path we'd chosen. Twilight came, then night, and by the fire that evening, we spoke of our homeland, and despite my hatred of some there, this recalled my love of the Forest, my thoughts of my brothers and sisters, unknown to me, and of Alienora. It gave me an unfortunate hope that night as I slept. It clouded my resolve, my march toward a lonely death.

By dawn, I felt even greater sorrow, for, several days from camp, deserting our knights meant death whether we returned to the army's camp or continued on to the poisoned city. I did not feel a choice, once I had begun that journey to Hedammu.

The boy accompanied me as a pallbearer might a funerary procession, following close behind me, and mute, as if he were afraid to speak of our destination. I was too selfish to concern myself with his fate. I had seen children die in battle. I had seen them die of fevers in my home. I suppose in the back of my mind, I had a hope that his innocence would provide us with a miracle, although I was not so hopeful as to let this thought cloud my resolve.

I felt as if I already knew the end of this journey. I welcomed it. I welcomed the gaping mouth of Hell, for it could not be a worse place than this Earth.

Thibaud Dustifot carried the skin of water, and had stowed a bit of salted goat meat in his pack and among his various pouches. We stopped to sleep, and I daresay that we had rough nights, for storms swept off the sea within a few nights' travel. During daylight hours, we had to be sure and avoid the Hospitallers, for many scouts and guards were about along the jagged hillocks and desert valleys. Then the infidel had to be avoided, although why I cared if I were captured, I did not know. Death was what I sought, but I suppose I wanted it in my own way and on my own watch. I did not wish to be at the mercy of the enemy, whose many tortures were nearly as well-known as those of my own countrymen.

We rationed the dried meat and water as best we could. The bread, which grew harder and tougher to chew with each day, might last perhaps a few more days if we were careful. I began to imagine that someone did, in fact, follow us, although I never saw anyone. The heat of the sun was intense during the day, while the night was often cold and stormy. It was strange weather, and my superstitious nature began to get the better of me. In weak moments of my resolve, I began to imagine that the Devil truly was along this road, and that his eminence's castle truly was ahead of us.

I found Thibaud's attention to my welfare touching, and I begged him nightly to return to the camp.

"You are young enough that you may be forgiven this desertion," I said. "Do you wish to die?"

"I wish to serve my master," the boy said, and drew out a bit of bread for our supper.

✦ 9 ✦

IN a few more heartbeats, the light of day would be swallowed, and the breath of the living would cloud the air. It was said, according to my fellow soldiers, that the infidels believed a great dragon lived in the caves of the hills. It left its lair by way of the sapphire sea, drank the sun down into its gullet each night, and defecated the new sun through the bowels of the earth before dawn. But there was no dragon, nor was the sea full of jewels.

Hedammu, Mighty Fortress! Fallen from its height as a center of trade and learning and of the ancient secrets of the people of this region. A poisonous, pestilent whore of a city, long abandoned. The Devil's Horns. I saw its towers from a distance, and as had been reported, there was no watch and no guard.

It was a golden city.

It was a city of the dead.

The view from the crest showed the dying copper sky as the sun moved languidly toward the metallic blue of the sea. The wind, when it swept across the towers and hills to the east of the sea, seemed like a blasting furnace.

The boy and I approached the open gates.

At the north gate, drawn with blood, the symbol of the Cross. Beneath this a word that meant nothing to me. Yet, I remember it:

anguis

Beneath this word, a drawing of a spiraling circle.

Atop the gates, opened to welcome all those who wished to perish, the pagan scrawls of the infidel, and something older, gargoyles of women who had the wings of eagles and the legs of lions.

"You must return now," I said, turning to the boy. "It has been wrong of me to allow you to follow me here. You will be taken captive by the enemy, or torn at by wolves. I am not your master, nor am I one who can care for you."

Even as I said those words, I felt torn, with the heavy heart of one who has made the decision to die in some terrible way and now had turned back from it. The boy himself had saved me as I had once saved him from a brute of a master. On our journey, he had taught me—by his silence alone—that there were reasons to live. Reasons to return to the good fight, to the duty, to the call of mankind itself. A child like this was reason enough, and I saw in him all the things that had been neglected in my own childhood. He recalled for me, just in his manner and devotion, the preciousness of life itself, despite the hail and lightning of the road upon which all life must travel.

He took my hand, just two fingers, and said, "I am your servant, sir."

"You are not," I said. "I free you here and now."

"You are my father, then, for I have none," he said.

"I am no one's father. No one's son. No one's brother," I said.

He raised his small fists in the air as if to beat me, though he made no move toward me. "You are my father!" He bleated like a lamb.

The welling of his emotion moved me, and when he rushed toward me, I expected him to hit me in anger. Instead, he wrapped his arms about my waist and pressed his face against me. "Be my father. Please. Be my father."

In his voice, I was reminded of my own as a child, remembering my grandfather, and how I had wished he would never leave me and my family. Wished that if I held him tight or stayed with him, that he would not fall to the earth in the last quiver of life.

"I do not want you to die." His eyes shone with tears as he spoke, looking up at me.

"I suppose," I said, finally, letting out into the evening air what I had held for days, "neither do I."

* * *

I had come to die. I had not anticipated a boy of my own country teaching me about the last drop of goodness in the cup of life. That all that was terrible in the world could be made sweet again simply by one good soul. Yet I was at war within my private thoughts, for another part of me felt as if Thibaud Dustifot was a phantom sent by the Devil to tease me into remaining alive to watch other terrors unfold in the world of men.

◆ 10 ◆

THIBAUD and I made camp just within the gates. I decided that my duty to the boy was stronger than my duty to my own destruction, which would come, regardless. I determined that I would turn around on the road and find our camp again on an arduous journey back. I would give myself up as a deserter, throwing myself on whatever mercy the commanders might have—which was death, also, but of a slower variety—and I would claim that I kidnapped the boy at knifepoint, forcing him to accompany me in my desertion.

Whether that plan would work or not, I was never to know, for the next morning, I awoke, and Thibaud was gone. In the dirt, his small footprints ended not far from the cloak of mine that he'd used as a blanket.

It was as if some bird of prey had lifted him into the sky.

· CHAPTER 10 ·

The Tower

◆ 1 ◆

AT first, I had no fear for him. I believed he played a prank on me, or had awoken early and wandered about. But soon enough, I became certain that he had been taken by something dreadful. The legends of Ghul and of demon played havoc with my emotion, and the intense heat of the oncoming day added to my feverish thoughts. I began to go out of my mind imagining all that might have happened to the boy.

I searched the dead city, calling for him, crouching at each corner to look up the wall, or down into a crevice where a boy might hide, or glancing into the distance, hoping that he stood near a doorway, only to find a tall, broken urn rather than a boy when I approached.

I passed through what had once been the chambers of the living, but found not a trace of him.

I discovered a storehouse for great treasure—armor, as well as weapons—swords made of silver and some cast from gold itself. I became full of an unimagined fear at seeing this treasury, for I wondered what leprous king might live there, murdering soldiers and knights and bringing the spoils of such conquest into this great chamber. I was too fearful even to touch it. Truly, this was a place of poison, for otherwise, why had not someone stolen these riches? What man could resist, let alone an army? I had heard rumors that the Templars were wealthier than all the other orders of knights, and this fortress that had once been taken by them seemed to be an example of it.

Other wonders met me, including a great long courtyard with a reflecting pool. Thirsty, I knelt to drink from it. As I did, I remembered the stories of the poisoned wells, and wondered if I would die of this drinking. Had Thibaud not vanished, I would have no fear of death, but as the day continued, I became afraid, for his sake, that I might not live to find him. But the water seemed fine, and I felt refreshed from it.

Gently scalloped entryways led to rooms full of mosaics that played out both the religious dramas of the infidel as well as those of the Templars and the Teutonic Knights. Along soft walls of yellow stone, madmen had scratched, in various languages, words and phrases that were indecipherable by me, yet I saw the Cross, again and again, as well as scratchings of swords and of a demon with wings, reminding me of that foul creature that I helped raise as a boy from the well in the Great Forest.

As I went through the halls and temples and houses within, I found a curious area that was nearly unreachable. It was a catacombs beneath what was, by all accounts, the keep of this fortress. As I wandered its byways, I found an entrance to a series of chambers. These seemed to be graves or mounds of some kind, too deep to peer into from where I stood. I could not venture into this snakelike chamber without risk of never leaving again, for it was hundreds of feet down, and I looked upon it from the edge of a corridor that simply ended as if it were a cliff.

I did not see any sign of the boy there. The smell of death was unmistakable, and I was glad to leave the area.

◆ 2 ◆

HALF-STARVED, I all but crumpled to the ground, longing for death or sleep. My conscience pounded at me, for I had, in my selfish loneliness, allowed a boy to come with me to that deadly place. Who could say what vultures or jackals lurked along the parapets or within the unseen chambers? What Ghul lived there? What enemy? What demons flew across the skies looking for the lost and unguarded?

I called for him, my voice echoing along the walls and the distant chambers, but did not hear his voice in return. As twilight drew close, with a dusty wind howling through the empty doorways and along the abandoned chambers, I became more desperate, afraid that I had brought the only goodness left in the world to a horrible fate.

With the seeping darkness of night, I heard him calling from one of the many towers. As I glanced tower to tower, I saw a slight flicker of light at some distance. Calling to him, I followed the faint cry of his voice to one of the great towers at the south end of the city, overlooking the sea beyond the cliff.

When I reached the tower, I pressed open its rotting door.

• 3 •

A T the base of the tower, on a low wooden table, there was a wide, shallow bowl. Within it, a greenish fire burned along the surface of scented oil. An unlit torch lay in a stack, as if I had been expected.

I heard Thibaud's scream, a loud, piercing shriek, followed by silence.

I quickly lit the torch from the bowl and took the winding, narrow steps up the tower two at a time. It seemed an hour before I reached the room at the top of the steps, and when I did, I felt faint from the terrible stench there.

I have seen Death in people—in the diseased, in those who are leaving the world for their reward, in the men in battle who, with limbs torn asunder, lay fighting for their final breaths. But this stench was stronger than even that. It was meaty, this stench, like a slaughterhouse.

As I went in the room, I did not see the corpse I had half expected to stumble across, from the smell.

There, bound in heavy chains, lying in straw and filth, was the most beautiful woman I had ever seen.

◆ 4 ◆

HER hair was the color of wheat and sandstone, and cut like a youth's rather than a maiden's, combed to the side in the Syrian way. She was the most beautiful infidel I had ever seen—for I knew on sight that she was not of my countrymen or even of Christendom. Her eyes were dark; her lips were thick and drawn slightly across teeth as white as burning sand. She wore a rent and tattered garment that barely covered her body.

She twisted in her bonds, away from the light of the torch, so that I might not see her brazen flesh. As she turned, I noticed that she had been branded across her left shoulder: it was a mark that one of my fellow countrymen might use for cattle, a cross with a Latin word beneath it.

"Who has done this?" I asked. I removed my cloak and draped it across her shoulders so that she could again turn to look upon me without shame of her nakedness.

Her breath was sweet against my face. "Help me, please," she said. "He will be back tonight, I am sure of it, he is a devil."

"Does he have the boy? A boy?" I asked.

She glanced furtively to the left, then the right, among the piles of straw as if someone might be hiding there. "Boy?" she asked.

"A child."

She nodded. "Yes. A boy."

The cloak slipped from her shoulders. I saw the pale flesh around her breasts. I looked back to her eyes. She wept without tears. "Please. Hungry. Thirsty." She motioned toward a corner of the room. I glanced in that direction and saw a wash bucket. "Please, he will kill me when he returns."

"Who is this scoundrel?"

"A demon."

She held out her arms, with the chains attached at the wrists.

I took my short sword from my side and tried to saw, then hack at the chains.

"That will not do," she said. "He may return. You must cut at the flesh of my wrists. Please. He comes at night."

She bit her lip and made but little noise as I cut the edge of her wrist with my dagger, and snipped at the flesh of her left hand until she could slip it beneath the manacle.

"The blood," I said, tearing off a strip from my cloak and wrapping it around her bleeding wrist.

She watched me as I took care of her cut.

She locked eyes with me, for I tell you she was beautiful even in her pain, and my heart beat rapidly. I no longer saw this foreign maiden, but remembered Alienora herself, in her glory, in her purity. I felt blood rush to the surface of my skin, an enveloping warmth, as I beheld her. She reached up to touch my cheek, cupping her hand there, a finger touching the edge of my lips. She smelled of roses and lavender, with something else, something musky and sensual, like myrtle beneath the sweetness. I wanted to stroke her face and wrap my body around her. *Alienora, is it you? Alienora?*

Perhaps if I had not thought of Alienora, I would not have looked away from this maiden, feeling a kind of shame and revulsion at my own feelings. My fury over life and how it had dealt with me rose up for a moment. I saw something in a pile of straw, just behind and to the right of the maiden I had rescued. Just a clump of straw, nothing more. Perhaps another bucket, turned over, that had been covered.

Then, I saw the small hand.

◆ 5 ◆

M Y mind could not understand why a small child's hand would be in the straw. Or why I had forgotten the reason I had climbed the tower in the first place.

I pushed her aside and went to dig in the straw.

From it, I drew up the body of Thibaud Dustifot.

My boy.

In my heart, he had become my child.

I held him in my arms and wept. I pressed his small broken body to mine and let out a moan so loud that I felt as if the world were breaking around me, like glass, like the fragile thing it was.

He had been torn at the throat as if a wolf had taken him in its jaws and shaken him until he was dead.

♦ 6 ♦

THE damsel fell upon me from behind. Her lips touched the back of my neck. Her teeth dug into my flesh, clamping like a she-wolf on its prey. I dropped Thibaud's body, anger welling up in me at once.

Against my will, I felt, beneath the initial shock as the teeth punctured my flesh, a burning in my blood. Feeling as though a lion had leapt upon me, I struggled against my attacker, reaching to my side for my sword, but weakness had entered my body. I had no strength in me. I had no vitality. I thrashed about, but her teeth dug more deeply into my flesh until I felt her connect to bone.

Finally, like a deer in the hunt, I fell, and she continued her attack. I looked at Thibaud's face, empty of life. Gone. I had come to meet Death, and Thibaud had gone before me, his small hand in Death's great claw.

I closed my eyes as the demon continued to hold me fast.

My body would not obey my mind, but gave in to a writhing ecstasy of the demon's piercing bite. I felt as if she were stroking me intimately.

I experienced a dreadful arousal throughout my body as my excitement grew, as the blood pulsed from the wound into her sucking mouth, the noise of which was disgusting and piglike. I fought against her, but all my muscle had gone slack. I had become unable to direct my own body against the creature from Hell.

When many hours had passed, she was gone, taking the boy's body with her.

Weakened, an empty vessel drained of most of my blood, I closed my eyes and prayed for death.

But it did not come during the day or night.

But she returned, with food and water to keep me alive. With caresses and bites and a terrible ravenous look on her face as of a starving woman who has just found a larder full of meat.

◆ 7 ◆

H ER bondage had been a game to entice me to rescue her so that she might enjoy attacking me. This creature loved her games, and when she drank from me, she smiled, and laughed, and taunted me with how easily I had been fooled.

I did not know how many nights passed.

All the sins of my life seemed to have been washed in her ministrations to my body. All the memories I had, save one, seemed to have been burned away from me. I no longer thought of war or the small body in the straw or a distant beloved maiden I had left behind, nor did I remember others. This creature swallowed those sketchy details of my life. She took my sense of self with her, my understanding of my station, of my world, even of my temptations. I had no anger; no fury; no destructive force within me. Neither did I have happiness nor hope.

All that was left was pleasure.

Any heaven I knew became the heaven of my wound and of her lips and of the tearing of her sharp teeth into my flesh, which sang with pain. Heaven existed in her drinking of my blood. When her lips parted, my heart beat faster, and I felt my loins lift as if meeting a mate. If I had had the energy to beg for her, I surely would have.

She drank heavily, staying at my neck for several hours. She drained me of blood, which seemed to flow like a river from my body into her mouth. My leech, my lamprey, my parasite taking, taking, taking. As she took, my mind went to a safe place where it could not be touched by her, or by grief, or by the memory of Thibaud's body, so empty of blood that when I had lifted him, he had felt like a rabbit in my arms.

I watched myself as if from above, looking down on the woman whose constant sucking against me became numbing by dawn, when she abandoned me to the straw.

Too weak to rise, I slept through the day until sundown, when she returned to me.

When the demon-woman came to me again, she brought bits of raw meat and a pitcher of water. I ate and drank greedily, like a wild animal. Yet, this brought me no strength, for she took as good as she gave, with her small sharp teeth, which were like twin daggers of jabbing white bone.

She pressed her sweet and bitter lips against my flesh. I felt as if the pleasure flowed from my being for hours at a time, though only minutes passed between us. She drank slowly, deliberately, sipping and lapping at my wound until I felt wave after wave of heightened joy. My body went into seizures, of both pleasure and sorrow, and yet my memory of it is of the best feeling that life ever offers one.

I longed for her and I despised her. I loathed this creature, yet I had become addicted to her bites along my throat. There was no pain from them anymore. I felt numb there, but a numbness growing from heat that kindled my flesh. I was not in love with this monster, but in her thrall, bewitched. She enslaved me through this bewitchment.

I knelt before her, and kissed her feet when she entered my prison nightly. She took my chin in her hand, lifting it up to her face. I saw both death and life in her gaze, but more, I saw the drug I had begun to crave, the sweet liquor of her breath as she brought her mouth to my wrist to drink, or to my throat, or even to my chest, where she drank from my nipple as if I were her mother, giving her the milk of my body, my blood. I had no great fear of death, as those who have ever been beneath the power of some great intoxicant, stimulant, life-enhancer, can understand.

Perhaps my eyes were encircled with dark smudges, perhaps my lungs wheezed with the effort of breathing, perhaps I had lost weight in the days and nights of my captivity. The delicious feeling of our union, of her mouth to my flesh, of her taking me into that mouth, pouring from my throat to hers—it was all I required of life. I had no life and no light in me—I survived merely to give her what she desired of me. I would be her table, her mount, her servant, her food, her drink, her thing, an "it," lower than vermin, to be consumed at her bidding. I would flay myself for her pleasure. I would wound myself with a thousand little knives if it brought her lips to my thighs, to my ankles, to my back, under my arm, at the nape of my neck. She encompassed me, and I willingly allowed her to swallow all I had. And yet my body created more blood for her. She was as insatiable in her thirst as I, in my offering.

We played games between us in seeking a new patch of flesh for bleeding. I played my role well—I found a place at my inner thigh from which she had not yet drunk. I showed her the slight pulse of artery that lurked beneath the skin. I seduced her with my veins, and she played the innocent who would submit to my desire to give her more blood. Another night, we lay together, her face in the cradle beneath my arm, against the faint tufts of light hair there, her incisors pressing into the tenderness of flesh. She drank all of me, or so it felt, and still I lived.

We barely spoke a word between us, but it did not matter. I could have lain with her, pressed my flesh to her greedy mouth for an eternity. The silence without was broken by the richness I experienced within my soul. I saw great cities of vast kingdoms that I had never before seen. I had visions of creatures that swam beneath the sea, monstrous but beautiful beasts, and of a woman who wore a shroud of darkness and a gold mask on her face. I saw this woman who held me as she sucked at my blood, but many centuries earlier, sitting within a temple on a cliff's edge, with cracks in the earth below her stone seat, and the mist of gases coming up.

With these visions, I learned her name—she was called Pythia, and I saw her differently in my mind while she drank from me. I saw her surrounded with serpents at her feet, wearing a long tunic that barely covered her, her breasts exposed, gold around her neck and arms, shaped also as snakes. Behind her, a statue of a man who wore a diadem that was like the sun itself. It was a pagan temple, and she was a priestess of some kind. In the vision, she began to move as if in a dance, but a dance as I had never before seen. It was erotic, then, by turns, vulgar, and I wondered if, in this vision, she was a temple harlot or a great leader. I could not tell. But the feeling I had while watching her was of ecstasy.

And then, when my mistress had drunk her fill of me for the night, and I felt the swoon of dawn arrive, the visions and the wonderful pleasure eroded. We lay together, entangled, I with my straps and ropes to keep me safe or trapped, and she with her cold flesh pressed against me, my lover, my murderer. There, I held her as the day wore on beyond the walls of my tower.

I forgot my past, I forgot my mother's fire and the Great Forest of my childhood, forgot the Barony and even my Alienora. Forgot my brother, and dear Thibaud, and my companion Ewen, who had been with me through so much of my youth. All of them became a dream that I had been told.

For all I knew I had been a slave to this woman named Pythia my whole life, from birth. She was all that mattered. I was nothing. I was less than nothing. I was beneath the contempt of the lowest creature. My only offering was the blood that flowed through me. If it sustained her, and brought her joy, that is why I lived. If she took pleasure from me, it was more than I could have expected. Sleep came or did not come for me. Sometimes, I lay there, a long endless day without light, and yet knowing that the sun rose high beyond this tower prison.

Night came slowly, with pain in my joints as I began to desire her mouth to my throat, or the warmth of her spit along my forearm, and that pressure from her sharp teeth just before my skin gave way to the razor edge. If I could not feel her feeding against me, I would choose death. During the day I might feel self-revulsion, but come the evening, I would want only her and serve only her and be what she wanted me to be for her. She was my all. She was my reason for continuing to live.

My life force waned, yet I wanted nothing from life.

"It is the blood," she whispered to me as she sucked the sweet nectar from my neck, now unshaven and bristling with several days' growth of beard. She spoke inside my mind, as if we were not separate, but bound as spirits.

She told me: *While you live, you are mine, you are my love, you are the dirt of my grave, you are the flesh that is my bed.*

Her presence flowed through my mind, through my memory, wanting to know of every adventure and thought that had ever come to me. Yet nothing seemed to be there—my thoughts were shadows in a cave of darkness.

I felt myself evaporate against her vibrating form—her teeth moved back and forth, sawing into me, tasting the fresh, newly made blood.

And then, one night, she did not return to me.

• 8 •

I lay there, craving her, knowing that she had abandoned me to death itself. Willingly, I would die. I was diseased, I had the plague, I was poison itself, no longer blood in my body. I had become a repository for some deadly liquid within my flesh. She had found me disgusting, judged me unworthy, now that she had her fill.

I lay there, weak as a newborn or as a man of nine hundred years. I tried to dream of her face and the feel of her upon me, using me, but I had nothing.

I lay that day, staring at the stones around me, wondering at my tomb, at my last moments of life. Yet I remained alive by nightfall. Just as I felt myself slipping from life, a dryness to my throat and a dislocation from my body, I saw her before me—a vision of unholy beauty. She had returned! Joy and hope for another night of bleeding brought the flicker of life to my pallid flesh.

"You are dying," she whispered to me, her lips near my ear. "But I have loved you for nearly one full moon, and I taste something within you that I do not want to send to the Threshold. Would you live as a monster, or die as a man?"

I tried to speak, but I had no words. Yet, she heard my thoughts.

"You will feel the pain of death. It is like a thousand needles, and within each prick of their dagger points, a thousand more emerge," she said, her voice like a mother whispering a lullaby to a feverish child. "It will stop up your heart and take the wind from your chest. You will have a fear that all mortals have at death, and you will not think that you will ever return here or into the world beyond the Threshold. But do not fear. Let death take your mortality from you. Let it have its due. What I will bring into being is a third being, between you and me, our child, and the child will be in you, and will be you. You will be the father of the child and the son, as well, and he will be you, yet he will not be you. Give me your breath, and take mine from me."

Instead of pressing her teeth into me, she put her lips to mine. I expected to feel the needles of her teeth, but instead she parted my lips with her tongue, and I felt a rush of air. A hot wind entered into my mouth, and forced its way down my throat. It felt as if invisible spiders scurried down across my tongue, along the moist tissues at the back of my throat. It was not simply breath alone, for something in it made me see her more clearly as it entered my lungs. This was some new ether that she had, and it began to revive me. I could not resist, and pushed at her because I feared it, but I had no strength.

My eyes went wide as I felt the burning at my lungs. She had set me afire within. I felt terror that I would incinerate from this heat.

She held me more tightly than I had ever been held—it was like bondage to another. I closed my eyes—feeling the submission to her, to her will, and suddenly a vision came at me in a lightning flash, all at once, perfectly made, every detail:

A man in priest's robes, with a staff in his hand upon which snakes entwined. An altar behind him, on which Pythia lay in royal splendor. We were in a great temple of some primitive civilization. And there was another—a woman whose face was covered with a terrible gold mask, a mask with a face upon it of some monstrous creature.

The priest said to me, "Alkemara."

I felt as if I were set on fire, tied as my mother had been, to the stake, with thorny kindling wrapped about my ankles.

The serpents that moved slowly along the staff he held suddenly became an encircling vine, and a small purple-blue flower opened from the rounded leaf of the vine.

The priest held an iron gaze upon me, as if searching within me for something he had been seeking for many years. He was a gaunt creature, with dark, reflective eyes. His scalp and face were shaven, and covered with tattoos savage and barbaric. He had rings through his ears and nostrils, and where his robe opened, I saw rings along his chest, as well. His fingernails were long and gently curved, thick and yellow. His robe was gold and red and black and, beneath the great moon above, it shone with a silver light along the sleeves of it.

When he spoke, his teeth shone black and shiny as if carved from some translucent dark stone and thrust into his gums. His eyes were black as night—no white to the eye, nor color. And yet for all this, he was a handsome presence, a powerful man. He had the look of a pagan leader, and when he held the staff aloft, I knew its name as if it held magick in its very wood.

It was the Staff of the Nahhashim, and I felt whispering voices. *Nahhashim,* as if others were there, repeating the word over and over.

As he stood before me in this burning vision, I saw great wings, as of a dragon, unfolding behind him. They blocked out the altar with their span. I remembered the demon that had been brought up from the well within the Great Forest. The priest had the same wings. They were leathering and slick like eelskin, but with great bony prongs that thrust out from the skin as the wings came to their full spread behind him, each finger of the wing ending in a bony talon.

I saw shadows, the ones who whispered the word *Nahhashim,* and all around the priest, there were other figures of men, but made purely of darkness. Another word they whispered, "Maz-Sherah."

The priest might have been the worst demon from Hell, with his great wings spread and those terrible shades of the dead all about him, whispering. Still I trembled not at the sight of him, but these other shadows struck me with a nameless fear.

The priest spoke within me, not with words of a strange language, but with a tongue of fire that spoke his words back through me, back into the mouth I had forgotten even existed—

"The Myrrydanai know of you from the breath. Already, they seek to destroy the All. The dark mother herself smells your flesh and blood. She will pursue you. Still, you must come. The Nahhashim await. The Kamr await. You must bring the vine and the flower that I might know you."

Pythia's lips closed. I exhaled into her, and she drew away.

The vision, gone. The priest, no longer in my thoughts. Yet it was as if he were there with the two of us in that tower. The last of his words were like ghosts, haunting me.

I spoke his words, in that ancient tongue that was unknown to me, and although I did not then understand their meaning, the words I remembered were *Alkemara, Lemesharra, Medhya, Merod, Myrrydanai,* and *Nahhashim.*

The look on Pythia's face was one of terror. It was the first I had seen her without a look of power or of deceit.

I knew at that moment what she knew.

The vision had been within her, and somehow, when she passed the breath to me, I had drawn it from her soul as if drawing water from a deep well.

Something within it brought dread to her visage, and she was no longer my mother, my goddess, my lover, my child, my mistress.

She was a vampyre, one of the foul demons of which I'd been warned, and she fell backward when she heard the words.

"No!" she screeched. She rose, her face still stricken. From her shoulders, dragon wings unfurled. I had not seen them before on her. They emerged from her back as she arched it, and suddenly, like the wings on that priest, they were at full span behind her.

She rose slightly from the ground, the great wings moving in a slow wave through the still, fetid air.

I suppose she wished to kill me then, but something stayed her hand. For the first time, I felt what all vampyres feel—it is called the stream, the connection between these creatures and their prey.

I had begun to feel that sense of otherness. I had begun, by inhaling the burning breath of Pythia, the journey toward death.

I lay back, unable to defend myself if she chose to slaughter me there. I experienced a winter's coldness invading my body. Then, it became like razors of ice cutting from inside my flesh, pushing outward.

At last, I thought. *I am dying. I am going to experience the end of all.* Whether my soul went toward Heaven or Hell, I had no care. Whether devils or angels had won the fight for my soul, what did it matter? Better to be in an eternity of torture that had purpose to it than the life I had led. The memories of life did not flood back as I went. I tried to grasp at something as I felt my life force leaving my body. I tried to re-member those I had forgotten. My mother—what had she looked like? I could remember the smell of her fire, but not her face. My brother, Frey, what was the last he had said to me? I could not recall. Would I see him in the afterlife? Would I meet any I had cared for there? Would I burn in the eternal fires of Hell? Yet, even these last thoughts made no sense to me as I felt winter overtake my flesh.

At the last, I saw a brief spark of blue, as if a match had just been lit, only it hadn't quite caught its flame.

A heavy darkness dragged me down into its hole, and everything I saw began to vanish in the valley of the shadow of Death. I smelled something that was like the memory of a rose—a scent so smothering and yet mild that I felt happy to go pursue its trail. The journey through death—candles being snuffed as if they were lit within me. My fingers lost the last of their tingling, and a heaviness turned my limbs to stone. A pressure grew in my chest. My mind had already be-gun to move with the swiftness of falcons into a darkness so deep that it began to turn light again and yet was neither light nor dark, night nor day, and a thousand colors grew as my body turned to ice.

And then, I died out, the last of the flame.

I awoke three nights later.

BOOK TWO

IMMORTALITY

I

VAMPYRE

· CHAPTER 11 ·

Resurrection

· 1 ·

M Y mortal life had ended in that tower, with the creature, the vampyre, taking the last of my life's blood, and giving me the breath of the life of immortal damnation. How many years and centuries have passed since that moment! The city of my rebirth is buried in sand, while other towering citadels have risen and fallen, like sand castles in a sweeping tide, built, destroyed, rebuilt, undone. Time itself changes with the first resurrection—for days become as minutes, and years, hours.

Mortality is a brief flickering of a lamp in a drafty room. The immortal existence is the fire that spreads in the wind, across dried grasses and dying villages. It destroys and seduces, it is the furnace of eternity within the figure of the lone creature: the man who arises from the dead.

Hunger and thirst seem amplified upon awakening.

The mind itself grows, expands, and encompasses more than the mortal mind ever could. Empathy grows, as well as a monstrous understanding of the prey and the dance it must perform with the predator.

But the first thing a newly risen vampyre feels is the shock of remembering the journey to death, to the Threshold itself, and the return into flesh is an unwelcome return.

Death is a whisper, an echo, but life is a tearing, ravaging imbecile, drawing one back to the flesh, back to the nerve and sinew and the beating of the heart.

Back to the blood itself.

◆ 2 ◆

I lay in a deep, open grave.

Above me, darkness.

I caught my breath as one who comes up from the sea after nearly drowning, and grasped for whatever I could—dirt and rocks beside me—to sit up so that the burning in my lungs would cease, and I could inhale deeply from the air. I leaned forward, clutching my knees to my chest. I was naked. Beside me, my tunic, cloak, and sword.

Someone had brought me to this place. From the tower to this home of death.

My lips were parched. I felt old beyond my years. I had only a slight memory of a dream—and as I gained clarity in my consciousness, I realized it was not a dream at all but the vision that Pythia had compelled me to have. The same vision that had frightened her so, though I knew not why.

The priest, with his eyes of shiny beetle blackness, and the figures in red and black and yellow that were painted upon his clean-shaved scalp, the small gold and jeweled rings that covered his earlobes and dotted his nose at either nostril.

"The Myrrydanai know of you from the breath," the priest whispered. *"Already, they seek to destroy the All. The dark mother herself smells your flesh and blood. She will pursue you. Still, you must come. The Nahhashim await. The Kamr await. You must bring the vine and the flower that I might know you."*

I opened my eyes, and looked up.

Closed again, I saw the priest from the vision. The words whispered to me, "*Nahhashim. Alkemara. Lemesharra. Merod.*"

And then I saw another figure in shadow, like a shroud, and I knew it was a woman and she held her arms out to me and I felt a terrible ice from her, and beside her, dancing shadows, and a whispering sound as of bats in a cave as they fly into the night. The priest's voice grew louder in my head, "She knows you are near."

I opened my eyes to darkness. The whispering in my head stopped. I began to see clearly through the dark. Far above me, another passageway. I had looked down upon these graves when I had wandered Hedammu looking for Thibaud. I had felt as if I were on the edge of a precipice then. Now, I was in the pit below. In some home of the dead.

I sensed someone nearby, although I could not then say how I felt the presence of another. No sound met my ears. I saw nothing as I looked upward.

I tried to rise, but my legs were too weak, and I collapsed.

Then, the rush of wind, nearly howling above me, as if a door had been opened to a sandstorm outside.

Whispering above me.

Then, the sound of a muffled scream.

A large bundle flew down to me from above.

I scooted backward.

The bundle: a maiden, completely bound head to foot with rope.

She stared at me in terror. Her face was white as milk, and she had open wounds along her shoulder and throat, as if a wolf had attacked her. Had Pythia already drunk from her? My heart beat fast, thinking of Pythia and of her ministrations to my own throat.

I wanted to lift the maiden up, but not for protection. I didn't see a woman's face so much as I began to see what ran beneath it—a dark, delicious elixir that was like fine wine and clear, pure water—the blood itself.

No longer man, I tell you, I had become a monster through Pythia's breath.

I crawled toward her. As I came closer, she opened her mouth to scream.

I turned her on her side. My fingers gently grazed her throat. The warmth I felt from her skin was comforting. I found the pulse of a vein near the whiteness of her collar. Had you told me that I lifted her to me like a barrel of ale and felt as if I might drink her down, I would have been amazed by your lie. I cared for this maiden and wished to cause her no harm.

I spoke to her kindly, my voice as weak as my hunger was strong. I simply asked for something of hers that she would be willing to part with—a memento of her existence. I promised her that I would release her after. I would release her from the ropes, I said. She could run home when I had that souvenir of her, that red flower of her throat.

A monstrous feeling in me arose. I fought it with all my might.

"Please," she whispered. She had said it in her foreign tongue, but something within me translated her words without knowing how I had done so. This was not the language of my home, nor even nearby languages I had heard in my life. Yet I had the newfound ability to understand other tongues. "Please," she begged, and began praying.

My compassion for this maiden overcame my thirst.

I nodded, and tore at the ropes and bindings that she might be free. The grave I lay within was too deep for her to scramble up the sides. My thirst for her blood increased—for I could smell the blood now, beneath her skin, soaking her organs and meats in its fragrant wine. Blood called to me. It called for my teeth to uncork it and to drink it down in one great draught.

Perhaps it was because I was a new convert to this alien tribe of the undead, but I pushed myself back against the dirt wall of my grave and allowed her freedom there.

"I will not harm you," I growled. I am certain that my visage was terrifying to the maiden as I went to her, scooping her up in my arms.

A woman, dark of skin with her head partially wrapped in a saffron yellow turban, her body cloaked in a fine cloth that wrapped about her to great advantage of her athletic figure, slipped down into my grave. She stood close, sniffing me. Her nostrils flared, then turned to slits, and I felt a strange heat as she came close to me. The heat turned almost into the feeling of tiny, light feathers grazing my face and throat.

She was not beautiful in the tradition of women of Christendom, for she was tall and thick of shoulder and thin of hip, and she had painted her face in a way that seemed too exotic for even the harlots of the armies. She was beautiful and too strong for a woman—she looked like a warrior, and though I had heard tales of warrior-women, I had not believed them until that moment.

When she began speaking, it sounded as if it were some strange tongue I had never before heard. Yet, the heat at my face and the feeling of being touched without being touched increased as she spoke. I felt vibrations in my ears, and I could understand each word she said. "Take her. Drink your fill." Her voice was like a commander giving orders to a soldier.

"No. I cannot," I said.

"You must drink," she said. "You will die without it."

"So be it," I said.

"You think she is like you. But you are not mortal. You are vampyre now, one of the fallen ones of Medhya. As am I. You are of the tribe. And she is not. She is a vessel of blood. You must drink."

As she spoke, the full force of her words hammered at me. No longer mortal. Vampyre. "I will die."

"Your instinct is to survive," she snarled, contempt in her voice. "You are weak. You are just being resurrected. You will be weak for several nights, even with blood. If I bound you to her, you would drink from her and she would die from it. If you drink from her now, she may live."

"Even so," I said. "I will not."

"So be it," she said.

Two other of the nightcomers slithered into the grave, as if on their bellies, like serpents. It gave me a chill to watch them, and to think that I was of their kind now. One, an older man of forty or so, thick of muscle and a chest like a cask, with a tangle of beard at his chin, and hair nearly to his back. He was unclothed except for rags bound about his loins. The other, a young man who looked as if he were a Turk, with the high cheekbones and piercing eyes of those barbarian people, but with the white-blond hair of the Norsemen. He was dressed in a simple tunic, and when he rose I saw his mouth open—it was filled with rows of fangs that seemed as if they were impossible to fit in his mouth.

These monsters moved closer to the maiden, who clutched at me, praying to her gods. The two males took up the ropes and bound her to my body so that my mouth and her throat were close.

"You must feed," the female vampyre said. "If you will not, I will cut her throat and force her life into your mouth. We do not let one of our kind suffer long. The prey also suffers when the predator lingers."

Then, more swiftly than I could comprehend with my mind, she and the others scrambled up from the grave.

"Do not leave me," I begged, my voice a dry rasp.

The female leaned over the edge, her gaze like ice. "Drink of her. Her suffering will be short. Yours, without blood, will be unbearable. We feel the pain of our tribe. Your newborn ache is with all of us."

Then, finally, she departed.

I was alone with the maiden.

Perhaps hours passed as I lay there, bound to the young woman.

Alone with her, who had given up all struggle, my lips so close to her throat, I could not resist.

"Forgive me," I said.

Without even being aware that I'd made the judgment, I brought my mouth to her throat. My teeth—which had, to my horror, grown into small points—sank into her flesh. I felt a pop of skin, then the blood burst into the back of my throat. I drew my teeth out as soon as I recovered from this uncontrollable instinct.

I had just taken a few drops, just a bit, but the maiden had passed out from either pain or shock.

• 3 •

MY first few nights were blurs of thought and memory mingled with the tastes of blood. I do not know what happened to the maiden who was my vessel, but one night I awoke, and she was gone, the ropes that had bound me, scattered on the ground beside me. I had still not left the womb of my grave, and though I felt strength in my body, I had not yet recovered from the first death.

The female vampyre brought me three men from a battle not far from us, each wounded and perhaps already dying, bearing wounds of others of our tribe—bites and tears along arms and legs and near the throat. I felt as if I were in a dream of dizziness and unquenchable thirst. My lips parched, I felt as if I were a hundred years old. Unable to move far, with a stiffness in my joints, I could barely crawl to the first man, whose body and spirit had already been broken by others. I did not pause to consider my monstrosity—my sense of humanity had begun to erode as my hunger and senses increased in their intensity.

I would even argue that all humans have this creature within them—this predator upon their fellowmen and -women, the monster inside that, if tapped, might reach a fever pitch and find sustenance with the blood of a friend or a lover. We fought in war and tore at our enemy. I had seen injustice disguised as justice and murder in the guise of religion. I had seen my own mother burn for the pleasure and sense of justice of others.

The monster lurked within humankind, and all around us, like a shadow that did not reveal itself until twilight, until the delight of the bloodthirst became overwhelming.

It is nature, after all, that requires the falcon to tear at the soft rabbit's throat and the hounds to run down the stag and attack it in a thicket. Was man any different? Were we not once human, those of us who had been resurrected into this new life, after death? Perhaps this was all there was of heaven—perhaps this was the realm of the gods themselves, for what in all of Nature and supernature fed from man's blood but the gods? What did we taste in Mass? Was it not the blood of our Lord? What did the surgeons leech from us, but our blood, to heal us by ridding us of the body's fluids? And what pleasure we took in offering our legs or arms to the leech that it might take from us that which was the only sustaining juice of the fruit of our bodies?

All, monsters. All mankind. We of this tribe of night, savages and barbarians, living among the dead, drink from the weak and dying, the jackals within human form. Did we not simply ignore the social convention of kindness and goodness and the falsity of differentiating between the meat and blood of the deer and that of man?

I followed the instinct that grew like fire from my soul outward, a fire that could only be contained by sprinkling the blood of sacrifice upon it.

Each night, for nearly a week, I drank from the soldiers' necks like a newborn calf sucking greedily from the cow. My nights as a monster had just begun, but even then I felt something more than murder and bloodshed. I felt a deeper connection within my soul, even as I sent a victim to his death.

When you have returned from the dead, you understand the doorway that death opens. Your mind grows from this knowledge, and the brief suffering of life is a gift to those who will travel to the Threshold, and beyond, to the journey of the soul.

While you, the creature who drank of the body, remain in the grave, conscious, aware of all you have lost and yet with a knowledge of your own destruction within you—of the price of immortality, which is the living death that does not end.

◆ 4 ◆

THE soldiers struggled against me. These were men who had spent their young lives in war, as had I, yet they were as full of terror as children in a nightmare.

My instinct rose and loved their fight as I drained them like great jugs, a glutton for the red elixir that filled me with strength and hope and a renewed love of the world. As I held one of them to me, tearing at his throat, I felt a communion with the soldier, who, as he lay there after, dead, drained so deeply from my thirst, had given up his secret to me, the wonder and pride of his treasure, buried as it was in vein and flesh.

I lay back, full, and felt as if I had never been so alive as I was at that moment.

During that first week of beautiful night and long sleep, I learned of the tribe I had entered when I had died, the first time. The other vampyres—I counted six or seven who gathered around as I drank—did not approach me during that time, except to look down on me from above my grave, as if I were some great curiosity.

It was dusk when I stirred from a sleep that seemed more like death itself, for it was simply an emptiness—as if I had lain down in my grave only moments before. The smells that greeted me were of earth and some malodorous ether, as if an animal had died nearby. Perhaps that animal had been me. Before I opened my eyes, I felt as if someone were staring at me. Yet, as soon as I looked, there was nothing but the grave of my rebirth around me. I had strength again—the blood had brought it. I felt a rich vitality in my flesh, and I longed to leave my resting place. I scrambled up over the ridge of the grave and saw a new world.

Great yellow stone columns spanned the spacious chamber and reached the ceiling a hundred feet or more overhead. Slits of windows let in the pink-purple light of the last of the sun, which lingered like a sword dangling above the darkness of my grave.

My eyes adjusted as the dark grew: all became light again, in my vision. I saw as a cat now, better the less bright the light. The earth itself had a luminosity to it, and was wondrous to behold: it was as if feeble mankind could not see the light that teemed in life itself. The movement of worms, of lice, of the smallest ant, the tiniest fungus—all of it created thin rays of yellow light such that I felt as if torches had been lit in the earth. I felt my eyes dilate, and soon, I saw more—the stones of the wall nearly four hundred feet from me, the other graves around me. I sensed that others were in them, also beginning to awaken to the night.

The thought panicked me only slightly: I, a monster among monsters.

I had not yet dressed, and was surprised to find that I had no self-consciousness about my nakedness as I had as a mortal man. In life, I had felt shameful without a tunic of some sort, but for the first time, I felt as if the flesh itself were clothing enough. I looked down at my body—it had whitened, and seemed to me like alabaster. I held my arms out in front of me and felt for life at the wrist, but there was none. Yet, I had the feeling of life in me. I felt a heart beat beneath my breast—blood still pumped. Life existed, impossibly, in this body that was neither dead nor alive. I felt the stirrings of nature itself, as I often did upon waking, and I wondered at this new existence, this damnation: why would it exist if it were truly evil? Why would I feel young, still, and even happy, after death had taken me?

What madness possessed me that I laughed when I arose and wished for nothing other than something sweet and warm to drink?

I had been afraid that I would be wholly demon. That my need for human blood would turn me against myself. But this awakening from the grave gave me the feeling of utter joy: yes, I knew I would need to drink from a man or woman that night. Yes, that might mean the death of that person. But what did it matter? What was death, after all? It had taken me, but left me behind at the same time. I experienced a sense of freedom that no living man could ever feel. I loved humanity in this.

My mind raced as I stretched—would I take down a youth, like a lion running after a young gazelle? Would I make a beautiful woman give me the gift of her blood in exchange for a night of passion? Would I grab a young man—another soldier, perhaps—of sinewy muscle and hearty laugh? Would I bring to them the knowledge of their own mortality, their vulnerability—or would I bring them tidings of their power as the source of my new life?

My love was death. My death was love. I brought death to mortals with this new incarnation, and it felt like a gift when I drank from them.

If I were a demon, then why did I still praise God? Why did I begin to understand that other gods roamed the world, as well? Why had my thinking changed, and why did I feel this unleashing of instinct as a beautiful force denied mankind?

Why did I still feel as if life was worth living, if I were not truly alive for the first time in nearly twenty years?

Death was the battlefield. The bodies of my brethren had been scattered over its great field of blood. I was not dead, not in the sense of death. I was not alive—yet I felt more life in me than I'd ever known. My mind expanded with the thought: death, useless death, was what mankind brought. Mankind was a plague against itself. I was a newly reborn creature then—I was a lover of man and woman. I appreciated what they offered, and I wanted to take it, with care, with kindness, as a lover takes the maiden's chastity and holds it close. I wanted to hold a man in my arms while I drank of his red juice, kiss a woman's throat before sensing the pulsing vein, then delving into her for that finest of liqueurs.

There was no madness to these thoughts. I felt as if I were not abandoned by God, but that I somehow, with my vital fluids, was intertwined with Him. I had eaten of the fruit of the tree—not of the knowledge of good and evil, but of the knowledge of the life after death. Not in some unseen spirit realm, but here, on this Earth, in the very heart of the land of the dead.

The thirst overwhelmed me soon enough. I felt as if I had never fed in all my days, and that if I didn't find blood soon, I would dry up like the last bit of kindling in an oven.

The others around me arose, as well, some swiftly, some slowly. Their figures looked beautiful to me—the males were muscled and possessed a beauty that I had never seen in mortal men. The females had that undead beauty also, that glamour of seduction that was no doubt needed to lure prey. Beautiful and damned and full of energy that was like a heat mirage of air around their forms. They did not resemble corpses or even demons—they looked like the gods of the Earth, possessing the vitality of life in their movement and upon the surface of their flesh.

I longed to speak with them, to ask them of this existence and their journeys, but they moved swiftly—swifter sometimes than sight itself. They showed no interest in either me or their companions in this demonic realm. Instead, they had gone up the passageways, to the world above.

A woman arose, whose skin was dark and whose hair was braided. The one who had first spoken to me of the need to drink of life. She wrapped a cloak of tattered raiment about her and briefly glanced at me. Her eyes were yellowed, and her parched lips parted, as if to speak. For a moment, I held hope, but when she opened her mouth, it was to bare the fangs of a wolf. She wrapped a cloth into her hair, which became a turban when it was done. Then, she crawled up the side of one of the tall columns and moved across the ceiling of this graveyard dungeon until she'd reached the slit of a window. She pressed herself through it—she was remarkably slender of waist and hips, and she moved like a cat.

I dressed, then, feeling the need to hunt, leapt toward the upper passageway, moving like a spider, my fingers and toes gently touching the stone, and yet somehow adhering so that I might climb a sheer wall.

• 5 •

THE lights came up more brightly until it was no longer night, but a false daylight, yet with a skewed perspective—colors had been changed, and what had been red was yellow, what had been blue was white. As I emerged into the courtyard, the moon seemed an orb of darkness, and the sky was lit where there were no stars. Where the stars existed, only pinpricks of black.

The rest of my newfound tribe had fled into the night. They would find the traveler on the road, or the dying soldier still on the field, and drink their fills. I, too, set forth, smelling the musk of the undead as I followed the invisible trail.

Through the night, I sensed a gathering of my tribe within a few leagues, and so I moved along what felt like a warm, invisible stream of air—that stream that my tribe sensed and kept within. My mind moved with it, as did my body, and soon enough I found the others. Four or five of my brethren had gathered near a dying soldier who had camped at the base of a rocky hill. They had torn off his armor, and one female demon raised an ax as if in victory, dancing near the fire alongside which the man had only recently eaten his last meal.

I stepped closer to the soldier—the rich smell of iron in his blood overwhelmed me. It was like smelling a boar roasted for many hours on a spit. It made my mouth water. I felt the pain again—my incisors had begun the painful growth that might not stop for days. But it was a pain I could take, for it increased my thirst. I greedily pushed the other vampyres from this unfortunate man. His throat and collar were brightly colored with his blood. The mouths and chins of my fellows, smeared with the stain of life, their lips smacking like hounds with the kill of a fresh stag. I grabbed his shoulders, drawing that delicious milk of life to my lips, but when I saw the man's eyes, I recoiled.

He looked at me with utter sadness. He was not yet dead, but he was well on his way to that place. I knew instinctively that to kill him would be a kindness—a swift kill was not the norm for my kind. The instinct within me knew that to drink from these cups of flesh was a gourmand's pursuit—sips as well as guzzling, a taste or a drunken swallow. But a swift kill was not what I should want, because the taste was better when life still moved in the blood.

But I knew this man. I loved this man as a true brother.

I recognized him, as if a long-buried memory had surfaced.

· CHAPTER 12 ·

The Sacred Kiss

◆ 1 ◆

IT was Ewen, my friend, my companion, and I felt sorrow for him, and yet a distance from the world of mortal man so that I had no pity. He recognized me in the firelight, his eyes seeming to glaze over, then brighten again as if he were fighting within himself to hang on to life.

"Aleric," he whispered. "Aleric. Take me. Take me. Take me where you go."

"I can't," I said, whispering this in his ear. "I love you, my friend. But you do not want to come to this place. We are demons. I am no longer Aleric. Let me drink the last of you and keep you from this world."

"Please," he whispered. "I don't want to leave you. I don't want to go. I want always to serve you. I searched for you. I followed your path."

But I could not let that be. I wept as I drank from him, the dual tears of one who wishes peace for a friend—to put him out of the misery of the pain of death, to open the door into whatever comes after—but also, I wished to feed. Does the shepherd not name the sheep of his flock, yet pick the finest spring lamb for slaughter? When he sits down to eat that meal, does he not remember that lamb, and the sweetness of its youth, even while tasting of its death? So I tasted Ewen, his rich aroma like the exotic coffee of the East, like the wines of my homeland, the iron within him proving a gentle metal to my tongue, like the edge of dull blade, the sweetness of anise and of the meat he had eaten that day.

I learned that night of the memory that comes with the blood. Not the memory of those we drink, but the memory of our own mortality, the riches of it, and its poverty, too. The innocence of childhood, the touch of a mother, the love of flesh, and the hatred for self. All of it returns in a flagon of blood, drunk to quench an unquenchable thirst.

Life is the blood. Health is the blood. It is the drink of the gods, and all who have drunk of it for sustenance do not hate those from whom they drink, the vessels of mankind.

Love was my feeling then, and even caring.

I was not a ravager of this man—I ravished him.

I pressed my teeth against the much-torn flesh, and sucked hard against those ragged flaps of skin. He became the vessel of my life. It was a form of love that humans can't ever understand because they think of life and death as opposites, when life is death, death is life, love is death, death is love, immortality is hell, and heaven is death. All of these thoughts washed through me. I felt his love for me in his blood as no man had ever given of himself before.

When I drew back, the blood across my chin and throat and chest, and saw a look of astonishment around me. The other vampyres stood as if watching, and I wondered if it was at my greed.

But when I looked back down at Ewen's face, I knew: I had not yet stopped his heart. He still had a flush of life in him, and I saw an intense beauty to this last moment of existence. He was more beautiful then than any maiden—even than Alienora to me. He had the beauty of what I would learn was the Threshold. The Threshold was the doorway between the living and the dead. Once passed through, there was no coming back. I looked at him and another instinct came to me—I wanted him with me. Ewen had been there, and he had no doubt camped there because he had tracked me and intended to find me. He was my link to mortal life, and I could not let him go. I could not let him die as little Thibaud had gone, at the hands of these creatures.

I could not.

Call it selfishness or fear or loneliness, but I wanted him again for myself, for my friend.

Instinct rose in me. Remembrance of Pythia as she pressed her lips to mine.

I would bring him into my world and make him one of our tribe.

◆ 2 ◆

I brought his head nearer to me and parted his lips with my fingers. His eyes fluttered open. He looked at me as one drugged.

I felt he knew me then, and I felt his acceptance.

Without further hesitation, I pressed my lips against his, locking to them as I remembered Pythia had done.

Like a viaduct, passing water through a new channel, I exhaled into his slightly quivering form. Another force made itself known to me—from my lungs, a power I had not felt before. My breath. The passing was in the breath itself. I passed this to Ewen, whose lips caught mine in tenderness.

I felt the slight grasp of his hand at my shoulder, then at my chest. His hand was cold, but warmed as I breathed into his lungs. The flow of the stream from my mouth to his increased, and I felt as if I might never stop, but instead lost myself in his mouth, down his throat, inside him completely, losing my body and spirit so that he might breathe again. His arms went to my back and drew me closer to him. I felt his desire increase, a furnace beginning to glow red. I felt an unseen presence there with us—whispering to me of the secrets of the stream, of the flow between vampyre and human, of passing the breath and the Death-that-was-Life to another.

I felt a terrible pounding in my ears, and a tender weakness in my loins. He wasn't just drinking breath from my mouth. He swallowed my essence. I felt his delight at this plunder of my force—this sucking at my core, my fundament—my being. He was my child now, my baby, and my birthling into the undead. I felt the third presence, the creation of a new being within him from the giving of breath. He would forever be connected to me by my essence.

He inhaled greedily from my lips as a man who has been smothering seeks air, and the suction this created began to pain me. I remembered Pythia, how she drew back, breaking the connection between us, breaking out of the sacred stream that bound us. I felt excruciating pain as I felt his tongue searching the edges of my teeth and lapping up to the roof of my mouth as he tried to get the last of what I offered. But I used all the strength I had left, and threw myself backward, away from him.

Something else, another memory of Pythia, as she gave me this life-in-death: *I saw the great city called Alkemara, shining in moonlight, and the priest, with wings as oily as eelskin, spread wide behind his form. In his hand, the Staff of the Nahhashim.*

Behind him, a figure lying upon a stone altar.

In Pythia's streaming into me, she had shown me something secret, something terrible, and I did not know what it meant.

A woman stood there, naked, beside the wing-shrouded priest, her face covered with a gold mask. From her full breasts to her taut waist, down past her gently rounded hips to her slender but muscled legs, her sun-darkened body was soaked in blood. The vision had the quality of a dream, for parts of it were vivid, and other parts seemed only half-formed. I saw the gold mask clearly for a moment: it had a woman's features, with her mouth wide and her tongue out, her eyes wild and wide. Behind the slits of the mask, I saw darkness where a woman's eyes should have been.

Something drew me to her. My sight moved as if it had wings, toward the masked woman, who stepped aside to show me the altar. I moved unbidden into the realm of the altar on which a young woman had been tied with strips of leather. Clothed as if she were royalty, she wore a cobweb-thin robe. Around her shoulders, a turquoise cloak with gold thread sewn through it. On her scalp, a headdress in the shape of a hawk. It was Pythia herself.

Then, this stream-vision of Pythia, which had flooded me when she offered me her open mouth and blood and breath, at the moments between life and death, vanished like smoke.

Shadows arose around the altar. Greedy shadows that tried to grab at the headdress and the robe, and I felt as if they turned to me, watching them from some distant time and place. The whispers of these shades became like flies at my ear—*"Nahhashim, Maz-Sherah, we know you."*

• 3 •

A ND then, the vision of that place exploded into brilliant light.

I was again with Ewen, my lungs burning, my body, cold and empty.

He sat up, a curious grin on his face, wiping his hand lazily across his mouth. His face was suffused with a radiant glow that I had never before seen.

I felt weak, and fell back. I looked up to see the other vampyres over me, watching.

They had looks on their faces as if I had frightened them.

One among them crouched beside me. He had a canine look to his face—his jaw was long and stretched with the thorny cusps of teeth that had grown too long. He had thick dark hair that fell below his shoulders, some of it swinging around his face. Tattoos of disks and strange symbols encircled his throat and his muscled arms. His clothes were of a type that I had seen on soldiers from Byzantium, but perhaps he had stolen these from one of his victims.

He grasped my wrist. "What have you done?" he asked. I felt his yellowed, twisted nails going into my skin. "What is this?"

"He is my friend," I said.

"This is impossible," he said, looking with wonder at Ewen, whose eyes rolled back into his head, showing only the whites. "Only the Pythoness can bring us into the fold."

"I did to him what she did to me."

"No," gasped another, the dark woman who wore the turban. "She is the only one."

"He will die," another said, watching Ewen's eyes close slowly, and the last shudder of life move through him. "He will die, and rot like all the others."

"We should drink the last of him," the tattooed vampyre said. "He should not die with blood in his body." As he crawled forward, his slithering reminded me of a snake. I felt repulsion, because I knew I would become more like him and less like Ewen as the nights unfolded. I had become some dark vermin, a plague on the world.

Yet, there was a great fluid beauty in his movements. As he approached Ewen's torn throat, he sniffed, his nostrils flaring, and he turned back to me. Then, looking at the turbaned female, said, "This cannot be."

The female stepped over to Ewen. Straddling his chest, she bent down to bring her mouth near his. She sniffed all around his face and throat.

She shot me a suspicious glance. "Who taught you this?"

"The one you called the Pythoness," I said.

"How?" the tattooed vampyre asked.

The female leapt up from Ewen and came to me, pushing me back down to the ground. "Did you see anything? Did you see the city?"

Remembering the altar and the priest, I nodded. "I saw a man and an altar."

The female looked up at the others, who came closer to me as I lay beneath her weight. "You learned of this . . . the Sacred Kiss . . . from her?"

Before I could answer, another female vampyre stepped forward. She was lean and pale, and had a look of disgust upon her face. "We should never have taken him from the tower."

"Rat ash," the tattooed one muttered as if it were a terrible oath. "She abandoned us."

The turbaned female atop me touched my forehead, then leaned into me, sniffing again. She whispered, "You would be dead if not for us, newborn. Your Pythoness abandoned you so that you would not feed if you rose from the first death. We knew of you and found you in the tower."

The other female spat. "The Pythoness was right to leave him there. He brings evil upon us."

Others began murmuring above—I watched their faces and saw anger and confusion.

The one pressing her knees against my shoulders to pin me to the ground let out a shrill cry, which silenced the others. Then, her face coming close to mine, she said, "What do they call you?"

"Aleric," I said. "The Falconer."

An enigmatic smile crossed her lips, and she showed her teeth. "Well, Falcon, tell me what the Pythoness showed you."

"She drank of me until I had nearly lost all my blood, and had little breath left in my mouth and no vision in me. And then, she pressed her mouth to me, and breathed both death and life into me. And as she brought this warm stream into my throat, I saw a vision of a great city of an ancient time. I saw a woman of ripe beauty wearing a terrible mask of gold, and beside her, a holy man with the wings of a dragon, and in his hand was a staff that seemed entwined with serpents. And behind them both, an altar of lapis stone, and upon it, Pythia herself, like a prisoner waiting for sacrifice."

"Alkemara," the turbaned female gasped, glancing at the others.

I nodded. "The City of the Alkemars is what he told me. The priest. And there were terrible shadows that whispered to me. I saw them just now when I sent my breath into my friend's mouth."

One of the others nearby said, "The Myrrydanai. They come."

"No," said the tattooed one. "We would feel them in the stream."

"Other strange words I do not understand," I said. "*Nahhashim. Maz-Sherah*. I do not know the meaning of the vision, but Pythia drew back from me suddenly. I felt she had not known how I shared her sight of that place and those people. She shrieked at my knowing of them, and I watched great wings grow from her shoulders. She flew up into the night, crying out as if I had not been meant to see these things."

"She gave you eternal life," the turbaned female said. "The Pythoness created all of us, to watch us extinguish."

"But what of the vision? The great city?"

"It is no more," the tattooed vampyre said. "It is a memory of the ancient world, a moment from another age. We have heard of it. But none . . . none has had the vision of it. Or of these things."

"He lies," the other female above me said. "She sent him to destroy us. She left him there. She knew we would feel his stream and find him. He is a trap for us."

"But the Sacred Kiss," the turbaned woman said. "None of us can manifest it."

"We have all tried," another vampyre said, a handsome man who stood holding Ewen's sword. "We have longed to bring our lovers to be with us. Instead, we send them beyond the Threshold."

"He is the one," the turbaned woman said, as she looked to the others.

Another said, "How can it be?"

"Bloody Turks! There is no 'one,'" the tattooed vampyre growled. "Nothing but a lie."

"All lies," the standing female said. "There is no Maz-Sherah. Alkemara is a fable. It is like the gods. They do not exist, but we create them so as to not fear the Extinguishing."

"You have heard the voice of the dark mother," the female atop me said. "The one who seeks to destroy us since she first gave us life."

Others mumbled assent to her words. The tattooed one spat out, "It is our damnation that speaks to us."

"She has a voice of thunder, and we feel her lightning in the stream itself," another said.

"She sends us to the Extinguishing," the female said. "I tell you, he is the one. It is as Balaam told us." She commanded one of the vampyres to go find more to drink, for I was weak. She held me in her arms, but I kept my eyes on Ewen as she raised me.

"You must feed again before dawn," she said.

"The Maz-Sherah," one of the vampyres said, a sense of awe in his voice. "Balaam muttered about the Maz-Sherah too often. But I thought it was a dream."

"If he is the one," said the tattooed one, "why doesn't he bring the knowledge? Why is he weak? Why don't we recognize him?"

"The dream is not yet flesh. He has not yet become," the turbaned vampyre said. "The priest breathes through him. Our dark mother who wishes the end of days fears him."

"He will bring destruction to us," one of the others said. "He will bring her wrath upon all who drink blood."

◆ 4 ◆

THE snarling female above me was named Yset; the long-haired one with the tattoos at his neck was Yarilo; the youth with the sword, Vali. The turbaned vampyre's name was Kiya, she told me, after naming the others around us. She had once been the wife of a merchant who traveled the seas. But she had been transformed nearly a hundred years previous, by the Pythoness. The city of Hedammu had been overtaken with plague, then, but there was no disease. It was simply the Pythoness's hunger. The oldest of the vampyres in Hedammu was named Balaam, "But his time is near," Kiya told me. "He has weakened, and we bring him blood, for he can no longer hunt. But I will tell you more of that another time," Kiya said. "You must feed and rest."

After a while, they brought a woman to me, who lived in an encampment along the trade route several miles farther. She shivered as they held her tight, and drew her clothes from her slowly, presenting her to me.

"Drink of her," Kiya said. "Drink long draughts, and don't hesitate to finish her. She will bring you strength and blessings."

I took to her throat. The prey clutched me as I did this, for as I knew, it was not unpleasant for our victims—as the leech clings to the legs that wade the marsh, so I clung to her throat and caused her little pain, though I made a mess of her. Drunk, sated, I fell back into Kiya's arms and felt the antidote to my torment course through me again.

Hours before dawn, I was strong enough to stand, and I lifted Ewen into my arms. Like a wolf pack, we raced back across the barren

land, to our home, Hedammu, the poisoned citadel that had been uninhabitable for nearly a century, by all but those who had become legend in this region—the jackals of the Devil.

• 5 •

I laid Ewen down in the ditch that was my grave and went to Kiya
who called to me in the stream, which invisible flowed through and
held all vampyric beings of the tribe. "I want you to meet the oldest of
our tribe," she said. She led me down to where a large stone circle
sealed a low-ceilinged chamber. We drew off the stone and crouched
down to enter.

"He was a great king once," she whispered.

There, on a bed of clay, lay a corpse, its leathery skin torn at the
curves of his elbows, while the thinnest skin along his scalp blistered
and peeled.

She knelt beside the dead man. When she touched him, his jaw
seemed to drop, and his lips curled back slightly. I saw the long fangs
of our tribal brother. Kiya glanced up at me. "He was beautiful not
long ago. He had long golden hair, and a strong body—like yours." As
she said this, she touched my chest, and her hand went to my throat.
"Do you feel his stream?"

I closed my eyes, her fingers lingering at my shoulder. I felt the
heat of Kiya's stream, but nothing more.

Then, a gentle, nearly imperceptible feeling, as of some small insect crawling along the back of my hand.

"He cared for me, as I care for you," she said. "A king of a tribe of
men who are no more—slaughtered, as so many men will be. Like you,
he had come, an enemy to this land. And as she did with you and I, the
Pythoness drank of him and brought her life into him. And as you and
I shall one day, he lies in the dust, never again to rise."

"We are immortal," I said. "How . . ." But I could not form the
words to ask the question I dreaded.

"While we are young and strong, we are no better than wolves and
jackals. When the strength fades, and the years pass, our hell is within this
flesh. For us there is no death. It has been denied us at the Threshold.

This," she said, turning again to wipe the drops of red sweat that had accumulated at his tattered brow. "This is our destiny, if we are not destroyed by men. It is the Extinguishing. We live forever, whether or not our minds continue. We grow weak and feeble. To some it comes fast, and they are dust soon. To others, like Balaam, it is slow."

"Has he lived many lifetimes?"

"Not so many," she said. "We live longer than men. But we do not live as we are now, forever."

Her eyes shone as she watched him. She crouched beside him and pressed her hand into his. "Here, hold me," she said, offering me her free hand. I took it in mine, and immediately experienced a sensation of horror. I felt as if my hand in hers were liquid, and flowed into Balaam, as he lay there, barely a breath coming from him. I felt a shivering cold and the feeling of movement as if I'd touched the sloughing skin of a sleeping serpent.

More than anything I'd experienced in immortality, this struck to my heart in a way that no human experience had. Though I had wept for my mother, for my brother, for my grandfather, and for loss of Alienora, when I felt what Kiya passed from this vampyre as she tightened her grip on his hand and on mine, it was not the terror of the Extinguishing of a vampyre's existence but the sorrow of an enormous diminishing of light. It was as if the stream between the three of us, in weakening, had drawn something from within me that had been dormant in my previous existence. I understood sadness in a way that was not destructive, not self-loathing, not vain, as had been my mortal feeling.

We were one in the stream. His loss, the loss of this creature's facilities, his power, his memory, all of it was my loss as well. Kiya's, too, and though I did not then understand why monsters such as ourselves should be pitied, still, I felt it, a great pity at the loss of this immortal, at the terror he faced, for, without hearing it from Kiya's lips, I knew. I knew.

The Extinguishing was worse than the pain of a thousand deaths.

It was existing into eternity, locked in a cage of all that would fall away and turn to dust.

"Mortals journey, when their flesh fails them," she said, softly. "Their skin is their cloak, and when they shed it, their souls travel across the Threshold. We cannot abandon our flesh, once we have resurrected. The flesh and the bone and the blood—the body—is our heaven and our hell."

I felt his youth and his childhood, his years as a vampyre, both the darkness and the light of his existence, the tearing of the fabric of memory as much as the tearing of muscle.

This is the vampyre's curse: the atrophy of the body, which comes, eventually, when cut off from the source of the tribe. Cut off as we, in that graveyard city, were cut from the womb of our being.

"He told me of the Maz-Sherah," Kiya whispered. "When I was young to the night. He told me of vampyres that live thousands of years. Thousands upon thousands. He knew of the legends from others who had turned to dust before my resurrection. I did not believe him, nor did I care. But I have been many years beyond age itself. I have seen others, like Balaam. I have watched them fall from youth and beauty, to this corpselike death-in-life. And then I have watched their bones crumble. Their eyes dry to raisins. Their throats become gnarled and twisted so that they cannot drink, even if blood is poured down their gullets."

"We are monsters," I said. "We live as demons, and deserve Hell." I remembered the winged demon brought from the well of the Great Forest. A vampyre, far from its tribe, in its Extinguishing, at the bottom of a dark well. I remembered the men as they cut off its head, and burned the creature. I thought of the dark ash as it rose into the sky, when I had been a boy, and not known of this other existence. I wondered if even that creature had continued to exist within the thousands of motes of ash that had spread in the fire that day. "We are monsters," I said.

"You would not say that if you had lived as long as he," she said, tightening her grip about my hand. As she did so, I felt how he diminished, moment by moment, even as I knelt before him. "Do you not feel it?" Tears streamed down her face.

The emotions flooded through me as I felt his loneliness—like a sparrow caught in a thorny bush—wings beating against the pain, and a mind racing with fear and the inability to escape—until I was overpowered by it, and I felt my heart open within me. Open in a way it never had as a mortal.

I saw the three of us as one, again. As one being, separated only by flesh. I felt a union, and an understanding, and still, fear and torment. Something within me grew—a seed had been planted, just by the simple act of holding Kiya's hand, of feeling what she felt through the vampyre as he slowly extinguished.

The terror was as nothing.

I felt brotherhood. Absolute brotherhood. A bond, a tie, and I could look at the bones of the vampyre and see my other half, just as surely as I could with Kiya. Not even a half—I could see my whole self within them. The stream had brought me their pain, their fears, their loves, their losses, their monstrosity, their humanity.

I had become a vampyre, more than I had ever been as a man.

I felt a burden, yet one I was willing to shoulder.

Providence had brought me there. Brought me into the realm of the damned.

Brought me into the court of the Devil himself.

And yet, I knew that even there, even among the creatures of darkness and blood, there was light. I did not understand the light, nor did I then believe it was a light of some holy or unholy flame. All I knew then was that it existed, and it wavered in the stream itself. The stream overwhelmed, it brought a mystical sense of purpose and communion to our tribe. I was powerless to resist its pull, and it opened me, opened my conscious mind, opened the deeper caverns of my being so that I began to feel as if I had the perspective of a god, cursed to feel all suffering, to understand all pain, and to be called to it, drawn to it, a mystery of existence itself.

My eyes closed, I was in the stream, and a vision came to me.

I saw, briefly, a great serpent, in my mind, a great turning creature, encircling the tree of life itself.

And it was not a thing of evil, nor was it purely good, but it was All.

I opened my eyes, feeling panic and the shiver of recognition all at once.

Kiya held me. She told me that all who were vampyre passed into the Extinguishing after a century or so. "You are the Maz-Sherah," she whispered against my ear. "I know it. You could not give the Sacred Kiss if you were not. You are the messiah of our tribe. You must be."

I held her, and felt the erosion of the flesh of the vampyre called Balaam.

LATER, we returned to our resting places. I helped unwrap her turban, her dark braids of hair falling to her shoulders. I lay down beside her in the Earth.

Before the sun rose beyond our columned tomb, I asked, "What is this city from my vision?"

"Alkemara is a legend only," she said. "It was swallowed by the Earth, cursed by the gods of every nation for it was the place where the priest ruled."

"Who is the priest?"

She smiled, an enigmatic curve of her lips. "These are all things that we do not understand. Legends passed from the old vampyres to the younger, before the eldest go into the Extinguishing. The priest is a king of some kind. The Priest of Blood, he is called. Alkemara was a land of beautiful maidens, and strong warriors. The Alkemars were the daughters of the priest. The Pythoness was one of his daughters and a priestess of that lost city."

"You say I am the one," I whispered, smelling the copper of her hair and the fragrant oil upon her skin.

"Yes, the Anointed One—the Maz-Sherah, in the language of the Kamrs. All we know of this Maz-Sherah is that it will come as a great bird to devour the Serpent and return dominion to our kind."

"How?"

"No one knows. Perhaps the Pythoness knows, but she won't tell us. She has the power to change her shape, and to move through the night sky like a column of smoke or a dragon. It is a power that none of us possess. She has abandoned us because of you, I think. When she felt what you had in you. You are the great bird. You are the falcon itself. She must have felt it in your stream. She must want to destroy you, even now. You are in danger, for your presence will surely mean the end of her existence. She is more than a thousand years old. None of us exists so long. The eldest among us does not reach much past one hundred years, and there are times when men hunt us, and kill us easily in our graves. And the Extinguishing . . ."

"What is it?"

"It is a journey none of us wishes to take," she said, a sadness in her voice.

"But it is not death? And yet," I said, remembering Balaam, "it is not life."

"The Pythoness lives eternally. But we were born from her without the power of the source of our tribe. We live young, powerful, for a time. But the Extinguishing always comes. We become as nothing, for our bodies rot, and yet we cannot lose life. Even as our skins fall, as our bones break and crack, still we exist. And we remain imprisoned even as the dust overtakes our remains. We are . . . extinguished . . . but without thought or control or mind. And yet our life, in the dust, continues, as a living death that cannot resurrect."

"The source is this priest," I said. "I was told that I was born from a line of priests."

"We are dying out, all of us. Men grow stronger. I grow weak. Even I cannot outrun some horses, and if dawn is near, we are at our weakest. They hunt us as we hunt them. So, we fear the sound of men and the bull roar of the battles that come closer to our home. If you are the one, then you can bring us the power and knowledge that have been lost. That is the meaning of the dream. The Priest of Blood, of our bloodline, sleeps in Alkemara, but it is a necropolis of dread, and none of us dare leave our resting place to go find out if the legend is true."

"In the stream-vision," I said. "I knew the priest's name. It was Merod. He held a staff of great power, and I knew its name. It was encircled with snakes and was called the Nahhashim."

"Nahhashim," she said, her eyes dimming. "The gates. The gates."

Even as she spoke, I felt the night's death coming on, and the birth of morning. I closed my eyes, listening to the last of her words, and remembered those terrible shades that whispered of my destruction. *Nahhashim,* they whispered, *Maz-Sherah, we know you now.* Their figures spun before me in dreams, and the day grew long as I slept.

When I awoke, I was alone.

◆ 6 ◆

K IYA had already left on the night's hunt.

I sat up, sensing someone nearby. I went to look at my earthen bed, and there lay Ewen. I felt the edge of his cheek, but life-in-death had not yet come to him. I covered him with a cloak and went off to hunt. After the blood-feast, I sat with Yarilo and asked him more about all that I had seen in my visions.

"Prophecies of ancient times that cannot leave us any more than the races of men can forget their ancestors' time in the caves of the world," he said. "It is all rat ash." He laughed when he saw my confusion at this term. "You've never seen a rat burn?" he asked. "These legends are all rat ash. They are meaningless. Our kind sleep among the dead and drink from the living and the dead for survival. Men hunt us, for we are their enemy. It is our damnation. There is no more."

"You believe we are damned?"

"My friend," he said, a vulpine grimace on his face, "we cannot bear the sunlight. Men may cut off our heads as we sleep in the day and thus end our lives. Or stake our hearts that we might not leave our graves. Or they may bring us out into the rays of the noonday sun to turn us to ashes in the blink of an eye. Even their silver destroys us. We feel powerful, for we hunt them, but they hold the power. We cannot run far from them if they are great in number. I have sat upon the hills, watching our kind run from the sunrise, while men on horseback attack from the north. I have watched the Extinguishing of many. There are fewer than twenty of us left, yet decades ago, there were nearly seventy among our tribe. From those I learned that hundreds existed before me. All have gone to the Extinguishing, but before they did, they were tormented and tortured by the very men who would call us demons.

"When extinguished, the torment does not end. This is why I am happy to drink from their children. To take a baby up and sup before its mother, then take her to my bed for a drink, and feel her terror and the suffering of her thoughts before the last of her blood is drained. I am the demon, and the monster. Though we have no great dominion, nor can we survive well without a deep grave or a hidden tomb, they fear us. We, who take only when the thirst is strong. I have seen a thousand men die at the hands of a thousand others. And yet, they do not feed on what they kill—they simply slaughter without purpose."

"Yet, you were once like them."

"Indeed." He nodded, his long, thick hair falling along his shoulders so that he looked every inch the barbarian. "I was perhaps the worst of them. I slaughtered my own family in order to take what was rightfully mine. This citadel, itself. Yes"—he laughed—"this was my father's city, taken by him when his army came from distant lands. It became mine when I assassinated him. I was the last king here, and now, I am the servant of its tomb."

"Why does Kiya think I am this Maz-Sherah?" I asked.

He gave me a look that held much contempt. "She is old. She will enter her last days soon enough. Perhaps I, too, will have great faith in the Maz-Sherah when I face my Extinguishing. Perhaps we all believe in ancient legends when we have nowhere else to find comfort."

◆ 7 ◆

AFTER the night's hunt, I sat with Ewen, as he lay lifeless against me. I remembered our homeland as I combed his dark thick hair with my fingers—my first sight of him in the Baron's house, with his ill-fitting tunic and his ready smile. The days of labor near him, and seeing him as someone in need of my protection. Our growing friendship, as I watched him turn from boy to man on the battlefield. I worried, too, that he would not return from the Threshold, but would continue the journey onward. I felt helpless there with his corpse and selfish for not wanting to be left alone with these vampyres. I wanted one of my friends, one of my countrymen. Someone who understood when I glanced at him. Someone who reminded me of all I had loved and lost in my years of life and death.

In the early hours before the sun rose, Kiya came and sat beside me, touching Ewen along his throat and shoulder, as if sensing a return to life. But there was nothing.

"We lose much of that," she said, her dark eyes flickering with wisdom as she watched me.

"Of what?"

"The love. The caring for mortal life." She smiled. "How you hold him like he is your brother. I had a child when I first died, and I didn't want her to be one of our tribe. But I still cared for her, and held her close to me. But soon enough, you forget. Perhaps years pass. It has been so long, that I do not understand the passage of time in the way I once did. You begin to see the past as someone else's dream. I thought at first that I could not be a monster who drank the blood of the innocent. But I soon found that instinct was more powerful than resistance."

"And your daughter?"

"I had forgotten who she was, and could not recognize her by the time she was sixteen. She had grown lovely, and lived in the desert with her uncles. But when we descended upon them, I took her first, and drank the rich blood that I'd given her at birth. I fought with another over the last cupful of her juice, and it was only when I had the last of it that I saw that child's face again in the dead girl in my arms. Even now, telling you, it does not offend my conscience to have done this. She had been my daughter, but I sent her to the Threshold intact. Though I tasted her fear, it wasn't more than an hour or two before she crossed over—and it's in that other country, from which no one can return without the Sacred Kiss, where she will find joy that could not be had in this place."

I gave her a moment's reflection, but her tales made me want to know more about the mysteries I had begun to manifest in visions and dreams. "Tell me more of the City of the Alkemars."

Kiya's faced was shadowed. "It is our lost homeland, where the legend of our kind was of our power. It holds the great temple of Lemesharra, the aspect of Medhya as goddess of the hunt and of bounty, where the Priest of Blood ruled."

"Tell me about Lemesharra. About Medhya."

"She is the great mother of Myrryd, a country that is no more but that existed for thousands of years. Its history has been wiped from the history of the Earth. Three kingdoms of priests and kings bowed to her. Their descendants envied her, and stole her flesh, and her blood, and the wealth and treasures of her mines, which made her powerful among other lands. In revenge, she cursed all that had been taken—including the Serpent, her beloved. Those who took the flesh were cursed to be shadow as she had become. Those who stole her blood became our tribe. And she cursed the Serpent above all others, for infidelity to her. The priests of the Serpent suffered the worst fate. They were the first beings to enter the Extinguishing. But Medhya has three faces. Lemesharra and her sister, Datbathani. Three in one, she is, and only as Medhya will she destroy us. But these are fragments of legend and dream. Even those who have already extinguished could not tell me more."

"Why would the Pythoness not wish to tell of these stories?"

"She is under the influence of Medhya. She is a being turned against herself. Perhaps she suffers an ancient hurt. For she resurrects us to this life, then watches as we perish many years later, as if delighting in the ends of her own children. Just as Medhya does."

"But we can find Pythia. We can reach for her in the stream."

"Pythia has left us. That is what I feel of her in the stream. She has left for some distant country. She is terrified of you, Maz-Sherah. Falconer."

"In the morning, before we slept," I said, "when I told you of the Staff of Nahhashim, from the vision. You said, 'gates.' What did you mean?"

"*Nahhash* is the old tongue for snake, and there is a rift between two great mountains, beyond the Plains of Vazg. It is uninhabitable by man or vampyre at this pass. It is called the Gates of Nahhash, for it is merely a snake pit and nothing more. Although there is a well for drinking there, it is surrounded by vipers and even the caravans do not take that route." Then, she felt for the tender indentation at the base of my throat, which was affection among this new race of beings I now called my own. Her hand felt like fever upon my skin. "You stole her stream and saw the city. You have the power of the Sacred Kiss. That would not have happened if you were just like the rest of us."

"But there's nothing wrong with the rest of you. I am the same."

"Eventually, even the blood does not give us strength. I am the next oldest, after Balaam. How much longer will I last?" To look at her while she spoke, I was amazed. She looked as if she were a woman of twenty-five. "I've watched others reach this, and pass it, until they can only drink from the dead, and that blood offers no strength. Before you came, there was one named Paolo, a monk whom the Pythoness had taken and brought here seventy years before I received the Sacred Kiss. I knew him when he still could recall the past, but I watched him lose his vigor and his will to live. I watched him become truly like a jackal, sucking at the marrow of a bone, drinking from rats and street dogs just to survive another night. Eventually, his memory gone, his words choked in his throat, he slowly began to fall apart. His skin sloughed, and his eyes sank into their holes. I watched as his jaw, which had become long and thick, dropped into his lap as he took his fill from blood I had brought him. They say we live, even in motes of dust. Think of the terror of that. Of a life that is no life, splintered and broken like shards of pottery, unable to move, unable to feed, to have thirst but nothing to slake it. To have being, without form or control."

"It is like death," I said, and thought of Balaam in his tomb.

"I will show you what it's like," she said.

◆ 8 ◆

SHE took me deeper into the chambers beneath the Earth, until we were in a tunnel low and filthy. As I followed her, we came at last to a chamber that was like a tomb.

Bones, and the dust of the dead lay in heaps. One corpse had only recently begun decomposing. Another was just turning to dust from crumbling bone.

"We bring them here when we can," she said. "When their ashes haven't blown across the sand. When the mortals haven't taken their bodies to burn. We do it that they may lie together and remain untouched. Even Medhya cannot find them here. One day, Falconer, I will lie here in this garden of ash, among our ancestors of Hedammu. If we do not go to the Gates of Nahhashim to try and awaken the Priest of Blood, you may one day lay your friend's body here and you will know of all that you might have done."

I felt a pang of guilt, for I did not think I was the Anointed One the tribe had awaited. I knew myself to be a poor boy grown into a dark world, murdered, and brought to vampyrism. I had no royal blood in me. Nor did I have a legend attached to my history. I simply could be nothing more than a creature of the dark, as was she. My eyes welled with tears as I contemplated the enormity of this place—of the vampyric brethren who had fallen in this chamber. Who lay with some degree of consciousness but without movement or power or ability.

It was the worst kind of hell I could imagine. Unending life, but a life that had no hope, no vitality.

She crouched down among the dust, touching it lightly with her fingers. "I can feel my own waning, in the stream. I have less than a full moon left before it begins. When my time comes, I will lie down among them and take my place. I will not fight it then."

"A full moon," I said. "How can that be?"

She turned to gaze up at me. "Balaam ran with the hunt just nights before we found you and brought you to your grave. It is fast, when it comes. The body falls suddenly. It is not a horizon in the distance for me. A hundred years goes by in a heartbeat. I have seen much, drunk much, but I do not want to face this. I know what I will become." I felt such heaviness in my flesh—as if the stream had changed between us. As if a great weight were upon me, simply from her sorrowful glance. She touched the underside of my throat. I felt her heat, her pain. "You are the Maz-Sherah that has been prophesied for many lifetimes. You are the only hope I have. The only hope for our tribe. We must find Alkemara, Falconer."

"Is it enough to survive?" I asked. "If we are all meant for this living dust?"

She put her face against my hands. Then, she turned away. "You had the vision. You bestowed the Sacred Kiss upon your friend. You cannot deny these things. Nor can you pretend they mean nothing. Balaam told me more before he lost his voice completely. He told me that the darkness of our tribe held a sacred light within it, though none could see it."

"And the light?"

"It is the Maz-Sherah," she said. "It is the one who is burdened with the vision who burns brightest. But more than this, Falconer, there is a darkness deeper than the night. She is our mother. Not the Pythoness herself, but the one who created her. She is darkness itself, and her wolves move as shadows. She seeks to destroy us, to take us into the Extinguishing, for as each of her children turned to dust, she grows in power."

· CHAPTER 13 ·

The Legend of the Lost City

· 1 ·

I SAT up that night to hear the stories of my tribe. Kiya brought me the full force of my vision of Alkemara, the lost city, and told me of the Gates of Nahhash, the rift between towering mountains in a land that seemed to be at the ends of the Earth. The others gathered around after feeding and sat in a circle with us.

"You must be careful of silver," Vali said.

"Silver?" I asked.

"It does not reflect us. Silver will destroy us if it enters our blood by way of sword. In its presence, we are helpless," Kiya said. "The legend . . ."

Yarilo interrupted her. "Legends, fables, folktales. It does not matter its origins. It is enough that it is the one precious metal that can be used against us easily."

"It is cursed for us," Vali said. He glanced to Yarilo as if expecting a challenge, but got none. "It is part of Medhya's curse of us."

"The mines," I said, remembering Medhya and the wealth of her land.

Kiya nodded, ignoring Yarilo's gruff manner. "Her priests stole her wealth, and she laid her fury within silver itself that it might forever pain us."

"As superstitious as fortune-tellers," Yarilo said. "There are those who claim it is the curse of Judas in the silver. Or that the silver is of the sunlight that burns us. It is simply a poison to us. Curses or no, I say it is the light thrown by the silver. We are pained by intense light."

"It is the curse," Vali said.

"You believe in the Great Forbidden," Yset said to Yarilo, who grunted in assent. She glanced back at me, slyly. "It is the drinking of another vampyre's blood, for it would not merely destroy the drinker and the one who gives the blood. We are connected through the stream. Our blood is also of one line. To drink of another of our kind brings disease to all of us. It burns through the stream and sends many to the Extinguishing." I learned more of Yset. In her mortal life, Yset had been a slave of a great empire, but soon enough drank of those who had kept her in bondage.

Vali, the beautiful male, with a sleek catlike quality to him and the muscles of a lion, had come down with horsemen from the East, to raid Hedammu. Instead, he had been plundered by the Pythoness, who kept him to herself for many nights. "She bled me slowly. Small cuts all along my body," he said. "We pleasured each other for nearly two moons before she took my life and brought me the Sacred Kiss."

"It was your strong thighs she wished for," Yset said, laughing, reaching over to scruff his hair. "She did not let pretty men pass without tasting of them first."

"Beauty is her downfall," Vali said.

"Beauty is treachery," Kiya said, rising up. "We must hunt."

I sat there, holding Ewen's lifeless body, praying to the darkness that he would return to me.

◆ 2 ◆

WE had passed the fifth night after I brought my breath and blood into Ewen. I wondered if indeed I had passed the Sacred Kiss to him. I did not feed at that time, for I had drunk much in the previous two

nights. I waited, and listened, and tried to understand this new existence and these vampyres, my tribe now that I had left the world of
men and women.

I felt the urgency of their mission: they had been waiting for the
"One" and had had their dreams answered. Was it me? Was this my
destiny? Or simply another illusion from that great stream among
our kind?

"Maz-Sherah," voices whispered in my dreams.

I had seen clearly the Priest of Blood when Pythia had bestowed
her Sacred Kiss upon me. In her breath I had taken a sip of that stream
she had held, and I knew her fear of me then was that she, also, knew
who I might be.

Then, the sixth night after the Sacred Kiss, Ewen looked up at me,
his rich warm eyes glazed with the passage back from the Threshold. I
leaned over to whisper to him of what he had become, and how he
must drink.

The sixth night, I knew what must be done.

* 3 *

B UT first, I had to bring Ewen into our world. He awoke with that
languid thrill that was common to us. He did not rise up with the same
fears and awkward confusion as I had. His body glowed with the life-
in-death, and I held him a while as he began to breathe slowly, catching his breath now and then as if he expected it to stop. I told him of
who we were, and what it meant, at least to the extent of my knowledge. I didn't know, I told him, about Medhya other than that she was
our mother, but that a creature called Pythia, or the Pythoness, had
brought me to this. Then I told him of the others.

I brought him a youth from a distant village, tied hand to foot so
that Ewen might easily take him and drink deep. After he'd drained
that vessel, Kiya brought him a short, rough-looking thief who had
been caught trying to enter Hedammu to steal its legendary treasure.
Ewen, feeling strength, wrestled with the man, rolling about on the
floor, nearly laughing. He took too easily to this new existence, and it

surprised me, for I had to wrestle with my mortal memories before the instinct took hold. Ewen was a natural vampyre. He pinned the thief down and pressed his teeth to the man's collarbone, ripping into his flesh. When he had drunk enough, he leaned back, arching his back and letting out a great whoop as if this were a victory in battle. He had a look of delirium upon his face and giggled when he saw me nearby.

He rose and began doing one of the old dances that the soldiers would sometimes do when together at the night's fire, after drunkenness and joy had taken them. His body shone with the glimmering blood. The others of our tribe gathered around him, licking it from his flesh the way a bitch might lick her puppy when born. All the while, his face clenched in pleasure. He seemed to have more spirit in him than I had seen in his mortal life.

Again, I remembered Pythia's words to me, of how by bestowing the Sacred Kiss, a third being would be reborn from the stream between the two of us: the vampyre was the child of the ancient breath and the new body.

A wholly new incarnation.

Watching him embracing the others, taking to this new world and way of being so swiftly, I envied him, and loved him more. When he saw me watch him with this beaming pride, he drew away from the others and nearly ran over to me, his arms around my neck. He laid his cheek against my throat, and whispered, "I thought I had lost you forever. Do not ever leave me now."

* 4 *

WE spoke more of all that we knew. Kiya and Yarilo spoke more of the Maz-Sherah, and Vali and some of the others engaged Ewen in games of swiftness and tests of his new skills. He had much of the vampyric energy in him. He crawled quickly up the walls to the ceiling above, then dropped down, landing like a cat in front of me.

"I love this new world you have brought me to," he said. "I love the thrill of my lips against a stranger's throat and the shooting of the first blood on my tongue."

"Do you not think we are demons?" I asked.

"Better to be a demon up from Hell than to be dragged to Hell by one," he said. "I was not desired by the Church, nor would I have entered Heaven. I was bound for Hell as it was, my friend, my only friend. I have done things and been done to so that I believed in my mortal life I should never find redemption. But now—now, I have the world. I have the night. I have all."

"Then you forgive me."

"I bless you, Falconer," he said. "I breathe with your breath. I am your servant. Your will is also mine. You are this Maz-Sherah."

"Ah, don't talk to me of that," I said. "I am not the savior of these creatures."

"You are," he said. "You are the light in the darkness. Can you not see it yourself? Your destiny brought you here, to vampyrism, just as mine was to follow you, to serve and protect you as you cared for me in our mortality."

"What if it is all a lie?" I asked.

A shadow crossed his face, as if I had hurt him in some way and yet he did not want me to see the hurt. "We are newly born here. We are brothers, and these creatures are our tribe. I can feel it in the stream, even if you cannot. Mortality was the lie. This is truth."

"No," I said at last. "I feel it, as well. I feel something more terrible than the Extinguishing that comes for our kind. I feel a sense of some terror beyond the stream that connects us, my friend, though I do not know the origin of this fear." I did not speak with him more that night about the dread I had begun to feel in my heart. I had a heavy darkness within my mind, a blind spot of some kind, and in it, as dawn came, I would see Pythia pressing down upon my chest, her talons about my throat as if to stop up my breath completely. I saw shadows where there were none, and felt the presence of spirits just as the sun began to take the day—of shades that were not ghosts, nor were they devils, yet these seemed to be nearby at dawn and at twilight. Yet no others sensed these beings in the stream, nor did any speak of them when I asked if they had noticed unusual shadows.

What I did not then know was that they were agents of yet another darkness, another world of nightmares.

◆ 5 ◆

I should write here of other manifestations of the changes that occur after rising from the sleep of death. All the strictures and confinements of the world of men are gone: one may laugh and yelp and take and have what one wishes. All property of mankind are the toys of my race. All flesh is beautiful, and even as my friend held me and I laughed against his scalp, I felt the love we had for each other grow stronger—and it reminded me of my love for Alienora. All love was the same love, just as all drink was the same drink. This awoke desire, although it was not the desire of man, but the desire for the stream itself.

To go into the stream, to wade into it, and explore its depths, is the greatest union of flesh that can be known. Greater than the act of physical love, and with greater pleasure. It knows no boundaries, no senses, yet it is smaller than a sparrow, this stream, and when you move into it with another, the union is unbreakable. The act of sex is a mere shadow of the stream itself—it is the distant, trickling echo of it—and when Ewen and I went there together, in the stream of each other's existence, I knew that the bond we had forged could not be broken. I drew back from him, breaking from him, from that feeling.

The sensations leftover from the stream were like the shameful afterglow of sexual union.

I felt myself opening to others in the stream, whether these were vampyre or mortal—it didn't matter. My taking of blood allowed me to stream into humans. Just the nearness of another vampyre brought us into each other's streams, the invisible connection of our tribe, one to the other. A touch between vampyres was filled with sensations that surpassed all sensual delight and warmed the blood in our bodies while barriers broke down.

All love was taken and devoured and brought forth again within the stream itself. I could smell the blood of the fresh kill within Ewen, my laughing youth in my arms, and we wrapped ourselves together in the grave and let morning take us into oblivion.

I would write more here about Ewen's first night, but even then my mind drifted back to the vision of this Priest of Blood.

Time was short. When I watched Kiya in the night's hunt, I sensed her fears of the Extinguishing. I felt it as if it were the brush of a raven's wings against my shoulder.

But what pushed me further toward seeking out Alkemara and its secrets were humans themselves.

◆ 6 ◆

MORTAL raiding parties had been coming to our home city for more than a hundred years. Although the land had been sown with salt, and the wells poisoned, and the legends of the blood-drinking corpses, as many called us, of the Devils, as the religious named us, were always among the ignorant people of the villages and cities even several hundreds of miles away, still humankind wanted to capture this fortress. I had seen the treasury when I had been mortal, though I could not visit again once I became vampyre, for the silver of it was a great danger.

In the stream itself, when I drank of a mortal, I had begun to sense something else, as well. Something that had begun to infect those of the area. I could not know then precisely what this new plague within mortals might be, but some strange drive had led them to seek us out. I suppose there was vengeance as well, although I did not then have the conscience for this (for in vampyrism, conscience is for your own kind, not for the vessels from which you drink.) But Yarilo had taken a thickly armored knight from a distant camp and brought him back to us half-dead.

"What do you know?" Kiya asked.

"He was the leader. Their commander. They are coming to burn us," Yarilo said. Lifting the man's head to his face, he said, "Tell her. Tell her what you've told me."

Still, the man wouldn't speak.

"I will enter his stream," she said and bent over his body, taking his forearm to her mouth. She parted her lips, showing her gleaming teeth. She pressed her incisors down into his wrist. A burst of blood, like the juice of a pomegranate met her lips and face. He gasped, and opened his mouth. A groan of pleasure came from between his lips. Kiya kept watch on his face, modulating her drinking of him as his groans grew, then subsided, until they were moans and whimpers as if she were taking his seed from him. Finally, she emptied him as he cried out in a terrible howl that echoed through our tomb.

She dropped his arm to the earth. She came to me, her mouth still full of his blood, and leaned forward to press her mouth to mine in a kiss. His blood rushed into my mouth, then back to hers, and in his stream and her stream, I saw what the man had known.

I saw the others who were coming to destroy us, with crosses and fire and sword. In this stream-vision, *I saw those shadows that whispered, spiraling in clouds of dust around the coming army.*

Afterward, she said, "Whether you are the One or not, it doesn't matter. You have the power of the Sacred Kiss. You stole the vision from Pythia's stream. You are called Falconer, and will be the great bird that will devour the snake and bring us our deliverer—the dragon. The snake is Nahhash, the name of the staff you witnessed and knew by name. And it is a desolate wasteland of serpents. Our tribe does not need to extinguish beneath the weapons of mortals. Those shadows of darkness are coming with the men. They know you are here. You are in danger. We cannot waste a moment more. We must follow your vision. Let us go to the Gates of Nahhash."

◆ 7 ◆

BEFORE we left, Kiya and I went to bid farewell to Balaam. We knelt beside his body and touched his throat, feeling the vibrations in the stream of his immortal being. His bones had fallen from gristle, and his skin was by then nearly insubstantial.

Within moments, I felt a crackle of sparks at my hand where I touched him. I heard a strange voice travel the stream from my fingers to my arm, finally into my mind where I understood the language. "You. You are he," the man said within me.

It was enough for me to understand.

Kiya looked at me, her face lighting up as if she had heard the words as well.

I felt a surge of power within me.

"I will be what you need of me," I told her, and it felt like a sacred vow.

❖ 8 ❖

NOT all of the vampyres made the journey.

Truthfully, I did not want any of them, for though they were my kind, and though I felt them in the stream, I feared that the coming journey would be arduous, and I preferred to go alone.

Still, Kiya told me she had to go, and would show me the Gates of Nahhash themselves. Ewen, who I knew loved me as no one since Alienora had cared for me, likewise demanded my companionship for the journey. "I am your sworn servant," he said. "You are my sun now. My light. I will never leave your side."

Of the males, Yarilo and Vali came. Yset was the only other female to come. But the others did not share this vision or hope. They accepted their lot as blood-drinkers who could move as swiftly as lions, with strength greater than any one man, but did not hope for more and did not think about the Extinguishing to come.

I may have painted a picture of our tribe being of one mind, for the stream gave that illusion. But the currents that ran in the stream often revealed a certain mutinous regard for Kiya's leadership, or suspicion of my designation as the Maz-Sherah, which several had given up believing in decades before. And yet, we were a pack, and felt the stream between us grow. It is what I believe allows vampyres to survive at all—for if we did not form a tribe among our kind, the mortal world could easily wipe each of us from the Earth, one by one.

The six of us set off at the setting of the sun. We stopped at an encamped caravan along the mountain pass beyond our home and took provisions. First, we drank our fill of many of the boys who tended the horses and camels. Then, we took two men who seemed to be merchants of some kind—Turks, Kiya insisted, from the north—and bound them together. Vali carried them like slain deer on his back, and growled like a wolf if they began to struggle. We stuffed their mouths with rags to silence their cries. When we slept—finding temporary shelter within caves—we kept the men tied to and between us so that if they attempted escape, one of us would awaken and stop them. We rationed their blood, drinking as little as possible each night. Additionally, we had to find food for them so that they might recover each day and create more blood for us.

This gave me the idea of how my tribe would need to live. We did not have to kill everyone that we drank from—we could keep them as vessels, then have blood to drink each night.

Kiya laughed at me when I suggested this—she had just lapped at an open wound on one of the men's forearms. Her mouth was smeared with his juice, and she told me that the thrill of the hunt would be gone if we did that.

"It would not be sporting," she said, "and most of what I enjoy about drinking is the hunt for it."

"You are like a cat," I told her. "Playing with the mouse before taking its life."

"It is a game where both cat and mouse play a part, not just one or the other. Victim and victor are two sides of one game. Without either, where is the pleasure?" she said, then lifted the forearm for me to sip.

BEFORE dawn, when we had a moment alone before our cavernous darkness would take us to sleep, she whispered, "He is devoted to you."

I glanced over at Ewen, who already lay down near some rocks, making ready my own bed in the ground. "We shared a homeland and a war."

"It is good to have memory," she said.

Ewen smelled of a fresh kill and of poppies. I cradled his head under my arm. Kiya lay against my back, her face pressed into my neck. She was in my stream now, and I smelled her scent, mingled with my own, mingled with Ewen's. We were like a wolf pack, I suppose, held together by the thought that any one of us needed to feel the stream of the other to feel secure and safe in our tribe.

I closed my eyes, and visions of Alienora came to me, fast and constant, and it was as if I watched her from beneath a dark pool of water. She stood there looking down at her own reflection, not seeing me. I cried out in the beginnings of this dream to her, called for her to touch the water with her hand so that I might reach up and grasp her and draw her into the darkness with me.

The sleep came with the birth of light at the shadowy entrance to our day's newfound cave.

• 9 •

I awoke, screaming in the night.

Kiya knelt beside me, pressing her hands to my forehead as if reading my thoughts. The other vampyres were gathered around me.

"I saw . . ." I began to say, and then tried to put in words the horror from my dream. There were shadows against shadows, writhing toward me, and among them, a blackness beyond any absence of light—a form of a creature, snarling, but shining in the darkness as a beacon from Hell.

"Medhya," Kiya said. "You have seen her."

"The dark mother," Yarilo whispered.

"She speaks to you in dreams," Kiya said.

I felt a madness like no other overtake me. "We must not continue this journey," I gasped. "What I saw, what I know . . ."

"A dream," Kiya said.

"A warning," Vali grumbled.

"I felt it not like a dream," I said, shaking my head. "I felt as if she held me, and these shadows, like pools of water about my ankles, like shackles. Making me look upon her."

"She is the darkness itself," Kiya whispered.

"Eyes like burning embers within the dark," I said. "Her hair moved as if a thousand snakes writhed along her scalp. And yet she had no form beyond shadow."

"She lives in dreams," Kiya said. "Balaam told me that some saw her, but none remembered."

"We hear her," Yset told me. "Sometimes, like distant thunder, we hear her, and know she seeks our destruction."

"We must turn back," I said. "She is here. Somewhere. With us. Hunting us."

"No," Kiya said, bringing her hand to my heart. Her stream was warm against me. "She fears you."

"We will all be extinguished at the Gates of Nahhash," I said, feeling as if it were true. "That is what she showed me." I could not tell them all, the visions of our tribe, skin ripped from the bodies, blood flowing, bones twisted and turned outward, while life, unending immortality, continued even in that suffering.

"She would not come to you in dreams if she did not believe you were the Maz-Sherah," Kiya said. "Her only power is in dreams. If she were able to destroy us now, we would not even be on this journey."

But I was uneasy, for the dream of Medhya had seemed too real. Seeing Ewen flayed, his eyes torn as if pecked by birds, with shadows sucking at the marrow of his bones—the vision did not leave me as we proceeded onward.

Yet something of the dream gave me hope, for Kiya believed that the dream itself was a sign that my fate was there, with this tribe, and my destiny was surely within the place called Alkemara.

◆ 10 ◆

WE traveled nearly a week, running swiftly through the night, grabbing mortals as we found them, drinking greedily. We stole food from new kills and gave it to our captives, who had become addicted to our nightly feedings.

The pleasure of having a vampyre feed is rarely spoken of among mortals, but it is a delight to their senses. It awakens the life instinct for them, and this, in some way, makes them feel a pleasant well-being and purpose.

When one of the captive vessels looked at me after I had drunk from a new cut made along his shoulder, I could tell that he saw me as some kind of god who bestowed upon him a feeling of elation and meaning. Though we continued to keep them bound and gagged, the captives had begun to look forward to the nightly feedings and seemed angered if we found other throats to slash. Keeping them alive was easier than I'd expected, for though we may tear at throats and wrists, our saliva has a healing balm within it that is like a leech pressed to a wound. The wounds heal rapidly, and our pleasure at puncturing the old wound to taste blood was matched only by the heady drunkenness of the mortal vessel that gives him or herself to our ministrations. Kiya was right—we were the cats, they were the mice, but it was a game that required both victim and victor, predator and prey. I gained, on this journey, an enormous respect for our prey, for these two men who began to see us as their messiahs, who only asked a bit of blood in the night in return for the thrill within their blood and the awakening of some lost connection to the divine.

We had to elude camps of men, also. Soldiers, knights, armies—we saw them along the plains. I wondered how many of my old compatriots were there, preparing for battle, as we watched them from a bluff or the mouth of a cave. We were no match for groups of men, particularly ones with weapons and armor. The legends of our kind were exaggerated, surely, for although we could take a family down fairly quickly, if there were several people in a camp who stuck close together, it was not a certainty that we could take on all of them and expect to see another sunset.

Finally, nearly a new moon into our journey, Kiya raced up the side of a boulder and looked to the east. "There!" she cried out. "There! The Gates of Nahhash! If the city of your visions exists, it will be between those great cliffs, Falconer!"

♦ 11 ♦

T HE Gates of Nahhash were two sheer cliffs rising up like giant castles on either side of a narrow path. "It grows narrower still as it continues," Yarilo said. "Many times my father's army ventured here. There were legends of gold and ivory deep within its caves."

"Even then, Alkemara was known," Vali said, "though none knew it by name."

"There are places where the rock traps mortals," Yarilo said, pointing to the cliff's edge many leagues above us. "They say the old gods sit up and push boulders over to murder all who seek entrance through the gates."

"Is that where we go?" I asked Kiya.

"There is no 'where' in that place," Yarilo said. "The far side of this road leads to a terrible desert, many days' journey."

"If this is where Alkemara exists," Kiya said, looking at the sheer rock wall of the cliff. "It is beneath this Earth, not beyond it."

"If this is sacred to the Nahhash"—Yset ran forward to the base of the mountain—"then it is in the nests of serpents here, and if we follow their pathways, we will find the kingdom."

* 12 *

"It is a snake's nest," Yarilo said, reaching into one of the many crevices along the ridge of the hill. When he drew his arm out, strings of small, thin asps had unhinged their jaws, biting their fangs deep into the flesh of his forearm. He shook them off—all were dead. The venom of vampyric blood was greater than that of any snake's milk. Yarilo grinned, his sharp teeth gleaming in the dark light. "It's narrow. Too narrow."

"We can dig," Kiya said. "It's down there. Below us."

"How do you know?" I asked.

"Do you feel the stream?"

I closed my eyes and flared my nostrils, trying to get a feel for vibrations of life. I sensed the others with me, and even the wriggling and coiling of snakes within the ground and among the rifts of the caves. But no other stream came to me.

I was about to open my eyes when I felt it. A gentle tugging. As of a heaviness—a pull to the Earth. It was unlike the stream around us. It drew me to squat down and press my hands against the dirt. I opened my eyes, looking up at the others. "It's more than the stream. It sucks at the Earth. It's an emptiness."

"Beneath here?" Ewen asked.

Yarilo got down on his belly and placed his ear to the ground. "I feel nothing. No underground kingdom. No life."

"Not life," I said. I glanced up at Kiya. "You feel it."

She nodded. "It's slight. But it's like the sucking mud of a swamp. It wants us to find it."

Yarilo glanced warily between us, his brow furrowing. "We can't dig through the snake pit to get there."

I looked across to the Gates of Nahhash—the great tall sheer cliffs on either side of us. Pockmarks in the mountain wall—snake holes and hairline entrances to caverns all along it. "Somewhere here, there must be entry."

I glanced back at our captives—the two Turks, bound together. Our wineskins for the voyage. "Where the snakes are large and plentiful, there we will find the doorway to the kingdom. Bring me drink."

Ewen went and grabbed the men, dragging them to me. I sipped from the neck of one while Yarilo took a taste from the wrist of the other. Replenished, I withdrew from the throat and felt the strength return. The pull of the Earth had taken something from me.

Whatever Alkemara was, wherever it was, it was a vacuum that would steal our strength and what energy we had. We had already begun to recognize this. It filled me with a nameless dread, for we would need power to awaken the sleeping priest if we found him.

"Drink your fill, now," I said to the others who stood watching. "Drain them. You'll need strength."

"Shouldn't we take them with us?" Vali asked. "What if we are trapped there? Shouldn't we have them?"

"Whatever roams the fallen kingdom, it will not let mortals through," I said. "Drink now, and hope it lasts us the journey."

The others gathered around the two mortals, each taking a place near the source of blood, whether neck or heart or shoulder or wrist or thigh. After the drinking was done, we sought out the place of the greatest of the serpents. The whole time, I felt as if we were being watched by someone—someone who followed us yet didn't interrupt the stream enough for any of us to completely sense this stalking form.

I saw it in Kiya's face—she glanced upward along the cliff as if expecting something to be seen there. Ewen reached for me as I climbed up the sheer wall, feeling as if I had the powers of a spider. He touched my ankle. I turned to him, and he said, "I feel something. Something is near."

I nodded, but had no idea what threat lurked nearby. When I had scaled perhaps a hundred feet up the cliff, using the myriad snake holes to grip as I went, and the energy from the newly drunk blood to move swiftly, a crevasse opened up, with a shelf of rock. As I studied this, I saw that it was truly a doorway—an ancient one, for it had carvings of strange figures along its edges, figures of women with wings and lions with the heads of children and the tails of crocodiles. Words, written above the doorway, carved into the rock, in some language long dead. Were they words of warning? Of welcome? I could not know.

I called to the others to follow after me. They did not move as swiftly as had I, and Vali fell twice. His agony on his second fall could be felt in the stream between us, and my head ached with his pain. Kiya clutched the sides of her scalp, closing her eyes. This was only the second time I had experienced the stream's negative aspect—that we were tied together in this afterlife, that our tribe was within one stream, held like clasped hands, one to the other.

Yarilo scuttled down the rock face as agile as a crab, and took Vali's arm, wrenching him up with him so that he might not fall again.

"I feel it," Kiya said, mysteriously.

I glanced over to her, just as she brought herself up onto the rock door's threshold.

Tension clenched at her face. "Something," she said. "Something's coming."

Suddenly, I knew what she meant.

What had been watching us from a distance descended along the wall of rock above me, pouring from the openings with clicks and a strange *shhh* sound. I glanced up the cliff and first saw a blurred motion of bone whiteness moving down toward us in a wave. It became more distinct as it approached.

Scorpions.

As large as my hand. Pure white, and with twin stingers hovering over their backs. Thousands of them coming toward us. I glanced down at Ewen, who struggled up the rock face, barely moving fast enough to make it to the doorway. He would be overwhelmed. The scorpions had already covered the threshold and begun crawling on Kiya, who madly shook them off. I went to try and help her. I heard Ewen crying out, and Vali, as well.

When I looked over the edge, I saw that the creatures had covered them, and were beginning to weigh them down. A stinger struck my foot, then a pincer. More stingers jabbed at my flesh. I felt the intense pain of both my own feelings and the others of my tribe as pain shot through our stream. The poison of these creatures worked into me, and I felt nausea as my blood fought against this strange venom that was unlike any other. It made my blood warm, then seem to boil. I pulled at the creatures, flinging them against the rocks, tearing at their twin over-hangs of spears, then I went to free Kiya from them. After I left her, I crawled downward on the rock, reaching, first Yarilo, who, once I pulled a massive scorpion from his face, had the strength to help Vali with his small demons. And then, Ewen, who I took up in one arm and shook hard so that the monsters would drop to the Earth, far below.

He was in the worst shape, and when I finally drew him up into the doorway, he rested in my arms while I plucked a stinger that had gone deep into the side of his neck.

"Why didn't we sense them?" Kiya asked, when we had all gathered at the mouth of the entrance.

"Perhaps," I said, "they're like us. Perhaps they are not alive."

"Who could create such a creature?"

"Who could create us?" I asked.

♦ 13 ♦

I watched the night sky with its pinprick stars above and the cliff opposite us. "These creatures are a warning. If we were human, their venom would have killed us. Whoever put them here did not think that those who have already been to the Threshold would exist to come here."

"The Pythoness?" Vali asked. His face had been restored to its alabaster splendor from the welts and scratches that had existed there just moments before.

"It must be another," Kiya said. "She would know we might find this doorway."

"Do you think she follows us?" Yarilo asked. He came to me, and sat beside me, gently stroking Ewen's hair. Ewen glanced up at him, then at me. I still felt pain within him, but his blood had stopped its raging within his flesh.

"She follows no one," I said. "If you had felt what I had when she offered the Sacred Kiss, you would know that she is far away from us now."

"Because she fears you," Kiya said, nodding.

"But the other one," I said. "Medhya. It feels as if she watches me, even now."

◆ 14 ◆

W HEN, at last, we crawled on our bellies through the darkness, we saw nests of vipers along rock shelves and among the deep pits along the way. They crawled across our backs and legs as we pushed through. I felt fangs going into my skin, and with each bite and injection of venom, one of the serpents died, drinking the poison of our blood. Holes crisscrossed the tunnel through which we moved, and eventually we came to a dip in the rock that opened into a larger space.

It was like a giant well within the mountain. When I looked up, there was no exit to the sky above. I sensed water far below us.

"We crawl down," Kiya said.

"Or jump."

She then sensed the water, also. "A sea," she gasped. "How, within the mountain, can there be this?"

"An underground passage of water," I said. "If the city was swallowed by the Earth, might not its waterway be also? And yet have you seen rivers that run beneath the Earth, as well? Perhaps this is like that."

She shook her head. "We've come all this way. But . . . water."

"We can go back," Vali said, crouching at the edge, peering down into the vast abyss below us.

"I am continuing on," I said.

"Water," she said.

I raised my eyebrows. "Perhaps."

Kiya said nothing then, but Vali called out, "We grow weak in water."

I nearly laughed. "Silver. Water. What good are we? Have we no strength in us?"

Kiya, angered by my outburst, spat back, "Do not laugh at what you do not understand, Falconer. Water does not harm us. We simply lose the stream within it. It takes much from us."

I took a breath, closing my eyes. Part of me wished to take Ewen and just escape this world, as I had wished to escape the world of mortals through death. Instead, I opened my eyes upon Kiya, and said, "Do not fear the water, then. I will be your strength." To the others, I shouted, "I will be the strength for all of you, if I must carry you each on my back across a raging river."

Yarilo roared with laughter, but Kiya remained angry. I tried to take her wrist in mine to communicate through the stream my respect for her, but she drew her hand back.

I leaned over the edge and tested my hand against the well's curves. "There's enough to hold. We can crawl down. Look." I pointed down the circular wall, and there, carved into the sides, was a steep series of steps, barely more than a slight raised shelf of rock. I felt that some engineer had planned this entrance—that it was not haphazard, not part of being swallowed by the Earth in a cataclysm, but of a plan. As if this mountain had been hollowed out by some great civilization, then, into which, it buried itself alive.

◆ 15 ◆

THE sight of us must have been extraordinary—six vampyres, heads toward Earth, arms and legs outstretched but bent, crawling down the well, clinging to juttings and holes within the structure, following the trace of indentations and narrow shelves that formed the steps down.

Near the bottom, there was the lip of a cavern, and a drop to the ground of perhaps twenty feet. I landed like a cat and remained crouching at the bottom, looking out at the wonder before me. Above, the cavern of many-colored rock, lit with luminous blue ore.

Directly ahead of me, the shore of a lake. Shingles and shells lay beneath my hands and feet. Other more substantial forms made of some kind of plaster also were underfoot. I lifted a flat disk, and turning it over, saw that it was a fragment of a white mask of some kind. Its eyes and lips were shell. As I glanced near where the water met the sand, I saw other broken masks also and proceeded to glance at each of them. Had they once adorned sculpture? Had they been worn? Were they of some heathen religion or of a theater's repertoire? I didn't know—something about them bothered me, for they seemed alien to me, and to anything human I had seen. Yet they were simply masks, most of them reduced to shards.

In the distance, more cavernous space and natural bridges of rock built so perfectly that they might've once been the outer walls of the kingdom. Before me, the water lapped gently at the sands—but it was milk white water, fairly glowing with minute particles of life, as if thousands of tiny white insects or prawns moved in the liquid. When I cupped my hands into it and brought the water up, it was as clear as any lake's. So, it was these tiny creatures—harmless—that made the color so white. When we had all arrived along the shore, we explored its edge, and presently, Vali found a barge docked at some distance as if it had been set there for us to find.

"See?" I told Kiya. "We don't need to swim."

It was little more than a large raft made of wood, but was large enough to accommodate four of us. Vali and Yset remained behind, for we could not risk them walking within the water, as it would drain them of any energy they had left. Yset touched the edge of my stream with her hand, and told me without words that she and Vali would guard the exit to this world at the center of the mountain.

We boarded the wooden vessel and pushed off from the shore. Yarilo and Ewen handled the oar and pike, pushing away from the rock walls, or digging into the sucking earth at the bottom of the water to propel us forward. The smells that came up from the water were of sulfur and a strange musty smell; from the caverns through which we navigated, an icy chill grew as we moved farther and farther from the shore. Just as we crossed beneath a spiked ceiling of glassy stone, Ewen caught my attention with a slight wave of his hand. I went over to him, at the back of the barge, and looked across the surface of the white water.

"Something's there."

"I can't sense it," I said.

"The water interrupts the stream," Yarilo said. Then, slightly startled, he pointed off to the other side of the barge. "Over there."

We watched the surface of the water as it rippled, then went still.

Kiya got down on her hands and knees and looked into the water. "I see . . . someone."

"Someone?"

"It's one of the Alkemars," she said, keeping watch on the milky water.

◆ CHAPTER 14 ◆

The Alkemars

◆ 1 ◆

WITHIN a few minutes, we all saw them—at least four creatures beneath the water's surface, lying as if on their backs, floating beneath the water. I had heard tales of mermaids, but had never expected them to have such monstrous forms. While the faces of these nymphs were fair and lovely, and their shoulders and breasts were as fresh and ripe as any young maiden's, gradually their pale flesh gave way to scales and fins, and barbs as catfish might have, while small barnacles clung to their sides and flat bellies. What would be their thighs melted together into one long tail like that of a crocodile.

"They watch us," Kiya said.

"They're beautiful," Ewen added.

"They're like us," I said. "See? They have the teeth." And indeed, their smiles were sharp, and the barbs of their teeth were like sharks'. "These are our ancestors, perhaps."

"They seem dumb," Yarilo said. "Fish. Monstrous fish. I wonder if their blood tastes of the sea?"

"Fish?" Kiya asked. "Or serpents? See their tails. They are like eels.

Or crocodiles. These are the sisters who guard the entry. They are not to be disturbed."

But Yarilo could not resist reaching into the water to touch the breast of one. Yarilo enjoyed his predatory touching—I had seen him do it with a maiden on the hunt. He had wanted to seduce her with his touch, and truthfully, he had drunk much blood from women who were enchanted by his handsome, rugged face and eyes that lit up like a cat's in the dark.

The Alkemar that he fondled grinned with the teeth of a shark. She rose up to meet his touch, and brought her face above the water. Her eyes were milky white with a yellow center almost like an egg yolk. Her skin seemed darker than it had beneath the water and was translucent in parts, so that beneath the skin, blood pumped, and streaks of nerves ran up and down just behind the glowing of the flesh.

She spoke in a voice that was nasal and nearly a shriek. A language like none we had ever heard came from her, and our senses could not at first decipher it. Kiya told Yarilo to pull back his hand from her—for he was cupping her face.

"She won't bite me," he said. "We're cousins, aren't we? You and I." He leaned over and pressed his lips to her eyelids, kissing her on each.

Then, her sisters rose up from the water, their heads above the surface, and as the white water spilled from them, I saw that they each had a green-gray color to them, like crocodiles of muddy rivers. Their tails, too, which whipped lightly a white froth at the surface. They had scales and prongs of gray-green flesh that were reptilian. These were not mermaids at all—they were as much serpent as the snakes in the outer caves.

As they chattered and shrieked among themselves, I realized that they'd surrounded our barge on all sides. There were nine of them all told, and I began to distinguish some of the ancient tongue they spoke so that words like *Alkemarizshtan* began to mean something to me.

"They are barbaric," I said. "Can you not feel it? They are not like us."

"They are just like us," Yarilo said. "Neither dead nor alive. Neither human nor quite monster. Aren't you? My sweet?"

I detected in him his intention. He had seen the blood, and smelled its vigor. These creatures had blood that we could drink, and his thirst had returned. Kiya must've felt it too, for I saw her nostrils flare. But I didn't trust their appeal, and these creatures were not human and might have been undead just as we were. Death could not feed from death without bringing death.

And yet, I sensed their life force. My nerve endings tingled with the desire to drink from them.

One of them crawled onto a smooth flat rock that jutted up from the water. She pressed her hands against the rock, swinging her tail lazily into the water. She cried out something, and I caught a few words that my mind was able to understand, something about "Damitra." At the sound of this name, another of the sisters looked over at her, then she glanced at the one nearest Yarilo. I didn't like this communication, nor the fact that Yarilo had abandoned the pike and Ewen had dug the oar against some rocks to keep the barge still. The stillness was bad. We were in their territory, and this was a dangerous world that had been buried centuries ago and was not meant to be found.

And then, I knew who had built the barge and left it. Left it for any who came. The Alkemars themselves. They were not simply dumb creatures of some ancient curse. They had an intelligence as a spider might in spinning her web, or a crocodile might, lying deep in the mud in order to fool prey.

"Her name is Damitra," Yarilo said, turning back to me, grinning. "She has told me. She controls the stream here."

I hadn't felt the stream at all among them. Had he? Was this monstrous creature really communicating with him through some form of the stream unknown to us? Or was it simply bewitchment?

I looked at Yarilo fiercely. "Let her go," I whispered with a harsh tone. "She is unclean."

He grinned more broadly, keeping his eyes on her face. "She is very clean." He laughed. "Look at how lovely she is."

I tried to reach over and pull Yarilo back, but it was too late. The liquid wriggling in the water swirled and spiraled in waves, like the beginning of a frenzy among sharks taking down a sea lion. The other

Alkemars surrounded their sister Damitra, the one that fascinated Yarilo, who leaned against her throat, sniffing for her blood.

And then the Alkemars leapt from the surface, grabbing Yarilo by the waist and shoulders as he leaned forward, pulling him beneath the water with barely a splash.

◆ 2 ◆

THE water's surface went still as glass.

Kiya swore, her voice echoing in the caverns. Ewen moved back toward me, clutching my arm. I knelt and stared into the water, trying to see them, trying to see what happened to our companion.

"I can't even feel him in the stream," Kiya said, her senses exploding, as were mine, as we tried to reach him using the only method we knew.

We could not go into the water, both because it would, itself, drain our strength, and also because none of us knew what these creatures might do.

I could not stand it anymore. Seconds had passed, and there was no sound. I dove over the edge, breaking the water's surface. When I felt the liquid pour over me, I felt ice both within and without. It was bone-chilling and did not just end my sense of the stream to my vampyre clan, but exhausted me as I swam within it.

As it was, I had no strength beyond ordinary mortal power, and even that was sapped. I swam through the milky sea, which was less murky beneath than above, and I saw them swimming away, each clutching him with their teeth, shaking at Yarilo's flesh as if they meant to tear him limb from limb.

They no longer resembled maidens in the least, but creatures called lampreys, which I have only seen once before in my life, as a boy when my stepfather had brought one home from the sea. The leechlike mouth with its rows upon rows of teeth, and that otherworldly look to them, as if they could not possibly be created from the Earth or Heaven or even Hell itself.

We all felt it at once: these were not merely daughters of the city of Alkemara.

They were infused with the spirit of the dark mother herself.

One of them had already sucked the flesh from his left hand, leaving shattered bone, and another had attached herself to his groin.

I swam to them, and tried to pull one of the miserable beasts from him, but she had him locked in an obscene embrace as if she were not a separate entity at all but part of his own flesh.

I could not breathe. I rose to the surface and gasped for air. I had traveled several feet from the barge.

Ewen moved the pike swiftly through the water, while Kiya rowed with the enormous oar. Ewen jabbed at the Alkemars as he went, thrusting the pike into them, then drawing it up to jab again. When I reached the barge, Kiya and Ewen drew me, gasping for air, up into it.

· 3 ·

SUDDENLY, Yarilo's face came up, breaking the surface—at some distance. He laughed, although his face had been torn to the bone.

"It is wonderful!" he shouted. "They are beautiful. There are more than you'd think. Oh, they've shown me all of it. All of the glory of it. It was a kingdom like no other."

Quickly, I grabbed the pike and guided the barge over to where he floated. I felt a faint stream again, among us. The binding of our kind. He had not yet been extinguished. He might survive, I thought, if I could draw him from the water soon enough. As I approached, something bumped the barge. Then, another thump against it. We could not move the barge toward him. In fact, we had begun to move away from him, as if on a cushion of air.

Ewen cried out, pointing to the water by the edge of our craft. The sisters were there, beneath it, drawing the barge away. No matter how I paddled or pushed off, their strength was greater.

There were not just several Alkemars beneath us, there were hundreds of them.

Perhaps the feeding on Yarilo had called them up, but suddenly the water bubbled with movement, and we saw these strange serpent-women swimming beneath the water, some drawing us away, others swimming in schools beneath the whiteness, all toward the place where the dark blood of our friend rose to the surface and drifted in a wake behind him.

"Yarilo!" I cried.

He looked over at us, not even aware that these monsters existed to keep all from the ancient fallen city. There was a bright pleasure in his eyes despite the tears at his scalp and along his cheek. Two of the reptilian maidens rose up, kissing his face all over. I could not bring myself to watch as one of them leapt above the water, her jaws unhinging like a snake's, her gray teeth slicing deep into his flesh. They were not like us, after all. They were not blood-drinkers. They ate flesh, and the flesh of the undead or the flesh of the living satisfied their needs.

To watch one of our tribe die was terrible. But to feel the stream—and the Extinguishing in the stream—was a thousand times worse. We felt the pain ourselves, within us, scraping at us as the Alkemar's teeth scraped across his skin until there was nothing but bone. Still, we knew, his life existed in that bone and flesh, and would never again be one being. Never have the essence of Yarilo.

Their faces were covered with his blood, finally, and the creatures no longer resembled in any way the beautiful maidens we had first seen. Their true forms had returned with their feeding.

They were soulless monsters with eyes that were empty and red and their jaws elongated into the crocodiles that no doubt had once been their totems.

These were the accursed of Alkemara, the daughters of the Priest of Blood himself, princesses to a kingdom that was now no more than a buried Necropolis, the female descendants of this subterranean world. Hundreds of sea serpents within this sea.

Hundreds of them, and none with the vampyre consciousness.

• 4 •

WE three sat together on the barge.

I held Ewen close to my breast, and Kiya pressed her lips against my throat for comfort. We felt the end of our fellow, and knew that

Yset and Vali, at the shore in a distant cavern, also felt the pain and searing of Yarilo's Extinguishing. The knowledge of the end came— not the mortal end, which meant a movement toward the Threshold and the world beyond. For us, there was no beyond. When we went, we died out, and there was no god or goddess to relight the flame. Our souls would extinguish.

We felt all this with Yarilo's passing.

Kiya began to chant the tribal song she had learned from one of the ancients who had passed when she was young. Although it was in a language of the Chaldeans, it translated as this:

"When Medhya arose
And found her skin torn
Her children wept and gathered their own flesh
To offer their mother
So that she might hide her shame,
And when they took her blood
Which held the power of eternal life,
Her children wept and set their hearts
On the underworld where the blood of the Earth flowed
That their mother might find sustenance.
But when they stole her children,
Medhya wept,
The Threshold denied them passage.
She begged the gods for flesh and blood
To avenge her children and her kingdom,
She lay at the Threshold, weeping,
For they could not cross into the land of the dead.
When she returned from the Threshold,
She gave her Sacred Kiss and her Curse
And we are now her children,
Fallen ones,
We cannot cross the Threshold again
Once we have returned from it.
Blessed is Medhya for cursing us!

Blessed is Medhya for her death-in-life!
Blessed is Medhya for our tribe of the Blood!
Blessed are our brothers and sisters whose light fades
Into the Extinguishing!
Medhya, our mother and creator,
Lemesharra, Datbathani,
Who drinks from us as we have drunk from her
When the twilight is upon us."

◆ 5 ◆

I felt more bound to my tribe now that I heard the words, and I understood why Kiya had remembered them. She had watched many vampyres go to the eternal nothing and knew that her time approached more quickly than she would have liked. The song-chant was a way of reconciling all of us to the fate of our kind.

At the end of this, the last of Kiya's voice echoed along the cavernous chamber. Ewen gently laid his hand across Kiya's throat, feeling the source of her stream. Because he was so young—not yet nineteen—and she was so old—her body was in its twenties, but she herself was passing a century, it was like mother and son, together, in empathy.

Then, with the Alkemars deep beneath the water, we turned our attentions back to the journey.

We pressed on, moving through the waters undisturbed. The Alkemars had done their feeding. We had lost one of our own to creatures of greater strength and power than our own kind.

What more would we face along the far shore?

◆ 6 ◆

OUTSIDE, it would be dawn. The rhythm of night and day had stopped for us deep within that mountain, beneath layers of rock and earth. Time had seemed to change altogether. As we floated onward, we kept watch for signs of the Alkemars again. Perhaps they drifted beneath the white water, waiting for a chance to come up again for more.

Ewen tried to sleep by lying flat on the barge, but found he could not—the motion of the very slight waves kept him from rest. As we rounded one passage, we were met with a strange sight—thrust in the water, and towering above us, statues that were as tall as any man.

Statues of four bulls stood, spaced apart as if they were at the entryway to some palace. They were made of what seemed to be basalt, and a wedge-shaped writing decorated their bodies. Kiya reached out to touch one of them, and her fingers came away with a fine dust. I noticed on the bulls' legs and haunches, there were small white crabs that looked nearly like spiders, for their legs and claws were long and slender. Their carapace resembled a mask of a human face. On the last of the bulls that we passed, we saw the legs of some rider attached—a child—where the top of the sculpture had been cut off.

We followed the water through chamber after chamber of cavern and low-ceilinged cave, until finally we came upon the end of the waterway. There was no shore, but instead a brown stone stairway rose from the water. It was long and built in terraced rows. We stepped off the craft and went onto the first step above the water.

A stone procession of men stood along the edges of the steps. These were no doubt slaves of some kind, carved into the rock. They held garlands of flowers and sheaves of grain, and beside each man stood an urn of some kind with figures upon it that must have been language. Serpents rested at their feet, coiling about their ankles.

It was the stairs of a ziggurat—and the wide tiers gave way to more narrow ones, until we were climbing the steps of some unfinished pyramid. Small lizards scurried about the recesses of the steps—lizards with shiny black skin and eyes that seemed too small for their diamond-shaped heads. My heart began to beat swiftly in my chest—I felt as if we were closer to our goal than I had expected. As long as we had survived the Alkemars, we would be safe.

As we reached the main landing of the steps, perhaps forty or so steps up, the cavern gave way to a larger space. It was not a pyramid at all—but a vast desert plain beneath a wider, greater canopy of mountain. Surprisingly the sun came through from a narrow gap in the mountaintop—high above us. It was like the center of a great cathedral, more gigantic than any mankind could devise. The mountain was completely hollow at this point. The crevasse above that admitted the sunlight cut it into a straight line.

A thin shaft of light formed a perfect wall before us, each end of it touching the rock face.

We would not be able to pass it until nightfall.

And yet, beyond it, we could see the blur of the city itself.

My vision failed me somewhat. I was still recovering strength from the underground waters, and the sunlight, which blinded us, didn't improve the situation for me. Ewen acted as my eyes, as best he could.

"It is a vast city," he said. "I have never seen a fortress like it. It shines like gold and has darkness in the form of giant stone figures all around it, at every gate. There are others there. Dead. Bones in a field. Like the brambles of the Great Forest—a Forest of Bones is ahead of us. In them, something moves, although I cannot see it clearly." Beyond that, he could not see more, for his eyes burned from the sunlight. Kiya's eyes were worse when seeing the sun's light, no matter how diminished that light might be, because of her age.

We chose to return to the edge of the steps, well above the water, to sleep until night came. As we lay down on the damp, slick stone, I felt leeches of some kind pushing against the flesh of my calves and along my feet. I glanced down—as soon as they tasted of my blood, they died. Ewen slept in Kiya's arms, and I kept watch for a bit, brushing off the dying leeches from each of them before finally succumbing to the little death of the day.

◆ 7 ◆

I dreamed that day of Pythia herself, who had made me and brought a third being into my soul—the vampyric self. I saw her face in its glory and power, as she pressed my mouth to her nipple. As I drew strength from her red milk, she whispered to me that I should not trust the vision, nor the legends, for the source of all power and of the prophecies were not as they seemed. A baby again, held by her, I looked up at her face. She was no longer that vampyress, but was the Queen of Heaven herself who held me, but not in the flesh, but of the statue that had been in the Baron's chapel.

And then, I saw another, behind the Pythoness.

The dark mother of all.

Medhya.

Her burning eyes.

"You will see your friends tormented until the end of days," she whispered.

I awoke to the night.

The sun had just set beyond the thin line of sky between the cavern opening above us.

As the darkness deepened, my eyesight improved, and I saw the Necropolis for myself.

II

ALKEMARA

CHAPTER 15

The Necropolis

· 1 ·

A S the moonlight from the chasm above us sent a glow of dark light along the distant citadel, I gasped—and I was not alone in my awe. I heard shocked sounds from Ewen and Kiya as they saw this new underworld.

Alkemara itself had once truly been a great city, for it towered into the enormity of the cavern, greater than any fortress I've ever seen. And yet, even so, it was in ruins, for its great marble columns had fallen, and the statues of its gods, the height of the walls itself, were in enormous broken pieces at its gates. The head of a jackal god, as large as any ship, lay beside its own eagle foot. The stone that had been shaped for these gods was like a dark onyx, only it had the properties of reflecting light from within the stone itself. On the path that my companions and I walked, more rubble had drifted and eroded from the great city.

The road itself was made of human bone—rib cages piled up to the left and right of us, and human skull fragments crushed into powder beneath our feet.

Thousands had died there, once, and perhaps hundreds more had come to discover the secrets of the place.

Between the bone, a strange vine grew, and blossoming from the vine, as if it were a flower of midnight, tiny perfect petals that were bluish purple to my sight.

Even more strangely, as we walked by this vine, I detected that it moved slightly—just a quiver—as any of us neared it or the bones. My curiosity got the better of me, and I crouched down, lifting a vine.

Even as I did so, one of the blossoms—as small as a beetle— opened up in full bloom. At its center, a dark red spot that grew veins like spider legs out into the inner petals. I could not resist its beauty or charm. I touched the center of the petal to feel the velvet of it. It was moist and of a fleshy texture, and emanated a slight scent of musk.

Too suddenly, the petals closed around my finger, and I felt a sharp sting. I withdrew my finger quickly. I did not feel a great deal of pain, but it was as if I'd pricked the end of my finger on a tiny thorn. A drop of my blood welled up, and the thinnest layer of my own flesh had come off and remained, a ragged particle of skin within the blossom.

"These flowers are vampyres," I said to Kiya, who had begun to walk ahead of me. I showed it to both of them. "It wants to drink from me."

Again, I remembered from the vision when Pythia exhaled into my lungs—*the Priest of Blood said, "You must bring the vine and the flower that I might know you."*

I tore the vine from the Earth, winding it around itself until it was a small bundle. This, I tucked into my pouch. I glanced at the bones nearby and lifted a fragment of one, also. It was sharp and rounded, and felt icy in my hand.

We were in a land of blood-drinkers; even the flowers drank it.

I could not fathom what god or devil had created such a place.

As we walked farther, we came upon mounds of skulls and low walls made up of human rib cages. More of the vines grew among the bone. The flowers were closed for the most part, but as we neared them, they began to open their petals. I sensed Ewen's fear. All of us had it, but he had it worse. Perhaps among mankind, we would not be as afraid of destruction, but this Necropolis was more powerful than we ourselves. It felt as if we were at the Threshold itself, and that if we went the wrong way or took the path to any other than the great entry gate, something more terrible than even the Alkemars and their progeny might await us with open jaws and scimitar talons.

Kiya grasped my wrist to stop me before I stepped into a recently rotted corpse. I looked down at the man—a thief of this ancient tomb, no doubt. The leech-creatures had sucked him dry, for he had their small, childlike imprints along his chest and belly, and his skin was tight against his organs and bones. His eyes were missing, and lips had been ripped from his mouth. "No one has come here and returned," she said.

"Mortal men," I said. "Nothing more. Our tribe has not been here." But I thought of Yarilo, taken by the Alkemars into the white foam, their pincers tearing his skin from him. The Alkemars and their kind had power over us. If they were a thousand years old, or a hundred thousand, they had magick beyond our own meager abilities. Whatever existed within this mountain was more than mere vampyrism. This was the world of gods, not of the living and the undead.

And then I saw a sight that filled me with a greater dread.

On poles, there were the skeletons of our brethren, hanging upside. The fangs from their broken jaws jutted upward. Buried in their rib cages, crude stakes made of silver. The left leg of each of them had been cut off and thrust between their jaws, a barbaric way to keep vampyres from returning from the Threshold. The strange vine had entwined through their eye sockets and moved up along their bones, the flower in full bloom as it twisted about the pelvis and bones of the right legs.

Extinguished. Tortured even in that nothing of the Extinguishing. Carved across their skulls, the word, *Maz-Sherah*.

◆ 2 ◆

"OTHERS have come before us," I said. "To fulfill the prophecy."

Kiya moved toward them and began cutting them down, careful to avoid the silver thrust between their ribs.

"There is only one Maz-Sherah," she said. "It is you."

"Perhaps I am one of many," I said. "Perhaps the dark mother exists here. Perhaps these . . ."

"Only one is truly anointed," she said. "These were false."

Suddenly, Kiya crumpled to the Earth as if her legs had failed her. I crouched down, wrapping my arms about her to hold her steady.

She did not have to say it. I felt it. Her stream was too weak.

She stared at the hanging skeletons of our tribe. I knew what she thought: she was near her Extinguishing. She had hidden any failings carefully. But she no longer could.

"I am able," she said, pushing away from me to stand again.

"Do not be afraid."

"I fear nothing," she said, her voice like steel. "Maz-Sherah."

She continued cutting down our long-extinguished brethren, and when she had them on the ground, she began to say a Medhyic prayer that their souls might find peace even in the endless eternity they now faced. She kissed each skull and drew the bones from their jaws.

Then she walked ahead of me, toward the city.

"What awaits us?" Ewen asked.

I saw terror in his eyes and felt protective of him.

"You have met death once," I said. "Do not fear it again. If this is a true prophecy, then we will see what we have come to see."

"The prophecy is for the Maz-Sherah," he said. "Yarilo is gone. Perhaps each of us will meet similar fates."

"We will find what we are meant to find," I told him. But I did not add that what we might find could be our Extinguishing. If our destruction would be at the jaws of the Alkemars, or among this poisonous Necropolis, it might not matter. I truly began to believe in my destiny. Perhaps the ripping at the stream, when Yarilo was taken, had begun this process. The leeches and the lizards and the deadly flowers might have been enough to keep human predators and thieves out. But whoever or whatever had built this kingdom had learned to weaken our tribe, as well.

We were expected.

I thought of the prophecies, and of Kiya's belief that I was the "Anointed One."

But whatever intelligence and sorcery had built this place, had also known that the Maz-Sherah would come, and had no doubt wanted "the One" to be alone, to have no defenses, and perhaps to extinguish in Alkemara.

With fallen gates before us, I led the way along the rubble of twisting road that ran through the luminous valley of bones.

◆ 3 ◆

A T the entryway, which was many leagues from where we'd first arrived at the great boneyard, we could better see the enormity of that city. The gates were two stone giants connected by bolts and crossbars, locked from the outside. They wore the armor of ancient warriors and were entirely naked in dress with the exception of helmet and chest plate and shield. They were the sentries, and with the exception of a few gaps near the base of the gates, they had not been touched. Whatever had buried this city within this mountain had come from within it, not from some enemy beyond its walls.

"It's a prison," Kiya said.

Entering through a long gap in the structure of the left-hand gate, we felt a current shift along the stream. We experienced a complete darkening of our eyesight and a blurring of the edges of things as if some gas were in the air that distorted what we saw. Shadows existed that could not be defined as figures or the last standing walls of a building. Statues that had fallen along the promenade were also of indistinct feature for no other reason than that our vision was impaired.

It was as if we were underwater—seeing this city was like viewing a shipwreck beneath the sea, where some shapes along the wreck were indefinable while others were perfectly clear. Great stone faces looked up through the hollow mountain, and the hands of giants—some marble, some basalt, some gold—lay upturned where they'd fallen during the cataclysm that had destroyed this land.

Along the walls, a labyrinth of pathways ran through chambers small and large, filled with more bones and fragments, more signs of life once lived. Some of the walls were painted with friezes that told parts of the story of the time. The images depicted a family or a brothel or athletic pursuits. A man embraced two maidens whose legs encircled his waist; a matron instructed handmaidens in their work; youths of beauty and muscle played athletic games with disks and balls and spears.

Walls without roof or doorway stood like pieces of a lost puzzle. Pottery in shards, some intact, lay among the jagged earthen floors. As we walked toward the center of the city, down the wide boulevards, we saw shadows imprinted against the walls themselves—shadows of men with their arms raised as if in supplication, of women clutching their children close, of horses and of dogs, as well as winged men like demons. Whatever had taken Alkemara, had dealt it many blows—from floods to earthquakes to this flash of light that had captured the shadows of the dead the moment before death met them.

Then, at the middle of this labyrinthine city, within a circle that proved to be a confluence of several roads, like the sun with its rays going outward, we came upon an enormous temple.

"There she is," Kiya said, pointing upward. "Lemesharra."

◆ 4 ◆

M A D E of black marble, domed at its top, with an arched entryway atop sleek dark columns, it was the tallest building in the city.

The statue of Lemesharra, herself, towered at its magnificent doorway. She wore the cloak of eagles, and her face was masked with gold that gave her the look of a jackal. Her headdress was a garland of flowers and leaves and fruits of the Earth. Her breasts were large and ripe, exposed beneath her cloak. She had wide yet inviting hips—the hips of the Mother Goddess, of the one who entices men to dwell there and bring forth new life into the world before destroying it. Entwined about her sandaled feet and up to her thighs, twin serpents with the faces of her other aspects, Datbathani, and Medhya, as Kiya pointed out, who knew how the tripartite goddess had been worshipped. Medhya, the immortal mother, Datbathani, the queen of serpents, and

Lemesharra herself, the bringer of life from death and death from life. A written language that resembled the prints of bird's talons as well as pictures of animals and men adorned her outstretched hands. In one hand, a young child rested; in the other, she carried a short, curved knife that was almost like a scythe, but with toothlike edges to the blade.

We passed beneath her immense form. I glanced up, looking at the towering woman who was the third aspect of the legendary origin of our race. I did not worship stone statues, no matter how tall, nor did I believe that Medhya or Lemesharra or Datbathani was here, in any of her aspects. But part of me wanted to believe that a single consciousness had formed our kind, a unique mother, a bloodline passed mouth to mouth, breath to breath, all the way back to this, our source.

The same mother who wished our torment upon us.

The same mother who came to me in dreams and whispered of eternal suffering.

WE pressed on, into the temple itself, which at first was a long corridor of yellow stone, then came to resemble catacombs, but without the bones of the dead. At the end of one part of the corridor, lay a central, domed room.

Beautiful youths and maidens stood in a semicircle before us.

• 5 •

I walked across the slick marble floor to them.

They were the product of a taxidermist's art. Some madman had created these stuffed creatures. They were as statues, frozen to the spot. I touched one of the youths, and his face crumbled in my hand, like dust from some ancient fabric. Then I pressed my hand to his bare shoulder, his arm fell and cracked into a heap on the floor.

We walked chamber to chamber. More of these repugnant statuary of some unimaginable hunt graced each. A woman worked at needlepoint in one chamber while a little girl and boy sat her feet. A student of some kind reciting to a scribe who wrote upon a scroll; two youths with leather armor upon their shoulders, dark swords in their hands, frozen in a battle; a man and woman in their mating; a youth dancing with his older mistress; a youth taking a small hand ax to another's throat for what seemed to be a bag of coins; in another, a naked discus thrower posed for a sculptor who had his carving tools against a large block of rock. The tableau of each chamber had a singular effect.

It was to haunt us.

To remind us of our mortal lives.

I looked to Kiya to see if her vampyric nature had erased any thoughts of this kind. I expected her to laugh at each figure, but she expressed a deep sorrow in her eyes. These humans were not our prey, and something in their aspects made me wonder why I felt such empathy, why when I could easily take the life of a youth or a maiden and drink so deeply as to drain them into a dried cocoon of flesh as a spider might its fly, why then did I feel anything for these people who had, centuries before, been killed and emptied and stuffed and posed?

Kiya said it first. "These are our ancestors."

It was a shock to hear her voice say it, but when she did, I knew it was true. These once-living statues had been tortured and killed, one might presume, then stuffed like an eagle or a lion for decoration.

Sorrow and even pity clutched at my throat. It was what made me clasp Ewen closer and reach for Kiya when she stopped at a doorway and watched the scene that had been set.

They were vampyres, as the hanging bones had been. Whoever had done this had destroyed them, then had mounted their bodies as trophies, obscene statuary, as if this were a demented child's playhouse.

◆ 6 ◆

BEYOND these chambers, another great hall came into sight. It had dark translucent walls, leading to an even narrower corridor that descended below, then rose again until, at its center, another domed room, completely empty of the engravings and carvings of the entryway.

The dome above was of an odd shape, and dark as the walls. It had a spiral of jutting stones within it, curved into the ceiling. The chamber was curved as the ceiling. Six doors led off this room, and the paths from them seemed to move upward. The doorways were arched and adorned with six serpents—each had a markedly different face and design. The first seemed to be a common asp, but its tail became crocodilian in the manner of the Alkemars so that it seemed to be a serpent of the sea. The second had small limbs, and its twin fangs were curved upward like a boar's tusks—this was the legendary salamander of fire.

The third serpent had wings and a tail that circled around itself until it came to a point—a serpent of the air, or dragon. The fourth was hydra-headed, and its many heads seemed like a woman's hair. This was the underworld's serpent. The fifth had no special designation, for it seemed a snake as any other, save for its tail, thrust into its mouth. And the sixth serpent image had the head of an eagle, the legs of a lion, the wings of a dragon, and its tongue, jutting from its beak, seemed to be afire. This was the serpent-as-gryphon, I suppose, or perhaps this spoke to a deity unknown to me. Even more remarkable was that each serpent seemed to be on its back, as if moving upside down, although their heads curved so that they were at least staring out at the world upright.

"Each to each," Kiya said.

I glanced at her and saw a worried expression upon her brow.

She explained. "Each doorway is meant for one of us, and only one of us."

"But there are six," Ewen said. "There are three of us."

"Six of us set out on this journey," Kiya said. "Whoever built this saw us coming, thousands of years ago. We are expected here, at this place."

I glanced at the doorways again. "But no one knew that all six of us would not arrive here." I remembered Mere Morwenna, having once told me about prophecy, and how it was not always the journey expected. Even this prophecy—it had anticipated six of our tribe coming this far. The guardians of Alkemara, those sisters of the milky water, took one. Vali and Yset waited on the far shore for us. Three of us had arrived, but there were six doorways into this oblivion.

"These doorways are traps," I said. I crawled up the side of the wall, to the edge of the dome itself. I looked at the room from that perspective, trying to see if there was any sign, any symbol we could not clearly see, that we had somehow overlooked. "We do not enter these new corridors. We do not have to."

Ewen glanced up at me. His face cheered me, for it was so innocent of the darkness that had seeped into my own soul. He reminded me of joy, and of home.

"The doorways were meant to separate us. Whether our destructions are down one pathway or another, I cannot say. But whoever built this temple understood that we would go down one path or another." I crawled along the upper platforms above the doors, where the serpents had been sculpted. "This chamber is itself important. We are at the center of the temple itself."

Kiya, whose sense of smell and heat was better developed than mine, began to sniff at the air. She went to the doorways, touching the stone carvings. She pressed her face against them, and said, "There has been blood in this room. I do not know when, but it awoke my thirst. It is old, and dried, but there has been much here."

Ewen crouched down, examining the stones of the floor. As he did so, I saw how the stones had been laid out in circles around one another, in a spiral form. I began to think that we'd been brought to the center of a great labyrinth. I closed my eyes, trying to recall the vision I'd had at the moment of my rebirth in vampyrism.

The altar. The priest. The woman wearing the golden mask. Pythia on the altar, to be sacrificed.

Then, I knew.

I leapt down to the floor and felt instinct take over as I wandered the spiraling pattern of stone. "Here. It was here."

"How?"

Kiya came over to me, bending down, crouching also, pressing the side of her face to the floor to pick up vibration and scent.

"I smell death," she said. "Nothing more. An old stink of blood, everywhere. These stones, washed with it over many lifetimes. But nothing more."

I pointed to the floor. "The altar is beneath us."

She sat back on her haunches, crossing her arms across her chest as if she were cold. She drew out her dagger, and pressed it against the stones. Scratches of dust and fragment came from it. "It's solid."

"To get here, we walked up the steep stairs from the milky waters. I have followed my dream too much. The temple is inverted. This is the lowest depth of it." I waved my hand toward the serpent doorways. "Those go toward the Earth, yet their paths go upward. If we followed the paths, I would surmise that we'd find the milky waters again. We have been descending underground since we entered the temple." Then I tapped on the floor. "This was once ceiling, and that," I pointed upward to the domed rooftop, "was a basin for catching the blood of sacrifice. See the way the stones in the dome spiral downward? It is a drain at its top, although this has been sealed."

"Then how do we go down, to the altar?" Ewen asked, rising from the floor.

"We go back," Kiya said, but her voice was filled with dread.

I understood why, seconds later. We felt it, in our stream. Something haunted this place. Some presence, heavy and smothering. It was as if we were inside some monstrous body, some breathing, living creature made of carved stone and filled with the bones of others. We each kept close to the others. I smelled the odor that Kiya had mentioned—like dried chrysanthemum and ambergris as well as putrefying corpses. It had grown stronger since we'd remained long in the domed room.

Something's changed, I thought, and wondered if Kiya could read me. It wasn't anything other than the sense that there had been an awakening since we'd arrived. The sentient being of this temple, whatever fueled it, whatever remained within it, knew we were there and had come to a state of growling wakefulness. All around us, this invisible presence became palpable, yet untouchable, unknowable. I began to think of it as male. I can't say why, but it felt masculine.

Ewen went to the wall by the way from which we'd entered and put his hands upon it as if to crawl up it, but instead, put his ear to it.

"It's a puzzle for us," I said. "The serpents. The chambers. There's something we've overlooked. Someone has put out a game for us. The pieces are all here."

"The vampyre statues," Kiya completed my thought.

◆ 7 ◆

WE returned along the narrow corridor to the chambers of the trophies, all stuffed and sewn room by room. I found a thin dagger made of material that seemed to be fashioned of amber—it was in the girdle of a man who held a maiden aloft and penetrated her in a mockery of sexual pleasure.

Kiya gathered up the sewing needle and skeins of thread from the woman in one room, and Ewen returned with coins in his hand. I turned these over and saw some ruler of old upon them. None of us could identify the words upon it, but there was no doubt that the coins were made of gold.

Still other things, mainly small, made to fit in a pouch were found; Kiya brought the scroll from the room of the scribe and student. Ewen brought the sculptor's tools in the tableau of the artist. In the chamber of the warrior scene, I took an enormous sword and scabbard. I lifted it up—it was of some heft and size, and I drew the sword from it. It was carved of a translucent black stone. Along its lower edge, the stone had been shaped like pointed teeth, and it was sharp to the touch. I hoisted it and bound the scabbard about my waist, securing it with a shoulder strap. I had missed the feel of a sword, and though we did not find them useful—for they could be clumsy in our attacks on prey—I did not want to leave this treasure behind.

When we'd gathered the finds, I said, "Some craftsmen has put these elements together. As if for us. An audience."

"To play a game," Ewen said.

"Each scene is meant to be understood," Kiya said. "The woman who sews is making a shroud. In the room where the scribe writes, knowledge is passed." She brought forth the scroll that she'd put in the sling along her shoulders. When we unrolled it, I could see the slight bits of hair along the parchment.

"Flesh," I said.

Kiya nodded. She pointed to the picture-writing up and down its length. Images of herons and of crocodiles as well as of jackal and serpent. Now and then, these were interrupted by the image of Lemesharra, wearing the same jackal mask that the statue at the front of the temple wore.

After we took our inventory, wondering at the uses of these things, we returned to the entry hall where we had first seen the stuffed skins of the vampyres.

They were in a ring, as they had been before. Kiya noticed something about them. "All of them are doing something. They are waiting for someone. Waiting on someone."

"These are servants of the one entombed here," I said. "Meant to stand guard against those who enter. They're meant to scare us, to warn us. Our tribe. Ancestors. These were extinguished, skinned, then raised again like scarecrows."

"As those outside were," Kiya said.

"The other Maz-Sherah," I added, feeling grim about our prospects.

I traced a wide circle with my foot at the edge of each of their heels.

Beneath a thin layer of dust I noticed interlaced designs on the floor below us.

"A seal," I said, withdrawing my sword from its scabbard. I traced what I saw as a door of some kind, a perfectly round reflection of the dome above us, and the dome basin far below. "Between where we stand and the last chamber we entered, there is another chamber. We must open it."

✦ 8 ✦

WE made little progress over the next two hours, using an ax, dagger, sword, and sculptor's tools, as well as other items gathered from the chambers. It would soon be daylight in the world. We needed to rest, and also to drink, but did not know how we would be able to do so. Had we come this way for nothing? Had we come to find a tomb that meant nothing, that contained nothing? This dust-thick chamber with its dead vampyres posed as if in some drama for our benefit?

The stink of death had increased, and although we were not living creatures in the mortal sense, still the smell of rotting death brought us no solace.

When we slept that day, close to each other there on the floor, guarded by the ring of the vampyre statues, I could not even sense the stream around us, though I knew it had to be there.

Somewhere beyond this temple, beyond this city and its mountain rock, the sun arose, and the seeping blackness of oblivion entertained me with its peace.

I awoke sharply, feeling as if my senses had become keen again. I sat up. Kiya, already up, gazed down at the circular seal in the floor. Ewen, beside me, coughed as he awoke, as if he could not breathe.

"I had dreams of terrible things," he gasped, when he had his breath again.

"Of what?" I asked.

"Of a mortal," he said. "One such as I have never seen. He watched me, sleeping, and put his hand upon my hair. He made me think I would end like . . . like one of these." He pointed to the statues near us.

As I rose, I thought I saw a handprint in the dust near where my head had rested.

Was it Ewen's? Kiya's? But it seemed larger than either of their hands. It struck me: someone else had been there. While we slept. I showed it to Kiya, and she nodded. "There is a watcher. But I have no sense of him."

"Who would watch us, but not destroy us?"

"A cat plays with its mouse before slicing it open," she said. Kiya got down on all fours on the floor, using the amber dagger to scratch away at a curve of the sealed door below our feet. She pointed out the edges where we'd worked on it the previous night—all our work was for naught, for it was as if the door beneath us had resealed itself.

I dusted off much of the door and saw that the designs in the stone seemed to be in small round shapes. "There is a key to this, I'm sure of it," I said. "But what is the key?"

Kiya brought the scroll out, unrolling it. It was as long as the door itself, but not nearly as wide. Yet, when she placed the scroll in such a way that it bisected the middle of the seal, the picture-writings seemed to line up with some of the carvings in the floor, although many were very faint.

"If only we could understand it," she said.

"There's the sword." Ewen pointed to the lower left hand area of the scroll. He was right—the black sword that I had secured to my waist had been depicted in the scroll. Likewise, we saw the sewing needle made of human bone and the thread of human hair among the images of jackals and birds. Then, three gold coins, which seemed to be resting over three perfectly small round indentations. An outline of what also might have been a human hand was depicted in the scroll, and beneath it, a very faintly similar shape in the stone door.

Then, as I put my fingers over the scroll, I noticed that by covering two letters of this strange alphabet I could make out some letters.

"Look." I pointed this out to Kiya, who was the reader among us.

"Aleph," she said, looking at the letter. She shrugged. Then, she covered the next four letters and came up with another letter. Then another, and another. Then, the letters stopped. The rest of the scroll was unreadable, full of pictures and wedge-shaped curves. "The only word it spells is a name," she said. "Ar-tep. Artephius."

"Is that a place?"

"A person, a place," she said. "Or perhaps the name is an indication of something else. It is of no consequence—it may be the signature of the scribe who created this."

"Give me the coins," I said, looking up at Ewen.

When I had them in my fingers, I removed the scroll, and placed three of the coins in the round indentations of the door beneath us. Then I took the sword and laid it down exactly in the arrangement of the scroll that corresponded with the door. We took each of the materials and did this.

"It's a map of some kind. This is a map for this doorway," I said. "Only . . . only it will not open."

"The hand," said Kiya. She put her hand, palm down on the indentation where it was meant to go.

Nothing happened. Ewen followed suit. They looked to me, and feeling that strange feeling of being "the One," I put my hand down on the stone, but nothing happened.

Then I arose and went to the guardians of the place, the statues of the dead vampyres.

I tore the hand off one youth and brought it back with me.

◆ 9 ◆

I set the hand into the recessed stone.

Suddenly I heard the turning of some mechanism, like the creak of the wheels and ropes of a trebuchet. It was an engineered doorway, and only when each item had been placed into it, would it begin to work. All around us, the bowls of oil lit up with fire, without benefit of fusil or flint, casting flickering shadows all around us. I pressed the hand a bit harder into the stone.

Again, the grinding of wheels and rope; the round doorway beneath us began to sink farther downward. I drew the scroll back, and we watched as the seal sank farther and farther—perhaps two or three feet down.

Then the room itself began to vibrate as if from an earthquake. Rays of etched stone appeared out from the round door, and as each appeared, separated from the one next to it.

The chamber itself began moving—its walls dividing, and the floor beneath us splitting as if run by some mechanism.

CHAPTER 16

The Tomb

• 1 •

THE walls around us moved with that mechanical grinding sound, then closed together so that entirely different chambers appeared beyond us—not the corridor back or forward, but other pathways. I had been wrong—it was not just one chamber level between us and the bottom level. It was a vast canyon of a room that stretched downward.

We each stepped onto one of the floor segments. The stuffed vampyres seemed to move in a strange dance—although no limb moved, their entire bodies seemed to float by on the great jagged plates of the floor, until much of the floor had been pushed back to the walls. We stood there as if looking down from a cliff. An icy wind rose from the chamber below. Near one edge of the newly moved flooring: a platform at the top of a stone staircase, leading downward to the center of the newly formed pit below us. We only had to step floor piece to floor piece to get to it, like hopping stones across a stream.

I grabbed up the black sword and went first into the icy depths of this new hell.

As I went, I was on guard, for I smelled death more strongly— mortals were within, flesh was there, and even blood. It was strong and terrible and not of the usual enticement of mortal blood, which was nearly erotic in its pull to me. Frost lined the steps so that we had to be careful not to slip. Some engine churned and spat, humming like a thousand bees. Although I would only learn of such things centuries later, it was a freezer of some kind—whether natural or unnatural, I could not then know.

A blue light began to form the farther down we went. Then, I saw what looked like white wheels and gears and locks shifting and clicking as if in some mechanism.

Human bones were stacked together in bundles, interconnected, some carved into rounded wheels, others a semblance of their former existence: femurs and pelvis and skull. They moved together, clicking, turning, the engine of this pit.

Who in Heaven or Hell had created this? It was an engineering marvel, and it operated without human hands pushing or pulling at it. The crack of bone, the hiss of some unseen steam (for how could there be steam in such a frigid place?), and the slight squeal of the turning gears all accompanied our descent. Only centuries later did I see clock- work that resembled this marvel, the great towns in Europe with their clocks that loomed above all else, with their work visible to any who went with the clockmaker into the tower. But none would be made of bone as this one was. It was as if it were the machinery of the Devil himself.

As the blue light brightened, I saw shapes and shadows along the wall. They became clearer as I descended closer to them.

It was a large chamber full of mortal beings. There were ropes of some strange red hue that ran between them, and around them like a spider's web. They hung suspended along the curved walls and wore masks of gold and silver upon their faces, men and women, youths and maidens. They hung like stags in the kitchen butchery after the hunt. Their flesh had been made so cold that it was nearly blue, with a limn- ing of frost at their extremities.

As I came closer to these mortals, I saw they were not bound in rope at all, but some kind of blown glass, in tubes that wrapped and curved about the bodies. Blood pulsed between these unfortunates. More than twenty such human cattle hung suspended like this. In their backs, was a series of thick blades thrust into their spinal columns, fixing them to the curved wall of the chamber.

My heart began to beat fast, for I was thirsty for what would sustain me, as I knew my companions would be. And yet, this terrible hanging garden of flesh and pulsing blood was beyond even our monstrous imagination. Ewen was the first to touch one of the maidens, just around her belly. "She's like ice," he said.

I followed the lines of glass tubing as it descended to a point behind the stairway. There, at its base, was a long, wide crystal box, of thick and workmanlike design.

Within it, the blurred form of a man.

Blurred, because it was surrounded by some kind of darkness or shadow that I could not fully make out. As I touched the crystal tomb, I heard Kiya cry out on the steps above me. I looked over at her, then in the direction she moved. It was Ewen—he had already pressed his teeth into a maiden's arm to drink from her.

The thirst had overwhelmed him, despite the danger.

Kiya grabbed him by the shoulders and drew him back, but he turned, and said, "She's good. The blood is *good*."

The blackest of blood soaked Ewen's face.

An image arose in my mind that was perverse and wonderful at the same time.

We were in a wine cellar. This was where he kept his best vintage.

Or someone kept it stocked for him. Some servant who had not abandoned him in his tomb.

For it had to be the resting place of the Priest of Blood.

◆ 2 ◆

THE interconnecting network of glass tubes curled and wrapped from body to body, thrust into the artery at the throat, at the legs, or straight into the area of the heart. The tubes all met and dripped into a large bulb-shaped crucible, as the kind I'd seen the surgeons use to heat when curing old women of maladies on their flesh. The blood welled there, and it was no more than a wineskin might hold. From this vessel, a single tube descending into the crystal tomb of the priest.

That was the darkness within it.

It was filled with blood. He slept in it, this priest-king.

It kept him alive, but entombed.

Who had been the architect of this mouth of hell? Had it been the goddess Lemesharra, herself? Her aspects of Datbathani and Medhya, the monstrous pagan goddesses of fertility and destruction?

But why would a vampyre do this? Why a god? This was all of mortal hand of some kind. It had to be. Only a mortal would be devilish enough to create these puzzles within puzzles. Only a mortal would slaughter vampyres for the sport of creating statues. Or hang them upside down and carve the word *Maz-Sherah* into their skulls to frighten us off.

For that had to be why this show had been staged. To keep us out or to slow us. To play with us.

Only a mortal would take his brethren, like these who hung around me, and turn them into a winter storehouse to feed a vampyre more powerful than all others. No vampyre would do it—it took away the hunt. Only mortal man tormented for long periods of time other men.

But the blood would not be so rich, would it? These bodies had been hanging for many years. Kept alive like meat in an icy environment, just enough to keep their sluggish blood manufacturing itself. Their bodies cool enough that the process of death was slowed. The tubes running between them such that they lived off each other's blood, as well, in whatever basic way a human might. But such living death would not last long. Whoever had done this had to replenish these bodies every several years or risk the blood stopping, surely. Mortal blood was not endless. The heart would eventually stop. The flow would thicken.

Someone, some alchemist of the world, kept this well-engineered chamber going. Some mortal. Or organization of mortals? A cabal of some kind? While we had slept during the day, had one or many been there, studying us, watching us? Perhaps even taking from us? In this underworld, what devil presided? It could not be the one in this tomb, for he could not rise from it. We were his rescuers, in fact. And yet, why would anyone who existed there let us awaken to the night? Why would any mortal man allow us to survive the day's hours?

Kiya approached me as I took in the chamber and wondered at its origins. "The watcher," I said. "It is some human being. Or a group of mortals. I would say this is magick, but it looks like a series of spinning wheels above us made of bone, and below, an alchemist's laboratory."

"The alchemy of Hell," she said.

• 3 •

THERE was no time to waste. I felt more than the chill of the place. We were in a trap of the kind made for rats, and somewhere the razor's edge was above us and might descend at any time. We had come to find our power and our source. We had come for the ancient sorceries of our kind.

We had been enticed. Pulled as if by magnets.

We all three lifted the lid of the crystal tomb.

Dark blood overflowed its edge.

I reached into the congealing blood, which was like tiny particles of red snow. I drew up in my arms the skeletal remains of the Priest of Blood. In the corpse's arms, cradled like a scepter, a great staff made of gem and bone.

⋄ CHAPTER 17 ⋄

The Priest

⋄ 1 ⋄

A SOUND like the rush of birds through an echoing hallway—we all heard it as I brought the body from the tomb of blood. As I laid the body down, I saw more clearly the staff that it clutched. It was the Staff of the Nahhashim that I had known of from my vision. I did not know what it meant, but I felt it must be of some magickal significance. It was this that I took first from the remains, having to cut the shackle at his wrists, then pry the bony fingers back from the staff. The Nahhashim staff was too important to the vision for me not to take it.

Surprisingly, the staff seemed very light in my hands, and warm to the touch.

The priest's body had been wrapped in some magnificent fabric—for I saw a gleam of gold filigree and a bright blue pattern in the bits that still remained and that had not been destroyed by the chilly blood.

His skull was oddly elongated, and his jaws thrust out like a wolf's, with great incisors that were nearly tusks, while the rest of his teeth were sharp and serrated like shark's teeth. As the blood dripped from his form, I saw that his eyes had been sewn shut. My mind flashed on the image of the vampyre woman sewing with the needle of bone. While his mouth had not been similarly sewn, it was sealed in its own way—a bone hinge and lock of some kind had been fashioned around and through his teeth. It was to become known to me as a trick of mortals who stopped up a vampyre's thirst by binding the mouth with bone that cracked, unhinged, then bound the jaw. His left ear had been sliced clean off, and the skin there was scarred and burned. Tattoos encompassed his scalp, and on his right ear, the piercing of many small jewels and rings had elongated it.

His shoulders seemed too bony, and when I turned the corpse to the side, I saw that there were strange protrusions of bones almost like pronged horns from between his shoulder blades, connected to a thickened spinal column. His wings had been cut off. The wings I had seen that Pythia possessed. He had once had them, but whoever had imprisoned him in this blood sleep had torn them from him as a child might tear the wings from a fly.

His chest was sunken in, and over his heart, metalwork of a strange design. It was a small sphere the size of my fist. Protruding from the sphere, a thin small blade that was thrust into the heart area. I reached out to touch it, but felt a strange repulsion—nearly a vibration—which made me feel sick to my stomach.

His legs were bound together, fastened with lengths of human hair that had been braided again and again to form a tight rope. And yet, it was easy enough to cut through—its purpose had been merely ceremonial.

Ewen leaned over the body, marveling at the tattoos that brightened as we wiped the blood from the body. The corpse had a particular sheen to it. Kiya quickly read the story of the tattoos in a language she understood well. "He is Merod Al Kamr, and he was truly the king of Alkemara. He began his life as a slave of the field. He lived in a fertile valley. He first heard Medhya's voice in the wind and found her flesh growing, a weed among grain. But it was the reading of what are here called the 'words,' and the stealing of the 'flesh of Medhya' that brought him into the realm of immortality."

"If he's immortal, then why . . ." Ewen began, looking at the skin drawings with wonder.

"He sleeps," Kiya said. "The sphere holds him, the blood feeds him. But he cannot awaken."

Then she turned to me. "You must open his jaws. He has been bound at the heart, at the mouth, and feet. His wings are shorn."

"Our tribe had wings as this?" Ewen asked.

"Wings, and more. I have heard that some could become wolves, and others ravens. Still others could enter a village as the plague itself and spread across human flesh like fire, drinking the blood of all within a single night. All the powers of Hell." Kiya laughed as she said this, for the vampyre phrase was that Heaven itself was hell, and Hell was heaven.

Ewen's eyes shone with excitement. "And we will have all this?"

I saw some danger then in Ewen's eagerness to embrace this ancient sorcery of vampyrism. "Treasure is to be used wisely," I cautioned. "What we seek should not cloud our judgment of it."

Kiya grinned, showing her polished teeth. "You are the conscience of our kind, Falconer. I am as hungry as a wolf bitch for this knowledge. My time is coming. But if we can discover the secrets . . ."

"The watcher," I said, cautioning.

Ewen glanced at both of us as if we had kept a great secret from him.

"Someone else is here with us," I said. "No vampyre would slaughter other vampyres to show us the trophies and scenes in the chambers above. Pythia may have known of this kingdom, and she may have escaped it. But some other agency is behind this. During the day, I believe this person or persons have watched as we slept."

"Then we must quicken our hand," he said, with alarm. He reached for the metal sphere above the priest's heart, but it was as if he received a shock—his hand was flung back, and he let out a brief cry.

Kiya moved closer to the sphere and sniffed at it. "Quicksilver."

"The man who made this sphere knows our weaknesses."

She got as close as she could to the sphere and said, "There's a slender blade running from it to his heart. It is keeping him from waking."

"We must remove it," I said. I drew the black sword from its scabbard, and nudged it against the sphere.

"You must be careful!" she said. "If the blade in his heart does not come out clean, it will destroy him."

I sheathed the sword again.

"The needle," Ewen said. "Use the bone needle. And the thread."

Kiya thought for a moment, then brought the needle out of her pouch. The hair-thread was just a few inches long.

She dipped the thread between the metal curves of the sphere until it came out the other side.

Although the quicksilver seemed to sting her a bit, she managed to grasp the end of the thread and draw it back up. Once she'd made a loop with it, she tied it in place. Ewen held it with his fingers. Then, she lay down beside the corpse and, using the long slender needle, pressed it into the nearly healed wound in which the blade had been carefully set. She was able to work open the wound. It was dry—no blood released from the corpse.

Then Ewen gently tugged at the sphere. It gave slightly. I looked at Kiya with some feeling of tension. Ewen tugged again; Kiya worked the bone needle a bit more about the blade.

Finally, the blade rose a quarter inch.

Then another.

And another.

A long slender blade emerged that had, at its sphere end, seemed of metal, but as it went down, was a slender glass tube with slight barbs along it as if to help keep it in place in the body. Quicksilver filled the tube. Thus, the engineer of this device had created something that would keep the priest in a state of constant dreaming, like the Extinguishing but without the destruction of the body or the ability to awaken and rise.

As the glass tube came out, a gassy emission erupted from the wound.

Then it closed, healing itself.

A foul stench rose up from between the vampyre's teeth. I swiftly went to break the hinged lock along his teeth. For this, I used the

sculptor's tools that we'd retrieved from the chamber above. I tapped
at the bone hinge, and it finally gave. His jaw, which had been broken,
hung down against his throat. Yet, as soon as his lower jaw was free, I
positioned it against his skull. It snapped into place.

I reached back for the Staff of the Nahhashim and held fast to it.
As I touched it, I felt a shock go from my fingers up my arm. It was as
if I held a live snake in my hands, and although it was some illusion, I
felt the staff wriggle as I held it, twisting as if trying to get away from
me. Still, I held it fast. The last of the blood fell from it, and I saw
white, ivory-like bone with carvings upon it, and this intertwined with
wood of some tree unknown to me. Embedded along its spine, also,
bits of amber and glasslike gemstones. At its tip, a bloodred stone that
seemed to reflect darkness.

I had heard of ancient mages with great power within their staffs.

And yet I did not know how to wield it, yet, or what its purpose
might be.

Nor did I did trust who this priest might be. I wanted to make sure
that if there was power in the staff, I had it on my side.

We watched while the body rippled as if serpents moved beneath
its skin. Then, blood pumped from the heart outward. His body filled
and plumped until a gaunt but living man lay before us. His skull
cracked and snapped and churned against itself, until the face was less
wolf-life, and more of the vampyre I'd seen at the altar in my dream.

He opened his eyes.

• 2 •

THE priest reached up, rubbing his eyes, which were milky white.

He seemed to be unable at first to see anything around him. He
rubbed his eyes once again, then one more time. He reached up with
his right hand for something, as if he could see a distant light. It was
his staff—he sought it, but it was not there.

I did not yet want to give up this prize. I reached out with my free
hand and grasped him by the wrist. His hand flailed, then relaxed. I
clasped my hand in his to show friendship and kinship. Quickly, I felt
the piercing of thorns—and let go of his hand quickly. Tiny barbs had

grown from his palms, and, just as quickly, receded into the leathery skin of his hand.

I reached to hold him again by the wrist. As I did so, the end of his hand became the head of a hooded serpent, which jabbed downward at the back of my hand. Although I felt some pain, I knew the poison would have no effect upon me, so I held him fast.

As if melting against itself, the cobra transformed back into a man's hand with long, spindly fingers.

He opened his mouth and rasped words in a strange language. His breath was as the worst death had to offer, and all of us coughed from it. Then it sweetened slightly—as I imagined his vital organs began functioning again. Our understanding of his language increased, and I heard him in a loud voice say, "Where is the serpent's progeny?"

Then I realized he had not spoken these words from his mouth but from his mind to my mind. I glanced at the others—had they heard him? But from the looks upon Kiya's and Ewen's face, I gathered that they had not.

I spoke aloud to him. "What is the serpent's progeny?"

"Nahhashim," he whispered within me.

"The staff?"

No answer.

"I have it."

"Who are you?"

"I am no one."

"No one is here," he said. "Do you not exist?"

"I am neither living nor dead."

"You are a child of Medhya. A fallen one of the great mother."

I did not reply.

"I am Merod Al-Kamr," he said.

"The Priest of Blood," I said.

"And you are my destroyer," he replied.

◆ 3 ◆

WITHIN an hour, we had cleaned him using our garments to dry the rest of his body as we might clean a newborn.

He rose, naked before us, and looked every inch the demon. He stood a full foot taller than I, and his skull seemed slightly elongated in the back as if there were some headdress beneath the skin. His shoulders though slender were broad.

As his skin grew and healed over itself, we saw muscles grow upon him like brambles beneath the flesh. The thinness of his body had become sinew and strength. His thighs burst heavily muscled, while his feet stretched slightly, with talonlike claws at the ends of his toes. The ear that had been torn from him grew back into place, and, as I watched, vestigial wings crackled and sprouted along his back.

The drawings and tattoos along his body seemed to be in constant motion, as if I could look at any of them carefully and I'd see the people within the drawings move.

The milky white of his eyes was unchanged. As he rose before us, he rubbed at his eyes again, and yet he still was blind.

"Give me Medhya's flesh," he said to me in my mind.

"I do not know this flesh."

"I smell it on you," he snarled. "Give it to me."

"I have no flesh other than my own."

I thought I heard the rasp of a laugh from him. Then, "It is a flower. It grows among the bones of those who have been sacrificed."

Remembering the carnivorous purple blossom, I told him I had gathered it up.

"Yes," he said. "I must have it." He reached out to me, his finger grazing my chin. I fumbled through my pouch, finding one of the crushed flowers and its bit of vine. I passed it to him without hesitation.

He took it, pressing the petals against each of his eyes until a dram of clear liquid pollen dripped from it. Still clutching the blossom, he lowered his hands from his face.

The milk of his eyes gave way to yellow, then began to turn dark, but with the red of blood pulsing behind them, shining beneath the black.

He could see again. As soon as his eyes shone with their red-black darkness, he grinned. It was a wicked, broad smile that showed enormous sharp, curved teeth.

He glanced at each of us, regarding us as a wolf might watch deer in the wood. Before any of us could react to his swift movements, he leapt upon Kiya, pressing his snapping jaws down upon her shoulder, ripping. She dug into him, biting back as best she could but barely grazing his flesh. She kicked against him, a blur of movement as he, his body still and tensed, drank from her.

Dark blood flew from his mouth as he dropped her, before Ewen and I could even reach her to save her from him.

She lay on the floor, blood flowing from her throat and shoulder.

His mouth, dark with her essence, still grinning, he kept Ewen and me at bay with enormous strength. "I drink from any I choose."

"You will destroy all of us."

He leaned his head back and laughed. As he did so, we heard a strange humming—and then gusts of flying insects came from between his lips, moving upward in a funnel of air, far above us in the chamber. Seconds later, they were gone.

"I am he who first heard the words of Medhya and drank her blood to enter into her stream. I may drink from all. I am your source."

"Are you mad? We have rescued you here, and now you seek to destroy your own kind!" I shouted.

"Vampyre blood carries with it great power," he said. "You may not drink of it, but I have kept the essence of Medhya prisoner within my body; I hold her hostage. She cannot destroy me as she might you if you drink from one another. You backward jackals. You are not worthy to be vampyre."

I stood up again, holding the staff up. "I am the owner of the Staff of the Nahhashim!" I shouted.

His eyes gleamed in darkness as he watched me. His neck moved slightly side to side, as if he were a serpent in its hypnotic movements. "You do not even understand its power, weakling."

"But I will use it as I wish."

His grin returned. Blood sluiced from between his teeth. "Is this what our tribe has come to? Such as you?"

"I am the One," I said, unsure of the truth to this. "The Maz-Sherah."

"There have been many Maz-Sherah who have come to follow the vision. There is no One."

"I am the only one who has freed you from your prison."

"If you were the Maz-Sherah, you would not need to speak. You would take from here what is yours and do what you are meant."

"I am meant to learn from you," I said.

"You are barely more than a boy. You are an apprentice to war, not even a great warrior. You have a heart that beats too close to the mortal rhythm. When the Maz-Sherah comes, he shall be more powerful than you."

"And yet, who has been imprisoned here so long? Whose kingdom was overthrown? Who created this machinery of bone and human harvest and quicksilver, to keep you in your cage?" I asked. As I spoke, Ewen reached over, lifting the threaded needle that carried the sphere and glass tube of quicksilver. He held it up at the end of a dagger toward the priest, though it caused him some pain to do so.

"You might be as afraid of the architect of this prison as I," he said. He lifted his left hand as if to make a sign. The sphere flew from Ewen's hand and smashed against a far wall. Ewen dropped his dagger as if it had burned his hand. "That alchemist has stolen the essence of immortality from me. And cheap sorcery like quicksilver does not daunt him."

"He has outwitted you, that is for certain," I said. Then, to Kiya, "Are you healed?"

She touched the edge of her shoulder where the flesh had been torn out. "The flow has stopped. It is healing, but slowly."

"Is the alchemist here?" the priest asked.

I nodded, guessing that the alchemist was the same mortal whose presence permeated this kingdom without ever having to make himself known.

"He has great power," Merod said. He lost his grin at this and spread his hands out, Christ-like, as if feeling for something in the air. "He sleeps now. He is not afraid of you. Or me. He may be watching even now."

"Or he has abandoned this place," said I. "He has allowed us to enter and wander, though he might have extinguished us during the day's rest."

"Perhaps then you are the One. For it might be to his purpose to let you find me. To let you raise me that he may strike us both down one night." He stepped closer to me, bringing his hands up as if he were warming them by a fire. "You are a mad vampyre. You do not know what I could do to you. What I could do to your friends."

I held the staff aloft. I could not understand what power it held, but he must have known it, for when I waved it in front of me as if it were a wand, he stepped back.

"I will kill him, and, if I need to, I will destroy you as well," I threatened.

"It is impossible. He has many protections," Merod said. Then he glanced up above us, as if expecting to see the alchemist appear.

"For a priest, you are an untrustworthy creature," I said.

"But I possess what you seek, do I not?" he asked, and the grin returned. Suddenly, nearly froglike, he leapt up to the wall where the humans hung. He broke off a length of glass tubing and drank blood from it. When he had slaked his thirst, he glanced back down, then dropped again to a crouching position among us.

As he stood up, he said, "My bed was a work of genius by the alchemist. Crystal can imprison us, for it is said to be of a hardness of water, which weakens our powers. He flooded the crystal tomb with the chilled blood so that it would torture me as I lay there in it, feeling it on my skin, my pores tried to open to drink it, but of course, could not. The quicksilver kept me in the state of dreaming so that I was aware these years of all that was in my kingdom. Of the tortures of my daughters and their transformations into those creatures in the waters, of the inventions he made that turned the altar into my tomb and changed the temple of the great Lemesharra, of the flashes of burning light that destroyed the mortals of my kingdom. He is a terrible being, and he has stolen knowledge from beyond the Veil and from our tribe, as well. Medhya loves him for all this, for her fury is never-ending. We are the children she has spurned, and he is the one who has been taken into her affections."

He went to Kiya again—this time, we were ready, and I thrust the staff between them. He stopped, but said, "I mean to heal her completely."

"Do not trust him," Ewen said, defiantly.

Kiya looked at me, then at the priest. "I have lived to see the end of many of our tribe, Priest," Kiya said. "I would ask that you heal me of this wound and teach us of what has been lost to us." She reached to my elbow, and I lowered the Nahhashim staff that she might approach him.

"When I drank of your essence," the priest said, "I tasted the end of your days, like the dregs of a wine goblet. Your Extinguishing approaches."

"I have few nights left," she said.

"If he is the Maz-Sherah, then you will have many, for he may bring to the tribe the power of the source."

"If you are our priest, will you not do this yourself?"

"My time is nearly gone, for I have existed upon this land for five thousand years, and although I continue in another realm, I will not extinguish nor will I pass the Threshold. But my fading has already begun, like the last of smoke from a dying fire. The Nahhashim is his. When he fulfills the final prophecy of which I know, he will be the one you must ask."

"What is the final prophecy?" she asked.

"It is only for the Maz-Sherah," he said. He stepped closer to her.

"He will kill us," Ewen said, looking as if he were about to leap upon Merod Al-Kamr.

"He will not," Kiya said. "This is the Priest of Blood. He can give us breath or take our breath from us. If he meant to destroy us, he would have as soon as he was free of the sphere."

The priest went to her and leaned again over her shoulder, as if to bite her. Instead, he spat upon the wound, and it quickly began to reform into healed flesh. Where the flesh smoothed, a tattoo formed, a strange red curved shape.

"We have come for the ancient sorcery," she said. "We cannot trans-form shape, nor can we run as wolves or fly as dragons. Yet all these things were of your kingdom."

"How have you heard of me?" he asked her.

"I heard from an old vampyre who went into the Extinguishing. Before he did, he told me that he had heard the legend of your impris-onment and of the kingdom of Alkemara from another of our tribe, upon her passing, and so, perhaps it has gone for a thousand years."

"More even than that," the priest said.

"I saw you in a vision," I said. "Of an altar, and of Pythia lying upon it to be sacrificed. And of a dark woman with a mask of gold."

He studied my face briefly, then glanced at Ewen who seethed with anger, and held an ax in his fist as if he might spring at Merod if given the chance. "Boy, do you mean to attack me with your weapons? Is this not your lord and master?" He waved his hand toward me. "Is this not your sovereign to whom you've pledged allegiance?"

Ewen glanced at me fearfully, nodding.

"I could snap your neck and feed on your skull and brains, as I have with other vampyres, and though my powers are at their lowest ebb, they are greater than yours," the priest said. "I would dig your entrails out." He lifted his hands, their yellow, curved nails long and ragged. "I would spread them out, then stuff them down your gullet while you choked until the Extinguishing came to you. You are a weak boy. Are you eighteen, even? Do you shave?"

"When I died, I was nearly nineteen," Ewen said.

To Kiya, the priest said, "You bring me novices. Young tribesmen. Are there no others of your age?"

"There are," she said. "But this one, called Falconer, is the only one to have the vision."

"When the vampyre named Pythia passed the breath through the Sacred Kiss," I said. "I saw all this and more. I saw your youth. I saw your temple. I saw your beautiful daughters as they once were. And Pythia felt terror at my seeing into her soul, into her knowledge."

"Yes, she would, that one." The priest nodded, a grave look upon his face. "But how am I to believe that you are the One?"

"Is there no test?" Kiya asked suddenly.

"Oh," he said. "A test. There is one such test. But its consequence is dire. It is baptism by fire, and the furnace entered is not so pleasurable as the rivers of Hell. If this Falconer is not the One, then he will burn as soon as he enters that realm. If he is not the One, all of you will be destroyed here. If he is the One, I will be destroyed. That is the prophecy itself. Already I doubt that you are the One, for six supplicants were prophesied."

"One has died by the hands of your daughters," I said. "And two wait for us beyond the white sea. All in all, six came to this kingdom, and whether dead or alive now, six have passed into the underworld of the Gates of Nahhash."

"Baz-ihiya-naai-lyat-nahh-ash," the priest said, his hands going to his face, covering it with shame. He wiped at his eyes, as if wiping a memory back. He pointed to drawings upon his body. "The story of our kind is written upon me. I am the living scroll." Then, suddenly, he added, "My time is short. You are the possessor of the staff of the Nahhashim," he said. "They were the priests of Datbathani, a face of Medhya, Queen of Serpents and the secrets of the Earth."

"And what is the power of this staff?" I hefted it.

"The Nahhashim holds many powers of the Serpent, and the Serpent protects its possessor."

"You were not protected," Ewen said.

"Had I not been protected, I would have extinguished. I was kept in the dreaming by the Nahhashim."

"What is the Serpent?" I asked. "I hear of the Serpent, but I know nothing of it."

"The Serpent is the father of our tribe, as Medhya is our mother. The Serpent gave us immortality and moves now through us. The wake of the Serpent as it moves its tail is the stream."

"Is the Serpent a god?"

"There are many gods. Some false, some true. The Serpent, when shedding skin, gives life to the gods themselves. And yet, the Serpent is not a god. The Serpent is beyond the meaning of god. The Serpent encircles the world and yet is not of the world we know. I feel the Serpent close, now that my hour has come."

"Why is your time short?"

"If you are the One, you are the reason. You were called in the prophecies the Maz-Sherah. This is, from an old language, the word for the Anointed One and the ritual feast. You are that Maz-Sherah. Many thousands of years ago the One was prophesied by Medhya's blood upon the skin of her priests. I heard of these prophecies and carried them with me on my body, for the words of Medhya are made flesh." Then he turned, and, beneath his shrunken wings, I saw, from his spine to his hind parts, the tattoos. Each bled into the next with scenes of distant kingdoms and people. "Look for the vampyre with the head of the bird."

I saw a primitive drawing upon him of a youth with a great sword, and a mask as of an eagle. Opposite him, the priest himself, his wings spread, his staff raised. In the next drawing, the youth had cut off the priest's head, and drunk of his blood. In the next, the youth had grown wings, and his mask had taken on the visage of a serpent-dragon. In his fist, the Nahhashim.

"I cannot drink from you, for your blood would be the destruction of our tribe," I said. "No vampyres can."

"I can, as the priest," he said. "And one other may. The Maz-Sherah. But first, you must pass the test of the Veil. But we must hurry. I do not like that the alchemist may be near. May be watching."

• 4 •

"THE magick is from the Serpent to us," Merod Al-Kamr said. "The salvation of our tribe from the curse of Medhya. To know it, to bring it, you must part the Veil. Do you understand?"

"I have heard once, from Forest witches, of the Veil."

"It is the billowing tapestry, more slender than spider's silk, that is beyond the stream and hides the world of the gods."

"How do I part the Veil?"

"If the wrong one were to part it, he would be immediately torn apart by the gods of many hungry mouths or would burn with a thousand suns upon him. But you may enter, Maz-Sherah, using the Flesh of Medhya."

"The blossom?"

"Its sting is death to mortals and sends the soul into the hungry gods' realm. But its juice allows us to see beyond this world. And from it, you will know if you are the Anointed, or the most damned of all creatures."

"It is the juice that brought your eyesight," I said.

"I have no eyesight," the priest told me. "All I see, I see within my mind, or within the shapes of the stream. My time will be gone soon. When you return from parting the Veil, you will know what to do. You must leave behind all fear if you do this. You must follow where the Glass within it takes you, to see what cannot be seen, or else the devouring monsters of that otherworld will find you."

He reached over to me, embracing me. I held fast to the staff, for though I had faith in our priest, I did not want him to seize the Nahhashim for fear that he would destroy us.

"Let go of fear," he said. "All fear. Let it pass from you like water." Then he whispered words of ritual that meant nothing to me, nor did their meanings translate within my head, for they seemed the mere guttural sounds of an animal.

He drew back, telling me to lift the blossom to my tongue and bite upon it. I did so, and a thick, bitter liquid shot to the back of my throat from the flower. Then he took it from my mouth as if this were the reverse of taking the wafer at communion Mass.

"You will first go find what your heart's desire is, through the Sight. Do not resist. The Veil, when it parts, takes you where your heart leads first. Do not be afraid. Do not speak to the visions you see. And if something terrible exists, some horror surrounding any you love, you must remain mute and keep from trying to shape the vision, for it will have consequence in the world that will not be as you will it."

"This will sting," he said, holding the small flower near my eyes.

• CHAPTER 18 •

The Veil and the Glass

• 1 •

I BRACED myself for pain, but when he squeezed the juice of the blossom onto my left eye, I felt only minor irritation. Then he applied the drop of liquid to my right eye. I waited for pain. The world went to mottled colors and shapes.

The burning shot along the edges of my eyelids as if red-hot pokers had touched just under the rim of skin there. I reached up to wipe my eyes clean of this awful feeling, but I felt as if my eyelids had sealed shut and no matter how I tore at them, I could not pry them open. Then I felt the Earth give out below me, and a bolt of light exploded within my vision. All the world went to white, and I was no longer in the temple itself, although I saw shadows of its statues and pillars all around me. In the air, rat-sized creatures that were of a rippling flesh, moved as if climbing over invisible rocks. The halls of the temple—which were now defined by a glassy outline that shimmered like a stream's flow—spread farther out, a long road.

Merod's voice accompanied me, and I felt his hand on my elbow although I could not see him. "You have parted the Veil, my child. You are in the Myrr itself, which is both paradise and hell. Do not be afraid, though you will see visions of creatures with many mouths and many limbs. You will see gods and demigods, all of whom are in twilight from the world. You may see spirits and Earth-children who have hidden behind the Veil when their times had come. Or you may see nothing but a vast desert of white. It is the realm beyond the Serpent, and its gate must be protected by you in all that you do.

"To part the Veil is to rip it, and each entry to it breeds monsters in the world. Just by bringing you here, there is a cost, elsewhere. A beast emerges at some distant place, or a plague, for you cannot rend the Veil without something escaping that was meant to be imprisoned or made powerless. When our kind was created, the Veil was ripped, and our race came into being. Even now, your entry here has passed the hand of death to many in the world, although I could not tell you of what kind or nature it has gone. But I have done this for you so that you might see what you desire and learn of your destiny."

I saw the pale shadows of forms—like white doves swimming through the white air. I remembered the milky waters of the Alkemars, and its tiny, barely visible insects, and wondered if these crawled the air now, all around me. The Alkemars themselves must have been born here, for how did creatures such as that exist? I was of this unseen world, as well, my blood, my vampyre blood, was of it. Above me, in the endless sky, a screeching sound, as of some great flying beast descending, a hawk dropping to catch prey. But I saw nothing.

Merod's voice at my ear, a circling gnat, "Do not fight the Glass itself, or it will break."

"The Glass?"

"It is of the world that was once here and died. It is now cracked and thick, but it shows much," he said. "It is not clear at all. You may trust what you see, or not."

Suddenly, I saw a flash of darkness. A black smoke blew across the white fog.

I saw a woman with flowing hair.

Alienora. My mortal beloved.

I watched Alienora while Merod spoke to me. She seemed to be speaking as well, though I could not hear her voice. She wore a plain shift, and a beautiful gown had been dropped beside her in straw. I watched as two dark figures came up beside her. Then, I recognized their habit and wimple—these were the anchoresses of the grotto, the Sisters of Magdalen. One brought a long dark robe to Alienora, and the other brought a small wooden cross attached to a rosary. Alienora, I realized, was looking into some bowl of water as she took both tunic and cross. Her hair fell down as if she had leaned farther over to look into the bowl.

Alienora donned the robe of the sisterhood. She had taken her vows! Through the Glass, I saw what she had done with herself. But it had been more than a year since I'd last seen her. She intended to join the Magdalens soon after I'd left, so this must be an older vision. This was the past.

I reached out as if to touch her, but instead I felt a thickness in the air, and her image rippled. "Careful not to break the Glass itself," Merod's voice warned.

"I want to touch her," I said. "I want to hear her."

"You may yet, but you must be cautious, for harm may come to both you and her if even a ripple passes along the surface of the Glass."

"How much time has passed? Is this vision of hours long past, or seasons?"

"I am not a keeper of time, Falconer. But smell her. Inhale her."

I inhaled as deeply as I could. I did not anticipate what came after— it nearly moved me to tears, the scent of her perfumed skin, of her hair, of the delicate spice that she pressed behind her ears, as well as the murky scent of musk and oil that was her body.

"What do you smell?"

"All I remember of her," I said. "All I know of her."

"Then she is near the time when you left. Perhaps a few months after," his voice said, then guided me to rise and move forward through this vision, into the Glass. "Follow the vision to its end," he said. "But you must beware of breaking the vision. It is as thin as the wings of butterflies, but as ever-tightening as a spider's web. Even while you move through it, it is enshrouding you with its strands. You cannot return through it. The last of it, when you are ready to leave, must be torn through, or you will be lost in the vision itself."

I moved into the rectangle of my sight, in which I now felt a stream unlike any other. It was smothering and heavy, and yet liquid in its consistency. I heard Alienora's voice, and other voices I recognized. I will write here what I saw and heard, and move with it as I moved through it then, for I cannot describe the sensations of it further. What I remember of it was how I saw and heard a series of events in Alienora's life that must have spanned a year or more, and yet, in my vision, lasted less than an hour.

"Something terrible has happened," Alienora said, awakening sharply from a dream.

◆ 2 ◆

SHE sat up in a bed made of straw, with a single thin coverlet over it. Candlelight flickered along the rock recesses of the cave of the Magdalens. I had never been inside it before, so was amazed at how well it had been carved over the years. It resembled an austere house of some kind, or a very clean catacombs, for I could see through the doorway to Alienora's small chamber that there were other rooms along a narrow hallway. The air grew heavy with incense, which seemed smothering to me as I witnessed this. The smell was, in some ways, more overwhelming than the vision.

One of the other Magdalens crouched down, squatting upon a low stool by Alienora's bed, bringing morning water in a bowl.

"He is dead," Alienora said. "The man I told you of. The boy I loved. He is gone."

"You must ignore these dreams, Sister. They are not sent from God or His angels. They bring you fevers, I fear," the Sister asked, her eyes ever-widening, and from her visage I could surmise that dreams in this order of women had great significance.

"My sins have been great." Alienora nodded. "The devils send me these dreams of damnation. But they are real. I cannot ignore them. Not when they are of the one I have sworn my heart to."

"You may not speak of such things," the nun said. "Turn your eyes to Our Lady. Leave off these blasphemies of your maidenhood. Have you not cursed your soul enough on his account? If he is dead, let the Devil take him. He has brought you nothing but sorrow." The Sister put her hand out, clasping Alienora's hand in hers. "You are in a new life here. Leave the old one, and the one who ruined you, to the angels. Your life as the Baron's daughter is of the flesh. Your life as a Magdalen is of the spirit."

"I fear for his soul," Alienora whispered, drawing her hand back from the nun's. "Shadows whisper to me of demons. Since I came, I have heard them. They tell me that his soul is hostage to deviltry."

"Dreams may bring prophecy," the Sister said. "But we may pray together here. Pray for all the souls lost to the Devil."

"He has been at war now for four months," Alienora said. Her complexion turned ashen, and she clutched the small cross around her neck, then kissed it. "The shadows show me things."

"Do you see?" Merod said within me. "The shadows know her. They taunt her. They sniff at her to find you."

The liquid air swirled, then settled. The Glass became clear again. Alienora knelt before a great dark statue at the very back of the Magdalen cave. It was of Mary Magdalen, I suppose, but her face did not seem blessed. Instead, the statue, which was black stone, was of a Dark Madonna. I had heard of this heresy, although it was not thought ill by many. Yet it was not what Alienora's Church would smile upon— the veneration not of Mary, Mother of God, but of her mirror twin. The image could not precisely be called Mary Magdalen, for the woman who had posed for the statue looked as if she were a queen of some country, and not of the humble sinner, the female apostle of Christ. Yet Alienora whispered the Ave Maria to this statue, and kissed her feet. Then, I heard her prayer aloud. She whispered in my mind, "Dear Lady, our Mother in the Dark and of the Deepest Places, let me understand the dream you sent to me. Let me understand what it meant. You know how I have sinned against the Almighty and the angels, and how I blasphemed the chapel of Our Lady in my father's house. You, Lady, know of darkness and of despair. You have knowledge of my sins. You understand the visions of angels and devils.

Please guide me now, and bless Aleric, who was the falconer of my father's house. Bless the father of my child," she said, touching her stomach.

• 3 •

I gasped as I heard her words and held my breath for a few moments. *A child.*

I wanted to look at her, to see her belly, to see how she had grown with child, but my vision followed Alienora's sight as she prayed, upward to the black Madonna. Her face was imperious, and in her hands was a small dark chest made of wood. In it, as Alienora's small white hands opened it, a dried human heart. The relic of the Magdalen.

Alienora leaned over, kissing the dried heart. "Hear my prayer. Save my beloved. Save his soul. Bring him to me. Cleanse me of my sins."

Another vision came up: Alienora, daily and nightly, at the foot of the Dark Madonna, praying for both her child and my soul. "I will do anything to protect him," she said. "Anything. Please bless him. Please protect him from the forces of Hell. Please bring him home to see his child." Her belly grew, and her weeping increased.

Then I saw the night of the birth.

Beyond the Magdalen's home, an enormous storm raged upon the marshes. Lightning flashed among the trees, and a great fire grew from among the oaks that stood sentry beyond the grotto.

Within the cave, at its mouth, I saw the flickering of candles and the shadowy figures of the Sisters as they tended my beloved's night of pain and birth. I felt my heart beating hard in my chest, and my mouth went dry as I watched the silhouette of my child's birth.

Just as Alienora screamed, nuns cried out with delight when they saw the baby's head.

The lightning flashed and, for a moment, I saw them all—several nuns gathered around as Alienora clutched at them, screeching at the pain. I saw a bloodied newborn in the arms of one of the Sisters. One of the Sisters shouted, "She still has not done. She still has not!"

Alienora screamed as if to rip the night.

The vision turned to white, and a new one came. I saw the trees of the Great Forest. A spear of sunlight broke through the thick branches and spread golden light upon the yellow and red wildflowers that carpeted the ground, surrounded with bursts of fern. I knew this place. It was near Mere Morwenna's cottage, near a brook.

Alienora, in her nun's garb, rode upon one of her father's white horses, swiftly across the Forest floor. My vision followed her as she went. She had no child with her, and I was sore afraid that my child might not have survived the night of storms at its own birth.

She dismounted near the grassy path that led to Mere Morwenna's humble home. She tied her horse to a birch just to the edge of the path. The house, a hovel really, seemed to be tucked into the arm of a low oak branch, sprayed with mistletoe across its roof, like a crown.

Mere Morwenna, her back stooped, and the veil across her face drawn down revealing a woman who looked to be a hundred or more, leaned against her rough-hewn walking staff as she stood by the deerskin-covered doorway.

"I saw you, child," the old woman said, brushing the strands of long gray hair back from her forehead. "I heard you were coming from the birds. Why are you alone?"

"I seek your help, Mere," Alienora said. "I've left the order. I cannot abide them."

"And you seek me out because you can abide me? I thought you were afraid of those of us who practice the Old Ways."

"I would not be here if I was. I was told you can help me."

"Help? How?"

"My dreams," Alienora said. "I have had them for months now. Even after the birth of . . . after everything. I have seen Aleric die and return from the dead. A darkness whispers to me, and will not let me sleep."

"You have come for the Craft. But you believe we are wives of demons, as well."

"I do not," Alienora said. She fell to her knees before the old woman. She clutched at her skirt with her hands, weeping. "I begin to see these things in daylight. The Sisters cannot help me. I have turned to God, but God does not speak to me or answer my prayers. I have turned to the Madonna of the Caves, and she is silent, as well."

"It was your family that has murdered friends of mine," Mere Morwenna said. "How do I know this is not a trick?"

"You have my word," Alienora said. "My father would have me imprisoned just for speaking with you. I would not risk taking a horse through the Forest alone if I did not think that my soul and the soul of my beloved rested upon your guidance. You know him. You have love for him."

"He was like a grandson to me, that boy, though I saw the destiny of clouds upon his face even as a baby," Mere Morwenna said. She closed her eyes, and began to cough. "I can feel him sometimes, though he is thousands of leagues away. His mother was special to me. They were of the old clans." She opened her eyes again, a harsh gaze. "What do you want?"

"I want to learn the Old Ways," Alienora said.

"For power." Mere Morwenna's voice cracked as she said this. "As your father seeks power by slaughtering others, so you seek power. It is in your corrupt blood. You want to become one of us, do you? To save his soul?"

"I know that the Christian God will not protect him. Will not save him. But I had a nurse as a child, named Nolwen. She was of the Forest."

"I knew her."

"She taught me about the goddess. About Cerne, as well. She showed me how to put the grain beneath the pillow to ensure the birth of a boy."

"It is a blessing that your father didn't have her tortured," Mere Morwenna said. "Go on your way, you Magdalen imposter. Return to your safe little cave or your father's household. Your dreams may not even be true."

Alienora's face darkened. She turned about and walked a few steps away from the old woman. Then she turned again, raising her fist to the sky as if cursing the gods. Mere Morwenna had never stopped watching her. "Grant me what I ask! I have seen such terrible shadows in my dreams that I cannot pretend they are born of fever."

Mere Morwenna lifted her walking staff as if it were a wand. She shook it with some violence in Alienora's direction. "Do you think that you can come here and demand to become an initiate in the rites of the goddess? That you can just decide one day that your beliefs do not bring you enough bounty? That you can avert destiny only by magick? And when you are done, when you have fixed your problem, will you not return to your safe sisterhood of ignorance and prejudice and live in a grotto that was once sacred to a great spiritual leader of our people, but now has been usurped by a conquering god? Do you think that statue you worship is of your religion? That is an ancient statue, a black stone, and though you believe it is one of your many Marys, it is truly something altogether different. Something that would make your skin crawl, my sweet misguided child!"

Alienora stepped back two or three paces among the tall grasses, shocked by the anger in the crone's voice.

But from the deerskin doorway, someone emerged. It was the changeling child, Calyx, grown to maidenhood, the one I had once looked at by pulling up the veil of a baby. She still wore a cloak and veil, and only her eyes could be seen. She limped slightly as she went to Mere Morwenna.

"Grandmother," Calyx said, her voice mature beyond her years. "Listen to her. I, too, have had dreams like these. It is a sign. The time of shadows is near."

"A sign of destruction," Mere Morwenna said.

The girl ignored her grandmother and went past her to Alienora. She took her hand up in hers and brought it up to her face. "You are on the path," the girl said. "You dream of the Falconer?"

Alienora nodded.

"He is lost," Calyx said. Then, to Mere Morwenna, she said, "She is meant to be among us. It is her journey. You know that you cannot interrupt what must be, no matter how you wish, for it will come to you with threefold vengeance."

Then her voice softened as she dropped Alienora's hand. Alienora looked at the palm of her hand as if stain had besmirched it. "You will join us on the night you call Lammas Eve, although it is a special night of Lugh, Lord of the first harvest. One will come to you within the grove of trees beyond the grotto. He will wear a mask, and you must not speak to him. He will blindfold you and raise you onto his mount, and you will ride with him to our festivities."

Calyx reached up and touched Alienora's forehead. She kept her hand there for a while, pressing her fingers about her scalp. "Your dreams haunt you. Shadows are upon you. You were meant to come to us, lady. You were meant to follow this path. You do not believe in what you have been raised to believe. You are full of dread and fear, and yet you still possess love. That is good. Love for children, love for yourself, love for the man called the Falconer, love for your father and brother and sisters, and love even for the Magdalens with their bitter darkness. Before you come to us, before you begin to understand the wisdom of the Old Ways, you must give up all that you love. For life is endless pain if we are too attached to things that pass and are lost. You will come to an understanding of what life is, and what is beyond it, in the Wisdom."

Then, the veiled maiden withdrew her hand. For just a moment, she reminded me of a statue as she stood there—where had I seen that statue before? Some small figurine, perhaps, maybe among my mother's things. She was cloaked from head to toe, with one hand up, palm out and the other also outstretched as if offering passage to someone. I reached out into the Glass, feeling as if I could touch the vision and longing to feel just once Alienora's skin beneath my fingers.

I had interrupted the vision—it rippled and swirled again, and I saw further into Alienora's days.

I watched as she appeared before a great gathering of the believers of the Old Ways. Though many wore masks on their faces, some did not. They had formed a great circle within a clearing of the Forest. All were naked, and Mere Morwenna herself was the priestess of these folk. I watched as Alienora became an initiate in the Old Ways, then followed her as she worked with the midwives and learned the lore of the Forest and field. It all had happened in a short span of time.

Winter approached, and I saw her again, but this time, she had begun screaming at Mere Morwenna's granddaughter. "You lied! Your goddess and gods cannot help me! Your power is useless! You are as damned to Hell as any in creation! My prayers are not answered, my dreams do not go away! I live among the Sisters and pretend with them, then come to your gatherings and speak your secret words, but it is as fruitless as the God of the Church!" Her face had taken on a strange aspect, as if she had not slept in weeks. I wondered about my child but had no sight of him.

When Alienora reined in her fury, Calyx crossed her hands, palms out to Alienora. "You have stolen our secrets. It was foretold that you would come, but I did not know what guided you. You do not love your offspring, nor the man you have lost. You have let your dreams rule you, and your fears are your master. That is not the path, and it is not the way of the Forest. You are bound, herewith, to keep the secrets of Bran and Cerne, and of the Old Ways."

"You witches have no power," Alienora spat. I had never seen her so angry, so bitter. "You are weak and deal in potions and spells and pointless ritual. I need more. I want more."

And then, the Glass began to fade in and out, as the sun might when clouds cross before it. I saw glimpses of things, of people, and a boy of two who might have been the son I had never met, although I did not know from the vision.

Finally, winter had come to the Forest, and there was my beloved standing amid the ice and snow. Her face was ashen, and her hair had grown wild and untended. She stood at the edge of a dark bog that was ringed by brambles and vines.

She spoke into the water as if it could hear her. Gradually, as I watched, her voice came to me in whispers, "You are more ancient than any in the Forest," she said to her reflection in the bog. "The shadows bring me here to call you from the deep. You are the one of shadows and darkness, upon whom I gaze among the Magdalen caves. You are the one carved in rock there, and I have heard from the great ceremonies that you were vanquished and live now in dark places. I have heard of a man who once came to you to beg for power, and you gave it to him that he might drive the invaders from our land. I call to you now, though it is forbidden of the Old Ways to do so. I call to you to come from the depths, to come from the darkness of your abode. I ask for your aid for I have seen terrible things in my mind, and I cannot rid myself of them. If there is power to save one who is damned, then I must have it, for I will not live upon this Earth without my beloved's safe return."

Then she began to chant in another tongue, which I could not comprehend, though my mind began to try to understand the words. It was some secret language that was impenetrable. Perhaps she had learned of it in the rituals of the Old Ways. Perhaps she had found it elsewhere, for there were always rumored to be books and grimoires of deviltry among the rich and noble.

Again, the vision dissolved, and another one came.

She stood holding the child in her arms. My son. A boy of perhaps two years. She wept as she held him aloft, and then she went to the edge of the bog, stepping into the water. The boy clutched her about the neck with fear. Tears ran from her cheek across his scalp.

In her left hand, she clutched a small blade that seemed to be made of a translucent stone. A ritual knife of some kind.

She raised it, and brought it down.

• 4 •

THE vision turned to red.

I cried out, reaching for her, and yet tangled myself into an invisible force that had the consistency of thick, cold mud.

I ripped through the vision, and it swirled about my arms. I saw flashes of images, faces of creatures the like of which I'd never before witnessed—some with wolf faces but the bodies of beautiful women, others with the bodies of rounded men but with mouths clamping shut and opening, all up and down their chests and bellies, with the

heads and horns of a stag where their phalluses were meant to pro-
trude; still other sights greeted me, each more fantastic and terrifying
than the last.

But worse, figures like shades of blackness, tall and wearing the
flowing robes of priests passed by, whispering to me the words, *Maz-
Sherah, we know you.*

A blur of these creatures drew about me as if they were a gathering
of sorts, or of a Forest with moving branches, in a circle around me.
And then I felt a crushing blow to my back, the like of which would
have thrown me across the room had I not been within the Veil. An intense burning feeling ran the length of my spine, then caught fire
along my shoulder blades. I felt as if my own geometry expanded in
some way—backward from my shoulders. Up from my throat I felt a
sucking at my breath, then my lungs filled with air again and seemed to
be lifting me up.

I became aware of my wings before I ever saw them. They unfurled like twin flags upon my back—leathery wings, slick with some
oil, and a great wingspan. They opened behind me with a crackling of
blue lightning upon my form. Within the whiteness, I rose slightly
into the nothingness, erect, wings spread, my arms moved into an outstretched position. I felt I was floating above the world, above clouds,
and yet the blurred dark creatures moved around me.

"When you, the Maz-Sherah, received the Sacred Kiss, these
shades were loosed from the Medhya's cloak. They seek all that protect you. They bring plague and fever with them. You must not let
your desire blind you." The priest, within my mind, whispered to
me that I would be the Bringer of Light to all the dark ones, the
fallen ones of Medhya, and the gods of the Veil blessed me, for I was
the Maz-Sherah. "You have but one task to complete the Serpent's
circle."

I felt his hands at my throat, as if to strangle me, although I did
not see him. "You must devour me," he whispered.

Then, the juice of that strange flower in my eyes burned slightly as
it diminished.

My sight returned.

The rip in the Veil had closed again into a white mist.

I lay on the floor of the tomb of Merod Al-Kamr.

• 5 •

I felt an enormous rage within my blood, and yet a surge of power in me threw me back to the floor of the temple. I looked up at the priest, who stood above me. "I have seen all that you have witnessed," he said. "The mortal you loved has taken the path toward the end of days."

"To save me!" I shouted. I did not notice how Kiya and Ewen watched me. "She went to God to save me. She went to the darkest pit of Hell to save me!"

"Perhaps," he said, nodding slightly. "But she is mortal. You are not."

He reached down to me, offering me his hand. I refused it, and instead, rose on my own. My body still exhibited arousal, and I had returned from the vision with the wings of the priest. In my hand I still clutched the Nahhashim.

"She murdered my child," I said. "To save me."

"Perhaps," he said.

I remembered Mere Morwenna's telling me of the Sight. Of its unreliability. "Perhaps it has not yet come to pass."

"She will pass the Threshold when she dies. Do not have sorrow. No mortal woman can love you. Your love would bring her death. Her love is darkening. You must not go to her. You must forget her. And any child that exists. I sense the shades around her, seeking the one who holds the heart of the Maz-Sherah."

"I cannot forget her. Not after seeing this. And my son," I said, as if I had forgotten a sacred vow, one of my former life. With it, the magnetic pull of my homeland, even there, in the underworld. "I must keep her from this fate."

"You must think of the others," he said, in a nearly harsh tone.

"What others?"

"Mortal and immortal both. I was not a priest to the vampyres, Falconer, but of humankind. I performed the necessary rites to keep

Medhya in darkness. The drinking of blood from mankind is sacred, and not to be abused as if we were wolves. Think of your life as a mortal man. You ran with the hunt, and you sought the boar and the stag. Did you not also leave them in spring and summer to mate and replenish their kind? So humankind must be allowed to sustain and grow. The Myrrydanai—who are the priests . . ."

"Other priests?"

"From Myrryd there came three castes of priests. I am of the Kamr priests, who are of the blood and whose Medhyic aspect is of Lemesharra. Lemesharra, who was known here as Lemesharra Medh-Kamr, by which it meant, Lemesharra, Mother of the Sight. The staff is all we know of the Nahhashim priests, who are of the Serpent and of Datbathani Medh-Nahhash, who is the Mother of Serpents. You now take your place among the Nahhashim and Kamr here before me. But the priests called Myrrydanai are those who have had their flesh torn from them by Medhya herself—torn and devoured for her pleasure. Like Medhya, they are shadow vultures that follow her darkness.

"The Myrrydanai are five in all, but they can grow into many as a shadow grows with the sunlight, for they travel by day as well as night. They do not drink blood, but instead drink souls. They are the most accursed, set loose only to Medhya's command, her bidding. She released them from the Veil because of your coming. They sweep the night to find those who will destroy you. But you will not allow it, for mankind brings us life, and we are born from human life, after all. Many vampyres may look upon mortals as flagons for drinking, but we must see them as sacred. Do you understand?"

"I have felt this sacredness," I said. "And yet is any life sacred with our kind?"

"Life is more sacred than are we," Merod said. "We are sent back to our bodies from the Threshold not as destroyers, though we may take life at times. We serve life and take it when necessary, but only as a sacrifice. For every life we take, we must preserve a hundred more. Just as the hunter preserves the deer of the wood after hunting the stag, so we must all be priests of blood, Falconer, and though we bring terror to mankind, we must also bring protection. All blood is drunk from the chalice of sacrifice. This is why Pythia destroyed me, with the alchemist urging her onward."

"Who is the alchemist?"

"A man who goes by many names, but I knew him as Artephius. He enslaved my daughter, turned her into his whore, and gained the ancient sorceries of stone and blood, which mortal man is not meant to possess. Medhya blessed him, and the Myrrydanai listen for his command. He wishes for the prophecies to be fulfilled as much as Medhya does. He built my cage. He took my daughters from me."

"You have great power," I said. "How could you be subdued?"

He didn't answer at first, then only said, "Perhaps someday you will know all. For now, Falconer, you have a journey ahead of you. You must know the final prophecy of the Blood of Medhya, for you will need to know it. It is written in my blood, within the vessel of my flesh."

Waiting for him to speak again, I felt a rush of wind at my back, pressing me toward him. It was more than wind—a wall of pressure, invisible, took me and I felt as if I were floating toward Merod Al-Kamr. His sorcery was strong, even without the staff of Nahhashim.

Finally, pressed against him, he leaned to whisper into my ear, "There is a final prophecy you do not know, Maz-Sherah. It must be broken. It is of the end of all mortal life and the destruction of the Veil and the Glass, a time of monsters and madness. The only hope is to raise the Nahhashim. And only the possessor of the staff may do so. But it will be at the cost of many. Sacrifices will be made. Sorceries will burn the skies. Many will extinguish. Many will fail. The staff is the source. You cannot let any other take it from you. You cannot give it. Keep it close at all times, for within it is something more powerful than even the Veil, though I do not know what it may be.

"You are the One, and as the One, you are the All. All, One. One, All. Understand what this means, and you will begin your journey. Medhya is gathering skins of humans, and her Myrrydanai swallow souls. They create an army of the spirit, using the Veil itself to bring the shades and banished demons into a monstrous existence. Even now they whisper in the minds of men, and seek to destroy those who have touched the Maz-Sherah. They are unleashing the Old Gods, as well, the beasts who have been held by the Veil for thousands of years. One day, the war will begin, and you must lead our tribe, and protect the flock of humanity both for their sakes, and for your own. You must protect those from whom you drink life, or life will be no more."

"I waste time here," I said, drawing back from him. "If what has befallen me has come to poison others . . ."

"You must first fulfill the prophecy," Merod said. "You are here for the Feast of the Passing."

I must devour you, I thought, *as you wish. I must cut you down and eat your flesh so that what you know and what you possess comes into me. The Nahhashim and the wings, they are aspects of the power. The resurrection of the loins is another signal of the source. But it is the essence within you, and your meat that is to transform me. But your blood will destroy me.*

Within my mind, he whispered, *The Anointed One of the Serpent may drink its own venom. My blood will become your blood. Your essence, my essence. All, One. My flesh retains the memories and the ways of Medhya. If you were not to kill me now, I would die before the next full moon beyond these walls. The One has come, the Maz-Sherah, the new priest has come, and my time is passed. Do not mourn me, for I have crossed many years of the life-in-death, and I am ready for my journey.*

Merod Al-Kamr, the Priest of Blood, the King of the Alkemars, bowed down before me, as a humble servant. I unsheathed the black sword and in one stroke swung it down upon his neck, severing his head from his body.

A rush of air filled my throat, and I heard his voice within my mind: *Seek the knowledge of the Nahhashim. When the One becomes All, the All become One.*

His head rolled beside my feet. I cautioned Kiya and Ewen to keep their distance, for I was not sure of what poison the blood might yet contain.

I lifted Merod's head and began the duty that had been set forth before me. With each bite of his flesh, I tasted the history of our kind and acquired the divine fire of immortality that had been denied us since the priest had been betrayed by his own daughter and her lover, the one called Artephius.

When it was done, and there was nothing but the bones of the priest, I began to feel his past, and his childhood, as well as a moment when he worked, a slave in the fields, and a great wind came up while a crescent moon lay along the horizon of the flat, fertile valley. And as the grasses moved in the wind's fingers, I heard Medhya's voice, and the words of the Blood that would transform Merod and begin our race, our tribe.

She whispered to me from the shadows, "Priest, you are mine."

As I stood there, drenched in blood, Kiya bowed down before me, as did Ewen.

When I asked them to rise, Kiya told me, "The falcon has devoured the serpent and has brought us the ancient sorcery. You are the King of our tribe. We feel it in the stream, even now, the change. You must anoint me. You are the source of our strength."

Instinctively, I went to her and held the Nahhashim against her loins, and against her breasts, and against her scalp, and finally, to her lips, and she tasted of it. And likewise, I went to Ewen, and touched him in the places of power with the Nahhashim. As I did so, I felt the Serpent, within the staff, wriggle in my hand, and a fire grow from it.

They, too, felt my stream come into them. Within their bodies I invaded their souls, and burned at the weakness there, bringing them the light of my internal fire, a fire stoked by the flesh and blood of Merod Al-Kamr and of the source of All, the Serpent.

They, too, felt the surge of power, of the Old Talents of the Fallen Ones of Medhya. What was once merely legendary, was the history of our race.

The Nahhashim staff seemed to glow in my hand with a blue-and-red fire as if the powers of old, rekindled, had themselves drawn strength from our tribe.

And when they had been restored with the abilities of transmogrification, of transforming into creatures of the night, of sprouting wings along their shoulders to fly like dragons above the trees, above cities, and to move so swiftly as to appear to vanish, they and I praised the Serpent above even Medhya. For Medhya, our mother, had cursed us, but the Serpent had bestowed blessing to our kind so that we might prevail among the world that was ruled by darkness. We praised Lemesharra Medh-Kamr, and Datbathani Medh-Nahhash, and the Priest of Blood, Merod Al-Kamr, who had not been extinguished, but coursed within my blood, the All becoming One in me.

We would be immortal for many more years than the century that Kiya had feared. We might not overcome the silver that held a strange power over us, which was the mined ore of the fallen kingdom of Myrryd, nor would we defeat an enemy by daylight, for the sun could still destroy us with its slightest glance.

But our tribe had been restored to its rightful place among the Medhya's children, and of our father, the Serpent who was within us, in the blood itself.

We stayed in that place long, but when at last we emerged into the night, having drunk our fill of the hanging bodies of Merod's tomb, Kiya said, "It's too late. It's nearly too late."

I knew what she meant—I could feel a movement in the stream, stronger, a pull backward. It was a call through the stream, back to the Hedammu, for our tribe had begun to suffer greatly.

The stream felt as if it were afire.

· CHAPTER 19 ·

The Whispering Shades

◆ 1 ◆

TAKING up the Nahhashim staff, I rose, my wings unfurling from my shoulders, brought about by my will. The others followed, and we three flew from the tomb and returned through the city of Alkemara to the milky sea. The barge we had abandoned no longer remained, but unfurling our wings—which came to us from our thoughts first, then grew swiftly from our shoulders as did the wings of devils—we flew above the choppy white waves, and though we heard the Alkemars calling to us, we ignored their entreaties.

Arriving on the far shore, we met Vali and Yset, who had stood guard all the while. They had tales of fighting off the Alkemars, who tried to reach them at the shore. After their anointing, we took off swiftly up through the passages of the mountains, emerging at the chasm's doorway through which we had entered into the moonless night. We flew, and felt both fear and an incredible freedom, for we had the ancient sorceries within us. Ewen flew highest, a great dragon he seemed above me, and Kiya remained just ahead of me, watching the Earth below for signs of any enemy. I felt bolts of lightning within me, as the flesh of the priest became part of my own flesh. Merod was not dead—he could not enter the Nowhere. But he was within me, I felt his presence with me, and his stream was like burning sand at my throat.

We moved fast, our wings beating with the dusty wind, traveling many leagues in minutes, and what had been a journey of several days on foot had become a night of travel by air. The memory of Merod's voice in my mind: *Medhya is gathering skins of humans, and her Myrry-danai swallow souls. They are creating an army of the spirit, using the Veil itself to bring the spirit to a monstrous existence. They already whisper in the minds of men, and seek to destroy those who have touched the Maz-Sherah.*

We began the descent as our birth-grave city Hedammu came into view below us. It was lit with many torches, and the cries of both men and vampyre. The stream felt like a boiling water within a pit, and it drew us earthward on a path of heat.

A battle raged below us.

♦ 2 ♦

A S the five of us descended swiftly into the midst of the fighting, I drew the black sword from its sheath, the Nahhashim staff in my other hand. I brought the sword down to the head of a soldier who had swung an ax against a vampyre who already lay dying.

I could not know then the author of this fight, or why my own countrymen—knights and commanders of the Hospitallers—had come to the poisoned city to find and destroy the tribe of the undead, but the Myrrydanai showed themselves between the light of the man torches and fires that had been set.

They were shadows of men with long, tattered robes and cowls covering their heads. They moved between and among the mortals, whispering as men fought and died. Their whispering was like locusts amid the battle. When I was not hacking at the soldiers who attacked, I was watching over the others of our tribe. I looked over to see Kiya slaughtering the human intruders who had come under the influence of those loathsome shades. Ewen, never far from my side, was gathering men up in twos and throwing them over the battlements, with the new-found strength of the anointing.

As the torches flickered, the shades of the Myrrydanai crowded around one particular man, and when I looked to see who it was, it was a knight, commander of this army, in full gear, with his great broadsword hacking at a vampyre whose arms had already been sliced away. When finished with the vampyre, Myrrydanai surrounded him with darkness. They possessed his flesh and raised his sword, pointing it toward me.

I flew to him, and became a wolf as I came down on his throat, tearing at his skin, all the while jabbing my sword between his ribs. Yet, even torn, he began speaking to me with the voice of the shadows. "Maz-Sherah," he whispered, "Your son will be a sacrifice to the Veil, so that we may multiply among you and among mankind. When the war comes, Maz-Sherah, you and your tribe of blood-stealers will be no more."

Then, in my human form, I held him there, and said, "What do you mean? Tell me of my son."

"Your son's blood will feed the dark, and your child will destroy you," the voice whispered from the knight's lips. "Despair, oh Hallowed One, for you have lost before the war has begun." And then, in a woman's voice, "Please, oh dear God, where are you, Aleric? Please, come to me. They're burning me!"

I recognized the voice as Alienora's own.

I sliced his head off neatly from his body and kicked it away from me. The remaining soldiers had lit a pyre of vampyres with their torches; but most of the humans were dead, and soon those that remained ran from the handful of our tribe, ran like dogs from Hedammu, out into the purple light that broke, heralding the coming sun.

· 3 ·

NEAR the great bonfire of bodies, we watched as the smoke rose and curled, and the smoky blackness bore witness to the shadows of the Myrrydanai as they rose up into the sky and traveled on vulture's wings across the sea.

Kiya had been wounded, but it would heal soon enough. Ewen flew down from a tower, his face and chest covered with blood. Yset's wounds from the battle had healed; Vali crowed like a madman and cried out for his lost brothers. We looked at the extinguished of our tribe, and the dead of the mortals, and had no words for each other. We carried those of our tribe who could be gathered up into the deep corridors beneath Hedammu.

We found that dreaded chamber filled with those who had already gone to the Extinguishing, and laid our lost companions down among the ash and bone. I blessed them with the Nahhashim, and called to Datbathani and Lemesharra to carry them to the Veil itself, though I did not know if the Nahhashim staff was powerful enough for such a prayer to be answered. With these five, we sealed the chamber as best we could so that should mortals find us during the day, they might not enter before we had awakened. In that chamber, I set the Nahhashim staff in the lock of the doorway, on the inside that it might keep out all shadow.

I dreamed in that sleep of a great serpent that moved through murky water.

At nightfall, I told the four left of our tribe of the war to come, of our mother, Medhya, who created us and would destroy us.

I told them of our purpose as protectors of the flock of mankind, and of how we must only take the blood necessary for our sustenance, as a sacrifice from a sacred creature of man and woman. Even as I spoke, I felt in the stream their resistance to this, for they had been a pack of jackals before the journey.

Would they be ready? Would they follow me as the Maz-Sherah, even with the power to bestow the Sacred Kiss? Might they not raise their own armies of our tribe and destroy me? How could I be the leader of these vampyres who would be nearly indestructible?

◆ 4 ◆

I knew I had to return to my home, to find Alienora and protect her from the shadows that whispered at her ear. My son might yet be alive, and I had a burning inside me to make sure that the Myrrydanai would not destroy either of those I had left in my past.

"You must stay here, and gather others of the tribe where they exist," I told Kiya. "You each now are able to bestow the Sacred Kiss. You will be the leader of Hedammu, and you must find other leaders to bring under our banner. Find us warriors, and princes, and those with rare talents. Find the scholars and those who seek to serve the Nahhashim."

"As you will it," Kiya said.

"We will speak in the stream," I said. "When you hear my call, come to me. Raise a great army, for a night comes when we will need to overcome a terror greater than either man or vampyre can fathom."

I took Ewen with me, for truthfully I could not bear a night's journey without him, and he, too, desired to see our homeland again with me.

We spread our wings out and flew beyond the city, beyond the cliffs, across the midnight sea. I did not want to think of the possibility of a war between spirit and flesh, but I knew it would come. I knew that, as I fulfilled the prophecy of the Maz-Sherah, so Medhya's prophecy of the great Last War would come.

Ewen and I slept that dawn in an ancient graveyard on the isle of Crete. We felt others of our tribe in the stream there, but did not have time to seek them out. We drank our fill from a maiden and her lover, but left them alive, yet weak. I spoke with Ewen about the nature of mortals, within the realm of the tribe. He lay with me at the first light, and when we drifted into dream, he whispered, "I would walk through Hell with you if you wanted it." His words reminded me of Alienora, and I dreamed of her, of our blasphemy in her father's chapel as we made love, creating the son whom I might never see. The dream left me with equal parts sorrow and hope.

We raced the winds by night, by day finding graves or tombs or shallow caverns. We continued to feel other vampyres nearby, unknown to us, clans within the great tribe, and it gave us hope, though we did not seek them out. We could not stop; I felt the urgency grow as we flew over cities ancient and new, barbaric and sophisticated in design, until, finally, on a night of storms, we sensed our village and the Great Forest itself, just beyond the horizon.

◆ 5 ◆

THE Baron's castle was afire in the night—again, I sensed the work of the Myrrydanai. Despite lashing rain, the fire raged, and lightning ripped at the black clouds rumbling across the sky. I closed my eyes as we flew over familiar ground, clutching the Nahhashim to draw its powers of seeking. I felt Alienora, and my heart beat fast. Human memory flooded my senses, and I wanted her more than I had ever wanted her before. All the feelings of youthful love had returned, and I began to scent her presence within the castle walls.

A strange voice came into my head, then, a voice I had heard but briefly in the Veil and the vision of the Glass—that strange veiled maiden known as Calyx. *"Falconer, you are too late,"* she said.

I ignored this voice—it could have been a trick of the Myrrydanai.

I followed a pathway of scent down into the castle, along the chambers, leading Ewen in flight. As we passed down the corridor with which I had once been so familiar, a place of desolation greeted us.

I ignored any other instinct I had, even a feeling of ice that had clutched at my chest. Alienora was there, somewhere trapped, caught, imprisoned in her own home. My son. I had seen him in the Glass. He might yet live. The vision might not yet have come to pass.

In the chapel. The very chapel in which we had made our child.

I landed, crouching, with Ewen beside me.

Alienora stood there, before the altar, naked as if she were the virgin sacrifice of some barbaric religion.

Blood on her breasts.

On the altar, her own younger brother.

His heart torn from him, still beating in her hand.

Alienora turned to me, with an inscrutable look upon her face. She had an unconscionable beauty—the radiance of a goddess of slaughter.

I knew in that second.

The Myrrydanai held dominion over her.

She was with them.

The shadows along the wall grew long, and I could not bring wings from my shoulders again. Nor did I feel my source of power within. It was as if ropes had been thrown over me.

I raised the Nahhashim, but as I did so, I felt a tugging at my fingers—and dark fingers grasped at it. The Nahhashim flew from my hand, carried by one of the shades to Alienora.

"The power of Medhya's blood imprisons the Nahhashim," she said, and brought the heart of her brother to her lips and drank from it as if it were a cup.

And then the shadows of the Myrrydanai surrounded us. *This is some unknown sorcery*, I told Ewen through the stream. *She has been given great power. She has forgotten her love. Forgotten her soul.*

The shadows surrounding us whispered a language that could not be understood, although it sounded like a chant—a ritual—a rite of binding, for the darkness began to smother me.

I felt the priests take me into their arms, covering every inch of me with their shadows.

All power had fled from my being. It was as if the Myrrydanai drank it the way the tribe drank blood.

I began to fade into blackness, terrified that I might be heading toward the Extinguishing.

A terrible shrieking erupted in the stream, then the dark enveloped me.

◆ CHAPTER 20 ◆

In the Well of Thirst

◆ 1 ◆

I AWOKE when the shadows had dissipated. I looked up, for my eyes opened skyward. But there was no sky. We were in a well of some kind. Torches had been lit near the top of it, a crown of fire high above us.

Muddy ground beneath us.

I lay against Ewen, feeling the despair, fearing the hunger that wracked my being. Many nights must have passed in that place, for my throat was a desert. I whispered to Ewen, who seemed as one tortured, "You must be strong. We must both be. We will escape from this. I know we will."

He had little strength to speak, but when he did, he told me that it did not matter to him anymore, whether or not he went to the Extinguishing. "May I die again soon, never to be raised from the dead."

"You must not think it," I said. "I did not raise the Priest of Blood from his captivity, nor did I devour his holy body to lie in this womb of hell. I saw, as a boy, another vampyre, also a victim of some supernatural treachery. I helped raise the creature into the light of day, where our former master, Kenan Sensterre, and his huntsmen cut off its head and burned its body. This is not meant to be our tomb, Ewen. We will not extinguish here, I promise you." Yet I was not sure if I could believe my own words. My eyes blurred with tears as I held him, feeling his shivering. We were as weak as fevered mortals. The Myrrydanai had taken much from us, and they now had the Nahhashim staff. I did not know how to use its magick, but I could be certain that they knew of its secrets.

I had handed it to them by stepping into the trap that had been set.

Within my mind, I raced through my blood memory of the priest, and of his words that were sacred to the Serpent. All, One. All, One. What did this mean to me?

My hunger drove me to madness, and while I embraced my companion, I thought of his blood, and how refreshing it might taste to me. *The Serpent may drink its own venom.* And yet, if I drank of him, he would extinguish. I could not do that. I have no doubt that he thought of mine as well, and I saw in the shadows of his face how he accepted the despair of this entombment.

All, One. The One in the All.

The priest's voice, in my blood, came up through my worst fever, smelling Ewen's sweet throat, knowing that less than a quarter inch beneath the skin, my tongue might taste the dark pure venom of the Serpent, the blood that had coursed through the veins of our kind for thousands of years since the first creation, when the priest himself, and yes, even Pythia, came into being, from the drops of blood of Medhya mingled with the venom of the beloved of Datbathani.

All in One. One in All.

All of us are One. The One is in the all.

Who is the One?

It is the blood of the Serpent.

It is our strength, from the Serpent.

The venom is the strength. The venom overcomes the blood.

I am.

I am, I knew. I am the One in All. The Maz-Sherah.

The All in One.

The one thing that had not been stolen from me, because the Myrrydanai did not know I possessed it.

The blossom. Crushed in the pouch at my side.

Called by some, the Serpent's Venom.

I reached into the pouch, bringing it out. I forced Ewen's lips apart, and bade him crush the dried blossom between his teeth. I had already tasted of it. He needed its juice.

After he had done so, I embraced him with a weary happiness. "I am the All. I am the One. When the One is the All, the All is the One," I whispered to him. "Drink from me."

He looked at me, gasping, his lips parched. When he spoke, his throat was so dry that his words were incoherent. "No. I will not. I would . . . I would . . . *die*."

"Drink from me," I commanded, and drew back from him. I brought my hand behind his head, and pressed his head toward my throat. "You have the venom in you. Mingled with the blood. I have it, as well. You and I may drink of each other, for the Serpent's Venom protects the blood. The Serpent may drink its own venom. You will feel the Veil, but you will not see it. Do not be afraid. Drink of me."

He resisted, but only slightly. I felt as if I were a mother bringing a baby to suck my teat. I brought his lips to my throat, keeping a gentle pressure upon the back of his scalp. I felt the graze of his teeth against my skin.

"Do it," I said. "Do it now, as I tell you. Do not hesitate." I forced his mouth so close to my neck that I knew he could smell the scent of blood beneath the skin, and the pulse of it. "I do not carry within me the blood of the dead, but the venom of eternal life. I am here, as the priest prophesied, to raise our kind to its previous glory, before the ancient wars of the gods, before the alchemist and the Pythoness betrayed the ancient of the tribe, when we kept the world of man safe from the devouring gods, in return for drinking from the vessel of his flesh. Drink from me and live. And grow in strength. And my blood in you, I shall also drink."

"Our brethren . . . the others . . ." he whispered to my throat. "They shall burn if I drink. We, too, shall burn."

"When you drink of me, not a thousand men or a thousand suns shall burn us," I said. "I have walked into a furnace and returned whole. I have fulfilled the ancient prophecy. I am the Maz-Sherah. I am the One. Drink now, Ewen, or you will be no more."

My palm grew hot as I pressed the back of his head, at the nape of his neck, hard against me, his lips to my throat. I felt his throbbing need. His lips parted. I felt his teeth grow to dagger points in anticipation of the rape of my skin.

He plunged himself into me. I felt the barbarous pain that my flesh had not experienced in many years, the pain of opening to another. My blood spat against his tongue. So thirsty was he that he made sucking noises as he drained the goblet.

I endured the pain. As it shot through me, it turned into a pleasure I had never before experienced. I lay down on my back, and he, crouching over me, kept his lips against the wound. I felt his thighs around my waist, and smelled the tender scent of him as I had not before. I grew weak through this, but my pleasure grew.

Finally, he groaned as I pulled him back by his luxuriant hair. His body shuddered against mine. I felt the excitement of flesh as he fell against my chest with his full weight. He gnashed his fangs, trying to get back to the pool at my throat that had ripped to my breast, but I pushed him away with the last of my strength. I saw a penumbra brighten around him, a halo of purplish light, as the life of our kind had come into him.

I had faith that this would not be the end of us, for I felt the prophecy live inside me.

All, One.

In thirst, I sought out Ewen's throat, and lapped my own blood from his chin and lips, then returned to the nape of his neck and plunged my incisors into him. I felt the bond between us that we would never lose, as we mingled together.

We were One. We were All.

All, One, I heard the priest's voice in my head, my grandfather of grandfathers, the mage of our kind, the ancient Priest-King of the Tribe of the Resurrected.

All, One.

The Source is within the venom you have drunk from the Serpent. Medhya's blood is a curse within us, but the Serpent's venom is our blessing. You are the Maz-Sherah, sacred of the Serpent and the Nahhashim and the Kamr who serve the venom.

I gasped, choking on Ewen's blood, and released him. I gazed up at the ring of torch-fire at the top of the well.

I felt power, a brief flicker of it as of the spark from a stone before fire erupts.

◆ 2 ◆

I am the child of the Great Serpent. I and my vampyre kin are the new priests of this blood. And the blood is a bloodline back to our Mother, the Dark Madonna, Medhya. We create from our taking in of blood a new race of beings. We are not the damned, we are the gods of the world of mankind.

I am the One. I am the All. I am the Serpent incarnate.

I felt my mind shoot off into another direction, as if my consciousness were an arrow shot from a taut bow, toward some unknown destination.

The first face I saw in this new world within my mind was a woman, a creature with a terrible visage, a mask of utter depravity, and along her shoulders, slender asps curled and twisted. As she reached up to remove the golden mask that hid her true face from me, lost in this trance within my mind, Ewen grabbed me, returning to my throat to tear through its newly healed wound, to drink of me.

In my mind's vision, the golden mask fell, and there she was, the Mother of Darkness, the Bride of Shadows.

The moonless night of her face stared at me as if she wished to destroy me.

Our Lady of Crossroads became the darkness of my mind. Not Medhya in her warrior aspect, but the Lady of Serpents, Datbathani Medh-Nahhashim, who was of the venom of the Serpent itself.

I lay back in that sealed well that was meant to be our eternal tomb, and felt my blood course from my veins to Ewen's lips and throat.

In the swoon of Ewen's leeching of my blood, I heard the voice of a man from somewhere above, beyond the seal of the well itself.

It was Merod Al-Kamr, speaking within my blood, for I had brought Merod into me and he lived in my flesh and I had his knowledge.

"Artephius is near," he said. *"You must not rest long."*

◆

This is the testament of Aleric, son of the accused and executed witch, Armaela of the Fields; the Maz–Sherah prophesied among the Kamr, the Myrrydanai, and the Nahhashim, who stole the cloak of flesh and drank the blood of the Great Medhya.

I, Falconer, the Eater of Merod Al–Kamr, who was called the Priest of Blood and was King of Alkemara; the rightful owner of the Staff of the Nahhashim and of the secrets of the rare flower called by the priest, the Flesh of Medhya, which contains the Serpent's Venom; I, the One and the All, the Anointed of the descendants of the stolen blood of Medhya, whose blood and breath is the soul of the vampyre race, who brings life to the dead, and death to the living.